Rescue Me GENTLY

A K Taylor

ABOUT THE AUTHOR

A K Taylor

A K Taylor is currently a wife, mother of three, and new to the writing world. With demanding jobs as a Customer Service Representative and a full-time wife and mom, she could hardly find the time to share her passion for true love with the world...until now. After years of *almost* doing it— now she can say she finally did. Dreams do come true, and her time to shine has finally made an appearance. Rescue Me Gently may be her first novel, but there are high hopes of many more to follow.

ISBN 978-0615916477

For my hero, Saul,
my heart is forever linked to yours.

ACKNOWLEDGMENTS

Marking this accomplishment off of my bucket list has truly been an immense endeavor, but a remarkable one. It has been an amazing journey for the last year, and I am truly grateful to those of you who stood by me while I took on one of the biggest projects of my life. I am especially grateful to the following people:

To my husband—Saul, my children—Andrew, Brett, and Chelsea...I love you all so much. Thank you all for your patience and understanding.

To my mother—Thank you for taking the time to read my words even when you're busy with all those grandbabies—lol (lots of love)...lol (laugh out loud).

To Chelsea and Keri—thank you ladies for proofreading my very first novel. I can't tell you how excited I am that it's finally done.

To my niece Heather—thank you for getting the word out there about my book. Word of mouth advertising is the best.

To the rest of my family, friends, and co-workers...thank you all for your positive feedback and your belief in me.

Prologue

Sit down, prop your feet up, and get ready to fall in love. Rescue Me Gently is sure to leave you breathless and left wanting more. It's an old-fashioned love story about a young woman who is faced with the one thing we are all faced with at one time or another—*when to give it up.* Hannah Brooke Stone chose to wait. She knew in her heart that one day when the moment was right, she would know she had found her soul mate; the man who would complete her and change her world.

Of course, Hannah is human, and we all know what that means. She's not perfect. She is a woman with needs, and those needs demand to be acknowledged. There are ways to calm a person's cravings, and she's found it. Her private moments ease the temptation of giving it up before she's ready, and her dreams give her a glimpse as to what it's going to feel like when she finds her one and only. With that said— she has been content living a lonely life, then things change; just like they always do.

Not only does she realize she may be a victim of her own morality, but she has an ex-boyfriend who betrayed her, a mystery stalker who won't go away, and a desire to give it up—to a man she's never met. It's like going to bed one person and waking up another. Suddenly, it's just too much for her to handle and there's nothing left to do, but get out of town.

She thinks a vacation away will help her put things back into perspective, little does she know, fate has a plan that will leave her breathless. The life she knew will soon be over. She's destined to be swept away by Conner Dawson, and it's going to happen fast; so hold on tight, and don't worry. When it comes to this man, she will have *no* regrets.

Table of Contents

CHAPTER 1 9

CHAPTER 2 19

CHAPTER 3 33

CHAPTER 4 49

CHAPTER 5 57

CHAPTER 6 71

CHAPTER 7 83

CHAPTER 8 95

CHAPTER 9 105

CHAPTER 10 117

CHAPTER 11 127

CHAPTER 12 141

CHAPTER 13 153

CHAPTER 14 161

CHAPTER 15 173

CHAPTER 16 181

CHAPTER 17 193

CHAPTER 18 205

CHAPTER 19 219

CHAPTER 20 229

CHAPTER 21 241

CHAPTER 22 251

CHAPTER 23 261

CHAPTER 24 273

CHAPTER 25 281

CHAPTER 26 291

CHAPTER 27 301

CHAPTER 28 315

CHAPTER 29 323

CHAPTER 30 335

CHAPTER 31 345

Chapter 1

Friday night was on its way to being a nice relaxing evening, and then she slams open the front door—almost throwing me into a coronary attack. If she only knew my heart was already in overdrive, she might have knocked on the door like any other normal person.

"Hannah! Put that book down, and let's get out of Oak Hill for a little while."

Baylee Parker stands there with her hand on her hip—tapping her foot and her eyes blazing.

I glance her way, holding on tighter to my new love affair.

"Not now, Baylee. I have a date with Maddox tonight." I laugh at myself...Maddox is the main character of my new erotica, and I'm burning up the pages anticipating his next move.

I sigh.

If only he were real—if only he were mine.

I groan at the reality of my life, at the man who is only real in black and white print, and realize how pathetic I must sound.

"Please," she begs, and I drag myself back to reality.

Looking like a goddess, she stands there showing off her five foot eight inches of pure-decadent gorgeousness. Her confidence and beauty is as voluptuous as her curves, and she is my dearest friend, but now is just not the right time for a night out on the town.

"I don't think I can, and you know why." I give her my serious arched brow look, but it doesn't work. She's pouting, and I'm destined to give in.

The buttery smell of popcorn is in the air, and the microwave dings, letting me know my snack is ready. "Get that for me, will you?" I grin.

She rolls her eyes and heads to the kitchen. I hear the door slam shut on the microwave, and she mopes her way back to me. Handing me the hot steamy bag, she then walks towards the couch.

"Hannah, I hate seeing you cooped up in this apartment. Please go out with me."

She's so *insistent.*

I huff.

She mocks me.

Plopping down on my antique floral-print sofa, Baylee starts eyeballing me—*studying my every move.* I could run and hide, but my two bedroom apartment isn't going to protect me for long. My friend is determined and refuses to take no for an answer; *she's not going to give up.*

"We'll have a great time, come on...don't make me beg—*please don't make me beg!*"

She's begging and pleading, and I'm falling for it—hook and sinker. She's reeling me in, and I'm her catch of the day. Taking a deep breath, I hope she will take the hint and tread the line a little; this ole girl needs some breathing room.

I roll my eyes at her and lay back, getting comfortable in my recliner; *I'm not budging.* "You know that I *don't* want to run into him." I gesture at my book. "Besides, I want to finish this."

Baylee sits there—*Indian Style*—with her elbows propped up on her knees and her brain churning. She's trying to think of a persuasive argument that is going to win me over.

She is not going to win me over.

Blowing a wayward curl from her face, the glint in her eye proves she's come up with something.

"That's only an excuse, Hannah. If he try's anything..."

Sitting up straighter, I stop her mid-sentence and look her directly in the face.

"You'll what, Baylee? You won't do anything, because there is nothing you can do." My tone is angry...taking a deep breath I try to calm down. It's not her fault my ex-boyfriend is an absolute ass.

Two months ago today, Kris Tucker opened my eyes and *ears* to a whole new world. One that would erase every hope we had of growing old together or having any kind of a future. He may have shattered my dreams that night, but his betrayal had been going on for as long as we had been together. *I was just too blind to see it.*

My mind wandering, I remember it like it was yesterday.

I had gone out of town for a family reunion and got a little homesick, so I returned late Friday night instead of early Saturday morning. I wanted to surprise Kris, but little did I know he had a surprise of his own. I was so tired after a four hour drive and it was the middle of the night when I arrived. All I wanted to do was climb in bed and cuddle with my boyfriend, and that's what I intended on doing. The apartment was dark when I stepped inside, but to my surprise it sure the hell wasn't quiet. In the guest bedroom, somebody was doing the bump and grind and I couldn't believe my ears. First, I thought Kris had a friend stay over and help "house sit" with him, but then I heard those damn sounds that made me want to throw up.

"Oh, Kris…"

Thump.

"Harder…faster," she said breathlessly.

Thumpity…thwack…bang…bang.

"Is this hard enough for you, Sara Beth?" said the voice I knew as well as I knew my own.

I couldn't take anymore and neither could the hand-me-down bed that they were torturing. I opened the door, flicked the light switch on, and there they were. My boyfriend and the girl I now despise—both butt naked and going at it like wild animals. He was banging her from behind, and she was holding on to the headboard for dear life. I stood there with tears rolling down my face…*speechless.*

Sara Beth jumped up, grabbed her clothes, and took off. Kris tried to soothe my pain, but when his *filthy* hand touched my face I smacked it away. He left that night, and I've been trying to pick up the pieces of my shattered life ever since.

Pulling me back to the here and now, I hear Baylee mumbling.

"Over here," she says waving her hands in the air. "Are you listening to me?"

Deep in thought, I never heard her say a word.

"I'm sorry, what did you say?" I ask.

"Don't let him control you like this," she insists.

"Whap!"

Her plea is put on hold when our attention is swayed to the living room window. Both jerking in that direction, we watch as the baseball bounces from the glass to the ground. That's the second time it's happened this month, and the land lord is going to be pissed. At least this time, it only cracked the window, but just like before, no one comes to claim the roughly tattered ball. It will just lay there—becoming a fixture on the lawn until some kid comes along and steals it away.

Now, where were we?

Oh, yes...

"Nobody is controlling me, Baylee. I choose to be right here...right now."

She huffs.

And here we go again...eye to eye she's got my attention.

"Okay...how about this...let me take you out—my treat."

My brow arches.

"In that case, make sure you bring your credit card." I say kiddingly.

We both burst out laughing.

She means well, I know she does, but why can she just not take no for an answer?

Springing from the couch, she begins throwing her hands in the air like that might change my mind. "Hannah. I'm pleading with you. It will only be for a few hours," she insists.

Unbelievable.

She pooches out her bottom lip, and there is no denying that face is going to win me over. Ugh. She can manipulate me better than anyone.

"Baylee, please *don't* make me."

Now, I am the one pouting, knowing it's useless to even waste my time. I throw a piece of popcorn in my mouth and chew slowly…my mind wandering.

The thought of coming face to face with the sex fend himself makes my skin crawl. I resisted the temptation of giving *it* up, and I don't know why it was so hard for him. He couldn't keep his cock in his pants then, and now he can't leave me alone. He's the epitome of badness, and I want nothing more but to avoid him. Kris made a fool out of me once, and I'll be damned if I let him do it again. I believed we were saving our innocence for each other, and all along he was sharing his goods with every booty-bumping-drawer-dropping floozy in town. I guess that was his definition of chivalry. *Chivalry my ass—he was living more like a man-whore wannabe.*

Baylee clears her throat…pulling me away from the drama playing out in my head…*again.*

"I don't want to do this, but you're not going to give up are you?"

She shakes her head no, and then tilts it to one side, blinking her hazel green eyes and knowing she will not be defeated—not tonight anyway. She's gorgeous, determined, and I'm left with no more excuses. "The only way to get over him is to replace the jerk," she insists, grinning and showing off her million-dollar smile.

I roll my eyes and flip back to the page I had left off in my book; glaring at it, but not reading the words. "I really wanted to finish this chapter. It's just getting to the good part," I murmur. By now, my voice is a mere whisper.

"The love of your life is not going to jump off the pages of your books, Hannah!" she exclaims.

I gasp. She is right. I know she is. *Why does she always have to be right?*

"Besides, that tight little toosh of yours is going to shrivel up like a prune before a real cock can make it sing *cock-a –doodle-do!*" she cackles.

If looks could slap someone backwards, Baylee would be doing a back-flip this very second. Sometimes the girl is funny, but sometimes you just want her to shut the hell up. Now, being the perfect time to do just that.

"Uh…whatever, Baylee, you better focus on your own girly stuff and leave mine to me to worry about," I protest, throwing a pillow at her.

She rolls her eyes.

Baylee may not be a virgin, but she's been abstinent since she and her boyfriend broke up over a year ago. They were high school sweet hearts and voted most likely to get married. Ethan took her virginity on prom night our senior year, and afterwards she never felt the same about him. She thought she loved him, but after that night she knew she didn't. Three long years later, she finally got the nerve to break the ties with the man who loved her unconditionally. Giving it up to him was a mistake she has to live with for the rest of her life, and I promised myself that would never be me. Though there's no doubt her teasing did get my attention. I am probably the only twenty-two year old virgin in the state of Tennessee. Heck, maybe even the world.

Held captive by my own morals, my virginity has stayed intact. I believe in waiting. I believe in love. I even believe in soul mates, but more than anything, I believe in giving it up on my wedding night, but the older I get—the longer I wait, I can't help but wonder if it's the right thing to do. I am a grown woman, a needy one at that—I'm craving orgasms more by the day since Baylee introduced me to my little vibrating wonder. *That thing can work miracles.* But to be loved by a man…one that leaves me breathless—wanting more—craving his skin on mine and vice-versa; that is what I want more than anything. My heart longs to be entwined with his…whoever *he* is.

My eyes stare back down at the pages, but my heart continues to long for something more. I crave to be loved by a man who hungers to have me all to himself. The thought sends inviting warmth all over my womanhood. *Ah,* maybe one day...I can only wonder if *he's* out there somewhere waiting to be found. I can only pray that he is.

My friend stands there staring a hole straight through me and willing me to tell her what she wants to hear. *Why does she have to be so persistent, and why do I have to be so gullible?*

Through gritted teeth, I smile and face the truth. There is no more denying it. "Okay, okay. I, Hannah Brooke Stone, from Oak Hill, Tennessee, am a sexually frustrated woman dying to give it up to a man who will love *only* me. The only way I'm going to cross paths with him, is to get out of this apartment, so you win. I'll go."

She is ecstatic, and I'm a nervous wreck.

"Great! Pick me up at nine, *you sexy southern belle you*," she insists, throwing the pillow back at me and adding a little of her own country flare to the words floating from her mouth to my ears. That girl has looks to kill and a voice that can trick a city-slicker into thinking he's a redneck drunk on love. I laugh at my friend as she finishes her demands. "Oh, and dress casual. We're going to Joe's Place."

"I thought *you* were taking me out?" I ask.

"I am, but I'm carless...I had to drop mine off at the shop this afternoon, and it won't be ready until Monday. Don't you remember anything, Hannah?" she laughs.

Oh, that's right...she got rear-ended last week—only minor damage, thank goodness.

"Yes, but that did slip my mind. Okay, but here's the deal," I reply, having stipulations of my own. "I'll drive there, but you're driving back, Miss Designated Driver. I got a feeling I'm going to need a drink." I let out a deep, defeated breath and wait for her response.

"Deal," she says, dancing her happy dance and slamming the door as she leaves my apartment.

I sigh, but it doesn't help.

I fold over the corner of the page in my book to mark the spot I'm leaving off, and down on the end table it goes. *"Stay put lover, I'll be back soon."*

Baylee is pleased and I guess that makes me a good friend again. I wander back to my room, moping and dreading the night ahead; *at least one of us is happy.*

Nine o'clock is only two hours away. What am I going to wear? I fumble through my closet looking for just the right outfit and finally come across the perfect cut-off blue jean shorts and tank top. A blistering-hot summer night calls for lots of bare skin and just right for where we are going.

Stripping down to nothing but my panties, I go to the bathroom to get ready, and there it is. My reflection is staring back at me. Some say I am the mirror image of my mom, and that is okay. She is a beautiful sexy woman. I have her auburn hair and her clear-blue eyes that drive men crazy, but my hour-glass figure—well, those bragging rights are all mine and my worn out Pilates mat proves it.

Sometimes, I wish I was a conceited, vain, cold-hearted woman, and then maybe I wouldn't think twice about true love, but no such luck...I'm me and that means my heart is waiting to be swept away.

I strip out of my lace thongs and step into the steamy shower. It is hot, and suddenly I realize so am I. This ole *southern belle* might be a virgin, but she's also a girl with needs, and right now those needs are demanding her attention. My mind begins to conjure up some kind of an incredibly gorgeous beast of a man. Tall, dark, handsome, and romantic...*I like where this is going.*

My fake reality sets things in motion—begging my hands to wander and play along. This is just what I need to sway my thoughts from the night ahead. As I close my eyes, my sensuality is awakened as *he* begins to massage a luscious smelling shampoo into my hair, causing sparks to ignite all through my entire body. It feels so good!

I laugh at myself, shaking my head. *This is crazy...*oh, well...what good is having an imagination if you can't put it too good use?

Continuing on...

What masculine hands he has. They are covered with bubbles, and he's running them up and down my needy body with long gentle strokes. After spending moments massaging out all the knotted up areas, he makes his way to my tight firm bottom. Whoa! That tickles. His long fingers find their way to my sides and around my waist; thus, making me gasp because I know where he's going next.

Tiptoeing around my navel, he's getting closer the lower he goes—and yes, finally, he's hit a homerun...sliding into base, I can hear my inner self cheering him on. My sex clenches in, sending my clitoris—no my love-button, into an orgasmic induced heat wave. It's sweltering down there between my legs, and I'm on the verge of a magical moment.

I close my eyes...bringing my fantasy to life—at least in my head.

Oh Yes! He's going to make it happen, and of course my well-groomed womanhood is heating up and ready to explode. I can feel my body tense as though I'm really going to feel such pleasure, and suddenly my eyes pop open, and I let out a *glass-shattering* scream. The hot water that *was* cascading over my body is now freezing cold. What the heck! My fantasy has ended, and I'm reminded that I'm in a hurry anyway. I jump out of the tub, leaving the orgasm behind, and grab a towel to dry off with. Next, I pull my long thick hair up in a wrap and leave the memory of what could have been behind.

I hustle out of the bathroom and step right into my bedroom with one thing on my mind. Walking towards my bed, I start searching for my phone. *Where did I put it?* Not on the nightstand...not on the charger...where the...ah! There it is lying between my pillows. Leave it up to me to always forget where I put something.

I shake my head at my forgetfulness.

Looking at my cell, I see that I have two calls from an unknown caller—*that's weird.* Dubious as to whom it could be, I throw it back on top of my thick, white, feather-filled duvet and go about my business. *They will call back if it's important.*

If I'm going to get ready, I need a mood setter—*candles and music* it is. After lighting my favorite vanilla scented pillar, I grab the remote and turn on the radio. Maybe that will get me in the frame of mind to go out dancing...*or not.*

Taking my time, I stroll over to my vanity table and pull out the bench and sit down. I wrinkle my nose at the thought of putting on make-up...*maybe I'll go without it tonight;* it's so hot. I scowl at myself, never thinking I'm pretty enough to do just that, and at the same time, hearing my mother's voice in my head. *Easy does it, Hannah...only a little bit goes a long way.* She always said my face was like a delicately sculptured piece of art, and there was no need to make over what was already flawless. I smile remembering how much I love her, and that settles it. A little blush, mascara and lip gloss is all that is going on this canvas tonight...no need to get all painted up anyway, it's not like I have a date with a man or anything.

I gasp at the thought of feeling sorry for myself.

Glancing over at my clock radio, I realize just how late it is getting. I better get a move on, or Baylee is going to give me an earful.

Hurriedly, I blow dry my amber-colored locks, throw on my clothes and spray down with my favorite perfume—taking a moment to steal a peek in the floor length mirror when that's all done. Running my fingers through my hair one last time and that does it...I'm ready whether I want to be or not.

"Okay, Hannah...you can do this," I tell myself while looking at my reflection. "It's now or never."

Breathing in, I take one last whiff of the vanilla aroma smelling up my apartment. One blow and the three-wick candle stops flickering, and I'm rushing out the door like a crazy woman—*right into a night that embraces the unknown.*

Chapter 2

After about a half hour of driving on the back roads of Nashville, Tennessee and almost getting lost in the dark, there it is. Joe's Place all lit up and surrounded by lots of cars. The popular country bar and grill is crowded more than usual.

Baylee's excitement is beaming all over her face. "Wow! I never expected it to be so packed."

I shake my head, laughing; *neither did I.*

"Baylee, I know you said there was live music, but this is crazy. Where am I going to park?" My eyes scan the area, looking at each and every vehicle.

No! It can't be.

Abruptly, my laughter comes to a complete halt. My nerves—my thoughts…there's a boxing match going on in my head, and my heart is trying to play referee. Looking ahead, I see what looks like Kris' 4x4. My stomach begins knotting up…trying to get in on all the action.

"Maybe I don't need to be here." I point so that she too will see his truck. "If he's in there, then I don't need to be."

"Hannah Brooke Stone. Don't you dare back out on me now! You are a grown, vibrant, sexy, young woman who is better than some sleaze bag like Kris. Now, put your big-girl panties on and let's park," she demands.

"But!" I exclaim.

She puts her hand over my mouth and finishes her plea. "You cannot run the other direction every time you see him. Besides, I deserve a night out with my best friend."

She's right…*again.* I can't resist her pleading, and I find a parking spot close to the front.

After shutting off the engine, we open our car doors to the blaring country songs playing on the jukebox. The sound is coming from inside, and it is loud and inviting even in the outside air.

And that smell. It's all over the place: food, beer, cigarette smoke—bad cologne. I had almost forgotten all about the odors that come along with barhopping. I really hope it's not that bad inside. The first thing I think about is my hair and how bad it's going to smell when I leave this place. It's like it sticks to every strand—meaning I'll have to wash it at least three times to rinse the stench away.

I roll my eyes at the thought of it.

Each deck of the three-level colossal building is wired with speakers vibrating to a rhythmic beat. The sound of music is drawing us in, and before I know it Baylee and I are dancing our way towards the crowded club. We climb up the long flight of stairs in search of the entrance to the lounge. There's the door. It swings open, and out comes Kris with some girl. They never notice us, and we both sigh with relief. He lets out a huge burp, and she snarls her nose up in the air.

I'm so glad I don't have to put up with that anymore.

A few more steps and we make it. Pushing open the door, we inhale nothing but food. The grill is fired up, and the smell of burgers is in the air. I smile when I see the signs. *No Smoking Inside* is displayed across the room—one on every wall. That must be a new rule, and *I love it.* Baylee breathes in deep, releasing salivating words. "Smells delicious and I'm starving."

Just like the decks outside, the inside is packed with people who are ready to have a good time. Girls are hanging onto their guys, and the guys are eyeballing the chics on the other side of the room. *What is up with that?* I shake my head—moving along. My eyes are taking in every detail—from floor to ceiling and everything in between. The walls are decorated with pictures of all sorts of country singers. Some of which have even stepped foot on the same floor I'm standing on now. There's one hanging over the bar with Joe standing in the middle looking like he owns the place...*and of course he does.* He has a nice set up here, and by the looks of all these people it's getting even more of a popular place to hang out.

"Are you hungry?" yells Baylee.

I can barely make out her words over the loud music, but luckily, I'm pretty good at reading lips. "Actually, I am."

"Great, I'm famished. I think I'm going to have the burger. What about you?"

"Uh-huh, that sounds good. Double that order." I grab my belly and realize it's growling at me. *I guess the popcorn is long gone.*

"Follow me, I see a couple of seats over by the bar." Baylee grabs my arm and holds on tight, leading me through the massive crowd.

As we approach the barstools, I get a whiff of something that sends my toes curling and my insides swirling. The aroma from the burgers has been pushed to the side and that fragrance has taken over. I take a deep breath in through my nose and smell a mixture of something clean, fresh, energizing, and best of all—*addictive.* It's laced with a hint of musk and a luscious smelling man. *Who is that?*

This place is so jam-packed that I can't turn around. That's when I feel *him*; I take another deep breath—breathing him in like it's a life or death situation. *He. Smells. So. Good.* With his hand on my back, he's using my body to help guide him through the crowd. For a second, he's stuck; his body pressed against mine. There is an electrical charge flowing between us, and the friction is shocking every nerve ending I own. The next thing I know, he's yelling over the noisy room and his words are meant for me. "Man, if this room gets any thicker, Joe's going to have to build on," he says. His voice is playfully warm, and a little raspy. It's so sexy. *Who is he?* "I'm sorry for the tight squeeze, ma'am." My breath catches in my throat as the heat of his breath lands on the back of my neck. I want to turn around, but I can't. It's just too crowded. Sliding his hand slowly away, he's gone before I can get just a peek at who he is. I have no face to put to the mystery man, but that sultry-sexy voice is now stuck in my head.

Unexpectedly, I feel weak in the knees.

I take my place on the stool and turn around casually just to see if anyone catches my eye. The place is so full, and there is no telling who he is. I look around and breathe in deep. So many men, but not one gives off any sign of being the one I'm looking for. Disappointed, I swirl back around.

The breathtaking smell is gone, and I am left with nothing; not even a whisper of the scent that I found so captivating. *Just my luck.*

A high pitched voice from behind the bar gets my attention, and the next thing I know I'm face to face with *it.*

"Well, hello girls. I'm glad you made it. What can I get for you tonight?" Her voice screeching over the loud music is so annoying—makes me wish someone would turn *up* the jukebox.

It's her—Kendall. Standing there with her jet-black hair slicked back in a pony tail and dressed like a hooker; her beady brown eyes looking our way.

Damn, I forgot she worked here.

I roll my eyes, but only after hers leave mine. *Could she not dress any skimpier?* I mean really, her double d's about knocked me off my stool.

Baylee is ready to order and so am I, although the hunger in her eyes isn't just for food. She is in her element, and I'm by her side. Thank goodness she agreed to drive home after our night out. Just like I thought, my intuition was right. I think I hear a mixed-drink calling out to me now. Kendall struck a nerve. Damn it! I can't believe I still let her get to me.

"We'll have the burgers, no onions, and easy on the mayo. Oh, and I'll have a piña colada minus any alcohol." My friend rolls her eyes—showing her hesitation to leave off the rum.

Baylee looks at me and winks when she sees Kendall looking my way. I order something simple…not too strong. "I'll have a fuzzy navel with extra cherries—easy on the schnapps." I say it with a crooked smile and try not to be too friendly.

Kendall and I haven't seen eye to eye since I walked in on her cousin, Sara Beth, and Kris doing it doggy style in *my* apartment. For some off the wall reason, she thinks it's my fault because I didn't know how to keep him satisfied. Whatever! That girl needs to get a life and stay out of mine. I remind myself that I am here to have a good time, and I throw those thoughts back into that safe place I have locked away in my brain. *Now stay there!* I remind them.

My best friend, slash co-worker, and I sit and reminisce about the week we've had at the law firm of Jenkins, Jones, and Smith. We had put our forty-hour week in as legal assistants, and Monday it will be time to do it all over again. We have tons of new clients wanting their divorces final yesterday—so many we had to hire a part-timer.

"I don't think we get paid enough for the job we do." Baylee yells over the noisy room and tips her glass to mine. "Here's to having the weekend off."

"To the weekend off," I say.

The next thing we hear is the scrambled words of people chattering around us. The music from the jukebox has been turned off.

"May I have your attention please?" Most eyes turn to the man behind the voice, and the room slowly turns to a whisper—not everyone knows the meaning behind his question.

It's Joe from behind the bar. His voice is deep and demanding and echoing through the yellow megaphone. It's obvious he wants us to hear what he has to say. "I would like to thank you all for coming out tonight. Now with that said, who out there is ready to *party*?"

He pauses.

The crowd goes crazy. They are clapping, whistling, and swaying their beer bottles in the air and ready to get the festivities started.

And he continues...

"A very good friend of mine is here visiting for the weekend, and I convinced him he should play for you guys tonight. He's great. I know you will appreciate his love for music just like I do; so, if you will make your way out to the top deck…I think he's about ready to get started." He puts the megaphone down and makes his way outdoors.

People are yelling and chanting fanatically. You would think they had never heard live music before.

Baylee and I sit and let the crowd go ahead of us. We haven't finished our food yet anyway, and there is no way either of us is up to fighting all of these people. I'm sure we will enjoy the music from wherever we sit.

The hustle and bustle of the crowded room slowly thins out, and we make our way outside up under the stars…*ah*…I inhale the fresh air with my arm linked with Baylee's. *She's not letting me out of her sight.* We're thrilled when we find two seats fairly close to the stage.

The sun had set a couple of hours ago and the night air has cooled off a little, but the noise from the crowd is still echoing in my ears. Thank goodness for the spacious deck; I was beginning to feel a little claustrophobic sitting skin on skin with all those people. At least outside, I can breathe— especially with the occasional gust of wind that blows through ever so often. I take a long deep breath in, smelling the sweet scent of honeysuckle—one of my favorite parts of summer. *Oh, how I love this time of year.*

"So, I wonder what kind of music he sings," Baylee asks as she takes a break from sipping on her second virgin piña colada. The frozen drink looks mouthwatering, and suddenly, I'm wishing I had it instead of mine.

"As long as it's Country, I don't care." I take a sip of my drink…realizing just how strong it is. I guess the *bartender* did that on purpose. I roll my eyes at her, wishing she could see me this time.

Our girlish conversation is once again interrupted, and it's all because of that voice. It's super sexy. I turn as the lead singer walks past us adorning a microphone headset and sending his scent our way thanks to the breezy night.

That smell—it's him.

My jaw drops. I'm stunned by the majestic being before me. I'm hypnotized by his beauty, his smell—that voice.

Jumping up on stage, he starts his introduction of the band. There's Blake, Hunter, and Grace, but what's his name? Did I miss it? Who is that sumptuous man picking up the guitar? I don't recognize the others, but who cares; I want to know who he is.

I hope that Baylee can't tell, but I've tuned her completely out; I cannot take my eyes off of this heartthrob. He looks like a Greek God who has just dropped out of the heavens. Six feet of scrumptiousness and a body that gives buff a bad name—wow. Look at those arms—he must work out daily to have *biceps* like that. They are hard, big, and luscious—*just like the rest of him.*

And his hair...I love it—that gorgeous, vibrant, long, sandy-blonde hair. It flows just past his shoulders, and it is the perfect length to get my fingers lost in its wavy texture. Look at the way he jerks his head to the left to keep the strands out of his eyes. *That's a turn on all by itself.* As he sweeps it away, it's then that I notice the windows to his soul. They are an intensifying emerald blue-green color...just like the Gulf Shore waters. You can't help but drowned in them, and that is exactly what I am doing.

Suddenly, I'm engulfed by what the word infatuation really means...it should solely be based upon that man alone. He's perfection, and I'm not the only one who notices it. I tear my eyes away from the excellence before me only to see the wandering eyes of the hot-blooded women to my left and to my right. They are drawn in by his beauty too and are begging for his attention, but he doesn't give them the time of day.

My eyes are desperate to see more of him. They move up and down his body; memorizing every detail. I have never seen lips like that. They are voluptuous. Not to mention, luscious and plump and begging to be kissed; by me, and no one else.

What am I thinking? This isn't me…or is it? I've never lusted after a man before, but damn, he's F.I.N.E. Now, where was I? Oh, yes…

The black T-shirt he is wearing hugs him flawlessly; showing off the muscles in his chest, and my eyes can't help but make their way south to the rest of his *manliness* beauty.

Wow.

I'm suddenly feeling a sense of jealousy overcome me because of those jeans he is wearing. They fit him perfectly, and of course they leave no room for the imagination. Right there beneath that fly lays a bundle of hardcore joy. How does he keep it confined with just a zipper? My mouth is watering, and I can't help but choke on my own saliva.

Baylee tries pulling me back down to earth. "Wow, Joe has a friend like *that* and he hasn't brought him around here before?" I heard her, but this astonishing man has my undivided attention. Reminding myself not to be so rude, I manage a response.

"I'm. Sorry. What. Did. You. Say?" I ask her, without tearing my starry-eyed expression away from him.

Baylee shakes her head—laughing. She realizes I'm stunned by the beauty of this man who has stolen my attention away from her. Right now, in this very moment, I'm thankful for my friend's persistence. If I had stayed at home, I would be missing all of this.

The music begins to play, and the words come pouring out of that sexy mouth of his. *It is a country song, and I know it word for word.* Before too long, I'm singing right along with him and having the time of my life. Wow! He's good. He has a face like an angel and a voice like one too. I listen closely as he doesn't miss a beat of the hit song. I can't help but think he sings it better than the recording artist himself. I am in awe of his talent.

I'm swaying to the music just like the rest of the crowd, thinking I'll never be noticed but then it happens. He is dancing around the stage like he owns it, and then he looks my way. It is at that moment that I swear our eyes meet, and our gaze is locked on one another for what seems like an eternity. Then he does this thing with his brow...*oh my.* Up and down, fast and sexy, and making my heart race.

My breathing speeds up, and I'm twirling my hair around my finger, flirting, and getting his attention even more. I blink my eyes while batting my eyelashes and willing him to come hither. Playing hard to get has left my vocabulary, and that has always been my motto; *nothing worth having is easy, so work for it,* I always say. For some reason, I don't want him fighting for something I want him to have; *me*—how much have I had to drink? This isn't me.

He smiles at me.

I think I'm going to faint.

There is something about the way he is looking at me; what I'm feeling when he does. It's calming, yet exhilarating all at the same time. I feel so drawn to him, like a magnetic force is pulling me in his direction? Not only that, but it feels natural watching him while he's watching me...like we've met before. That's nonsense. I've never laid eyes on this man.

Baylee notices his stare and states the obvious. "I think he's looking at you." She's right and I'm speechless, but thanks to my last alcoholic beverage my imagination is running wild.

With his hot-smoldering eyes still fixed on me, I can see his desire. It is me. His thoughts are devouring my virtue at the same moment my womanhood is begging to be rescued. He grips the microphone and licks his lips in between the words of the song. He's drawn to me, and there is no denying the intense aspiration we feel between each other.

He finishes the song and leads right into another one. It's a perfect melody for lovers to dance to, and I'm not shocked that I'm longing to be in his arms and in his bed. As I'm deep in thought and forgetting that I'm a good girl with her virginity intact, I realize the star attraction has made his way off the stage and is walking through the crowd. Oh no! I mean, oh yes! He's headed in my direction.

Within seconds, I'm fanning myself with my hand and trying to cool down from all this heat, and I don't just mean the hot summer air. My adrenaline is flowing and my heart is pounding, making me feel like I'm having a personal heat wave of my own.

Suddenly, my head starts spinning, and I don't know if it's from the third fuzzy navel I just downed, or if it's because this sexy beast of a man is only a few yards away from me. I hang on to every word he sings as if he's singing them right to me, and I can't help but hope he keeps heading my direction.

There they are again. His flaming-hot eyes are hooked on mine, and my womanhood is screaming for attention. He has me all hot and bothered, and I can't control my thoughts. They are only of him. The sexiest man alive is heading right towards me, and I can't believe what he just did—*he winked at me.*

I breathe in and out, slowly and seductively; all while trying to calm my rapid heartbeat. This savagely magnificent creature has me second guessing my virtue and what it has meant to me my whole life. No one has ever done that before; Kris doesn't count. *It has to be the alcohol.* Yes, that's my excuse and I'm sticking to it.

The things I would let *that* man do me. Seconds later, he turns away and jumps back on stage. Great! So close, yet so far away. Disappointment wraps her greedy arms around me—laughing at how naive I am. *Did you really think he was coming for you;* her words tip-toeing around in my head.

As he continues singing, I just listen closely to the wild, yet tameness in his voice. He has captivated my attention, and it's obvious I did the same to him; so what if he turned away—he was entertaining the whole crowd, not just me.

Maybe fate has something fabulous in mind for me after all. I look up at the stars and wink; my way of accepting whatever she has in store for me and kicking little Miss Disappointment to the curb.

Time flies when you're having fun...I really did almost forget what that felt like. Up under the stars, swaying to the music, drinking more than I should have, the night is almost over.

Hours have passed since we arrived here at nine thirty, and the next thing I hear is Joe calling last call for alcohol. He closes up at three, and it's already a quarter till. That's crazy...seems like we just got here. Baylee and I have both enjoyed our night, and we didn't even care to keep up with the time. Of course I was too enthralled by the entertainment.

Hoping not to be noticed by her, I find my eyes skimming the area for the mystery man that is no longer on stage. Where did he go? Looking in every corner, every stairway, and every direction in between, I see him as we make our way down the steps and onto the parking lot.

He's climbing in the back seat of a dark gray SUV, and there's a woman there waiting. *My heart just did a belly flop.*

She looks like she's been crying, her mascara smeared beneath her eyes, and her blonde highlighted-hair looks like it's been brushed by a whirlwind. She's a hot-mess, and I can't make out who she is; *being three sheets to the wind doesn't help.*

I don't know what I was thinking drinking so much; it's left me an emotional wreck. *I wanted him to leave with me.* It's been months since a man turned my head, and I'm feeling jealousy that I shouldn't—and I think I'm even pissed.

The night was almost perfect, until now. First, he leaves with her, and then I hear the voice I dread the most; wait, maybe it's not so dreadful after all. If Tall, Dark, and Handsome doesn't want me—the man behind those words does. Suddenly, I'm thinking things I shouldn't, and my heavy consumption of alcohol is making me do it.

"Hannah! Hannah!" he yells.

All night long and nothing; not even an awkward glance from the man who has been a thorn in my side since our break up. Why does he have to bother me now, when I'm in this condition and not fully aware of my principals?

Walking through the parking lot, Baylee puts her hand on my back, but I shake my head. "It's okay," I insist, wondering if it really is.

I throw her my keys and tell her to wait for me at the car. Looking at me like I'm crazy, she leaves me alone to face him. *I'm really fixing to do this.*

"Kris, what do you want? He reeks of alcohol, but oh well, so do I.

"Come here, baby. Give me a kiss for old time's sake."

He's grabbing at me, and I'm doing pretty good keeping out of his grasp. If he gets a good grip, I may not be able to break free. *He's so damn strong, and I'm so damn drunk.*

And then it happens. The car carrying Mister Divineness himself drives by, and I get a glimpse of the woman's head resting on *his* shoulder. That's it. I'm tired of playing a losing battle with my inner self. I'm tired of being alone. I want what I've never had, and damn it...if I can't have it, Kris will have to do. I give in—falling into the arms of the man I've been fighting off.

Within minutes we're hidden away in a dark corner, and Kris is eating away at my neck and I'm letting him. He's managed to slip his hand down the back of my shorts, squeezing my ass as he gets a handful. He's hard as a rock and ready to go; he'll take me here and it doesn't matter that people are only feet away.

His other hand is up my shirt trying to get close to my breasts, and then my virtue is saved by his drunken words.

"I've always wanted to be your first, Hannah. I can't wait to open you up with my cock; you're going to be so tight—you're going to feel so good..."

Pushing him away, his words were my cup of coffee; sobering me up to the reality of what I almost let happen.

I break free from his hold and run back to find my friend; little do I know, he's chasing behind me.

"Hannah, wait!" he screams. I keep running.

"Get lost, Kris," I yell, but he doesn't listen.

Catching me off guard, I feel two hands on me. He turns me so quickly that I almost lose my balance. Before I can do anything, his lips are on mine, and he's got a grip on me I can't get out of.

Without thinking, my knee swings into action and thrusts into his manhood. I manage to break free, and he yells out in anguish while falling to his knees.

"Kris!" Baylee runs back towards us, and she is pissed. "Stay the hell away from her!" She places her hand on my back, kicks gravel in his direction, and tries to lead me away.

He doesn't give her a second thought, but he does to the girl walking by. She has more curves than a winding river, and that proves he is never going to change. I can't help but laugh and take pleasure leaving him with his throbbing *bruised-ass* balls. "You won't be using those tonight." I laugh.

At that moment, he knew I was more serious than I have ever been. After all these months, I can irrevocably, without a doubt, find humor in his pathetic ways. Finally, I am free. I no longer see him as the ex-boyfriend who betrayed our promise to each other, but as a wretched lonely soul who no longer has any control over me.

He lowers his head as though embarrassed, and without giving him a chance to take any more of my time, I turn and walk away smiling. *I did it!* I feel as though a heavy burden has just been lifted off my shoulders and life is worth living again. I jump in the passenger seat of my car and search frantically for the perfect song—flipping through my case of music like an idiot, I find it. At last! There you are girl; referring to the cd that is now in my hand. I slide the disc into the tray, hit play, and the rocking melody fills the air.

Baylee gets in and lets down the top. Rolling down the windows, we drive past Kris in my ole faithful convertible.

Of course the music is playing, and it is perfect timing as the chorus begins to play. I can't help but sing along. Please, please let him hear me.

You are a memory worth forgetting
There is nothing left to say
You are a lonely whisper in the wind
And I am getting away, getting away, getting away...

Kris stands to his feet, dusting off his jeans, and realizing he now has an audience. "What the hell are y'all looking at?" He yells, flipping his long black hair out of his face.

Three scrawny guys against a muscled-up dude like Kris...not happening; they're scared and it shows on their faces. They hustle away before he takes his humiliation out on one of them, and we keep on driving; leaving him to gloat in his own self pity.

I can't help but look in the rearview mirror and notice a woman coming to his rescue. Unable to make her out, my only thought now is how thankful I am that it's not me.

"Are you okay, honey?" Baylee asks.

"I am better than I've been in a long time," I whisper, staring out the window in amazement of what took place tonight. *I got my life back.*

Baylee and I make it to my apartment safe and sound, with no sign of Kris following us. We are both beat and ready for a goodnight's sleep. She goes straight to the guest bedroom, and I go to mine.

As I lay my head down on my pillow, my thoughts linger about a man I don't know—never thinking twice about the woman he left with. I go to sleep smiling with hopes that he will be in my dreams. Tomorrow is a new day. Maybe, just maybe I will find out who he is.

Chapter 3

Saturday morning comes way too early, and I'm up and out of the bed before I want to be. It's almost noon and my thoughts are of the new mysterious man that crossed my path last night. Who is he? It was the most amazing night—minus his departure and the encounter with my ex, and it is because of him. I wonder if I will ever see him again. I *have* to see him again. It's crazy. I'm longing for a man that I've never actually spoken to, but there's no denying the attraction that engrossed us both.

I exhale, allowing thoughts of him to settle in the back of my mind as I grab my phone and read the text I just got from Baylee.

Got up early and decided to go for a run...all the way to my house...lol...call me later.

That girl and her running; she is so dedicated. I shake my head.

I spend the morning dusting, sweeping, and mopping the front of the apartment. My little two-bedroom home may not be appealing to many, but it's mine and I think it's beautiful. Well, maybe not *beautiful*, but my independence forced me into showing my mom that she raised me right, and that I could take care of myself. Even if it isn't my dream home, I don't mind faking it in front of her. If she thinks I'm happy, she's happy.

Finally, my chores are done, and I make my way to the bedroom. It's a spacious room, but with all my second-hand fixtures it looks pretty crowded. The furniture came from an estate sale, and I was lucky to get the antique six-piece suit for a little bit of nothing. It may be old but it's paid for, and that's one less bill I have.

I can't help but eye my bag of goodies underneath the bed, and as soon as I do I'm reminded of my loneliness. One of those little one-inch vibrating wonders may temporarily ease my arousal from time to time, but how much longer will that be enough? Not only do I crave the thick hard thrust of a man's joy hitting that hotspot between my legs, but I also yearn to be loved by a man full of passion. It is becoming a craving that is getting stronger as the days go by, and it is a fact that I can no longer deny.

One day soon, I hope to find the man of my dreams, but for now I'm stuck wishing it could be the divine deity from last night. He is the pure essence of what the perfect lover should look like. He has just what it takes to be the star attraction in one of my erotica's. I smile; maybe even my life.

There is something about him that leaves me breathless just thinking about him; his face, the windows to his soul, his eye-catching manhood. And that voice. I fight the temptation to call Joe and find out who he is. I can't get him out of my head. *Hannah! Get it together!* My subliminal essence demands.

Perfect timing! I hear my phone ringing and my thoughts are put on standstill. I pick it up and the caller ID flashes unknown caller. Clearing my throat, I answer the call.

"Hello? Hello?" There is no sound and no one answers.

Hanging up, I throw my phone to the side and go to the spare room where I find my Pilates mat. A good workout is just what I need.

An hour passes and sweat is dripping from my body like I just had mad wicked sex, but of course I didn't. What I had been doing is exerting myself to the point of no return. Any other day a massive workout would have cleared my thoughts, but not today. My sixty-minute indulgence flew by and no luck, he is still there and taking up residence. What the hell am I going to do?

I need a shower.

I strip down and climb in; turning the water on as hot as I can stand it. The steam is filling the room fast, and I'm already starting to relax. Closing my eyes, I allow the water to flow over the top of my head, down my back, and I turn around to give my breast the same affection. Yes. This is just what the doctor ordered.

Before I know it, the shower head is in my hand and on full pulsate mode. The invigorating hot water feels fabulous as it hits my aching body, but there is no denying that little piece of me that has been deprived of the attention it deserves. I move the shower head from my waist to between my thighs and place one foot on the shelf of the tub so that my legs are wide open—*baring my essentials.*

The pounding water finds its way to my pleasure-area and begins to beat away at my throbbing love-button. It won't be long now; I know I will soon find my release. My mind is racing full speed, and it's then that I imagine *him* on his knees in front of me taking control of the situation. Oh yes! It's happening! The tension is building and all the stress is going to flow right out of me. Climax and then relax. Now, that is the best form of self medication. *Ah!*

I spend the rest of the afternoon reading, thinking maybe a little Maddox love would get *him* out of my head…but no such luck. Even all the passion my book portrays doesn't keep my mind from fantasizing about a complete stranger— *it's making it worse.* All I can think about is being tangled up with him up under the sheets—his bed, my bed, *it doesn't really matter which one.*

Blinking my way out of the daydream, I reluctantly lay my book down. *Sorry Maddox honey, I'll have to catch up with you later.*

While pacing the floors, my mind becomes more exhausted than my feet. I have to get out of this apartment and do something; *anything.* Maybe I should go see a movie. Yes, I think I will. I grab my tablet and pull up the website for the local theater. Glancing at their homepage, I find myself totally disappointed. *No. No. No.* Not one movie out of all nine is a chic-flick; most shows are either bloody horror films or rated G. *Ugh!*

As I'm tapping my fingers on the table beside me and watching the trailer of one of the least scary movies, I'm startled by the ringing of my phone. After almost jumping out of my skin, I check to see who it is this time.

It's only Baylee.

Getting a grip, I answer it—scolding myself for my reaction before I do. *Get it together, Hannah!*

"Hello." My voice is squeaky and I try clearing my throat, quietly with my hand over the receiver.

"Are you okay?" she exclaims.

"Yes. I'm fine. The phone just startled me, but I'm okay now. What's up?"

"How do you feel about getting out for a little while tonight? I came across a couple of tickets to see the *Sweet Men of the South*. Do you want to go?"

"You must have read my mind. I would love to go, but I thought you had a date." I exit out of the website...*no scary movie equals no rattled nerves for me tonight.* Thank goodness.

"Yeah, I did, but he stood me up again. I don't know why I even care anymore. So, will you really go with me?" she asks, determined for my answer.

"Of course I'll go with you. I can't wait. Text me the details and I'll pick you up."

"Okay...I'll see you in a bit." She hangs up without saying bye or giving me a chance to either. I shake my head at my friend. She really is one of a kind.

Staying busy is the best way to keep that mouthwatering mystifying man out of my thoughts; surely a roomful of *sexy* strippers will do that. I hate that Baylee's date stood her up again, but I'm more than happy to take his place.

With my top down on my convertible, Baylee and I enjoy the fresh air. The temperature has dropped about ten degrees from last night, and the breeze outside is refreshing compared to the scorching heat we've already had so early in the season. It's going to be a hot summer. The weatherman has forecasted rain this evening…maybe he'll be right this time.

After a half hour drive up under the stars, we make it to our destination. Women are lined up with their tickets in hand and waiting to enter the *ladies only* affair. Twenty minutes have passed, and finally we're walking through the front doors.

The music is bumping, and the walls are vibrating to the beat of a song I am not familiar with. I can't hear myself think much less hear the words that are pouring out of Baylee's mouth. I motion for her to follow me to a table on the other side of the room. The music is still loud, but at least now we can have a conversation.

Making our way to the tall round table, we sit down on the stools adjoining them—feeling like we're the star attractions thanks to the flashing lights that are coloring up our space. The music, the scenery, even the smell is getting us pumped up and ready to have a good time.

"We'll be talking about this night when we're old and gray and trying to keep our teeth in," Baylee laughs, but I know deep down her joke is one of her biggest fears. She doesn't have a vain bone in her curvy structure, but her beauty has taken her places some women can only dream about.

A wicked grin breaks through my tightened lips as my mind once again loses its train of thought. I picture myself gumming my future husband's pride and joy and putting my teeth back in when I'm done. Then I realize that's not funny at all, and I make a mental note to see my dentist at his earliest convenience. *Call Dr. Pierce first thing Monday morning.*

"Baylee, we'll find our fountain of youth one day, and we won't have to worry about aging." Trying to banish her thoughts of a future she feared, I point to the center stage. The bouncers are clearing it of empty bottles and of the women who have already clearly had too much to drink. The show is starting, and we are both in desperate need of some serious entertainment.

From out of nowhere, comes a mist of smoke that fills the area quickly, and the disco lights are flashing brighter to the beat of the music—now splashing the whole room up with the vibrant neon colors and taking the spotlight off of us.

Horny women from every corner start screaming, and suddenly everything goes pitch black. Seconds later, the darkness disappears; the music changes out, and before our eyes are five of the sexiest masked men ever—bare-chested and showing off their assets. They may be easy to look at, but nothing compares to what I watched last night.

Damn, he's in my head again.

My mysterious heartthrob is the personification of sexy. Why can't he be up there stripping down to his bare essentials? *Ah!* What a sight that would be. I gasp, wiggling in my seat. Just the thought sends my womanhood into craving what it's never had. Mmmm...

Focusing, I force myself to pay attention.

The men take control of the stage as they rock out to one of my favorite songs. Before we know it, they are stripping down to their thongs and dollar bills are flying in the air everywhere. I can't help but notice a woman yelling from close by; waving money in both hands and getting the attention of one of the dancers.

"Hey you, hot and sexy, please give me some of that sugar!" she yells and he prances her way, his face now in front of hers— teasing her with his mouth, so close to hers she can almost feel it. He licks his lips, running his fingers down his chest and landing there. Yes, he really just slid his hand beneath the string holding his bulge in place—tempting her to shove some of the cash between the thong he is wearing and his oil-slicked skin.

And she falls for it—earning her a kiss to the cheek; the exotic dancer just made her night. Dancing away, he's left her thrilled and her friends are jealous, but they still laugh right along with her.

I shake my head laughing, and then I notice him.

An enigmatic, yet somewhat familiar dancer makes his way to our table. Without giving me a second look, he is all up in Baylee's business. He is giving her a lap dance she is sure to never forget. As he grinds his well-endowed cock up and down her bare thighs, I can't help but notice her tensing up. What is *her* problem?

Quickly, she grabs a napkin from the table and sticks it in between the cheeks of his ass. He removes it in a flash and dances away. I give her a confused look, but she is not to be reckoned with. "I need a drink!" She shouts over the loud music and motions for the waitress.

She orders her favorite drinks and downs them one by one. Baylee is working on her fourth piña colada when I finally get the nerve to ask her what is wrong. "Baylee, talk to me...what happened?"

She takes a deep breath and says, "Look."

I turn around to see one of the guys dressed in a pair of tight fitting jeans, boots, and a cowboy hat. He is wearing a bandana to cover his mouth and is swinging a lasso in the air. Some bull riding song is playing over the sound system, and I still can't figure out what the big deal is. As he dances, I realize he is the same one that visited our table earlier. The daggered-heart tattoo on his left bicep clearly gives him away.

And then it's like someone slapped me across the face with a reality check. A flashback of our latest pool party comes to mind, and now I know why the stripper looks so familiar. It is Tyler; the only man that Baylee would give up being single for, and he has stood her up for two weeks in a row now. No wonder she isn't in the mood she was in when we first arrived.

"It's Tyler. I can't believe he is stripping now," she says—confusion written all over her face.

Patting her back, I try sympathizing with her, but it is not working. She is hurt and she is pissed. Tyler may have stood her up, but it is clear she is far from over him.

"Baylee, maybe he needs the extra money." My empathizing words not making her feel any better. *I feel so bad for her*. She really looks heartbroken over this jerk, and I'm longing to kick his ass. "Cheer up girl. We are here to have a good time, remember." I hold my glass up as to give a toast, and she clinks hers to mine.

"To good times girl." Her words are well spoken, but I know her heart really isn't backing them up.

Rocking lyrics continue to croon over the sound system, and the dancers have stripped down to their last routine. The night has flown by and the show is soon over. Thank goodness I had enough sense not to finish my third mixed-drink over an hour ago. Needless to say, my friend would be feeling the wrath of a hangover tomorrow. I couldn't blame her for over doing it; after all, she is heartbroken.

I am finding it hard to make it to my car with Baylee, as we are fighting our way through the restless crowd. She is too drunk to know she is tripping over air and almost taking me down to the ground with her. To my surprise, I hear a voice calling my name from not too far behind us. It is him. Tyler. The one person I really don't feel like dealing with right now.

"It looks like you could use a hand," he says, trying to be helpful.

Lifting Baylee in his arms effortlessly, he makes his way to my convertible. In my quiet voice I whisper to him, "You have a lot of explaining to do, but not to me. She deserves an explanation of why you stood her up. I know you will give her one as soon as she sleeps this off."

I open the door to the passenger side, and he sets her down with ease. He even leans over to buckle her in, and before leaving he gently moves the hair from her face. As I watch him, I can see something in his eyes that gives away his feelings for her. Maybe he does care after all; if so, what is his problem?

Glancing in my direction, he notices I have put my index finger to my lip—his sign to say goodnight. He waves bye.

I start my car and begin to back up, when I realize something is caught in the wiper of my windshield. I jump out to retrieve it, and it's a sealed envelope. *That is so weird.*

Ripping it open, I find a legal size sheet of paper folded up. After unfolding it, there's no doubt the large boldface words get my attention. Left to right, my eyes read the dark print.

I'M WATCHING YOU HANNAH.

My stomach catches my heart as it dives into the acidy pool below—*I think I'm going to throw up.* My heart slams back into my chest. I will not be scared—fear will only get me in trouble. I take a deep breath and tear my eyes away from the print.

I search the area closely and see nothing out of the ordinary; just a lot of women trying to leave like we are. Kicking fear to the side, I grab my phone and call the one person I trust the most—my brother. Landon works as an officer at one of the local police stations, and he will know what to do.

After the third ring, he answers and I tell him about the note.

"Sis, you did the right thing by calling. Be cautious of your surroundings, and don't trust anyone you don't know. I'll have a patrol car keep an eye on your street tonight," he says as I pull out of the parking lot.

"Thanks, Landon. I always knew you were good for something." I laugh trying to keep the fear out of my voice. I don't want him worrying, and I really don't want mom finding out about this so I have to be convincing. She's always trying to get me to move back home, and this would be good leverage for her to hold over me.

"Landon, keep this between us. Please don't worry mom." I continue talking to him, and he agrees; our mother does not need this burden to carry.

Meanwhile, on the drive home, my brother the cop suggests the unthinkable. "Hannah, do you think Kris would stoop this low?"

My heart sinks even thinking he would, but I try to reassure myself and also Landon, that Kris is finally ready to move on. I recollect the last twenty-four hours I've had, and deep down I know my ex-boyfriend would make me his all over again if I would allow it.

"No, Landon. Kris isn't that stupid or desperate for that matter."

He exhales...thinking about my situation I'm sure. I know he'll do what he can to get to the bottom of this. I trust him whole-heartedly...not only is he my brother, but he is a damn good officer.

My eyes are drawn to the dark cloudy sky; it's lightning in the distance, and the wind is picking up. This is it. Our first rain in weeks has arrived. It starts coming down, a few droplets at first, and then it's like the clouds opened up to water the thirsty dry grounds. Hands up to the weather guy; he knew what he was talking about this time. It's been a month since the last good rain, and this heat is burning everything up. I just wish it could've waited until I got home...just a few more minutes and I would have made it.

I flip on my windshield wipers. "Are you still there?" I ask patiently.

"Yeah, sis, I'm just trying to figure this out. Are you going to be okay alone tonight?" His voice is worried.

"I'm not alone. Baylee is with me." I leave out the part about her being passed out drunk in the passenger seat of my car. I'm not sure how much help she will be if I am being attacked, but she's here nonetheless.

"Great. Well, call me in the morning and let me know you survived the night, okay," he demands.

"I will, Landon," my voice almost a whisper. "Thank you."

"Any time, sis," he hangs up without saying bye.

As I pull onto Macon Drive and head toward my building, I see a glimpse of what looks like someone leaning on the door of my apartment. It sends shivers down my back and I think long and hard on whether or not I should keep driving. Paranoia is trying to step in, and I'm fighting it tooth and nail.

I slow the car down and notice a tree limb swaying back and forth and catching the rays of the street light above. That has to have been what I saw. This storm is pretty brutal, and trees are swaying in the wind all around my apartment complex. *I'm sure that's all it was*. I convince myself it is okay and continue pulling in. I really need to get Baylee to bed, and now is no time to chicken out of going home.

The rain has eased up to only a mere sprinkle, and if I hurry I can miss the next down pour. I can hear the thunder pounding in the distance, and the lightning looks like varicose veins splitting in every direction all over the dark sky.

I park the car. Hurriedly, I help Baylee out of the passenger side and hold on tightly to the pepper spray I have attached to my key chain.

My eyes are skimming the area closely and watching for anything out of place; everything looks normal. I exhale, letting out a sigh of relief as I make it to my door, pushing it open, and letting go of my friend for just a moment.

While trying to get my key out of the doorknob, a bolt of lightning strikes close by causing me to jump. I blink my eyes and take a deep breath and listen as the thunder rolls for what seems like minutes.

Baylee manages to stumble her way across the room and falls to the couch. She is fast asleep and soon it will be my turn.

I turn to lock the front door and notice a piece of paper caught underneath it. I pick it up, unfold it, and there are those large bold letters again. This time my stomach slams into my heart as I read the threatening words.

ARE YOU SCARED YET?

I promptly lock the door and realize that it was a person's shadow I saw after all. I'm being stalked and scared doesn't begin to describe what I am feeling. I am freaking the hell out.

Quickly, I grab a blanket from the hall closet to cover my friend with, and then run to the safety of my own bedroom.

Refusing to shower this late, I throw on a T-shirt and climb in under the covers; securing them tightly around me and sealing my eyes shut. My only way of closing out the fear that is now haunting me, until I'm fast asleep.

It's dark and I can't see in front of me. I'm fighting to control my breathing, and suddenly, I realize I'm restrained. My wrists are above my head, and the more I try to move them the more I can feel the metal cutting into my skin. My legs are opened wide and propped up towards my hips. I try to relax them, and I soon acknowledge they too have been carefully tied to something I can't get out of. There is a silky soft piece of cloth covering my eyes, and that confirms it; I've been blindfolded. I struggle to release myself, but it's hopeless. My mind is racing, and my heart is pounding. My lips are moving— I'm trying to scream, but not one word escapes my mouth.

The only thing I can hear is the heavy breathing of what sounds like a mongrel of a man. He breathes in, and he breathes out; with every stench of his nasty breath hitting my naked body; *my naked body*. This can't be happening. He sounds as though he could ravish me like a seven course meal.

I struggle, but there is nothing I can do bound to this bed. I feel helpless knowing this monster is going to take the most precious gift I could give the man I love on our wedding night— my virginity. The thing I dread most is upon me. I can feel his hands grabbing and rubbing me in places only I know personally. I twist and turn over and over again, and suddenly, I feel as though I'm falling from the sky.

"Wake up, Hannah!" yells Baylee, as she shakes me back to reality. "You are having a bad dream!"

My eyelids are heavy and I struggle to open them. Finally, I manage to rise up and realize I'm soaking wet with sweat. I look out my window to see the sunrise peeking through the horizon. The storm is over—so is my nightmare.

The clock on the wall says it is 5:43, and I can't believe it's already morning. I yawn long and hard, realizing I'm not ready to be up at this hour, but I am thankful she woke me from that horrific dream.

Baylee has slipped away, and I can hear her in the bathroom. Her body is beating her up over the indulgence of alcohol she consumed. Once she's done flushing the last of it out of her system, she returns from the bathroom with a glass of water in each hand—one for me and one for her. "Are you okay, honey?" she asks.

My brow creeps up—almost in a straight line. "Shouldn't I be asking you that?" I ask.

"I'm fine," she says. "Now, tell me what had you fighting beneath those sheets."

After catching her up on that weird-ass stalker crap and the details of my nightmare, we laid in my bed facing each other. Being the good friend she is, she stays until I fall back to sleep. And that's exactly what I did—right up until noon; my only dream this time was of a dark sultry voice bathed in sexy. I wake up smiling, and it is to an empty bed. Baylee is gone, but she has left a note.

Hey, Hannah Banana ☺
I didn't want to wake you, so mom came to pick me up.
Call me later.
— Baylee

That means I'm all alone. Looking around my room, I see the bathroom is only feet away. I really need to go. Damn the fear. I will not let something or someone control me this way. I jump up out of bed and go to the bathroom to take care of my business. Once I'm done, I shower and lounge around the apartment for the rest of the afternoon doing what I do best—*reading, surfing the net, and thinking about the man with the singing voice.*

By six o'clock, my mood is better than it was this morning. I cozy up on the couch and decide tonight is a perfect night for a pizza and a chic-flick.

I pick up my tablet to go online and order my favorite pizza, and I see that I have new alerts on one of the social networking pages. It looks like they are the same ole requests— nothing exciting. Then, I get to my messages and see that there is one from a person I don't know. There is no picture and the name reads Just Me.

I click on the message.

*Are you thinking about me like I'm
thinking about you?*

I gasp out loud and start talking to the screen, but more to myself. *"What the hell? Who is this?"* Oh no! It dawns on me it has to be the stalker. *"No! No! No! Why is this happening to me?"*

I continue talking to my tablet as though I'll get a response. I try to think of any enemies that I may have made recently, but none come to mind. This just does not make sense. Then, it happens. I'm startled by the pounding on my front door, and a sense of fright runs through my entire body. My pulse races and I feel like I just choked on my heart.

I cringe at the thought of looking through the peep hole, but here goes nothing. I grab the flyswatter—*the flyswatter?* This jerk is causing me to lose the only thing I have going for me; my common sense. Closing one eye, I peek through the tiny opening with the other.

There's no one there.

Yes it is.

Damn those blonde curls that bounce up out of nowhere. It's Baylee. I let out a deep sigh of relief and open the door.

"Hey, girl," she says. Baylee looks at me and she can quickly tell something is not right.

"Uh, oh. What's wrong now?" She questions me with words but more with her eyes. *Her eyes always give her away.*

Feeling aspirated, I pounce back down in my recliner. "Look at this." I show her the message that I found waiting on me.

She reads it, and then reads it again; her eyes scanning for any evidence as to who it may be. "That's crazy Hannah, but don't let this idiot get the best of you honey. You are stronger than this, and besides, you've got the flyswatter to swat their butt with."

We both burst out laughing—putting fear on the backburner and changing the subject. Oh how I loved the way she could find humor in just about anything; even when my life depends on it. If only I could be so confident. Baylee keeps me company for the rest of the evening, and we spend it watching one of our favorite movies. It is a tear jerker, but has the best ending—just what I needed.

Chapter 4

Manic Monday flies in like a whirlwind, leaving the weekend to now be only a memory. Mr. Jenkins is out of the office sick, which means a double workload for me, and today is one day that I will welcome the extra duty. The more files I have to focus on means the less time I have to dwell on whoever the hell *Just Me* is.

For the most part, yesterday was relaxing; just not long enough. I think I had too much excitement in one weekend, because I am still so exhausted; emotionally, physically, and in spite of everything that's going on, I can't get *him* off my mind.

Thoughts of a man I want to know kept me up half the night. The other half was consumed with dreams of the moron that is trying to invade my personal space. Three days ago my life was normal...boring maybe, but drama-free and no worries. Now, that's all changed. It's as though I'm seeing the world through someone else's eyes, but I'm not. *This is my life.*

I'm startled by a knock at the door, and my thoughts are paused. I look up to find a young delivery boy holding a vase full of colorful roses.

Brushing an unruly strand of hair away from his dark brown eyes, he looks lost and confused.

"Ms. Stone," he says in a shy kind of way.

"Yes, I'm Hannah Stone." I smile.

"I have a delivery for you ma'am." He swallows hard, almost like he's nervous.

I grab my purse and hunt down a five-dollar bill to tip him with, and he graciously hands me the vase—accepting the cash and leaving.

I'm left curious and questioning someone's generosity.

It's not my birthday, so why is someone sending me flowers? Maybe it's the sexy-singing-stranger that I can't get out of my head. I shake off the thought and realize how absurd that sounds. *He doesn't even know my name.*

I take a deep breath in, and I am quickly reminded I don't like the smell of fresh flowers. Although these do look like they were picked last week, the scent still reminds me of a funeral home.

After sitting the arrangement on my desk, I look to see if there is a card attached.

"Ouch!" I didn't mean to scream, but I pricked my finger on one of the stems looking for the card, and now it is gushing blood. I grab a tissue and blot the redness away—taking time to add a little pressure so that it doesn't come back. Finally, the bleeding stops, and I open the small sealed envelope. I pull out the card and read the words.

Hannah,

Red *is a <u>reminder</u> that I am always watching you.*
Yellow *symbolizes the <u>yelling</u> you will do.*
Pink *is for the <u>passion</u> you will never experience, it's true.*
White *represents my <u>willingness</u> to torture the pure virtue right out of you.*
Violet *stands for the <u>virgin</u> you will no longer be.*
Black *is for the <u>bitterness</u> you will feel—brought on by me.*

Sincerely,
Just Me

Suddenly, I can't catch my breath and my hands are trembling terribly. I hadn't noticed Baylee standing in the doorway until she spoke up.

"Hannah, what's going on?" I can tell by the look on her face that she can see the fear in mine. I pass her the card, and I find myself sitting all too quickly.

"Honey, this is messed up. You need to call Landon and officially report this." There is fear in her eyes and anger in her voice. Both of which, I am feeling. I know she is right, but the thought of being stalked is still trying to sink in. Why would anyone want to cause me harm?

"Yes. I. Know. I. Will." I could hear the words come out of my mouth, but did I really say them aloud? Now, I feel like I am really on-looking someone else's life—*this cannot be mine.* "I need to go. Please let the others know I'm leaving for the day, and tell Mr. Jenkins my vacation has officially started."

I don't give Baylee time to respond. I grab the vase and throw it in the trash next to my office door. I have to figure out what to do next, and I can't do it here. Walking out the door, I can hear my friend calling after me, but I don't have time to deal with her. I'm out of her sight within seconds.

I pull on to the highway and notice the young delivery boy walking along the sidewalk. Without thinking, I swerve into the gas station close by and throw my car into park. I get out and run towards the boy, and I realize he's looking at me like I am some kind of a crazy woman.

"Are you alright lady?" I hadn't realized how young looking he is until now. The poor kid must think I'm a real nut job.

"The flowers you gave me. You delivered them to me, and I need to know who sent them. Please." I am pleading with a boy who can't be over fifteen, and he's looking at me like I have lost my mind.

"Look, lady. I don't know who the guy was," he mutters. His voice sounds as confused as I am, but I'm desperate for answers. He has to know, so why won't he just tell me?

Desperation is all over my face. There is no denying the blinding fear in my tear-filled eyes, and I know this poor defenseless kid sees it.

He takes a deep breath, letting it out slow and easy. "All I know is, I was at the skate park, and so was he. He asked me if I wanted to make some fast cash, and I took him upon his offer. All I had to do was deliver the flowers to you." He jerks his head to the right. He does that a lot, trying to keep the hair out of his eyes.

I examine him closely. Eyes don't lie...they just don't and his aren't.

"Do you remember what he looked like? What was he driving? Please, just try to remember." My heart is racing and it's hard to control my breathing, but I have to. I have to be in control right now; that is the only way I'm going to figure this out. I don't realize I have a hand on each one of the boy's shoulders with a grip that has to be hurting him, until he starts to squirm.

"I didn't see the car, but I think he was Chicano: dark eyes, black hair, young...maybe in his early twenties," he says. "I'm not really sure though."

He's scared and confused, and none of this is his fault. The boy jerks out of my grasp and takes off so fast I can't stop him. Suddenly, I realize I have an audience and several of the onlookers are young men. Some are Mexican, while others are biracial; then there are the white men whose skin has been overly kissed by the rays of the summer sun, and they are all peering through eyes that could be his.

Crap! I turn around and run to my car. What if he's here watching my every move now? He will know just how terrified I am, and that is the last thing I want him to know. I have got to keep it together or the stalker will fulfill his plan. *Think, Hannah! Think!* Screaming the words inside my head, I plan my getaway while trying to pay attention to my surroundings.

Speeding away, I recall my earlier words to Baylee. I left the office saying my vacation had just started. Maybe that's not such a bad idea after all. But first things first—I have to make this official.

I pull into the parking lot of my apartment building and before getting out of the car, I call my brother.

"Hi, Landon. It's me." I clear my throat, so that he can't tell I've been crying, but it doesn't work.

"Sis. What is it? What's wrong?" His demand heard loud and clear and needing answered.

"I think you need to send a car to my place. I would like for you to be here, and I'll explain then."

Sitting in my car with my head on the steering wheel, I can't hold back the tears. I don't understand why this is happening to me. Fear is not an emotion I deal with easily, but it is one that I take seriously. Scared and confused, I try coming up with a plan of escape.

Moments later, I am brought back to reality with a tap on my window.

It is my brother—my big, strong, fearless brother. I didn't see the patrol car pull up beside me due to my deep thoughts, but I was happy for their quick arrival nonetheless.

Jumping out of the car, Landon grabs me and embraces me with a brotherly hug that can make any girl feel safe. Oh, if only I could feel this way after he let go.

"Hannah. What happened?" He questions me…part cop, part brother.

I start with the second note I found at my apartment door, and I can see the disbelief in his eyes. He realizes I didn't inform him of this when we talked yesterday.

Without explaining why I withheld the information, I went on to tell him about the message on my tablet and the flowers with the threatening card attached to it.

He shakes his head and introduces his partner.

"Hannah, this is Mark. He's going to make a report of everything you just said. We will get to the bottom of this. I promise."

I nod.

The officer asks questions and takes notes when he sees fit. Of course, the first question he asks is the last one I want to hear.

"Do you have an ex-boyfriend or …" I stop him before he finishes.

"No. Kris would not do this." That much I truly believe. I have to believe that much.

He proceeds to ask me about anyone who may have taken an interest in me lately. Someone that maybe wants more than I'm willing to give.

I remember *him,* Joe's friend, and my thoughts go back to Kris. There is no way it's either of them. It can't be. Hell, I know it's not the man from the bar. The unknown calls started before I ever laid eyes on him. The calls have to be coming from the stalker, and I refuse to believe that is Kris.

I look at Landon, and he's trying to get me to cooperate with a tilt of his head, but I'm done. I'm not answering anymore questions.

"I don't know who the jerk is, but I'm finished talking."

I can't help but still feel a sense of shock. I cannot believe this is happening to me. I like to consider myself a good person. I never bother what's not mine, and I try to stay away from any form of drama.

All I want is to fall in love, live in a quaint little house with the man of my dreams—I don't even need the white-picket-fence, but now some sick and twisted pervert is putting a chapter in my life that I don't want there. It's time to turn the page...*now, but how?*

"Ma'am, I think that will do it. We will send an extra patrol car out this way to keep an eye on things, but you call if anything else happens."

"Okay." I whisper, standing there frustrated, worried, and scared like crazy with my arms crossed in front of me. Mark seems nice enough, but a patrol car isn't going to make me feel any better at the present moment. "Thank you, officer. May I have a moment alone with my brother?"

As I turn to look at Landon, it's as though he can read my mind.

"I think you should get away from this place for awhile. Maybe you can stay with mom or even crash at my place."

Landon means well, but I really don't think he knows me as well as he thinks he does sometimes. I refuse to go back home or stay in an apartment with him and his two other flirtatious roommates.

"I'll think about it and let you know. Thanks for coming."

We say our goodbyes hurriedly because the officers are called away on an urgent matter.

I rush into my apartment and take a quick look around before shutting the door. I don't see anything unusual. I take a deep breath and lock the deadbolt.

Moments pass while I stand in the living room and go over the last few days in my head. Finally, I know what I have to do. I go to my bedroom and grab the lock box from the top shelf of my closet. Inside I find my passport, birth certificate, credit cards, and some extra cash I had put away for an emergency. Yes, a vacation it is—not sure where, but I'm getting out of this town as soon as possible.

While still in the closet, I bend down and grab my luggage set and start packing. This is crazy. Where am I going to go? I don't know, and I don't care as long as there is sunshine, a beach, and far away from this craziness. I am in desperate need of a little me-time, and this stupid drama is getting left behind in Tennessee…that's for damn sure.

There's nothing more to think about. I'm packed and ready with no real destination in mind, but that's not going to stop me. I decide to drive up to the Nashville airport in the morning and pray they have an open seat with a destination to paradise.

Chapter 5

It is a beautiful morning and the skies are clear—that means all flights should be on schedule. I make my way into the lobby of the airport and gasp at the massive crowd. The lines are long and full of anxious people ready to board the planes. There is no way there will be an empty seat with so many people waiting.

The steady rhythm of footsteps echoing in my ears will not get me off track. I am determined to get away, and that's exactly what I'm going to do—one way or another. Making my way to the end of the line, I stand there looking lost. Waiting as each passenger in front of me shows their id at the ticket counter and the agents pass them through to security. Oh, if I can only be so lucky and they have an extra seat going *somewhere.*

While waiting, I text Baylee to let her know I'm going to get away for about a week, just so I can try and figure things out. I don't want her coming around looking for me while I am gone. I would hate for her life to be in danger just because of me. Showing my mom and Landon the same respect, I text them saying I will be extra busy for the next few days—*that way they won't be surprised if they don't hear from me.*

Now, back to figuring out my destination…

Glancing around the loud overly-packed terminal, I notice most people are dressed in shorts and tank tops and others with Hawaiian style shirts. *Hawaii.* Oh, how I've always wanted to go there.

I look at the board and notice there is a flight that leaves in three hours headed to the islands. I mentally start counting how much money I've got, and I know I have enough to cover at least two weeks—that includes the credit card I just activated this morning. Finally, paradise isn't looking too far away. Now, if they just have an empty seat and a ticket with my name on it.

Despite the long line, it seems to be moving pretty fast. I'm at the front of the line before I know it, and it's hard to believe no one is standing behind me. The attendant, whose name tag reads Molly, looks at me and offers her assistance.

"How may I help you today?" she asks, standing there with a perfectly tucked bun on the top of her head. The strands of her hair are platinum blonde and go well with her sparkling-blue eyes. She is well-groomed and very pretty.

"Molly, I would like one round-trip ticket to Honolulu please."

My desperation is bleeding through with demanding words, but there is no way around the fact that I really am desperate to board that plane—*any plane for that matter.*

She looks at the computer screen, and I can hear her fingers typing on the keyboard. She's hitting the keys over and over again—desperately seeking out a seat just for me. I can see her answer when she looks back at me. Once again, *eyes never lie.*

"Ma'am, I'm so sorry, but that flight is booked solid," she sighs.

"Oh, of course it is. But could you please look again? Maybe there's been a cancellation that you hadn't noticed before," I beg, and there is no doubt in my mind that I will get on my knees if that's what it takes. I have got to get out of this town and desperate times call for desperate measures.

A look of hopelessness must be all over my face, because suddenly she looks speechless. Not to mention the sudden warmth that has just come over me…must be the late reaction to being cooped up in this line for so long. No, that's not it. It's though I can feel someone watching my every move, but I'm far from scared; just curious. I look ahead and to the sides. Nothing.

My attention goes back to Molly, but before she can answer me, a deep-velvety-smooth voice from behind me speaks up.

"Molly, there is an empty seat next to mine if Miss Stone is interested," he says.

Her eyes are locked on the man behind me.

"Yes, of course, Mr. Dawson," she answers him quickly...almost too quickly, as though he's somebody to be intimidated by.

I turn around.

Whoa!

Wide-eyed and stupid, my mouth drops open.

It. Is. Him. The breathtaking beauty from Joe's Place is standing there like a piece of perfection...*yep*; I would say that's pretty intimidating.

He opens that gorgeous mouth of his and I really have to focus on what he is saying— my mind is fighting a losing battle, you see. I keep telling myself to play hard to get, but my heart keeps tempting me and begging me to just give in; have a little fun—you only live once, right—funny how a girl's train of thought can be swayed from one direction to another just because of a good-looking man.

"We meet again, Miss Stone," he says calmly, like we've *really met before.* No words grace my lips—only a nod in his direction confirming what he said. I stand there gaping like a complete love-sick idiot—mouth still wide open. He clears his throat, allowing a slight devious grin to peek from one corner of his lips—*all just to get my attention.*

"I'm sorry...what did you say?" Trying hard to pay attention—my eyes move back and forth from those dreamy eyes to those kissable lips.

"Miss Stone, am I right?" His voice so raspy-smooth.

"Uh, excuse me— " I mutter, *now* trying to clear my own throat. "Yes, I'm Hannah Stone."

Fight it, Hannah! You can do it. Pay attention to the man and not that. My subliminal essence taunts me...begging me not to falter. His tongue glides across the bottom half of his lip...and that's it; I do better when I'm eye to eye with him. Face to face, looking his way as he looks mine...now I can listen to him.

"The seat is yours if you want it, and it won't cost you a dime." His voice is dreamy—seducing me into saying yes. Not to mention my heart is whispering uh-huh, while my thoughts are screaming *be careful.*

He eyes me intently—waiting on my answer.

"Well, what do you say?" he asks.

His gaze is smoldering—piercing right into mine, and I can feel the tension building. It's getting hot in the well air-conditioned lobby, but only between the two of us. He continues licking his lips—now gently scraping at the bottom voluptuous half with his pearly whites. He's teasing me and I'm letting him. I can't help but wonder if he can see the pure lust in my eyes, so I quickly blink and try to get it together. I manage to let a smile spread across my lips. *That's a good start,* since the words refuse to come out of my mouth.

My heart is racing, and suddenly I feel a massive incandescence overcome my entire body. Oh. My. Goodness. At the moment I can barely breathe, but I have to answer him. I take a deep breath, letting it slowly slip out between my lips.

"I would love the seat if it's available, and of course I'll pay for it," I whisper.

"I assure you that will not be necessary." The tone of his voice shows off his smooth talking abilities while he watches me—smiling and trying to read my every thought...*and then we're interrupted.*

"Ms. Stone, your passport please?" Molly tries again to get my attention. "Ma'am?"

"Oh. Yes. I'm sorry." Immediately, I reach across the counter to retrieve it, and I realize I don't even remember handing it to her in the first place. Before I know it, I've lost my balance and I'm fumbling and down to the floor I go.

Damn the bad luck.

Oh, no. He extends his hand out to help me up. For a split second, I am tempted to turn him away and get up on my own, but my heart is being drawn in by a force stronger than my own will power. I can't resist looking into his vibrant eyes; they match his shirt and are hypnotizing me—I have no control. So hot—and beautiful, very manly-beautiful. He defines the art of manliness—dressed in an intense emerald blue-green long sleeve shirt. It buttons up and the collar frames that perfect face of his—and those jeans…oh damn, he's sexy.

He kneels down, getting closer so that I can breathe him in and that's all it takes. I reach out and take his hand, never acknowledging the stares we are getting. In this moment, nothing else matters. All that does matter is how much I want to get to know him, and now is the perfect opportunity.

As he guides me up, I do the unthinkable. I slip, falling down again and bringing him down with me. *Am I really this clumsy, or did I self-consciously just do that on purpose?* Okay, now my pride is out the door and humiliation has stepped in. I'm so embarrassed. I can feel my face turning ten shades of red, and it's as hot as a heated oven—as well as the hot-spot between my legs.

I lay there pinned beneath him, looking him in the eyes as he glares into mine and can't help but imagine our bodies joined at the hips—naked and connected. Our breathing is erratic and the electricity between us is familiar; the attraction is there—just like it was that first night. *I knew it wasn't just the alcohol.*

He can't read my mind, but at this moment I feel like he knows my thoughts are all wrapped up in him; not to mention my arms, legs, and womanhood. Ah, my scorching hot womanhood. It is throbbing with desire and waiting to be devoured. What am I thinking? Only a slut would be having these kinds of thoughts; not a woman who has been saving her virtue for true love. My inner self scowls at my girly stuff—telling her to calm the hell down, but little Ms. Girly Stuff isn't giving up without a fight…she scowls right back and forces Ms. Self into hiding—*at least temporarily.*

I can feel his chest expanding as his breathing gets heavier. Mine does the same—my breast now pressing into all that muscle. He looks down—getting a better glimpse of my cleavage. Inhaling deeper, he cuts his eyes straight back to mine. His hot breath sweeps over me as he exhales. I take a deep breath and smell sweet cinnamon-deliciousness.

"Miss Stone, I've had a few women fall for me in my time, but none have ever brought me to my knees—*until now,*" he breathes.

"Err...I apologize. I can be so clumsy sometimes." My voice smothered with nervous tension. Laying here, in the middle of an airport lobby, the most desirable man blanketing me with his lean body and I can't find one freaking sexy-smart thing to say.

"Don't be sorry, Miss Stone. I'm not," he says—not budging.

My eyes widen and that deep dark cavern between my legs is burning up. *Oh, snap.* I think he's got a hard on. *He does.* He's as turned on as I am. As quickly as I can, I scoot myself out from beneath him and begin gathering up all of my personal belongings. Attraction is one thing, but a whore I am not. I will fight these feelings one way or another. Ms. Self resurfaces—patting herself on the back for a job well done.

Before I know it, he's up and squatting in front of me. My eyes now glued to his. I think I'm in a hormonal state of shock. *"Get a grip, Hannah!"* screams the little voice inside my head. I can't look away if he doesn't stop looking at me like that. His bright eyes are so intense—showing off a happy-horny-bad-boy gaze. He licks his lips. I swallow hard.

"Let me help you with that," he demands.

"Thank you," I murmur.

Forcing my eyes away from his, I reach for my cell phone and put it in my purse. His hand brushes mine—sending a splashing-tingly feeling from my head to my toes. He hands me my lipstick—then my mirror. I grab my notepad, never noticing what he grabbed next until it was too late. No, not those; my tampons and the *condom* that Baylee snuck in my purse. I remember her words....*Always be prepared, Hannah; you never know who you might run into.* I roll my eyes...if she only knew who I ran into.

Still squatting side by side, he takes my hand in his and guides me up. His grip is so tight, and I'm so humiliated. I could just fall off of the face of the earth right now. *I can't believe I did that.*

I glance at the attendant and begin apologizing. "Molly. I'm so sorry. This has not been my week."

She winks at me; almost like she's assuring me that my week has just gotten better. "There is nothing to be sorry about, Ms. Stone."

That sexy stern voice of his interrupts our girl moment, and before I know it, we are both hanging onto his every word.

"Thank you, Molly, but I'll help Miss Stone from here." Unlike me, he's far from embarrassed. By his tone, I think he may even be slightly amused. *Just like a man to find humor in a moment like this.*

"Of course, Mr. Dawson," she says, forcing herself not to stare.

Unexpectedly my heart skips a beat and picks back up like a fast moving train. What is this man doing to me? No man has ever had this effect on me? *That look—that smell— that voice...w*ait a minute. How did he know my name, and why *is* Molly so intimidated by him? Realizing he knew my name before the attendant ever mentioned it has thrown me for a loop. The next thing I know he is picking up my luggage and ordering me to follow him. I am not use to taking orders from strangers, but for some reason I am now.

"This way, Miss Stone," he demands, and I humbly obey.

Without hesitation, I follow close behind this mouth watering creature. Tall, dark, and handsome has nothing on what I'm looking at. His ass wears those jeans perfectly. They are skin tight and perfect for showing off his manly *assets.* And that strut. He glides with a dominating confidence. I bet he leaves every girl begging to submit to his every desire. All of a sudden, I'm craving to be that submissive. Naughty but true. A hungry smile takes control of my lips and the fight is over. Just because the attraction is amplifying every hormonal fiber of my being, doesn't make me a whore—it makes me human.

I wave goodbye to the girl who has just been a witness to this unforgettable moment in my life, and the look in her eyes says it all. She would trade places with me in a heartbeat.

Suddenly, I realize I'm running away from one stranger and right into the arms of another. As crazy as that is, the direction I am headed seems to give me peace. There is no sense of fear; only an indescribable energy that makes me feel like I can conquer the world.

I am taken by surprise when it is a private jet with his name on it—Dawson—in big black letters. *Crap! Double-hellacious-crap.* He owns his own private plane—no wonder he offered me a free seat. *I am so out of my league.* Rolling my eyes at my own stupidity, I try to soothe my broken heart. A man like him and a girl like me…rich man…poor girl— *only in fairytales.*

Pulling me out of my train of thought, I notice someone waiting at the entrance. We are greeted by a beautiful blonde stewardess who looks to be around my age. She leads us into a cabin that is immaculately decorated with a style suited to the man before me. It is absolutely breathtaking—the creamy leather seats trimmed in 24 karat gold—the matching sofa—the wood paneled galley—the big screen television. My eyes do a double take—*was that a king size bed in the other room?*

It looks like a penthouse suite in one of New York's finest hotels, but it's not. "Wow. It's beautiful. Are you sure we're really on a plane, Mister Dawson?" I ask while my eyes are still focusing on the bedroom.

When I turn to look at him, he looks past me. His eyes darken over with desire as he stares at the bed—then back at me. He catches my gaze…pulling him away from whatever it was he was thinking about.

"Yes. And please, call me Conner," he advises. A ghost of a smile appears at the corners of his lips, and here I am grinning ear to ear. He must think I'm crazy.

Take a deep breath, Hannah! He's rich and you're not; so don't get your hopes up.

"Conner Dawson—A strong name for my new hero; Hannah Stone—the girl you just rescued in more ways than you will ever know." I extend my hand to his as in any formal introduction—so what if he already knew my name. His palm now pressed against mine...we shake. *That stinging breathtaking feeling*—it is pure pleasure. It is the same electrifying sensation from the bar and in the airport lobby—I could really get use to that charge. His expression is screaming with wonder. He feels the connection. I knew it—screw the money, it's only a thing, and I will not let it stand in my way.

"I don't know if I can live up to your hero expectations, but I'm glad I can help get you to Hawaii. You should have a seat and prepare yourself for takeoff. It shouldn't be long now," his voice is demanding but seducing me all the same...*and he releases his tightened grip from mine.*

I do as I am told but not without taking my eyes off of him. He is so easy to look at. Like a beer-loving alcoholic, I have just found my very own addiction. It is him, and I am drinking every inch of him in during my very own personal *happy hour.*

I reach for my seatbelt, but he beats me to it.

"Let me do that," he insists.

"Okay," I breathe.

Gently, he buckles me in and takes my breath away once more. He has to lean over me to snap the 24 karat gold buckle in, and when he does I get the chance to breathe him in. How can he smell so divine? Is it really possible for someone to smell that intoxicating? And that face...that body—he's so perfectly handsome. His strong lightly-stubbled jaw line—high cheekbones...*his wet lips.* I am in so much trouble—how will I ever talk myself out of not wanting that man?

He catches me admiring him from out of the corner of his eye—but he doesn't budge. He takes his time fastening me in good and tight. *I think he knows what he's doing to me.* He does. That smile he's trying to hide proves it.

Rolling my eyes, I fight off the urge to lean into him. Cracking a mischievous grin of my own, I glance out the window at the place I am leaving—almost thankful that I was ran out of town by an idiot. It's so weird the way things happen. Sometimes fate really is watching out for us.

Or is it?

My romantic moment is interrupted by long legs and high heels. A beautiful, rather tethered-looking woman makes her way to Conner, and he turns and greets her with a kiss. It may have been on the cheek, but nonetheless those voluptuous lips of his landed on her.

I feel my claws coming out, and my kitty tightens between my legs—begging me not to start a cat fight...*like I really would anyway*—I long to be a lover not a fighter.

"Hillary, you made it. I was beginning to wonder if I was going to have to send a bounty hunter out after you," he says—seriousness more on his face than it is in his voice.

My heart feels as though it has just skipped three beats. I can't breathe, and suddenly I'm cursing beneath my breath at a woman I've never laid eyes on before, *or have I?* That hair—is it her? Could it really be the woman from the car? This cannot be happening, but it is. I imagine her with blown-away hair and a bad make-up job, and that confirms it. It is her.

I look at the woman he calls Hillary. She looks at the stranger he's invited along on their trip. Then her eyes move to his. She's got a quirky grin on her face, and I don't think I am going to like her very much. Quietness fills the air. Hillary is watching Conner and vice-versa, and I can't help but watch the two of them. Then, she breaks the silence.

"Take it easy, little brother. Daddy would have my hide if I didn't come along—as well as my allowance."

Did she just say little brother and allowance in the same sentence? *Yes, she did.*

I exhale. I can breathe again. She looks to be in her early thirties, and she still gets an allowance. Ugh! Some people just have all the luck.

"Hillary, I would like for you to meet Hannah. Hannah, this is Hillary, my older sister." His voice is so freaking *sexy* and even sexier now that she's his sister.

I smile in confusion as they both laugh at some sort of inside joke, and I extend my hand to hers. I can't help but notice bruises on the bend of her arm, as her hand meets mine. She sees the look on my face; pulling back—a helpless smile creeping across her face. "It's nice to meet you Hillary. You really can't be much older than Conner. I would have guessed you the younger of the two."

What was that all about? Anyway, from one woman to another, I know my lie will win her over—even if it really isn't true.

Wow. Conner must be older than he looks.

Hillary laughs and thanks me for the compliment, but states she is *only* eight minutes older than her baby brother. They are twins and have just recently celebrated their twenty-sixth birthday. Surprised and left speechless, I never would have guessed that. If I were a betting woman, I would have guessed there was at least eight years difference—not minutes.

It isn't long before I am all caught up in the love connection this beautiful duo share. They have a bond that is much like the one Landon and I have. They talk. They laugh. And it is truly captivating. A love like that is undying, non-judgmental, and truly never fails. I guess they sense my eyes and ears are all up in their business, so it isn't long before they include me in their conversation.

"So, Hannah, how do you know my brother?" I am taken by surprise and not sure how to answer her question. Thank goodness my new found hero sees the desperation all over my face and rescues me once again.

"It was down at Joe's Place. We *bumped* into each other there and again this morning at the airport. She was desperate for a flight to paradise, so I offered her one."

Nibbling lightly at his thumb nail as the words escape his mouth—his hungry gaze is looking my way. Conner wiggles in his seat, props his right foot on his left knee—his only way of adjusting himself right in front of me and his sister. He's got a growing bulge in those jeans and it's all because of me. My subliminal essence cheering in my head—*he likes us, he likes us.*

"That's right, just what he said." He catches me starring at his crotch…I can't help myself.

He wiggles again.

My kitty tightens.

Our eyes locked…mine on his…his on mine.

Hillary watches me as I watch her brother. "So, Hannah—did you know that my brother could have any woman he wants, but he chooses to work his ass off for our father instead of having a personal life?"

His gaze leaves mine and shoots across the cabin to his sister.

"Enough, Hillary—I don't think that is necessary," Conner demands. He puts a stop to his sister's taunting before it gets carried away—even she shows a side of intimidation when it comes to him.

I guess he could see me squirming and trying to hide my discomfort; although her words didn't make me feel that way. It was the reminder of what I actually woke up thinking. My thoughts were of the stalker and how I was going to survive his threats. My little getaway is only a temporary fix. I will have to face the cold hard truth that someone is out to get me, and the thought alone is hard enough to take.

Okay, enough of all these depressing thoughts. I refuse to think about what's going on at home until I go back….now back to seducing him with my *come hither look.*

We haven't been in the air long, and the stewardess comes around with cocktails and pistachios. I sip on a piña colada and try to prepare myself for the long flight ahead. Before I can get too relaxed, Hillary starts in with more questions.

"So, Hannah, where do you plan on staying while you are on the island?" My eyes go from the woman who asked the question to the man who is listening with opened ears. I look back at her...gasping a quick breath and confessing. "I actually haven't thought that far ahead yet. This trip is a last minute, much needed getaway, and needless to say I didn't know where I was going when I got to the airport much less where I would be sleeping when I got there."

Her eyes widen and she nods her head. She looks at her brother who has concern written all over his face, and then back at me. They don't ask any questions, leaving it up to me to fill them in...and I choose not to.

"Well, enough said. You are staying at the penthouse. There is plenty of room, wouldn't you agree, Conner?"

Slowly, I turn to look at her brother who looks speechless.

"Conner!" Hillary raises her voice, but just to get his attention.

His penetrating glare piercing straight through me. He's trying like hell to figure me out. *I think.* "Hillary. I don't think Miss Stone will feel comfortable spending the week with complete strangers while she's on vacation. I'm sure we can help her with her own accommodations if need be it."

"That is pure nonsense, Conner. She's flying hours over the Pacific Ocean with us, so why can't she sleep under the same roof? Besides, she traveling all alone; I'm sure she would like the company."

Hillary sure is persistent, but that's okay. I'm glad she's on my side. The heated tension in the room thickens, and our desire for one another is begging to be calmed. I feel it. He feels it. Our body language says it all. His hands grip the arms of his seat. The tips of his fingers are turning white from the pressure, but the color in his cheeks is flushed with a burning need to be all up in my business. I watch him as he watches me. My ears long to hear him say yes, but my body craves to feel him say it. What will his answer be? He is trying to be in command of his emotions, but this may not be something he has any control of. I can see it burning deep in his eyes. He is scared he'll not be able to contain the passion that is brewing inside of him. He hesitates, but he gives in. "I suppose she's got a point, Hannah. You are more than welcome to stay at the penthouse if you like."

I let out a deep breath of relief.

Is this really happening or is it just another one of my fantasies? The sexiest man alive has just become my lifesaver, and I feel like I'm the heroine in my latest erotica. Can it get any better than this? If I'm dreaming, I don't want to wake up. I have to snap out of it. *Answer him already,* my inner self demands. "If you are sure I wouldn't be in the way, I would love to."

There's that laughter again. "In the way? No, Hannah, you will have your choice of three huge master bedrooms. The penthouse is *GINORMOUS.*" Not only is Hillary young and beautiful, but she doesn't mind flaunting their wealth.

"Then it's settled. You will be our guest," he says, exhaling heated breath. The reassuring look on Conner's face makes me feel at home, but there is no denying the desire in his eyes. He may have his game face on, but I know he wants me and my subliminal essence is cheering him on.

I'm overjoyed and I know it's obvious. Without a doubt, this is sure to be a trip neither of us will ever forget.

Chapter 6

A soothing voice coons over the intercom—waking me from a peaceful nap. It only takes a second for me to realize where I am, my head now resting on the shoulder of Conner Dawson's. Quickly, I sit up straight and listen closely as the captain makes the announcement...never looking *his* way. *I can't believe I did that.*

"Ladies and gentleman, our destination is just ahead, and it is a lovely 85 degrees. Please prepare yourself for landing as we will be doing so in approximately ten minutes."

I have to apologize.

Getting the nerve to look him in the face, I turn and there he is watching me.

"I'm so sorry, I never meant to fall asleep...much less use you as a pillow."

His lips curl up, causing his eyes to do the same.

"Glad I could be of service, Miss Stone," he says, patting my hand and sending a lovely current all through my body.

His charm has completely won me over. A huge grin takes hold of my lips, causing his smile to grow even bigger. I force myself to look away from him, and glance out the window.

The view from the plane is breathtaking, and I can't wait to walk barefoot on the beach. I can't wait to feel the hot sand between my toes and the lapping of the ocean water hitting my legs. The closer we get, the more colorful the scenery. Flowers are all over the place. The fresh beautiful kind that every bride would love to have on her wedding day. The same sort of flowers I have pictured in my very own wedding. They are bright, beautiful, and breathtaking—*and they are everywhere.*

"Hold on tight." Conner places his hand over mine, and I cannot help but gasp when he does—neither can he. Our eyes do that thing again, and we are once again consumed with each other. Skin on skin with this man is all it takes to awaken my senses. I absolutely love the way he is making me feel, and I can't help but crave more. Instead of answering him, I smile and do as I am told.

It is a smooth landing, and as we depart the plane there is a slick black limo waiting to take us to the penthouse.

Conner introduces me to the driver whose name is Finn.

"Aloha, Ms. Stone, welcome to Honolulu," he tips his hat.

I smile at his greeting. It is surreal and it is true? I am *really* in Hawaii.

"Aloha, Finn," I say.

As he takes our bags and puts them in the trunk for safe keeping, we get to know each other. Finn is a local resident of the island, born and raised here. He was named after his great-grandfather who was from Tennessee. By the smile on his face, it is easy to tell he is proud to share the family name with an ancestor he had never met.

His age shows from the fine lines that have been etched over time in the crevices of his face, and the streaks of gray that are in his hair. Though he doesn't come from money, he is a man to be respected just because he is our elder. It doesn't take much to see the admiration Conner has for the driver, which in lieu makes me have that much more respect for this mysterious new man in my life.

Before getting in the car, there's one last thing to do before we head out. Finn adorns us with fresh, beautiful, brightly colored leis—a reminder that they still believe in the perfect Hawaiian greeting.

And off we go.

The drive is about twenty minutes to the hotel, but I don't care. The view from the car is even more beautiful than it was from the plane. The sun is setting, and it is resting upon the waves of the ocean; it won't be long before the stars are radiating through the clouds as the sky gets darker. The trees are swaying back and forth in the breeze—almost like they are welcoming me to their homeland.

I am almost disappointed when the driver announces we are minutes away, but when I look ahead I am amazed at what I see. There is a massive driveway that is lined with tall palm trees wrapped with white lights. It is the perfect lit path to the amazing hotel and casino resort that will be my home for the next week. I can't believe my eyes. I'm mesmerized by the inviting exquisiteness of it all.

We pull up under a paved breezeway, and the limo is quickly approached by a tall man with a stocky build. He has short black hair, and he wears a well-groomed goatee on his chin. He opens the door before Finn has a chance to step out of his. We step out onto the pavement.

The man greeting us is the concierge, and immediately he has someone take our bags. "Mr. Dawson. Ms. Dawson. What a pleasure it is to have you back."

Conner shakes his hand and motions for me to come closer.

"Thank you, Henry. It is always good to be back. We have a guest who will be staying with us in the penthouse." Henry's eyes are on me. He is looking me up and down and checking me out. "This is Miss Hannah Stone. Please instruct the staff to treat her with the same respect they would me or my sister."

"Of course, Mr. Dawson, I'll make sure of it." Henry stretches out his hand to mine and welcomes me. "It is my pleasure to meet you, Ms. Stone. Welcome to Dawson's Hotel and Casino Resort."

Oh my. I realized back on the plane that Conner and his sister must come from money, but I had no idea they would own a place like this. The last few days have been so overwhelming—*the stalker, Kris, and now this.*

My heart...I can hear it beating.

Whoa! I feel like I'm swaying...but I'm not moving. My head...It feels like someone is turning cartwheels up there. Everything is spinning—I've got double vision. *I've never had double vision.* What the—and everything goes black. I'm out cold.

When my eyes open, Connor is holding me in his arms with a cool rag on my forehead. "Are you okay?" His eyes boring into me—almost as though they are trying to resuscitate me back to life.

"What happened?" The question is only a mere whisper leaving my lips.

"You passed out, and luckily I was close enough to catch you before you hit the ground," says the man I am totally mesmerized by.

I look at him like he is crazy, because I have never passed-out a day in my life.

"Really?" I ask. "I feel fine. I don't know what happened. Maybe it's because of the long flight and skipping lunch." I was scared to put too much food on my stomach while on the plane, so I opted out of having the grilled chicken breast that was served earlier.

"Henry, send up some soup and sweet tea," Conner orders. Then he lifts me in his arms and carries me to the nearest elevator where Hillary is waiting with the doors wide open.

"You're going to have to quit rescuing me like this, Mister Dawson. A girl could get use to this sort of thing. Now, please put me down before you hurt your back."

His sister stands there laughing.

"Have you not looked at my brother?" asks Hillary.

I glance her way and then back to him. All I want to say to her is everything I can't. I don't recall ever being so taken by a man's looks. His perfectly lean powerful body is now etched in my memory forever. Therefore, I need no reminder of how buff he is, and frankly, I do not appreciate her putting me on the spot.

I can feel his muscles flexing as he holds me, and I can't help but admire his strength. My eyes are studying his face. He's worried, and the way his eyes are twitching and his nostrils are flaring with his every anxious breath confirms it. He's concerned about me.

Part of me doesn't want him to put me down. I want him to carry me to the closest bed and take what no other man ever has. I want to be skin on skin with a man that I barely know, but suddenly trust more than anyone. *Breathe, Hannah. Just breathe.* I remind myself quietly in my own mind. As far as Hillary's remark goes, I think personally she just likes bragging on her brother, and I can't blame her for that. He *is* something to brag about.

The doors close and the car starts the transport to our destination. I watch the numbers light up, and finally they stop on the twenty-eighth floor. The elevator doors open wide, and we step through the foyer and into a huge open floor plan.

Wow.

It's beautiful.

The décor is stunning—all black and white furnishings; with the exception of the Murano blown glass vases sitting around the room. Each one filled with freshly cut flowers and adorning a rainbow of colors. Bringing the room to life, the plants brighten the whole area, and there is nothing dull about this black and white set up. I can so see myself never leaving this place. It is breathtaking, and I can't wait to see more.

Then, the unthinkable happens. He puts me down and my feet hit the floor.

My inner self pouts, but not for long…thanks to her.

"Hannah. Follow me and I will show you around." Hillary is anxious—grabbing me by my arm and tearing me away from *him*.

"Careful, Hillary!" he calls out.

"I'll take care of her, Conner…don't worry so much!" she yells back.

I take a deep breath and hold on tight.

I can't help but get all giddy; she's like a young girl having a sleep over. She leads me all over the suite, dragging me room to room and showing off its massiveness and its beauty. It is beautiful beyond measure, and I can't believe I'm really here. The flickering candles…soft music in the background…*breathing the same air as him*; what more could a girl ask for?

She leads me to a room that I fall in love with, and it is the one I choose to make mine—and best of all, his bedroom is right next to it. She leaves me alone and a short while later he's knocking on my door.

"Hannah, may I come in?" he whispers.

My heart—it's no longer beating at a normal rhythm. Instead, it's racing…and it's all because of him.

"Come in," I reply.

He opens the door, holding a tray in his hands.

"It's getting late. I just wanted to say goodnight before I go to bed, and I noticed you hadn't had a chance to eat your soup."

He has changed clothes and wearing nothing but a black silk pair of pajama bottoms—loose fitting but hugging him in all the right spots. His abs are screaming to be looked at and that's what I'm doing. They are spot on perfect: hard, lean, and adorning a six pack. He's gorgeous from head to toe, and I want to taste every mouth watering inch of him—forget the soup.

"Thank you, Conner." I grab the tray and my hand brushes against his. There's that awesome vivacious feeling again. Turning away, I place the tray on the table by the bed, and look back at him. "Goodnight, Mister Dawson." I mouth the words, but my mind is blaring *come to me lover boy*.

He turns away, closing the door behind him.

I lay back on my pillow, forgetting all about the soup, and close my eyes with nothing but Conner Dawson on my mind.

He is on my mind and in my dreams, and the morning comes all too quick. I must have slept really hard because my body is tense and it's hard to move. I am worn out from the trip; not to mention all the rocking and rolling that went on in this bed last night.

I look around the room, and I'm amazed at the mess. The bed has been practically stripped of the quilt and sheets that covered it and four out of the five pillows are lying in the floor. I'm utterly astounded at how much twisting and turning one person alone can do and shocked when I realize my head is at the opposite end of where it was when I closed my eyes last night. I think back on my dreams, and they were filled with a very dominating man who craved me as much as I craved him; that man was Conner and he liked to play hard.

A massive tingle goes straight from my lower belly to between my legs when I remember the sensuous, mouthwatering torture he put me and my kitty through. Lying back down, I gasp, remembering the leather flog he teased me with and how much I loved letting him have his way. I can't help but wonder if every virgin desires what they've never had, or if it's just *me* and what this handsome man does to me.

I close my eyes, trying to rewind the dream that has me longing for a much needed orgasm. Without realizing where my hand is, I suddenly feel my sex clench as though it is going to explode. I can't help but notice that my fingers are hot and wet and gliding over my clit. Before I can finish what I started, I jerk my hand from out of my panties and realize how humiliated I would be if he were to walk in.

After jumping up out of bed, I rush to the bathroom to wash away the evidence of where my hand had been—taking time to splash some cold water on my face, hoping that will drag my butt back to reality. It was only a dream...*just a dream.*

Minutes later, I'm headed to the kitchen.

Conner's not standing there...neither is Hillary, but someone is. *Who is she?*

I'm startled by a woman who must be my mother's age. She is dressed in black and white and covered with an apron to match her attire. Behind her is an array of fresh fruit, muffins, croissants, and bagels. I start salivating just looking at the juicy mouthwatering pineapple waiting to be devoured.

"Good afternoon, Ms. Stone. May I get you some coffee?"

"Please, call me Hannah, and did you just say afternoon?" I'm confused.

"Yes ma'am. It is a quarter past twelve, so I think the morning is behind us now. My name is Leilani, and I work for Mr. Dawson. Please let me know if there is anything I can do for you."

She seems nice enough, but I can't help but wonder where *they* are.

"Thank you, Leilani. If I may ask, where is Conner and Hillary?" I ask, looking around the room.

"They headed out early this morning—said something about meetings all day."

"Oh...okay, thank you." My response to that is short, but what else am I supposed to say? *Why did they leave me here?*

After thanking Leilani, I can't resist the layout in front of me. I grab a plate and cover it with fresh fruit and a croissant. I am famished, and I am starting to get embarrassed from all the growling my stomach has been doing since standing in the kitchen. I guess I should have eaten the soup after all.

She smiles and goes about her business, leaving me to help myself. It is the most divine, delectable fruit I have ever put in my mouth. I have to make myself stop, or I will be too miserable to go to the beach.

I can't believe I have slept half the day away. I need to hurry if I want to get started on my Hawaiian tan.

I take the elevator down to the lobby, and I must look like a lost puppy when I step off because Henry is fast to my rescue. "Ms. Stone, I hope your day has been great so far. What are your plans for the afternoon?"

"So far so good, Henry. How about your day; has it been great or what?" I ask, smiling back at him when he laughs out loud.

"Yes, Ms. Stone, it just keeps getting better and better. Now, how may I be of service to you?"

I look around the crowded lobby, searching for a sign that says *this way to the beach,* but there's not one in sight. "I need to feel the sand between my toes and the sun on my skin...if you could point me in the right direction I would be a happy girl." I say…my eyes still in search of an answer of their own.

"Of course, Ms. Stone, please follow me."

Henry leads me through the elegant lobby and out the door to a breezeway. It leads to a private beach that only guests are allowed to use, and I can't help but indulge in the thought of being exactly that. If Baylee could see me now, jealousy would rip through her just like the fear I felt barely forty-eight hours ago. She's always wanted to go to Hawaii, but has yet to talk her parents into paying for it.

I thank Henry for his generosity and walk to a quaint little area with a large umbrella and lounger. I place my belongings there and decide to take a walk. It is just as I pictured; the sand is hot, and the water is cool. It is a perfect intoxicating mixture that I cannot get enough of.

After about an hour of walking along the shore, I decide to join in on a volley ball game. They are a person short and are excited when I said yes. I love the game, but love it even more since Kris isn't around. Between him and all the other drama in my life, a vacation away from Tennessee is just what I needed.

It was like kismet running into Conner at the airport— perfect timing, along with the ideal man.

I spend the next few hours showing off my experienced moves that take my team to victory every time. I guess all that time spent playing the game in college paid off. I can't help but gloat when the guys pick me up and throw me in the air chanting my name. I feel like a true champion.

Afterwards, I grab a grilled chicken salad and a frozen margarita and enjoy a late lunch beneath my umbrella. The breeze that comes off the ocean is soothing and relaxing and before I know it, I have no control over the nap I am taking.

As I drift off, I feel more peace in this moment than I have felt in the last year. There is no Kris begging for my attention, no stalker watching my every move, no job demanding my time—*only me time.*

From a distance, I can hear the flapping wings of birds flying by and the ocean water lapping up against the sand,

and there are times I can even hear what sounds like bongo drums and singing from not too far away. The breeze has more of a chill to it and the heat from the sun isn't as intense as it was earlier, and where in the world is that tick-tock noise coming from? The pounding of the drums gets louder, and suddenly I feel sticky and wet all over. I hear Conner's voice calling my name, but I can't find him anywhere. The next thing I know, that wet sticky feeling I felt has a smell to it, and it smells just like dog breath. Gross! My eyes pop open and the cutest little boxer puppy is licking me all over.

I can't help but laugh, rubbing the four-legged pup behind his ears—*then I realize the moon is shining bright; where did the sun go?*

Oh. My. Goodness. It's dark. I quickly look at my *ticking* watch and it is almost nine o'clock. I know Conner and his sister must be wondering where I am.

I grab my things and head to the breezeway, and I can't help but notice a bonfire surrounded by the same group of people I played volley ball with earlier. One of the guys is going at it hard on a set of bongo drums, and now I know why I couldn't get that sound out of my head. I remember hearing Conner calling my name, so I quickly look around to see if I can get a glimpse of him. Nothing. It was only his voice I heard in my dream.

I rush up to the penthouse, and the only person I find waiting on me is Leilani. She greets me with a smile and offers me something to eat. "Thank you, Leilani, but I would love to shower first if you don't mind."

"Of course, Ms. Stone," she says. I make my way to my room and to my surprise my luggage has been unpacked and neatly put away. As much as I love someone waiting on me hand and foot, I know better than to get use to it. This week is sure to go by faster than I want it to, and I would be back to cleaning up after myself in no time.

I walk to the chest of drawers and choose to wear my pajama shorts and a tank top, and then I head to the huge bathroom that is connected to my room.

After getting in the hot shower, I realize I have gotten a little burned from being in the sun. I know it won't be that way for long though; luckily my skin tone matches that of my moms, and I know I will be golden brown by morning. At least I hope so.

Conner comes to my mind while I am dressing, and I think about how his day had been. I can't wait to see him. Hurriedly, I dress and towel dry my hair and make my way back to the kitchen. *Hopefully he's here by now.*

Leilani is sitting at the table drinking a glass of tea, but still no Conner and Hillary. As disappointed as I am, I don't want to be rude to this lovely woman who has been nothing but nice to me.

"I feel so much better; there's nothing like a refreshing shower after a day at the beach." Leilani laughs and again offers to fix me something to eat. I really am not that hungry, so I opt to just have a small bowl of cereal.

We sat at the table for the next two hours, and I listen to stories of her childhood and she listens to mine. Even though there are two and a half decades between us, we have a lot of things in common. One of which, we are both hopeless romantics.

Chapter 7

I **toss and turn** for what seems like hours, and I still can't sleep. Looking at my phone, I realize it's already a quarter till one, and I'm wide awake. Why can I not get *him* off of my brain? He's running through my thoughts like there's no tomorrow, and I feel like a school girl crushing for the first time.

Actually, this really is a first for me. I've never been so consumed with anyone or anything in my entire life. He's like the wake-up call I've never had and my well-rested body feels more alive than ever. I know so little about him, and I long to know more…like what in the world is keeping him out so late at night?

My mind goes from tiptoeing around what his business duties entail to chasing after what his personal affairs might be. Without a doubt, I want to be the center of his attention—forget everything else.

In a moment's notice, I'm fantasizing about Conner Dawson. It's only natural that fantasy turns into a dream, and before I know it I am riding him hard and he is yelling my name as he pushes deeper inside my needy womanhood. I am hot and wet, and the more I feel him slide in and out of me, the wetter and hotter I get. His long, thick, joystick is hitting all the right spots—as good as it feels…I don't want to unravel just yet. I don't want the feeling to end. I want more of him—all of him, all night long. His strong masculine hands are all over me. Rubbing my back and then squeezing my butt. Within seconds, he has me on my knees and pounding me from behind—making me love every voluptuous inch of his manly part. It is stretching my girly stuff to the perfect size—making him the perfect fit.

The next thing I know I'm rubbing my head, and there is a throbbing that won't go away, and I don't mean the orgasm that was building between my legs. My head is hurting…what the hell just happened?

Really? Did I *really* just fall off the bed? My dream is over as quickly as it had started, and I'm startled when I hear someone yell my name.

"Hannah!"

Lo and behold, those strong masculine hands that were just in my dream are now lifting me off the floor.

"Are you okay?" he asks.

Conner sits me on the bed, and once again I am humiliated in front of the one person I can't stop thinking about. He leans over and turns on the lamp.

"Other than my pride being shattered, I'm okay. Thanks again hero. I'm beginning to feel like I have my very own *super hero*. What am I going to do when you're not around, Mister Dawson?"

He can't help but laugh as he brushes my wayward hair away from my eyes. "Super hero I'm not, but I do seem to be in just the right spot at just the right time lately. Looks like that beautiful face of yours may have a little added color when you wake up in the morning."

He places the hair behind my ear and allows the knuckle of his middle finger to glide down my cheek; all the way to my chin, slow and easy, before pulling away.

Did he just say what I think he said? *Yes, he did*, and as he caressed my face he innocently made me yearn to be touched elsewhere. I think I just quit breathing. Who's worried about a little bruise when the sexiest man alive just called me beautiful?

There it goes again. My heart is racing, and my belly is tingling. The effect this immaculate being is having on me catches me off guard every time and I love it.

I pick up my phone to check the time and its half-past one. "Are you just getting in?" I asked…squinting my eyes at the bright light coming from the lamp.

"I haven't been in long. I was on my way to bed when I heard something go *bump*. I rushed in and found you on the floor. Guess you don't like the bed much, huh."

I smile and agree with him.

"Ha, ha. That is it." I try to laugh the humiliation off. There is no way I will tell him the real reason I landed on the floor. Clenching my sex in, I'm reminded of my dream and what it felt like to have him going at it caveman style from behind me—filling me with his manly pride. Ah, what a feeling; spiraling down from an imaginary orgasm leaves me wanting to go back to dreaming. At least then, maybe I'll spiral down from a real one.

I can feel my face blushing, as though he can read my thoughts. I guess he can see the crimson-color now shading my cheeks too, because he excuses himself just that quick.

Dismayed that he is no longer in the room, I grab the quilt and lay back a bit too quickly. Instead of my head hitting the pillow, it hits the wall, and I'm reminded of the knot I already have. Now I have a throbbing ache in two spots. "Ouch!" I yell out, not using my quiet voice. I realize he had to have heard that, and sure enough he did. I hear his footsteps and he is just outside my door.

Pushing it open with one hand and holding an icepack in his other, I can't help but notice the grin that he's wearing.

"Hannah Stone, did you just bump your head against the wall?"

His smile is contagious, and before I know it, I'm wearing one too. "Yes, Conner Dawson, I did, and you have found me out...I may just be the clumsiest girl you've ever met."

We both laugh as he makes his way back to me.

I watch him as he strolls closer, and I'm overwhelmed by a mad, passionate, toe-curling desire to throw myself at him.

If only I had the nerve.

Sitting on the edge of the bed, he pushes my hair away to show the spot that is beginning to swell. *This is definitely a butterfly-effect-kinda-moment.* I can feel the fluttering pulsing through my veins, making my heart race...my breathing...oh, my...*am I even breathing?* Closing my eyes, I do my damndest to relax.

Blinking, I focus on him.

He places the cold icepack on my forehead and fluffs the pillow behind me. *Thank goodness...now I have an excuse for those peek-a-boo bumps that keep popping up all over my body.*

His hand brushes against my shoulder.

It's like my skin is screaming "rub me, rub me," because he does just that.

"Should I adjust the air, you feel a little chilly?" he asks, trying to rub the tiny spots away.

"No, I'll be fine once I get back under the sheets," I whisper.

His hungry gaze follows the cover all the way up my body...my feet...my legs...my waist...and then he pulls it away from me.

"Lay back nice and slow," he demands with one hand behind my neck guiding me down to keep me from bumping the wall again and the other one tucking me in with the duvet. Gently releasing both hands, he continues to take care of me. "Look at me, Hannah, and tell me how many fingers I'm holding up."

My eyes look ahead and see two fingers only inches away from my face. "Two...or is that one and I'm seeing double?" We both laugh. "I'm fine, Conner, really." I try reassuring him, and by the sparkle in his eye I think I have.

For a moment, he sits there just watching me. Maybe he's wondering if he should stay and lookout for me, or maybe he's trying to figure me out. I start to speak, but he beats me to it.

"Well then, I guess I'm no longer needed here...sleep well, Hannah." He leans over to turn out the light and whispers goodnight as he closes the door behind him.

"Goodnight, Conner." My murmured words so low I doubt he heard them.

I lay there in the dark, the moonlight peeking in between the curtains and cannot go back to sleep. As usual, my mind is running a marathon, and I'm trying to get some shut-eye.

I can't help but think about life and how sometimes it has a plan of its own. No matter how determined you are to make it go exactly how you want it to; there are times when it just doesn't go that way. Sometimes things happen that change us in ways we never expect—turning our world upside down and causing life to be everything it never was. On occasion that's a good thing, and every so often it's not, but I have to admit this new man in my life is making me feel like a brand new woman; and that's not just good—that's awesome. He makes me want to run around naked and tempt him with my girly stuff. I laugh out loud at myself and realize I'm wet, and I don't mean down there.

The homemade icepack is now full of water and has somehow sprung a leak—interrupting my thoughts and causing me to leap up and out of bed. I go to the bathroom, hoping to empty the rest of the contents down the sink. By the time I get there, the bag is barely full and now I have a mess to clean up on the floor.

On bended knees, I begin mopping up the water with a towel. I'm just about to stand up, and it's then that I hear something. It is music, but where is it coming from? I rise to my feet and open the bedroom door. It's dark in the hallway, but there is light coming from somewhere. I tiptoe closer to the living room and see Conner sitting out on the balcony with his guitar in his hand and a pencil resting between his lips. The melody he is playing is beautiful, but nothing I have ever heard. He pauses for a moment, taking the pencil from his mouth and leaning over to write something down. I realize he is writing a song, and I'm blown away at how talented he really is.

He begins once again to sweep his thumb over the strings, and I can't help but notice the candles dancing in the wind. His hair is moving right along to the beat, and I admit it is a beautiful sight. I lean back on the wall, admiring him as he does what he loves.

Lightly, he strums the chords—never realizing each sweep of his thumb is more than just music to my ears. Every note along with every lyric is playing a part in sweeping me off my feet and standing here watching him is like witnessing a love affair with more than just music. It's like watching a man pour his heart out to the world. All too soon, seconds have turned into minutes, and those minutes have turned into a whole half hour. Lost in the magical moments that are passing way too quickly, I never notice what's behind me—*an elegant sunset painting.* My tilting head hit the picture—thus sending the 16x21 framed artwork to the floor.

"*Err...*" I growl out loud at my clumsiness.

Cutting his eyes in my direction proves he overheard the fallen clatter. I swallow hard as he spots the frame at my feet—even harder when he jumps up and heads my way. "Hannah!" he yells. "Are you okay?" Storming his way through the doors and past the sofa, he flips on the hallway light.

Slowly, I bend down to pick up the picture and my *heart.* He's there—eye level. I force myself to look directly at him. "I'm fine, but I'm not so sure about the picture." Glancing at the glass—we both sigh. *It's not broken*...but I am—broken into a million pieces of heated bliss. *Why can I not fight my attraction to him?* Oh, yes...because he looks like that. Squatting there, shirtless, his chest muscles flexing and his long thick eyelashes batting—I realize he's too beautiful to be a man...seriously, no wonder my hormones are fighting a losing battle. I'm a woman...he's *all* man. It's only natural for me to be having these kinds of feelings.

Rising to our feet, he hangs the picture back on the wall. "I thought you would be sound asleep by now," he says, now looking back at me and not the picture-perfect painting he just put back in its spot.

"No, not yet, I heard you playing and..." My whispered words interrupted by his.

"I'm sorry, Hannah...I didn't mean to wake you up. I don't usually play this time of hour, but I was inspired and when inspiration hits I have to put pen to paper and thumb to string," he says, smiling his way deeper into my heart.

"You didn't wake me up. I haven't been to sleep yet."

"Really?" he asks. "I left you over an hour ago."

"I know, but my wandering mind refused to let me drift off to sleep, so I've been wide awake since you left. You're playing was a welcome I didn't expect in the middle of the night."

His grin warms my heart.

"Well, you should've joined me outside instead of hiding away in the dark. I would have welcomed the company." He sends his brow into a dancing invitation. "Would you like to join me now?" he asks, holding out his hand.

"Are you sure? It's really late."

"I'm positive. I'm not going to be at it for much longer. There's just a few kinks I need to work out, and I got a feeling it will go smoother if you're sitting out there with me."

"In that case, I would love to." Whispered words pass from my lips to his ears as I take his hand.

"Great!" he exclaims. "Follow me, Miss Stone."

Leading me to the balcony, I have a seat next to him. He immediately has the guitar in his hands...his fingers picking away at the strings. A beautiful upbeat melody flows through the air—and he stops only to write down a few notes along with a few words. After about fifteen minutes of watching him go back and forth between the strumming, humming, singing and the writing, he's almost done.

"You're so good at that. I wish I had half of your talent," I confess, as he takes a quick break.

"Practice makes perfect, Hannah...but a beautiful girl sitting next to me makes it even easier. He smiles—*while winking.*

Smiling back at him, I blush—*and then yawn.*

"I. AM. SO. SORRY." My tired words making him laugh. "I guess a lullaby is just what I needed to remind me of what I should be doing at this time of night."

Eyeing me with wonder, he looks so curious. "Are you sure I didn't bore you into being sleepy?" he asks, showing off a questionable glint in his emerald beauties.

"Bore me? No, Conner Dawson—you just took my breath away."

Oh me. I wonder if he knows how sexy that heated gaze is. If he doesn't...*we do—referring to me and my girly stuff down there.* He continues eyeing me with a look of desire, and I can't help but squirm in my seat. It's time to call it a night.

"Thank you for letting me admire your work up close and personal, but this ole girl better get some shut eye. I would hate to sleep the day away tomorrow while I'm in paradise."

"That would be an absolute disaster, Miss Stone. Please, go get your beauty sleep," he pauses. "Goodnight, Hannah."

"Goodnight, Conner."

I can't resist standing by my bedroom door only to admire him for a few more minutes. *Oh, how I wish he were mine.* I bet I'm not the only girl wishing that right now. I'm sure Conner Dawson has his very own personal fan club. I roll my eyes at the thought of another woman wanting him as much as I do. Quickly, I get the thought out of my head, and my attention goes back to him.

Oh my…licking my lips, I watch as he calls it a night. Those black silk pajama pants…damn, I wish they would hang just a little lower—then maybe I could get a glimpse of that tight ass of his as he's bending over putting his guitar away. He closes the notebook and places it inside his guitar case. Walking over to the edge of the balcony, he runs his fingers through his hair and admires the night sky…the casino lights…and all the beauty that surrounds it. Only a short minute later, he turns around and picks up his things. Determined to go unnoticed, I slip back inside my room when I see him leaning over to blow out the candles.

As quietly as possible, I shut the door and jump in bed before hearing the glass doors from the balcony close. He's inside the penthouse, and I can hear him walking down the hallway; humming the melody and memorizing his work. Within seconds, his footsteps have stopped, and he's right outside my room. Secretly, I hope he opens the door and seduces me, but he doesn't. He walks away, and I force myself to go to sleep.

I had good sense to set my alarm on my phone this time, and it is ringing in my ear at seven thirty a.m. on the dot. There is no way I am going to sleep the day away again and miss out on seeing Conner before he leaves for work. I reach for my phone, and when I do I notice a note and a bottle of ibuprofen.

Good morning, sunshine. Thought you might need these after your encounter with the floor last night. Hope you're feeling ok and get to enjoy your day.

Conner

Not again. I missed him again. I am beating myself up for oversleeping, and at the same time I'm trying to figure out where he got the energy from to get up so early. He had less sleep than I did, and he was still up before dawn.

I take a deep breath and grab my tablet. I need to check my messages and make sure no one is desperately trying to get in touch with me. I snarl my nose up at the thought of the stalker that I left back in Tennessee and go to my favorite social networking site. There are no new alerts, only a new message that I am scared to open. I take a deep breath and click on the icon. It is Baylee. Thank goodness.

*Dear best friend. I'm worried about you.
It is not like you to not call. I haven't seen or
heard from you since your text. Please let me
know your okay.*

Poor Baylee. I know she's probably freaking out, but what do I tell her? I decide the less information the better. I don't want to put her in any danger. I choose to message her, but I don't tell her where I am. My message is short and sweet, just to let her know I'm okay.

I am doing okay, Baylee. Please don't worry. I am out of town, and I will be back in a few days. Promise I'm okay. Hope Mr. Jenkins is making it without his assistant. Let him know what's going on with me, if you haven't already. You are the best friend ever, and I love you for caring. Thank you. Oh, and please let Landon know I'm okay too. Thanks again, BFF.

I hope she is able to smooth things over with Mr. Jenkins. It was wrong for me to up and leave like I did, but I had to. Losing my job is the last thing I need to go back home to. He has to understand my abrupt departure.

Okay. No more dwelling on Oak Hill. I promise myself to focus only on the present moment and the week I am spending on the island.

Thank goodness I don't have to worry about booking a flight home. Conner and Hillary made it clear that the jet was at my disposal, so it looks like I'm stress free for the next few days. Now…time to get busy enjoying this vacation.

I climb out of the way too comfy bed and make my way to the bathroom. I look in the mirror, and Conner was correct. Above my right eye is a small knot that is already turning three shades of purple. Ugh! Great. Leave it up to me to fall off the bed in the middle of an amazing dream. But then again, it got me a midnight visit from the star attraction himself.

A ridiculous smile spreads across my face.

I can't help but wonder what it would be like to have him in bed, and if he would be as good as he was in my dream. I bite my bottom lip and back to reality I come. *Wishful thinking Stone; don't get your hopes up.* Ugh! Shut up you! *My mind, my thoughts!* Shaking my head at my inner self, I go on about my business.

After pulling my hair up and throwing on my beach clothes, I go in the kitchen, and there she is. Leilani. I feel like I am having a déjà vu moment, because she is standing in the same spot she was yesterday, with the same scrumptious layout behind her.   Thank goodness it is because I am starving.

"Good morning, Leilani." Strolling her way, I reach over and grab a bottle of water.

"Good morning, Ms. Stone. I hope you slept well." Before I can answer her, she notices the small discolored knot above my eye.

Her motherly instinct steps in, and she is immediately in front of me checking it out.

I assure her I am okay, and it is nothing to worry about.

"You kids, now days you are tough as nails—nothing fazes you," she laughs and returns to her daily duties.

Smiling back at her, I grab a bagel and make my way out of the kitchen.

"Bye, Leilani. I'll see you later," yelling with a mouthful of food, I step inside the elevator and head to the beach.

The day goes by fast, and it is pretty much a repeat of the day before, minus the afternoon nap. I walk the beach gathering seashells and playing volleyball with my new found friends.

After a long day of hitting the ball back and forth, I am invited to join them at the bonfire where we sip on piña coladas, devour roasted hotdogs, and share stories of our pastimes. I am enjoying myself so much that I don't even think to keep up with the time.

When I do look at my watch, it is already close to midnight. I decide I better say goodnight to my friends and go upstairs. It is only minutes after my head hits the pillow that I am sleeping like a baby. The last twenty four hours took me from well-rested to just the opposite. I truly am worn completely out—physically and emotionally.

Chapter 8

"Rise and shine beautiful,"** he says. His voice tempting me to wake up, and my body begging to obey; finally, I submit. Though, as slowly as my eyes open, they shut even quicker. The blinds have been drawn, and the sun is beaming in—showing off the beautiful morning and causing me to blink uncontrollably.

Eager to see the man calling out to me, I force myself up. Stretching, yawning, and rubbing my eyes until it's not uncomfortable to keep them open. I search the room over, and there is no sign of Conner. I know that was his voice I heard, or *was* it just in my head? My eyes scan the room, and suddenly I feel like I'm losing my mind, but then I see *it*.

On the table, I notice a hair clip that has a big, bright, pink flower on it, and attached to it is a note from him. Immediately, a grin spreads across my face, and after reading his words I have to read them again to convince myself they are real.

Good morning, sleepy head. Hope you had a better night's rest last night. I have a busy day ahead of me, but I would love for you to spend this 4ᵗʰ of July evening with me. Until then, I have got your day all planned out for you. I don't feel as though I have been a very good host and would like to make it up to you if you will let me. Henry has all the details, so please meet him in the lobby at nine o'clock sharp· If you have other plans, I completely understand·

Conner

P·S· You do this thing with your mouth when you're sleeping, and I have to admit it's kind of a turn on· Hope to see you tonight·

Like a child, I'm on my feet and jumping up and down on the king size bed. I hold the note close to my heart and clip the flower in my hair. Scenarios of what my day will entail devour my thoughts, and my excitement knows no boundaries.

I leap off the bed and run to the mirror to check for drool. Gross, but what else could it be that I do with my mouth? Drool free. Thank goodness. My mouth curves into a massive grin while my heart does a happy dance.

The woman looking back at me no longer looks lost and lonely, but instead full of life. I take a deep breath and exhale. Today is going to be a great day, and I cannot think of any place I would rather be. I can't wait to see what Conner has planned for me. I gently take the clip from my hair and undress so that I can get in the shower. Nine o'clock is only forty five minutes away, and I don't want to keep Henry waiting.

Leilani isn't in her usual spot when I pass through the kitchen, but the layout is there just like before. I grab a protein bar and a bottle of water and head down to the lobby to find Henry.

I see the back of someone admiring a beautiful scenic picture of the islands, and there's no doubt it is the man I am looking for. "Now, that's a beautiful picture if I do say so myself." Standing behind him, I too appreciate the artwork. The artist really brought out the natural beauty; showing off immaculate detail of the exquisite flowers that are all around the island.

"Ms. Stone, you are right on time; thank you for your promptness," Henry says, turning and facing me. He places his hand on the small of my back and leads me to the front entrance of the hotel. There, we see Finn waiting with the limo.

The driver greets us with a tilt of his hat and a good morning hello as he opens the car door. I slide in, and to my surprise, Henry follows. He pulls out his smart phone, makes a call, confirms *my* appointment, and hangs up...just that quickly.

"Okay, Ms. Stone, first things first," says the concierge. "Have you eaten breakfast?" I recall the protein bar I inhaled while on the elevator.

"I did eat. Thank you."

"Great. You have a 9:30 appointment at Michael's, and it is best not to be late."

"Michael's?" I asked, confusion in my voice. "Who is he, and why am I going to see him?"

Looking at Henry, I can see the humor in his face. When he smiles, so do the little lines around his eyes. He really is a pleasant man. No wonder Conner has him escorting me today.

"Madam, you are going to enjoy a day at Michael's Luxurious Hair and Spa Resort. If you don't know the definition of being pampered, you will when you leave. First, you will relax and undergo a ninety minute massage, and that will include a hot-stone treatment that will leave you feeling like a brand new woman."

I gasp with widened eyes. I know he finds me hilarious. I can tell by the smile that he's now trying to hide. Closing his eyes and shaking his head, he can no longer resist the temptation of laughing. He lets out a cackle, and I can't help but join him.

At this moment, Henry and I are bonding. Not only is he an employee of the Dawson's, but he is now my friend, and I can never have too many of those. I listen closely as he continues.

"Next, you will receive a manicure, a pedicure, a therapeutic facial, and last but not least you will get a fresh new hairdo." He clarifies that these are the instructions of Mr. Dawson himself, and he's here to make sure I follow through. Somebody pinch me, because I have got to be dreaming. I have never been pampered so much in my life, and I have to admit I almost feel like somebody's somebody. I take a deep breath, anticipating my new makeover and how I am going to thank the man behind it.

Looking ahead, I can see a tranquil place just off the road, and it's sitting on the beach. There's a huge tiki hut, no, make that enormous, and it is surrounded by not only trees and flowers, but also the ocean. It is so inviting. Just when I'm thinking how I wish I was there, it's then that I see the sign— Michael's Luxurious Hair and Spa Resort.

Wow. Suddenly, I'm more excited than I was just seconds before and Henry sees it. He can't help but laugh out loud— *again.* Maybe, that means he likes me—either way, I can't wait to get that hot-stone treatment.

Moments after arriving, I am introduced to Michael himself, who in turn introduces me to Greta. The owner is a petite man in his mid-thirties and seems very confident around a woman I try not to be intimidated by. Greta is at least five foot and ten inches tall and has more of a man's build than Michael.

Standing in the lobby, Henry by my side, I can hear soft music along with the light sound of flowing water. There's a smell in the air too, maybe a mixture of eucalyptus and coconut. I'm not sure, but it's very soothing as is the setting before me.

In every corner, I see plants and floating candles.

Looking above, the ceiling fans even look tropical; adorning big brown banana leaves of their own. They really aren't leaves, but they look like it. Between their breeze and the one coming off the ocean, you can barely tell it's a hot summer day in Hawaii.

"Ma'am, if you will follow me we'll get started now," says Greta. *Her voice is even deeper than it should be.*

I tear my eyes away from all the beauty, to look at the woman who will have my life in her hands for the next hour and a half. *I can do this.*

"Enjoy yourself, Ms. Stone. I will be here waiting when you're done," says Henry, as he sits down in one of the chairs by the entrance.

Glancing his way, my brows raised, I crack a smile, and wave goodbye.

He waves back.

Walking down the hallway on the right, we approach the place where the flowing water is coming from—a surreal, man-made pool of water. It's big enough for three or four people, but there is only one woman there enjoying it. It's made for relaxing, and that's what she is doing in the perfectly stone sculptured hot-tub. *Looking over at Greta,* I wonder if the lady will let me join her. *Yeah, right!*

Anyway...

Steam is filling the air, circling the woman as she stands beneath a shelf that is trickling water over the sides like a waterfall. Standing there, the H_2O cocktail recycles back and forth, over and over again, and what her skin doesn't drink in, the pool surrounding her does.

And we keep on walking.

I am almost petrified when Greta leads me into a private room and asks me to strip down to my bare essentials. I must be looking at her like she is crazy, because she smiles and hands me a white robe to put on afterwards.

"I'll give you some privacy and return in a few minutes," she says.

I debate on whether or not I should do as I was asked, but then Conner comes to my mind. He planned this, so I'm sure

I'm just overreacting. I strip down to nothing but my panties, and wrap the robe around my near-naked body.

Greta returns just like she said she would, and I'm taken by surprise when she leads me out another door. My feet hit the sand, and I realize we're on the beach.

The site is exquisite. There are two massaging tables resting beneath a large tent, and of course there are even larger trees shading the whole area. Next to the tables, are smaller ones that are covered with the necessities that Greta will be using on me. Things like exotic oils, rocks, and even items I can't quite make out.

Carefully, I lie across the table and remove the robe I am wearing; pulling the thin sheet up to my waist—exposing nothing but my back. Woman or no woman, my boobs are mine, and I don't care how private this area is; nobody's getting a sneak peek.

Alright...here we go. Her hands are on me and my eyes are squinting shut; nothing open but my ears, and suddenly all they hear is the lapping of the ocean water. Wow, this may not be so bad after all. I feel my body relaxing; enjoying the serenity of it all and letting the stress go. Greta's pretty good...hands up to her; *you go girl.*

The next hour and a half fly by, and I have to say that woman earned every penny she made. I didn't realize just how stressed out I was until she got a hold of me. There was tension balled up in places that I didn't even know I had, but not anymore. Relaxation is covering me and begging for company. I can't help but wonder, *is it time for my date yet?* Smiling, I prepare for my next endeavor.

The next few hours went by just as Henry said they would.

When it came time to work on my hair, I opted to keep my long length with a trim to the ends, a few chunky highlights just on top, and include some bouncy curls. I remember Baylee's curls and how she is always incredibly beautiful. I am hoping to be just that when Conner lays his eyes on me tonight.

They did an astonishing job with my makeup too. After looking in the mirror, I noticed the spot above my right eye. The bruise is no longer visible and my face looks flawless; finally, it's time to go find my escort.

Calm, cool, and relaxed, I strut to the lobby and find Henry sitting there waiting on me. He has a magazine in front of his face, but I can see him cutting his eyes in my direction. He's impressed and showing off a pleased look when he lowers the latest edition of celebrity gossip to the table beside him.

"Mr. Dawson will be very pleased, Ms. Stone," he says, walking towards me and escorting me out of the resort.

"Thank you, Henry," I say, blushing.

Now that my spa treatment is over, I wonder what the rest of the afternoon will consist of. We've been driving for a few minutes, and Henry is in control of my destination. The scenery is beautiful. I can't help but envy the people who get to live here.

It doesn't take long before we make it to our next stop. There is a strip of boutiques that could make a girl go in debt. But even all the fabulousness before me doesn't stop me from craving the man who has planned my day perfectly.

Inside me, something eager and greedy is trying to surface. My body is desperate to see him…to feel him…to thank him in person. A smoldering desire to beg him to take what I've never given is consuming my thoughts.

"We're here," says Finn, jerking me away from my fantasy.

The limo pulls up to the curb and the driver turns off the engine. Finn opens the door, and out goes Henry and me right behind him. "So, where would you like to start, Ms. Stone?" asks the concierge-escort-friend-man named Henry.

I look at the high-dollar boutiques and know right away I did not budget for this. There's no way—one dress alone would probably cost me three months rent.

"I don't understand. I mean, I can't afford to…" Henry stops me before I can go any further and states that I am not to pay for anything.

"The sky is the limit, and the only thing expected of you is to not turn the gift down." I stand looking in awe of all the stores, but inside I'm screaming with irrevocable excitement. "Madam, may I also add that your dinner date will be at a luau, so you may want to consider that while shopping."

Amazed at Conner's generosity, I remember the pink flower clip and decide to get something to match it.

I look around at all the hustle and flow of the busy sidewalks. They are covered with extravagantly wealthy women who snarl their noses up at me when they check out my stunning apparel. I'm wearing cut-off shorts and a T-shirt, with flip flops to match. *Shoot*— I was irritated with myself for not thinking ahead. I should have dressed better— I hope I haven't embarrassed Henry and Finn.

Never in a million years would I have thought I would be going on a shopping spree. But I am, and it is all because of him. My sexy, rich, new man-friend is paying for a much needed makeover, and I can't help but wonder why.

Maybe he thinks I need to *look* like I come from an *aura of wealth* in order to be his date tonight. My heart skips a beat, and I put the crazy thought away. There is no way that is it. I laugh at myself thinking he would probably take me anyway he could get me; dolled up, Plain Jane, or over easy. I feel the connection just like I know he does, and the money and good looks are just a bonus.

I don't realize how late it is getting due to my overwhelming shopping adventure. It is amazing the things you can buy when you aren't afraid of spending your rent money. The last boutique is the one that sells me my apparel for the night. I choose a long, flowing, white skirt that rests right above my ankles and the shell anklet that I will be wearing. I top it off with a hot-pink strapless top that not only shows off my belly button but will also match the hair clip Conner had left for me.

Okay. I think I am luau ready, but am I ready for the affect I am going to have on him when he sees me? Will he be pleased, or will he think it's too much...*or not enough*? I can't worry about that—it' almost time to meet him, and there is no going back now.

Finn drives us back to the hotel, and Henry helps me with my bags. He leaves me at the penthouse and instructs me to be back downstairs within the hour; the limo will be waiting.

After freshening up, I put on my new outfit and walk over to the oval mirror next to the closet. Perfect! Everything fits the way it's supposed to, and my hair and make-up still look as good as ever. I am ready for my date with Conner, and I can only hope it will be the first one of many.

Standing here admiring my own reflection, I imagine him behind me. His left arm banded around my waist, while his right hand moves my hair to the side. Closing my eyes, I can almost feel the heat of his breath glide across my skin.

My eyes pop open.

What am I doing here? He's waiting on me.

Giggling to myself, I grab my flip flops and head downstairs. Finn is waiting by the backdoor of the limo with that contagious smile of his spreading across his ancient face.

"Ms. Stone. You look stunning."

I hug him for his compliment and slide inside the backseat after he opens the door.

He shuts it behind me.

All of a sudden, I am so nervous. *What if Conner doesn't see in me what Finn does?* He is the only man I want to see me that way, and I am scared to death that he won't see me that way at all.

Trying to grasp hold of my confidence that is now flying out the window, I get a glimpse of myself in the rearview mirror. *I really do look like my mother.* That gives me just the boost I need to put little Miss Confidence back in her place. After all, my mom is the most stunning person I know.

The thirty minute drive is over, and I have made it to my destination. Only seconds after putting the car in park, the door on my side opens. His hand is the first thing that I see, but it is his eyes that get my attention. If eyes could smile, his would be—*so would mine.* Allowing my fingers to interlace with his, the *first-date-wow-effect* consumes me...the current flows from my head to my toes and everything in between. I cannot believe I am here...with him—Conner Dawson...*my date, my lifesaver, my hero.*

Chapter 9

I **step out of** the car, and his grip tightens. Our fingers are entwined, and he can't take his eyes off of me. He is speechless and that says it all. I can feel a trickle of sweat on his palms, and I think he may be as nervous as I am.

In the background, I can hear the chattering voices of a crowd and the vibrant sound of music. It sounds like somebody's having a party. A massive grin spreads across my face as I look at him.

He releases my hand, but only to place a beautiful white lei around my neck; within seconds my hand is back in his.

"Wow. You are even more beautiful than I imagined you would be, Miss Stone." The words rolled off of his tongue, and I listened closely as each syllable made its way to my ears.

"You're not so bad yourself, Mister Dawson."

We laugh as we stroll through the most amazing flower garden I have ever witnessed. It is beautiful and landscaped by a genius. The garden surrounds a huge stocked goldfish pond that seems to have no ending. All this beauty is connected to a three-story home that sits right on the beach. The home is not a house…it's a mansion and its brand new.

We walk to the back where there is a huge buffet of food and drinks, and people are everywhere. There is an array of exotic hula dancers and fire knife dancers for our entertainment, yet none of it compares to the man that I am here with. His beauty out does it all. He is dressed in dark stone-washed blue jeans and a white T-shirt that shows off the muscular perfection beneath it. Around his neck, there lies a fresh-flowered lei that intensifies the color of his dreamy eyes. He is barefoot and happy, and he is mine for the night.

"Some party. Who are all of these people?" My eyes wander the area, and no one looks familiar.

"Let's see." He points to the left and then to the right and then to the group that is dancing along with the hula dancers in front of the band. There are architects, landscaping groups, home interior designers, and a few friends that have just come to celebrate. Of course, they are all celebrating not just Independence Day but also a job well-done. It is obvious that a lot of the guests here are the geniuses behind this thrifty new home.

"Wow. Which one is the lucky owner?" I giggle and raise my eyebrows—trying to figure it out on my own. It's not like I will know him or her, but I can't wait to put a face to the luckiest homeowner in Hawaii.

He looks at me with his hand still in mine, and bends down to speak softly in my ear. He smells so good. It is hard to focus on anything he is going to say with his body so close to mine. "Me." His word a mere whisper; his hot breath like exotic air hitting every nerve ending I own. The man is seducing me and doesn't even know it. *Yes he does.* Of course he does. Looking around the grounds and back at him, I see the resemblance. Every Adonis should have his very own paradise, and now he has his. Surrounded by beauty, head to toe, wall to wall, this man seems to have it all.

"Now I know why you've been a stranger the last couple of days." Thinking back on his long days and late nights, I imagine him here giving orders and telling the crew exactly what he wanted.

"Yes, Miss Stone, I have spent a lot of time here in the last seventy two hours." I scan the area looking for his sister, but she's nowhere in sight.

"And, Hilary, where is she?" I ask.

His brows arch as he takes a deep breath and lets it out.

"Hillary had some personal business to attend to. She said to tell you goodbye, and that she was sorry she couldn't say it in person." His answer has a hint of disappointment to it, but he tries to cover it up in his voice. Needless to say, his tell-it-all eyes are saying something else. *What is going on with her?*

I nod my head and smile; continuing to follow him as he leads me to meet his guests. Introductions are made along with new friends. I watch and listen as they all have the utmost respect for the same man I do. He really does have it all. Money. Power. Friends. Family. Respect. But one thing I've noticed is missing—a ring. He isn't married, and evidently he doesn't have a special girl in his life other than his sister. Could it be that my path has finally crossed with my soul mate? This is all happening so fast, and I want to stop time before the week is over.

Leaving the guests to enjoy the party, we stroll along the beautiful grounds.

"Pardon me, Hannah," he says with a disturbed look on his face. Moving his hand from my back to the front pocket of his jeans, he pulls out his vibrating phone. He looks at the caller i.d. and then back at me.

"Don't mind me, please, take the call," I gesture with a nod of my head.

Answering the phone, he walks a few feet away to block out the sound of the music—*I can still hear him.*

"Conner Dawson speaking," he states in a very authoritative manner. "I see. No, continue as planned. I will be in the area in a few weeks, and I expect the matter to be taken care of," he says, pausing while he listens to the voice on the other end of the line. "No buts about it. Get the job done, or I will find someone who will!" he demands roughly before ending the call.

Trying to give him the privacy he needed, I turned to watch the entertainment. Within seconds, he's strutting his way back to me. *There he is*—his strong masculine hand now resting on the bare bottom half of my back. I close my eyes for a split second only to lavish in the decadent feeling that consumes me when his skin touches mine.

"My apologies, Hannah." Conner says softly, now running his fingers from one side of my skin to the next.

Stomach fluttering—eyes rolling as my body reacts to the attraction that I no longer have any freaking control over. That damn feeling feels so damn good. And I take a deep breath—exhaling as I turn to face him.

"Please, don't apologize. Business is business. I completely understand."

Gazing at me with a look of relief, he begins guiding me back to the party—*hand in hand.* "Well, thank you for understanding, Miss Stone." His lips curl up into that glorious smile that I love.

"So, Hannah, what do you do for fun back in Tennessee?" His curious question making me blush—thinking about my erotica reading. *Gosh!* I really have been leading a pretty boring life lately. Not that I don't like my reading because I absolutely-without-a-doubt *love* it, but there is more to life than sitting alone pouting over some deadbeat loser that ripped my dreams away and reading about hot sex and wild passionate love affairs that aren't mine.

My sex twitches at the thought of having a wild passionate love affair and *hot sex* with the man who is holding more than my hand—I can't explain it. The feeling I get when I'm with him is suffocating me in a good way. I feel so alive.

"Well, as you know, I've been known to show up at Joe's Place from time to time. Other than that, my life's pretty laid back. I don't get out a lot, but I do love to read so that takes up a lot of my time.

"Reading is good," he states. "I've been on many adventures in my time and never had to leave the privacy of my own bedroom—*all thanks to a good book.*"

I cock my head in his direction—*way up there.* He winks at me—grasping my hand tighter as we stroll amongst the guests.

"I would love to hear about those adventures, Mister Dawson."

Throwing his head back, he tries to manage his tasseled hair that is now windblown from the breezy night.

"Maybe one day, Hannah, but for now...*let's dance.*"

Leading me directly to the all *naturél* green-grassed dance floor, he begins rolling his hips to the beat of the bongo drums—twisting back and forth to the same rhythm of my rapidly beating heart.

Oh my, oh me. Suddenly, I feel the need to be standing in a pool of ice water with an air conditioner vent blowing all over my bare-naked body. I'm so hot...well, make that my womanhood—it's smoldering down there.

Admiring the view and forgetting to get my own groove on, Conner sachets directly in front of me, places one hand on each of my hips, and starts gently forcing my body to sway to the left and to the right. I can't help but burst out laughing. It's contagious—he's grinning ear to ear.

"That's right, Hannah. Just like that. Listen to the music...feel the beat pulsate through your veins. Swirl those hips to the rhythm." I'm swirling with his hands still in place. He watches me as I watch him—his burning desire to be up in my business is shining through in his heated expression. "Do you learn this quickly at everything you do, Miss Stone?" he asks with a wicked-sexy look all over his beautiful face.

"Depends on what that something is, Mister Dawson," my cheeks flushing crimson at the way I'm looking at him. I can't help it. I swear if I was a *naughty* girl I would pull him away to a perfect little hiding spot—peel his clothes off...no make that *rip* his clothes off and have my way with him all night long. "I do give my all...sometimes I can grasp things, and sometimes I can't. Dancing with you is easy," I say breathlessly.

"Likewise," he replies.

The beating of the drums stop and is replaced with the upbeat sound of music playing from the sound system. One song after another Conner keeps me moving... *All this booty twisting is wearing me out*—and that look he keeps giving me has my adrenaline running a freaking marathon.

And the last song is over—and I'm thirsty.

"Where can a girl get a drink around here?" I ask, gasping sticky dry breath...*ugh, I have a chronic case of cottonmouth.*

"That depends on what you want," he says, pointing to the right at a huge display of iced-down buckets sitting around. "Alcoholic beverages are to the right and anything else is to the left."

"After all that shaking, I'm thinking I better go left," I rasp.

"Left it is," he laughs.

Leading me to the bottled water, he grabs a twenty ounce container. Opening the top, he then hands me the ice cold drink.

Forgetting that I'm a *lady*, I turn the bottle up and down half of it—never taking my eyes off of him...he looks at me hard.

"You were thirsty."

"Very much so—and *hot*," I reply, still breathless.

Taking the bottle from my hand, he whispers for me to turn around as a slow song begins to play. I eye him speculatively—turning slowly until he's standing behind me. Gently, he pulls my hair up off my neck—holding it to the side. I jump as the cold bottle rolls from one side of my neck to the other and across the top of my back; and as his manhood lightly sweeps across my ass. He's dancing back there, so naturally I begin to sway along with him. Gently he begins to blow on my wet skin—cooling me down and making me singe with desire at the same time. I feel my body quivering.

Leaning in closer, I can feel his breath trail up to my ear. "Are you still hot?" he asks bluntly...*seductively*

If he only knew.

"I feel much better," I murmur. "Thank you."

The next few hours we laugh, talk, eat and dance the night away on the beautiful green lawn...and shortly before ten o'clock Conner walks away only to make himself the center of attention.

Oh my.

Sitting on a stool with a crowd encircling him, he begins playing his guitar and serenading us with the song he had been working on the other night. He glides his fingers across the strings as the words leave his lips. I can't tear my eyes away from him—*neither can he fight the temptation of staring at me.* A few minutes pass—the song ends, and he makes his way back to me.

"You're really good," I say as he puts his arm around my waist.

I close my eyes and take a deep breath...*that feeling.* It's like nothing I've ever felt.

"I love to sing," he admits. "But, thank you."

I tilt my head back at him, but before I have a chance to say a word the show has started.

Thunder may roll and lightning may strike, but the sound of fireworks is echoing across the sky tonight—*such sweet splendor.* I absolutely love the 4th of July, but without a doubt this one has been the most breathtaking ever. The sky is lighting up with sparkling colors as far as my eyes can see, and I get to stand here and admire it all with *him.* Never have I witnessed so much beauty in one place: Conner, the island, the house, and now this. I'm surrounded by magnificence— what a perfect ending to a perfect party.

One by one, the guests are leaving, and before I know it Conner and I are the only two people left. Finn has even left...thanks to my date giving him the rest of the night off. He offers to give me a tour of his home, and I can't resist.

The inside is as gorgeous as the outside and even more breathtaking than the penthouse. *I really like all the earth tone colors.* From the bottom to the top and back down again, we make our way through the elegant house. Although, he never shows me his bedroom and I can't help but wonder why.

The home he built looks so much like him; extravagant but yet down to earth and breathtaking. Conner may come from money, but he doesn't let it control him. He knows when to be domineering, but he also knows how to let loose—unlike any other millionaire I know. Not that I know any other ones, but I have read about several.

It is hard to believe that having that much money doesn't go to his head. Though, he did mention earlier it was his dad's money that had funded his new home on the island, but I'm sure he has a hefty bank account of his own. Even if he depends on his dad for all of his money, I don't care. It isn't his money I want anyway…it's him.

The house was Conner's birthday present, and he was given the go ahead to design it as he saw fit. He did an amazing job, and I realize this is just one more thing to add to the list. The list of things he is *good* at that is.

The tour is over before I want it to be, which means my night is coming to an end. *Not yet. Please don't be over yet.* I beg, using the quiet voice inside my head.

We stand in the kitchen staring at each other, neither of us ready to call it a night. Finally, he breaks the silence. "How would you like to see the beach?"

"I would love to." Yes! He read my mind.

He leads me out the back entrance, but not before grabbing a blanket out of the hall closet. "Put this over your shoulders. There is a cool breeze coming off the water tonight. I would hate for you to get sick."

"You are so thoughtful, Mister Dawson. You seem to have taken really good care of me today. Thank you for everything."

"It was my pleasure. I could get use to spoiling you," he says, his voice as seductive as ever.

A flirtatious grin spreads across my face. I could really get *use* to this man spoiling me—by giving me his time—not his money.

He puts his arm around me after placing the blanket there first and leads me down a divided breezeway. It is lined with flame-proof bamboo poles that light up the whole area. To the left of the breezeway is a room big enough to be a guest house, and to the right is the ocean. There are palm trees on each side of our path to the white sanded beach, and Conner is correct about the breeze. There is a chill in the air that causes me to shiver.

We walk barefoot through the sand, and neither of us seems to care that it keeps getting between our toes. As we make our way across the beach and to the shoreline, I can't help but notice him collecting all the dry branches we come across. It peaks my curiosity. "What are those for?"

"Miss Stone. I mean, Hannah." He winks at me. "You are shivering, and I can't have you catching a cold. I'll have you warm in no time." He smiles, and it turns to laughter, and before I know it, I am laughing right along with him. We're walking along the beach up under a black sky lit up with twinkling stars, and the moment is splendidly romantic.

Only a few more feet and we stop, now just a short distance from his private beach house.

I watch him as he puts branch upon branch, rubbing hard and blowing gently, and he has a fire built in no time. *Why do I always have to think about sex when it comes to him? Branch upon branch—his body on mine; rubbing hard and blowing gently—sex itself; fire built—climaxing.* Is there anything that does not turn me on about this man? *Uh, no!*

I decide to share my blanket to keep the sand from getting all over our clothes. I take it from my shoulders, and lay it down—making sure not to get it too close to the flames.

We sit down and cuddle in front of the fire like star struck lovers—taking time to appreciate the beauty of heaven's canvas. The night sky sparkles, showing off the exquisite detail before our very eyes. God really knew what he was doing when he painted the world; such intense perfection that so often goes unnoticed. I close my eyes for a moment, taking a deep breath, and appreciating the magic moment at hand.

Conner clears his throat—only to get my attention.

"Harrumph."

Opening my eyes, I lean my head back to look at him.

"Where did you go, Hannah? For a second there, I thought you had fallen asleep on me," he chuckles. His laugh singing notes of its own. It's like music to my ears, and I could listen to it all night long.

"Just taking time to memorize this very moment; hiding it away right here, so that I remember it forever." Placing my hand over my heart, he wraps his arms around me even tighter.

The warmth of his body has me hotter than the flames from the fire, and it's so intense. I feel it, and I know he feels it too. *I absolutely love being wrapped up in his arms,* but there is a question I need answered, and now is the perfect time.

"May I ask you something?"

He nods his head.

"How did you know my name?" I scoot around, but just a little—there's no way I want out of his arms, but I do want to get a better look at him.

He smiles, causing a chain reaction. My lips curve into a massive grin of their own and then he answers me. "Miss Stone, do you really think I would let you cross my path and not find out who you are? My eyes met yours, and I was lucky to remember the words to the song I was singing. Before I left that night, I pointed you out to Joe, and he knew exactly who you were."

I nod my head, agreeing. "Of course." I whisper. We have a mutual acquaintance and his name is Joe. That explains it. "By the way, what *were* you doing in the Nashville area?"

I wonder if I'm being too nosey, but nonetheless, I am curious, and just like mama always says...*You never know, unless you ask.*

"Hillary and I were there looking to buy a major record label." His mind wanders and things get quiet; his fingers now making a trail in the sand...over and over again making a complete circle. Something is on his mind, but what?

The silence is interrupted by a gust of air. The wind has picked up, and my hair is getting in my eyes. Conner takes the clip from above my ear and pins the loose strands back so that they are away from my face; twirling a blonde curl while he's at it. "I really like what you did with your hair; the highlights bring out your eyes, and they already stood out on their own—very beautiful, Hannah, just like you."

"You're too sweet, Conner. Thank you." *Now, kiss me already.*

A slow blink—and then another; I'm drawing him in for what I want. He's just as guilty—smelling the way he does, looking at me with such burning desire; he's drawing me in just as much.

Watching each other—the soft tip of his finger has now left my hair, and is trailing down my cheek. My breath catches—this is it; I know what's fixing to happen; so does my heart. It's beating away like I've never been kissed before. Thinking back, I didn't feel like this—*I've never felt like this.*

Leaning in, slow and seductively, eye to eye, heated breath and a perfect night to share a first kiss—it's going to happen. His lips are barely an inch away now.

Cupping his hand beneath my hair, he pulls me into him...and that's all it takes. Our mouths are like a magnetic force not to be reckoned with, and we couldn't stop if we tried.

His soft, plump, beautiful, wet lips are on mine, and his tongue is devouring me within seconds. His kiss is gentle yet powerful, and with every flick of his tongue, I know he wants me as much as I want him. He has one hand on my back and the other one is moving up my skirt—in search of my bare legs.

Gently he lays me down on the blanket, and we make out under the stars for what seems like hours. His kiss is addictive, and I want more. He tastes better than he looks, and it takes everything in me to restrain from giving this man the one thing I have held onto for the last twenty two years; my sweet, sweet virtue. I pull my lips away from his, and lay my head on his chest.

It isn't long before we are both fast asleep underneath the moonlit sky. This night has been a diehard-romantic's dream come true, and I am living it.

Chapter 10

The blistering sun has shown itself, and shore birds are already flying around looking for their morning feeding. The water gently splashes upon the white sandy beach, and then back into the ocean just to do it all over again—back and forth, stretching as far as the waves permit. It is such a tranquil sound and a perfect alarm to wake up to.

The fire Conner built had burned out sometime during the early morning hours, but the passionate desire between us is still ablaze. I feel it. There is no doubt he does too. His arms and legs haven't budged; they are still wrapped all around me.

A content smile embraces my face, and I am so happy here—*with him.* The best part of waking up is the pleasure of opening my eyes and looking into the face of an angel. The perfect way to start my day and one that I could get use to.

I lean over and nibble on the lobe of his ear—tempting him with every flick of my tongue. He exhales. His breath is as hot as mine, but he never opens his eyes. I watch his chest. Up and down it goes—showing off how irresistible he is even while sleeping.

I want him awake. My lips part and with heated breath I whisper to him the same three words I read in the note he left me the other day. "Good morning, sunshine."

He flashes an amazing grin before he opens his eyes—a trace of laughter even parting his lips. Then he asks me a question that I need the same answer to. "Am I dreaming?"

I take a deep breath and answer him the only way I know how. My lips close in on his, and all of a sudden he has me on top of him—grinding his morning erection all up in my business. *Oh! That. Feels. So. Good.* And I don't have it in me to stop him...not yet; after all we are fully clothed.

After a long good morning kiss, he pulls away and his eyes are looking straight into mine. "Spend the day with me, Hannah."

There is no denying I want that more than anything, and he knows it. "I would love to, Conner." I kiss him gently but only a peck. "Anything for my hero."

Throwing his head back, he laughs out loud—shaking his blonde wary strands away from his eyes as he looks back at me. "This *hero* name calling is going to keep me on my toes...just how often are you going to need rescuing, Miss Stone?" he asks, arching his perfect brow over his right eye with a huge mischievous grin on his face.

"Well, I am actually a klutz at times, so it could be pretty often. You may have your hands full when it comes to me and my two left feet." Eyeing him cautiously, his hands trail from my back to my ass.

"Mmmm...I think I have my hands pretty full right now," he growls, squeezing both my butt cheeks and sending my belly into a fluttering frenzy.

"Yes, indeed you do—*really full*," I breathe, referring to the big butt my mama blessed me with.

"Being that I'm an avid ass-man, I think I'm going to like watching out for you," he confesses.

I blush. He flushes with desire.

A tickling sensation sachets its way all around my belly—one side to the other until finally its diving down and enveloping my womanhood. I gasp at the natural reflexes going on down there and even more at the growling noises now coming from my body.

"Err..." I cry out while grabbing my stomach.

Wide-eyed, his gaze is as hungry as my belly. "Sounds like somebody has a hunger for more than just an early morning rendezvous in the sand," he whispers, pulling me closer for some mouth to mouth action.

Our mouths meet—tongues twist...and then our lips slowly part.

"Sorry, Mister Dawson, but who needs food when I can get a mouthful of you." I swallow hard, but he likes my flirtatious behavior—his devious grin proves it...but he knows we both need real food if we're going to have the energy to keep this up.

"I agree, Miss Stone. You are pretty scrumptious tasting yourself, but we need to get you fed. I don't want a repeat of what happened your first day here." Conner takes out his phone to check the time, and when he does I realize I don't have mine.

"Oh no, my phone—I don't know where I left it." Panic is all over my face, and I wonder if I have any missed calls.

"Don't worry, Hannah. We will find it. Try to think of the last place you had it," he demands.

By memory, I back track my moves since I arrived here last night, and realize I didn't have my phone all night. Next, I remember the ride over, and I don't recall having it then either.

"It has to be back at the penthouse," I said.

Resting his head against mine, he steals a quick kiss before guiding me to my feet.

"I'm sure it is, sweet girl. Don't worry about it. I am sure it's right where you left it."

I sigh.

Conner grabs the blanket, and we head towards his house.

His newly built home is only a short ten minute walk, and we're there in no time. I'm shocked when he raises the garage door, and we climb into a classic seventy-eight Chevy pick-up truck that has been cleaned up and made to look brand new.

"Climb in and hold on tight. Baby boy here is meaner than he looks." Conner laughs and revs up the engine. He is right. This bad boy sounds like a monster. I buckle in and hold on tight to the handle above my head.

Conner takes a back road to bypass all the traffic, and I'm amazed at how well he knows the island. "So, how long exactly have you been visiting here?"

"Since I was a boy, we use to come here every summer and sometimes twice a year. I knew back then this is where I would make my home one day. Dad knew it too. That's why he built the casino and gave it to me on my twenty-first birthday. I've been living in the penthouse since, but we do so much traveling that I've hardly been there lately." He looks so peaceful, living the life he's always dreamed, and he *does* have his own bank account after all; not that it matters— just good to know.

I envy the places he must have seen while growing up. This small town girl didn't do much traveling unless it was to the lake or to Nashville, and that had to be on a special occasion. My mom worked two jobs to keep a roof over our heads, so there wasn't much money left to play with. I admire her for the memories I now share with her and my brother Landon. They are cherished memories that I will treasure for a lifetime.

My eyes maneuver over the bad boy driving this monster on four wheels; head to toe, I admire the length of his muscular body. I respect the way he handles the big truck; it's big and powerful just like him. "You look pretty good behind the wheel, Conner." He flashes his pearly whites at me, and I'm blinded by the beauty of his breathtaking smile.

"Hold on! This is a big one!" I barely have time to grip the handle tighter, and over the hill we fly. I feel like a kid on a roller coaster, and it's amazing. He did a good job of making me forget about my missing phone, but not for long. I worry that my mom has found out about the stalker and is trying to get in touch with me. I tell myself not to worry, and I try to do just that. *No worries. Not yet anyway.*

We pull up at the luxurious hotel and head straight to the elevator. Henry is in the lobby, and I know he realizes I'm wearing the same clothes I left here in yesterday. His eyes move up and down my body. I can't worry about that now.

My attire is the least of my worries. I wave and keep on going.

We step into the suite, and there is Leilani—cleaning and dusting a spotless room. "Good afternoon, Leilani." Our voices are in sync as we both greet the housekeeper.

He leans over and whispers in my ear. "Great minds think alike."

"Yes, they do." I smile and notice Leilani watching us.

"Good afternoon, Mr. Dawson. Ms. Stone."

"Leilani, Miss Stone has misplaced her cell phone. Have you seen it lying around anywhere?"

"Yes sir. It is on the dresser in her room. I found it under her bed while I was vacuuming this morning," she says, smiling when she notices Conner's hand resting on my lower back. I can't help but smile back at her.

A sigh of relief escapes me, and I rush into my room to get it. I have ten missed calls. Oh no. I slide the bar over expecting it to be my mom, but only two are from her. The rest are unknown, and that can only mean one thing—it is him. The stalker is bound and determined to make my life miserable.

Scanning over my messages, I notice there are several—some from Baylee, a couple from Landon, and one from my mom. Quickly, I text them all in a group message.

> *Sorry I'm just getting your messages. I have a lot going on right now—you know me, always busy doing something. Okay, well scratch that, but I really am busy. I promise to get in touch soon. Love you all ☺*

I hit send.

"See. I told you we would find it."

Shocked by the sound of his voice, I turn around to find him standing in the doorway of my room. Conner may have startled me, but I shake it off. There is no way I want him finding out about this. I don't want to scare him off, even though he doesn't seem like the type to get intimidated easily.

I fake a smile and excuse myself. "If you don't mind, I would like to freshen up a bit. I hear the shower calling my name."

"Of course, I will have Leilani make lunch." There is concern in his eyes, but thank goodness he doesn't burden me with questions.

"Great. Thank you." I grab some clean clothes and head to the bathroom. I barely get the door shut, and the tears start flowing from my eyes. The fear of going back home to that craziness has affected me more than I realize. I do not want to live my life like that. *I want to live it like this.*

Hurriedly, I turn on the water to keep the others from hearing my sniffling. A long cry calls for a long relaxing shower. I know it has to be a half hour before I make it to the kitchen, but I had to get it together before I could face Conner.

The smell of cooked pork is in the air when I open the door, and it smells delicious. Making my way past the breakfast bar, I see that Leilani has put together a barbeque salad and a mouthwatering pineapple smoothie. I know it's going to be appetizing.

That woman can work miracles in a kitchen. I can't help but wonder if she will be working at Conner's new house too; not that it is any of my business, but I still feel the need to quiz her. "So, Leilani, what do you think of the new place on the beach?"

My concentration moves from her to him as he sits down at the table across from me. He too has showered, and he looks good enough to eat. Forget the salad, there's prime rib at the dining room table and I'm starving for a taste of it.

She looks at me—then at Conner—then back at me. I can't help but notice how sexy her boss looks, and I guess she sees it all over my face. Ah, and that smell. That divine scent alone arouses my innocence, and before I know it I'm as hot as ambers in a burning flame. His sex appeal is shouting at me, and again makes me want to forget about what being a virgin has meant to me all of these years.

Leilani smiles and pats my back after she puts my plate in front of me. "I can't imagine a more beautiful house for Mr. Dawson. Maybe someday he'll find true love and have someone to share it with." She winks at me, but he doesn't notice.

Conner's eyes meet mine, and then his move to my mouth. I am licking my lips and biting gently on the bottom one. He is turning me on, and I feel as though I have no control over my own body anymore. I am too into the moment that I haven't noticed Leilani has left the room; he has all of my attention.

"Eat, Hannah, or I'm going to come over there and feed you myself," he says with his fork sliding against his lips.

"Don't tempt me—I might just let you," I tease.

He lets out a low growl, and I start feeding myself. We're both reminded that Leilani is just in the other room when we hear the washing machine start up.

Twenty minutes pass, and we have devoured our salads. The smoothies were just as good and our empty glasses prove it. Not only did we finish our drinks, but we sat and drank each other in as well. Memorizing every detail of the other and drowning out the music in the background.

"I want to show you something. Grab your bathing suit while I clean up," he demands—arching his brow up and down and causing my sex to clench in and out.

Jeez...even when he's bossy he's sexy.

Surely he knows I've spent the last two days on the beach. He has definitely piqued my curiosity though; what could he want to show me? "Okay." I pause—only for a second hoping he will give me an insight as to where we are going, but nothing. "I'll be right back," I say.

I excuse myself from the table and head to my room. I don't even make it past the kitchen sink, and he pulls me into his embrace. His luscious manliness is trying to breakthrough his zipper, and I know it won't take much convincing to release it. He is as turned on as I am—*and damn he smells so good.*

I breathe in deep while I have the chance.

Both his hands resting on my butt, he pulls me closer. No doubt he wants me feeling just how aroused he is.

His fierce gaze focuses—his desire shows...he's horny and doesn't mind sharing it. My body trembles—my kitty purrs, begging to let him break us in...but I can't do it—no matter how much I want to take him right here in broad daylight on the kitchen floor—Leilani is still here and the fact of the matter is—I'm still a virgin. *How am I going to break that news?*

"Mister Dawson, I think we have a visitor, and he's dying to introduce himself." Conner laughs at my joke and smacks my bottom.

"Go get your suit, baby girl," he whispers...growling like a tiger as I walk away.

The sting from his hand is more of a turn on than I would have ever imagined, and suddenly I feel as though we could both use a cold shower—or some playtime. *He makes me want to be a bad girl.* A naughty grin spreads across my face as I'm grabbing the most seductive bathing suit I own. If he wants to play—I'm game.

When I return from the bedroom, Conner is waiting patiently by the huge picture window in the living room. He is admiring the view and is deep in thought. I stand there wondering what he could be thinking about.

"I could look at you all day long and never get bored," he says, his voice a seductive whisper.

Though there is a sound in it that demands my attention. It is as sincere as the way he looks at me. It is then that I notice my reflection in the window, and he is looking directly at it. He turns my way—his seducing gaze glaring right at me.

Before I can appreciate the moment as much as I would like, his playful side is back. He sweeps me up over his shoulders and has me laughing out loud like a maniac.

He's in a hurry to show me something, and before I know it we're driving a way in his monster truck.

Chapter 11

I **cannot help but** notice that we're headed back in the direction we came from earlier, so I decide we must be going back to the house. When we pass it and go a half mile down the road, it's apparent my thoughts were wrong.

My breath catches as we turn down a gravel road that leads up to an open field. The setting is as picturesque as it is charming. The green-grassed area is home to the most beautiful horses I have ever laid my eyes on. They are all amazing, but there is one that catches my eye more than the rest.

"She's a beauty isn't she?" he says.

Conner watches me as I take in the scenery, mesmerized by the brown and white filly that has captivated my attention. She is grazing close by, and when she hears us pull up she stops to watch us as we make our way closer. Her mane glistens as the sunlight beams down through the clouds, and I find myself longing to take her for a ride. I can thank Baylee for my love for horses. We spent so much time at her grandparent's farm when we were teenagers, and it was there that I learned how to ride. It became one of my passions while in high school, and we visited there regularly.

Conner keeps driving until we make it to the stable that houses the stunning four-legged creatures, and that's when the words come pouring out of my mouth. "Shouldn't I have brought my cowgirl boots *instead* of the bikini I'm wearing underneath my clothes?"

I'm flirting and thoroughly enjoying it.

He glances my way, fire in his eyes and a low growl in his voice. "Maybe you should have," he purred. "But the bathing suit will have to do."

Squirming in my seat, I take a deep breath. That look...that sound—that man is deliberately trying to wind me up and turn me on. The urge to straddle him and not the horse is now tiptoeing around down there, and I find myself fighting to calm myself.

The sexy roughness in his voice settles and seconds later he's belting out. Once again, his laughter is like music to my ears, and it is contagious—the more it rubs off on me, the more I like it.

The truck comes to a complete halt.

Before turning the key, he revs up the engine. His laughing eyes show off his dancing brows—that's it...my heart goes pitter-patter right along with the roaring engine. A few pumps later and off goes the truck along with the T-shirt he is wearing.

My body freezes, but my eyes...well, they do what comes natural. I watch him as he peels the material away, giving me a perfect view of those washboard abs. Moving up—that chest. I think my heart just skipped a beat. I long to run my fingers through those tiny golden-brown curls, tempting and teasing him as I trace the thin line of hair that leads straight to his manly part. Taking a deep breath, I catch his gaze and he catches me licking my lips.

After a hot-smoldering moment, he grabs my hand. "Let's get going, Hannah. There's so much to see and so little time."

He opens the door, jumps out, and I follow behind him. We walk over to where the saddles are hanging, and he grabs one and sets it on the table close by. After choosing another one almost twice the size of the first, we make our way to a stall that is home to a big black beauty whose name is branded on the gate. He calls her Black Pearl, and that is exactly what she is. Like a diamond in the ruff, she stands out like no other horse here. She is as black as velvet and as soft as it too. She is amazing, and she is his.

He saddles her up and turns to go get the other heavy seat…never noticing that I had already grabbed it. Turning my way, he's shocked to see me holding the synthetic twenty-pounder. "Careful not to hurt yourself, that saddle is bigger than you," he rasped.

"I'm stronger than I look, Mister Dawson, but if you don't mind you can take it now and put it on her." I'm left breathless from the weight. *It really is heavy.*

He grabs it.

Turning back around, he sees the brown and white beauty making her way into the stable. She must be curious as to who the stranger is visiting her home, because she comes closer to check me out. He looks at the filly and then back at me.

"I think she likes you, Hannah. Guess I'm not the only one who recognizes a beautiful woman when I see one."

I'm flattered and it shows. My batting eyelashes and lip-curling smile proves it.

He saddles her up in no time.

"Are you ready?" he asks.

"I was born ready, Mister Dawson."

I brace myself.

In a flash, he has me in his arms and helping me up on my seat. Minutes later, he's got a bag of goodies packed and is sitting atop Black Pearl. The horse is ready for a good run, kicking up her hoofs as to say *"on your mark"*. Holding the leather reins in his hands, he begins to lead us away.

"Wait. You didn't tell me her name," I yell.

Without stopping, Conner calls out her name and leaves me breathless once again. "Heavenly. Just like you."

I can't help but grin ear to ear…he seems to make me do that a lot.

"Catch me if you can, baby girl!"

Conner makes a noise with his mouth and smacks the black beauty's behind. His hair is flying in the wind, and even from back here he is a sight to appreciate. His golden skin radiates along with the sun's rays, and I watch as the muscles in his back flex with his every movement.

The person in front of me is not only smothered in sex appeal, but he is a man of prestige. He comes from wealth, immense power, and is bathed in superiority...yet, I'm getting a glimpse of a simple man who doesn't let all of that control who he really is. He's human just like the rest of us— and he's living life to the fullest.

I race to catch up with him, and when I do the grass has turned to sand. We are on the beach, and the horses love it as much as we do. The next half hour we don't do much talking; we just race up and down the shore enjoying the competition that is building between us. It is so much fun beating him with a horse I have never ridden, but I can't help but wonder if he is letting me win.

After a hard run, we slow down to a trot and enjoy the beauty of God's creation. It's simply breathtaking.

"Hannah, I brought you out here to show you something. Stay close and don't get left behind."

I can't believe what I am hearing.

"How can there be anything more exquisite than this?"

He smiles, knowing I am pleased.

"You haven't seen anything yet, Miss Stone," he whispers.

He races with the wind, and now I'm fighting to catch up. *I guess he was letting me win after all.*

We make our way back on the grass and come to an exotic area that is adorned with trees and flowers everywhere. I can hear birds singing, but can't see where they are coming from because of the tropical woodland in front of us.

There is a path we follow, and the closer we get to where we are going I can hear the trickling of water. I hear wings flapping and frogs are chirping. I feel like I am in a fairy tale, but this is really happening.

"Let's stop here," he says. "The horses can't make it through the bushes. We'll have to walk the rest of the way."

Anticipation is building and my excitement is showing. I can't quit smiling if I tried. Conner takes my hand in his and leads me to the bristly greenery. "Careful, Hannah, I'll guide you through to the other side." Sliding his fingers between mine, he gives me a gentle squeeze.

With the deep-green grass beneath our feet, he lures me down the tropical path. Slowly, he circles the pad of his thumb in the palm of my hand, over and over again. The sensation sends my heart soaring. His touch—*oh, that touch.* The current consumes me—the moment is captivating.

I exhale.

"Are you okay?" he asks, glancing my way.

"I'm good…just a little anxious," I breathe.

His fingers flex, squeezing a little tighter.

He pulls me closer. "We're almost there, close your eyes," he says, his whispered breath blanketing my neck.

Without hesitation, I do exactly that. I let him lead me the rest of the way. After a few more steps, it's time to see the secret that is hiding away from the rest of the world. "Open your eyes, baby girl," he whispers.

I do as I am told, but not without taking a deep breath first. I have a feeling I am going to be breathless when I see whatever it is before me. Slowly, I open my eyes and I am right.

Sculptured by nature, the landscape before me is breathtaking. This amazing place facing us looks like a little piece of heaven dropped out of the sky, and it is absolutely the most spectacular place I have ever witnessed. Due to the abundance of plant life, the area is secluded and truly hidden from the rest of the island.

Tilting his head, he watches my wandering eyes. "What do you think, Hannah?"

"I've never witnessed anything more perfect," I whisper.

"Come," he demands.

He leads me closer.

The trickling noise I heard has turned into gushing water. It's coming from the waterfall that washes into the perfect round lagoon that is just feet away from us. It's not a huge area, but just the right size to keep the two of us entertained for the rest of the afternoon.

The pond is surrounded by flowers, palm trees, and rocks big enough to sunbathe on. That water...it is the most amazing clear-blue color; I can see all the way to the bottom. I cannot wait to feel it soak into my skin.

Over to the right, I can see steam coming up from an enclosed area around a pile of rocks, and as I get closer I can tell that it is a small hot-spring pool. It is right next to the lagoon, but the water there is more for relaxing than it is for swimming.

I can't believe my eyes. Breathtaking beautiful is not enough to describe what I am looking at. Only one word even comes to my mind. Paradise. Yes. That sums it up. True paradise.

I'm speechless and overwhelmed. Without saying a word, I strip down to my bathing suit and jump into nature's swimming pool. Right behind me is the luscious heartthrob of a man who has stripped down to his boxers. I can't help but laugh knowing he didn't take time to change into his swimming trunks.

Showing off my backstroke, I admire the man who has blown me away. Not only with his looks, but also the kindness he has shown me. How will I ever repay him? What do you give a man who has the world at his beck and call? He is a man who gets what he wants, and this proves it.

The lagoon is inviting, but not as much as the waterfall. I swim over to it, and Conner follows me. His hard lean body controlling every mouthwatering stroke he takes. His masculinity is soaking in the water, and I'm soaking him in. He is the epitome of mind-blowing perfection. It is pure ecstasy watching him—*I can't help but stare.*

The water from above is pouring over the top and trickling down in front of us. Hard, but not too hard. We circle each other; laughing, splashing, and flirting. Enjoying not only the water, but also each other. Then, he disappears. Down he goes and seconds pass that seem like minutes. As clear as the lagoon is, I can't find him. Panic takes over my body, and I'm searching desperately for the man who brought me here.

Suddenly, I feel his masculine hands rubbing my body. My legs. My waist. My breasts. Up and out of the water he comes. His hands are in my hair, and his lips are on mine. Tasting me and drinking me in. I return it with deep exhilarating passion and pleasure; savoring every drop of him.

Our tongues twisting and turning...our kiss deepens with every stroke. It's an intense moment as he groans into my mouth, his manliness throbbing against my leg. He's hard, heated, and ready to go. His cock is searching for my virtue, and if I'm not careful he's going to find it. With every flick of my tongue, I devour him. I am starving for something that he can give me, but I cannot give in. I jump out of his embrace and dunk him under the water—swimming off and daring him to come after me.

"Catch me if you can," I yell out before going beneath the water—*and down I go.*

Moving through the lagoon, I swim as though I'm in some sort of competition. I guess in a way I am. There's no doubt in my mind that he's taking me up on my offer. I'm sure he's right behind me. The thought sends my hormones into overdrive. I wonder what he will do with me when he catches me. *Guess I'm about to find out.* I wiggle my foot that is now in his hand...*he's too strong—I can't break free.* Embracing my legs, he moves up my body—spinning me around until he's hovering over me. Our eyes meet—*it seems as though a thousand seconds have passed by.* I fight to hold my breath...it's so hard due to the fact my adrenaline is pulsating through my body like crazy.

Still beneath the water, his penetrating wide-eyed gaze continues to bore into me. His hair swimming around his face, he moves in for a kiss. Locking his mouth over mine, he forces his tongue between my lips. We share a hot passionate kiss while swimming to the surface.

Fighting the need for oxygen, our lips part and we both inhale deeply—allowing the air to slip out slowly.

"Gotcha!" he smirks.

I roll my eyes playfully. "I thought I was fast…but you're faster," I say breathlessly. "Where did you learn to swim like that?

"College swim team…I was the captain my senior year. No one could beat me –all four years," he admits, breathing hard but not as hard as me.

"No wonder, you swim like a fish…probably faster," I tease. "If only we were on a volleyball court and not the water. You're not the only one who was a captain their senior year…I was too; and let me tell you—*I kicked butt.*"

"No wonder you've got a rock-hard body," he says flirtatiously. "You must have worked out a lot.

"I did and still do."

That look of desire is peeking back through the windows of his soul…*it's time to change the subject.*

"Come on; let's go back down—the view was amazing."

He blinks, as though breaking out of a trance.

"I'll race you." He dives beneath the water, sending small rippling waves my way. Breathing in deep, I go after him— finally meeting up with him at the bottom.

The water is so crystal clear. There are so many tropical fish swimming around us—lots of butterfly fish and angel fish…all showing off their vibrant black, white, and yellow striped colors. The underwater plant life looks as though it's dancing in the seagrass meadow. There's so much beauty floating around down here. Even the bright yellow sponges stand out—especially with the dainty little blue fish gathering around them.

Conner gets my attention, pointing at the school of bandit angel fish swimming straight for us. They are the most beautiful of all—mostly white with a thick black band running from their eyes and straight across their bodies. The hint of baby blue splashed throughout their fins is really what makes them stand out from all the rest. The moment is so surreal as they get closer…swimming between our opened legs and around our waists. I don't want to leave—but I am in desperate need of air.

I grab his arm with one hand, pointing up with the other. He shakes his head yes.

Swimming to the top, once again we inhale deeply…gasping as the fresh air hits our lungs.

"That was unbelievable," I rasp, trying to catch my breath.

"I agree, the view is pretty amazing down there…but it is here too," he says, swimming closer my way until we're face to face. Leaning in, he kisses me hard and then gets me back for dunking him earlier. Pushing my head beneath the water, he takes off before I have the chance to pull him down with me.

When I come back up, he's showing off his perfect backstroke. So lean—so in control. I don't want to interrupt him. Instead, I swirl around in the water—turn a few flips and sneak a peek every now and again at all that sex appeal floating just feet away.

After a few invigorating laps, we climb up on one of the large rocks to rest, sunbathe, and talk.

"How did you find this little piece of heaven anyway?" I ask.

He looks around, and there is this look on his face that shows off just how sincere he really is. "Believe it or not, I think I was led here by fate. One day I was out driving and got out of my truck to go for a walk. I walked the beach over and over for what seemed like hours and was drawn to the path from there." He is as stunning to listen to as this place is to look at. "When I found it I was floored by its exotic beauty. In that moment, I knew I had found the perfect area to build my home."

A peaceful look adorning his face, he admires the paradise he chose to share with me. "You are the only other person who knows about this spot. If you tell anyone I will have to hold you down and spank that sweet little ass of yours." He laughs, reminding me of our previous encounter.

I laugh back at him, but I am also turned on from the memory of our earlier endeavor. His strong healthy hand hitting my ass didn't scare me. It made me long for his touch even more. I wanted his fingers to glide up and down my body and make me want him more than I already do. The thought sends goose bumps all over my sun-kissed skin and resisting him is getting harder by the minute. "Your secret is safe with me. It's the least I can do for the man who has done so much for me?"

"Excuse me for a moment," he murmurs. Conner disappears and returns with the bag he had packed for our trip. Inside, he pulls out a bottle of tanning oil. He opens the top, releasing a luscious-smelling coconut scent. It is the perfect addition to the perfect setting. "Do you mind if I rub some on your back?"

"Are you kidding? My skin could use a little tender-loving-care." I roll onto my belly anticipating his touch. The oil has been heated by the sun, and so has the huge rock we are laying on.

He unties my top, and one string falls to the left of my breast and one to the right. Instead of breathing, my body is screaming from within. *Yes! No! Stop! Oh, hell, just do it.*

The next thing I hear is oil being squeezed from the bottle and into his hands. Rapidly, he rubs his masculine hands together, and there they are—on me. Rubbing and gliding from one side of my back to the other. Up and down, over and over again. He doesn't forget my arms or my legs and gives them his undivided attention too.

My day at the spa has nothing on Conner's expertise. *Sorry, Greta...he's so much better at this than even you are.*

"In case you haven't noticed, Hannah, I like you," his whispered confession prompting my own heartfelt words.

I take a deep breath—*slowly exhaling.* "I like you too, Conner."

"There's something about you. You're different from other women, and I like that. Not many people can make me forget about the rest of the world, but for some reason you can. Why is that?"

My mind races. What does he want me to say? Here goes nothing.

"I'm just being me—*a little ole country southern belle from Tennessee* who doesn't like to be the center of attention. I'd rather sit on the sidelines and enjoy the scenery."

"Well, you've got my attention, Hannah. Now, what are you going to do about it?" he asks.

"I'm going to lay here and let you spoil me with the best massage ever," I giggle.

"I guess that means you like my roaming hands gliding all over your oil slicked skin," he breathes, whispering so close to my ear that the heat of his breath tickles my skin.

"Uh, huh," I murmur senselessly.

He stops...*great!* I shouldn't have opened my mouth. What is he doing back there? All that maneuvering around— *oh,* he's just getting more oil. I smile when I hear him opening the bottle and even bigger when I feel him squeezing the liquid up and down my body. After he puts the container back down, I can feel his hands back on me. Oh. My. Goodness. The next thing I feel is pure sumptuous joy. The weight of his exquisite body is on mine, and he is rubbing me with every mouthwatering inch of himself—his thick, luscious manhood included; *it is the best feeling in the world.* He has moved his hands from my body to the rock beneath us; helping to support his body from weighing me down too much. My womanhood is ablaze being this close to him, and even more knowing it is my body that has aroused him to such a hard, scrumptious, length. I can feel his manliness throb against my yearning innocence, and it is time for him to know the truth. I will not give into my desires today, and I will not let him think I am a tease. Here goes nothing.

"A girl can't get any sun if she's shaded by all that muscle, Mister Dawson."

He laughs and reluctantly climbs off of my body. That still does not stop my heart from longing to keep him there.

"I think I need to let you in on a little secret of my own, Conner."

I huff, preparing myself to let it all out.

"A beautiful girl with secrets...who would have ever thought that was possible?" Smiling that graceful seductive smile of his, he lies on his back propping his hands behind his head and gives me his undivided attention again. I can't resist laying my head on his chest. Besides, I don't think I can make eye contact with him when I reveal the truth. I can hear his heart beat. It is racing all because of me.

I can't keep him in the dark any longer and out pour the words—almost in a whisper, but I know he hears me. "I'm a virgin."

Silence is in the air and suddenly I'm scared of what he's thinking. I rise up but only to be pulled back down. Before I can get to my feet, he grabs me and brings me face to face with him.

"You are so beautiful—inside and out. It is that beauty that I have dreamed of since the first night I laid eyes on you. Hell, I think I've been dreaming about you my whole life. I just never knew who *you* were."

I am overwhelmed by his honesty, and he has my undivided attention.

"I guess I assumed you were, you know, experienced. You must think I'm a real jerk," he sighs, and I remember the condom he found back at the airport. *Baylee!* I make a mental note to remind her to keep her lubricated, frilly little cover-ups to herself and in her own purse.

For a man that comes from so much power, his tenderness comes straight from the heart. He is a good man, but a man with *needs* nonetheless. There is no doubt that there are women lined up everywhere, dying to be where I am now, and at this moment he's chosen me. *Why can I not just give into him—I want to give into him damn it!*

"Thank you for the compliment, but beauty is only skin deep, and sex is not something I take lightly. My virginity is something I am very proud of and thought you deserved to know the truth, and no, I think you are perfect." I hold my breath waiting on a response.

The windows of his soul are looking into mine, and he's moving my hair from my face so he can get a better look. "I have to say I'm pretty proud of you for holding on to it. I'm sorry if I am making it hard for you to keep it that way." His words are sincere, but it's not all his fault.

"I have been second guessing my morals since that first night at Joe's Place. My thoughts have been all wrapped up in you and what I wanted to do with you since Friday night." I watch him as he watches me. "I can't even get you out of my head long enough to sleep, because every time I close my eyes there you are."

He looks so serious, but sexy still the same. I don't understand why he will not say something. "Conner, I want you as much as you want me, but I can't give in. If I do, and..."

He stops me with a kiss and that's all it takes. I know he's ok with the shocking news, but something is funny. Laughing with his mouth still on mine, he stops to say what he's thinking.

"So, you dream about me huh? No wonder you were saying my name in your sleep the other night."

My mouth opens further, allowing him further access with that velvety tongue of his. Suddenly, I'm so embarrassed and praying that's all he heard me say—our mouths part. I can only hope he did not hear anything else. I have to change the subject, but at least now I know what it is that I do with my mouth that turns him on while I'm sleeping. *I say his name.*

"Basking in all this beauty has made me hungry. Let's go get some food before my belly starts yelling at me again," I insist.

"You got it, baby girl."

Leaning in, he gives me one last kiss.

I exhale, wanting more.

"Next time we'll bring lunch," he says.

Taking one last look at the beauty behind me, I can only pray that day comes; and if it doesn't, today will be etched in my mind for the rest of my life; a memory worth cherishing…today, tomorrow, and always.

Chapter 12

Stepping out into the hallway, a wild hunger sweeps through me. And I don't mean for food. Running into him caught me off guard, but the desire to lick him all over was something I was getting use to.

He was passing my room just as I was leaving it—my wandering eyes looking one direction and my feet headed in the other. Next thing I know...*Wham*—my face is in his chest, and his hands are clinging to my waist.

Breathing in deep, I take one last sniff of his appetizing scent before pulling away.

Quickly, I take two steps back.

Tilting my head, my eyes meet his. "Pardon me, sir...but you seem to be in my way," I say breathlessly.

I swallow hard, trying to force the drool back down. He really does look good enough to eat.

He liked that. His pearly whites prove it, but those dancing eyes...they're showing off his desire to strip me of the dress I'm wearing. My sex entertains the thought, aching with sweet pleasure.

His chest expands, and he exhales.

"You're excused, but it's going to cost you," he threatens.

My heart races as he wraps me up in his embrace.

Stealing a kiss, he dips his tongue into my mouth. Kissing him back, mine swirls around his. He pushes me against the wall, his hands now tangled up in my hair...slamming his lips harder into mine, he fights the urge to grind his hips all over my girly stuff. A few erratic breaths later, he backs away—adjusting the belt on his perfectly tight-fitting jeans.

"Are you ready?" he asks breathlessly.

My eyes widen.

I can't breathe.

He sees the look of despair written all over my face.

"For dinner, Miss Stone," he says, winking at me and making my heart wink back...in a matter of speaking that is.

I let out an exhausted breath.

Unsure if I'm feeling relieved or disappointed, I take one last look in the floor-length mirror at the end of the hallway. The aftereffects of our heated moment show in my tasseled hair. Twisting my locks back in place, my gaze turns to him. "I'm ready whenever you are, handsome."

He likes that too. Shaking his head, he leads me downstairs—my hand in his, just like a real couple.

We travel by limo to a crowded restaurant on the beach, and of course we are led to the front of the line. I can't help but feel bad for the people waiting, but I have to suck it up and realize I am holding on to the arm of Conner Dawson; the son of one of the wealthiest men in the country—maybe even the world.

We are greeted by the hostess immediately upon entering, and she knows exactly who I am here with. "Welcome back to The Crab's Den, Mr. Dawson," she says, never looking my way. Batting her eyelashes, she bends over to pick up the menu she dropped...*she so did that on purpose*—a girl and their cleavage—man's true weakness. Conner's not playing her game. He pulls my hand to his mouth, gently kissing it long enough until she notices. The woman is pissed...but being at work she tries to hide it. Putting a fake smile on her face, now she notices me. "This way please," she says.

We follow the hostess through the five-star restaurant and are seated at a secluded table on the deck facing the ocean. The cool breeze coming off the water is a welcome to us both. It was a hot day in Hawaii, and I don't just mean because of the sun.

The Crab's Den may be sitting on the beach and surrounded by aquatic décor, but it has a touch of class like no other place I have ever eaten before. I can't help but think that Conner and I were given the best seats in the house, not only is it private, but also very romantic.

The hostess removes the *reserved table* card and storms away.

I can't help but feel like the *girl who got the guy*...grinning ear to ear, I look his way. "I see you called ahead."

"I did," he admits, pulling out my chair before he does his own.

I take a deep breath in, smelling the candles that are masking the true smells of the ocean. Needless to say, it is breathtaking when I get a whiff of my date. I smile, appreciating the moment and longing for time to stand still as I watch him take the seat in front of me.

The menu has a huge variety of seafood to choose from, but we both opt for the all you can it King Crab Leg dinner; and a bottle of their best wine. While waiting on the food, we sit at the table hand in hand, conversing and speaking our minds—all while taking in the beautiful scenery.

"You're a very lucky man, Mister Dawson," I say, looking around at the breathtaking view.

"Indeed I am, Miss Stone. Indeed I am," he breathes, his voice low and seductive.

Our moment is interrupted by the ringing of his phone.

We both look at the glowing screen as he picks it up from the table. *That's funny. I never even saw him put it there.*

"Excuse me, Hannah."

"Of course," I murmur.

"Conner Dawson," he states after swiping the bar.

Looking his way, I see him gaping at me.

"What do you mean they won't accept the offer?" he pauses...listening hard. "I see. No, don't up it that much. I'm willing to add another 25k to it, but not a penny more. Make it happen," he demands, ending the call without saying bye.

"Sounds like somebody is giving you a hard time," I say, prompting him for information.

Conner's nose flares as he lets out a heavy breath.

"You could say that," he says dryly. "People can be so damn greedy. I have this project going on...it's one that can change lives in a good way, but all they want is more money."

I stare at him while taking a sip from the chilled glass of wine the waitress just poured.

"What sort of project is it," I ask, after swallowing the smooth cold drink.

"I'm calling it *Hooked on a Better Life*. It's a foundation meant to lure addicts off the streets...get them off drugs and educate them with hopes that they will never go back to that lifestyle. I have a dream to make this world a safer place, Hannah, and I'm willing to offer the tools to those who are willing to try."

"What kind of *tools* do you mean?" I ask with sincerity. This is really interesting.

"I want to build a complex big enough to hold at least one hundred people in every major city. If the occupants agree to my terms, they will be allowed to live there for one year at no cost to them. This is the length of time I think it will take to get them *dried out* and in a state of mind to learn some sort of trade. The first six months they are there will prepare them for the next six months that they will be required to go to work. Each person will be allowed to save their paychecks so that they will be able to make it on their own once they move out."

"That sounds amazing. It's a good thing you're doing, Conner. I hope it works out the way you want it to."

"So do I, Hannah. It has to work out," he insists.

His eyes watch me as mine watch him. The next thing I know, we're having a heated stare-down for the next ten minutes.

And dinner is served.

The legs are steamed to perfection and taste even more decadent dipped in the melted butter. We are both messy eaters, but so is everybody when it comes to eating these mouthwatering little creatures. The crab meat melts in our mouths, and we crave it more with every bite. I'm snapping and cracking crab legs and don't notice the two eyes watching my every move.

"You're pretty good at that. It will do me good not to get on your bad side," he chuckles, while cracking legs of his own.

I laugh at his joke while feeding him a piece of the sweet delectable meat. It's only natural when I rub my finger along his bottom lip to catch the mess that is dripping from his mouth. My thoughts are all caught up in the moment, and I am tempted to lick the butter off with my tongue instead of wiping it away with my index finger.

I know he can read my thoughts, and within seconds he is making it happen. He leans across the table to meet me halfway, and we share a very romantic kiss. He is delicious.

I pull away licking my lips, but only because we are interrupted by our waitress who has brought us our second bucket of crab legs.

Opting out of eating any more, we both sit back and finish our drinks. Sipping slowly and watching the splashing water beat upon the sand. It is so peaceful, but the night is still young, and I'm in the mood to get a little rowdy. I feel the *country* in me begging to come out and play, and the adjoining nightclub downstairs is the perfect playground.

He's thrilled when I share my idea with him, and quickly he pays for our meal. Before making our way through the doors of *The Hammerhead Cavern*, he calls Finn to let him know we're going to be longer than expected and to come back in a couple of hours.

The club is lit up with black lights everywhere; causing every neon-colored object to glow intensely. Center stage, right behind the band, is a massive hammerhead painting.

Alone it demands your attention—letting you know this is *his* place.

I have to admit, I really like the jellyfish dangling around the room; you almost feel like you're dancing right along with them beneath the ocean. As beautiful as all of this is, the most unreal, most amazing of it all, is the glowing dance floor beneath our feet. It really looks like we are walking on water...*Gulf Shore waters.* I glance at Conner's eyes and back at the floor...a perfect match.

With his hands on my waist, he walks me to the center of the crowded dance floor and starts showing off his moves. I can't take my eyes off of him—stunned that there is nothing this man can't do. He's good at everything. It just comes natural swaying to the music with him, fast dancing and getting caught up in the moment as if we were the only two people here.

The next two hours fly by, and we're both drenching with sweat. We have danced our butts off and burned off the calories from dinner—maybe even lunch too. The blaring music we had been used to all night has slowed down, and I couldn't be more pleased. I may be worn completely out, but this moment is what I have been waiting on all night.

Conner pulls me close to him, placing one hand on my lower back and the other gently on my face. Our eyes have a conversation of their own while our bodies beg to be one.

My feet follow his as he continues taking the lead, and we are now the star attraction—all eyes on us. I don't care and neither does he; we only have eyes for each other and that's all that matters.

The song is slow, and there is no doubt it was written by lovers. It's very romantic, and I can't help but tear up when Conner leans in and quietly sings the words in my ear. Between listening to him and the heat of his breath tickling my neck, well, it's the ideal aphrodisiac...I can't help but feel aroused. It has affected him too; the growing bulge in his jeans gives him away. He looks down at me—knowing I feel it, and he turns me around so that my back is facing him. Swaying back and forth, gently grinding into my backside and making me more aware of his arousal—*he wants me to feel it.*

Just when it's getting good…it's over.

Our heated moment is interrupted by bright lights and chattering voices. It's closing time, and Finn is just outside the door. Taking my hand in his, we walk away and make our way to the limo.

The night was perfect; the food, the weather, the dancing…especially the *dancing.* It is as great as the day we shared, and I am almost sad when it is over.

Conner is a perfect gentleman, walking me to my bedroom when it is time to say goodnight.

"Last night, today, tonight…it's all been great, Hannah," he breathes.

"Yes, it was amazing," I agree.

"Maybe we can do it again sometime."

"That would be great, but soon I'll be back home and you'll be here," my words making my heart pout. *There will truly be an ocean between us.*

Placing his finger over my mouth, he whispers the truth. "You'll only be a flight away…and I have business in Nashville to take care of anyway—*remember*…besides, we still have the rest of the week."

"I remember," I mouth with his finger still in place. My heart goes *pitter patter* thinking about spending my last days here with him.

Slowly, he leans in…moving his hand and taking my breath away with a splendidly romantic kiss. His lips are made for kissing, and I can't seem to get enough of them. Once we break free from the most impressive mouth to mouth action, I turn my back and disappear behind the closed door.

After a quick shower, I fall out on my bed and stare up at the ceiling. Women all over the world are dreaming of meeting someone like him. It is a dream I once had but am lucky enough to be living it now.

I gasp out loud, allowing a grin to take control of my lips. Climbing beneath the sheets, I fall asleep smiling.

We spend the next day sightseeing—including a little window shopping at a local store called *The Exotic Passion Parlor*—a shop he stopped in front of first...not me. I can't help but wonder if this is his way of slowly inviting me into his kinky little world. Could this be the kind of thing he gets into? Is he itching to get a reaction out of me, or is he just admiring the desires of so many others?

After watching him, there's one thing I'm sure of...he's the one with the mad sexual appetite. The hungry look of wild passionate lovemaking is swimming around his irises, and he has a yearning to calm it.

His hand grips mine—his thumb circling my palm; the crops—the sparkling cuffs—the exotic swings...there is a fantasy playing out in his head, and I am the star—make that the sex slave. I have no doubt he would restrain me and manipulate an orgasm right out of me if I would allow it. If I'm going to run—now would be my chance. Lucky for him, I am as turned on as he is. Standing there gaping, neither of us ever say a word...we just walk away craving to buy out the store.

Nightfall comes way too fast, and we finish off the evening in his casino. He can't resist showing *me* off and also his skills at the blackjack table. Of course I can't resist watching his *every* move; although it is a little intimidating when it comes to watching him play boss to his employees. He is strict and he is domineering, but there is no denying they respect the man known as Conner Dawson.

My adrenaline has gone haywire and my mind is overflowing with thoughts of him, our time together, and the paradise he has shared with me. I have gotten spoiled by all the attention and glamour. Then reality hits me. Tomorrow is my last day here.

Refusing to think about it, I continue having the time of my life. Hours pass by, and we have not wasted a minute. We dance. We laugh. We talk. I'm learning everything about him that he wants me to know and vice-versa. If only time would stand still and let me have him to myself just a little longer.

But like always, that's wishful thinking.

All too soon the night has ended, and we are at the suite before I know it.

Walking me to my room, he stands with me outside the door.

He looks at me, twirling his fingers around my curls.

I pull him closer, my fingers tugging at his belt loops.

"What a night," I whisper.

I look at him after saying those words, and it almost feels like I can read his mind. He feels something for me; I know it. *It's just happening so fast—for both of us.*

"Hannah, the last few days have been amazing. Thank you for sharing them with me."

"No, Conner. Thank you."

He kisses me goodnight, and we go to our separate bedrooms with nothing but our dreams to keep us company.

The morning peeks in between the blinds, and I wake up early knowing today will be my last day in Honolulu. My vacation is ending as quickly as it had started, and there is nothing I can do to stop it. I know tomorrow I will be on my way back to Tennessee and back to face the stalker. That is irrevocably the cold harsh reality of it.

I climb out of the huge bed and walk sleep-eyed to the bathroom. I freshen up with a much needed shower, and pull my hair up in a ponytail when that's all done. I don't have much of an appetite for food, but I do for Conner.

I leave my room in search of the man I am craving, but to my surprise, he is nowhere in the penthouse. Leilani is in her usual spot in the kitchen, and she is also the bearer of bad news.

"Ms. Stone, Conner had to leave earlier. There was an emergency at one of the other islands, and he traveled by boat to get there around 3 o'clock this morning."

Fear settles in where peace was, and I know she sees it on my face. "He said he will contact you when he has the chance, but he does not know when that will be."

My expression now adorning a hard straight line where a smile was only minutes before; waking up thinking I would see him was like a natural high and made me happy. Now, I have no control over the apprehension that has taken over.

I can see the worry in her eyes, and I know it is evident in mine. "Leilani, do you know what kind of an emergency would call him away at that time of night?" I murmur, my voice full of worry.

"No ma'am. I have been anxious to hear from him all morning, but nothing. He did say to let you know the jet would be fueled and ready to take off by 8 o'clock in the morning."

I feel as though someone just slapped me across the face—forcing me to face reality. My world is coming to an end and not just this unforgettable vacation. Is Conner really taking care of an urgent matter, or is he just trying to escape me? I wonder if he will even be on the flight back to Tennessee with me.

I grab a cup of coffee and walk out on the balcony. The view is amazing, but not as much as my time spent with him over the last few days. I sit down and rock back and forth in the bamboo rocker—my thoughts only of him. I have fallen for a man who is out of my league, and he is no where around.

What was I thinking?

My mind is in overdrive, and I can't get him out of my head. So what if he isn't here? I have lived my life without him for the last twenty two years and managed just fine. The independent woman I am will get me through. The past week has been incredible—more than incredible. I will cherish the memory of it forever, and I have him to thank for it.

Maybe I am overreacting. Maybe there really was an emergency that called him away in the middle of the night, but what if it wasn't, and he's off doing who knows what with whomever it is that pulled him away at that time. I cannot just sit here and do nothing. I'm going to drive myself crazy sitting here thinking of tales that might not even be. It's time to go somewhere, anywhere that will take my mind off of him.

I decide to do what most girls love doing. Shop. I realize I have not bought the first souvenir for my family and friends back home.

Chapter 13

I **take the elevator** down to the lobby and see Henry doing his job all too well. Meeting and greeting guests, shaking hands, and making each and every patron feel just as important as the next. I will miss his genuine kindness. It is not too often you meet someone who loves their job, but this concierge does. I think back on Leilani and Finn, and they too seem to have that same thing in common with Henry. All three employees were linked to Conner Dawson, and that sums it up—the perfect boss, equals the perfect job. No wonder they love it.

As I make my way out the doors of the lobby, reality sets in. The calm before the storm...a theory I have relied on since I was a little girl. That eerie, somewhat peaceful calmness is in the air, and I recognize it quickly. My intuition has not steered me wrong yet, and today it's giving me a glance into what's to come.

A tropical storm is on its way, making my last *full* day in paradise a cloudy, dreary one; kind of how I am feeling at the present moment. Despite the dark gray skies, I don't change my mind. I keep heading towards the strip; finally, making it after about a twenty minute walk.

Shopping is not having the effect on me like I thought it would. I make my way down through the strip of shops, up under the darkened sky, and go to each of them one by one. Everything I see reminds me of Conner, and all I want is for him to be here with me.

Hours are passing by, and with each visit I think I will find something different. Not so much. Almost everything looks the same. I end up buying a hula girl lamp, a few surfer-dude shot glass sets, aloha T-shirts, and the usual key chains and magnets. That should cover everybody, now time to get back before this storm lets loose.

Walking back to the hotel, I can't help but feel a little disappointed. All this retail therapy did not cure me of the anxiety that I am feeling. It is not healthy to be this consumed with a man. The thought of walking it off and spending a little money was absurd. With each step I take, I know I am a step closer at walking out of his life for good, and that is the reality I am faced with.

Suddenly, I am startled by the rolling of thunder and bolts of lightning in the sky. I am scared and I am alone, and storms are one of my biggest fears. I run as fast as I can back towards the hotel, but the bags in my hands are slowing me down. I decide to take shelter under a little tiki hut that serves mixed drinks and sandwiches.

The smell of the food hits me hard, and I realize I have not eaten all day. I order a hot ham and cheese melt and a fuzzy navel with extra cherries. While I'm eating, I cannot help but overhear the conversation of the two young women sitting across from me.

The cute one with the short blonde hair is joking about the guys who were flirting with them last night. The red headed one, which happens to be the more beautiful of the two women, assures her friend that there is only one man who is going to be getting a taste of her cookie. I cannot believe my ears. What kind of descent woman talks that way—especially in public?

I try to tune them out by focusing on the storm at hand, but then the blonde says the unthinkable. "Conner Dawson is not going to give you the time of day girl. He may be the most eligible bachelor in Hawaii, but you can keep on dreaming."

I choke on my sandwich when I hear his name, and I struggle to swallow it the rest of the way down. Ugh. My appetite is officially over, and I'm racing with the wind before I know it. I can't help but wonder if they are the reason he left in the middle of the night. Tears fill my eyes and run down my cheeks, blending in with the rain that is now hitting my face.

The storm is turning brutal, and I'm running faster. I am in the middle of a tropical downpour, and I must look like an idiot running through it. The hotel is in sight, and I see a hot shower in my near future; now if I could just get there fast enough.

It's not long before I am mentally and physically worn out. My mind is racing about all the things I need to do before my departure tomorrow, and I have got to get out of these wet clothes. *How could I have been so naive...Why did I have to fall for him?* I don't have time to dwell on that. The last thing on my mind is the least of my worries. So what if I'm drenched and soaking wet. I am okay with being a hot mess, and I could care less about the prying eyes looking my way as I enter the lobby.

Henry is where he was when I left; wooing guests in hopes that they will return. There is no doubt in my mind that they will. Who wouldn't come back to a place as flashy as Dawson's Hotel and Casino Resort? This place is incredible—just like the owner.

As quickly as possible, I make my way to the elevators; pushing the lighted arrows, I beg the cars to hurry up. In the background, I can hear the slot-machines dropping coins and the screaming people who are winning big. They are so happy—so excited.

The next thing I feel is an emotional-overload. I'm crying even harder and hating myself for it, and I can't help but drowned myself with questions. Where did my *happy* go? Why am I *gloating*? Most importantly, why the hell do I even care? Men will be men...my *dad* proved that to me a long time ago. Trying to compose myself, I wipe away my tears—anger taking over the sadness.

Pushing the buttons over and over again, I demand the doors to open.

Finally, there's the ding I've been waiting on. The shiny silver doors open, and my eyes are in shock. They focus and refocus; still not believing if what they see is real or a hallucination. The sight before me is unpredictable, but definitely not a figment of my imagination.

I cannot believe I am looking into the eyes of Conner Dawson. He has survived the same downpour I have and has managed to look sexier than ever. His hair is darker than usual, drenched from the rain water, and his eyes are shaded with fear. His wet T-shirt is hugging him, showing off the muscles in his chest, and my mouth is watering from all that sex appeal. He pulls me in, allowing the doors to shut before anyone else steps in.

He pushes the number twenty-eight, and then takes my bags from my hands; setting them down beside us. Through all that beauty, he still looks worried and confused and without a word his embrace ends the silence, and seconds pass that seem like minutes, and finally he speaks.

"Hannah! I have been so worried about you. Are you okay?"

I soak him in just like the rainwater did my skin. I can't break free from his hold; not that I want to anyway. All I know is in this moment, if I do let go he may fade away like in my dreams—*and the anger slips away.*

"I am better now. Although, I thought for a moment I was going to get washed away into the Pacific Ocean."

We both let out a whisper of laughter as he holds me tighter, and I am utterly breathless and loving it.

"Thank goodness fate stepped in and brought you to safety, Miss Stone."

He releases his hold, but only to rub my back with fast swift movements. He is trying to dry me off. When he realizes his hand is not soaking up the water, he gives me another tight squeeze—heating up the core of my very existence.

The ride on the elevator is short and quick, and we are at the penthouse within minutes. Leilani has left for the night, and the only thing to welcome us is the sound of thunder coming from outside. He picks up the bags, and we step into the foyer.

"Wait here. We need to get you dried off before you catch yourself a cold."

Conner puts the bags down and leaves my side, but only for a few seconds. He returns to find me stripping out of my wet clothes and hanging them on the coat rack that is hidden in the corner of the room. His eyes are locked on my naked body, and it is obvious he likes what he sees. His eyes move gracefully from one direction to the other as he checks out every curve I own. He's utterly speechless, getting his first full glimpse of my naked body. I stand there, breathing harder—my chest expanding—my feet glued to the floor. He can't resist gazing at my breast. He watches as each passing breath lifts my bosom a little higher.

My sex clenches, as his heated pride grows.

He fights the urge to devour me, his nostrils flaring from the erratic breathing that has consumed him.

Slightly blinking, he begins to break out of the trance. His eyes moving up…he walks my way with an expression that sends my body into a shivering frenzy.

Thinking I'm cold, he wraps the fluffy white towel around my shoulders, but I catch him by surprise. Chilled to the bone is one thing, but I'm burning up from the inside out. I push the towel to the floor—unable to control my desire, I give in. My hands are gripping his damp shirt and pulling it over his head. He's kicking his wet shoes off. Our lips meet with eagerness unlike any kiss we have ever shared. It is full of passion, and it is hot. Our tongues are fighting to taste each other, and it is time to ease this craving. Just a little taste and we will both be satisfied.

My fingers find their way to his fly, and down to the floor go his tight drenched blue jeans. Before I know it, he is carrying me into his master bedroom and heading to the large walk-in shower.

He turns on the water, and within seconds the room is steamy and seductive. We can't get enough of each other; even while he stands me to my feet on the porcelain-tiled floor our skin is still clinging together for dear life. Stepping beneath the spout, the hot sultry water cascades over our bodies, and the passion is consuming us both.

"I want to feel every part of you, Hannah," he breathes.

"I want you to..." I gasp as his long masculine fingers begin to make a trail over my skin.

Slowly, Conner's hands move over my body like they were made just for me. He is rubbing me and touching me in places that no man has ever ventured before. He caresses my breast with such intense passion, and the next thing I know he has my nipples between his fingers—pulling and twirling—making me hotter with every tug.

"I love your nice firm breasts...they're so big and round...so beautifully plump," he growls. "I'm going to suck them now."

I think I am going to scream for mercy when he glides his mouth down my neck—then to my bosom. With every flick of his tongue, I groan with anticipation. That suction...*wow*. I'm tingling down there, and he hasn't even made it *there*— yet. Without a doubt, I know this man is going to give me what no other man ever has—*an orgasm*. I can feel it growing, just like I can feel his manhood getting bigger and bigger.

The hot water continues biting at our skin—making our bodies that much more sensitive to what is going on. *It is such a turn-on,* and I'm so inexperienced. Right now my virginity is the last thing on my mind. I want this or *do I?* Hell, I don't know. I'm too caught up in the moment to care either way.

While his mouth is still focusing on my nipples, he moves his hands slowly down my body—feeling every inch of me. He's in search of something, and I can't wait until he finds it.

His fingers tiptoeing further down and around, there it is.

My body tenses as he reaches his destination, but then I relax and let him have his way with me.

"Ah!" I gasp as he spreads my legs apart; his search is over, and I'm in blissful trouble. *I'm really letting him do this.* My womanhood is screaming, and I almost explode when he inserts one finger into my vagina. In and out.

Slowly. Gently. Passionately. I can't help but gasp again; his fingers feel so good down *there*. He is in control, and he proves it when he massages my throbbing clitoris; faster and faster—soon causing me to find the release I have been longing for. My body tightens up, and I climax.

Seconds pass with my eyes closed and my head buried in his chest, as I spiral down from the deliciousness of what just transpired. I shake off the orgasm and hold on tight to the man who just made it happen. Thank goodness his lips are back on mine and giving me the strength I need to keep from falling.

Standing beneath the hot water spray, my pure essence is tested when I feel his body quivering with desire. He wants me wearing his manhood, and there is no denying it. I can't let him suffer, but I can't give away all of me just yet. That would defeat everything I've believed in since first understanding what sex, love, and marriage represent. Maybe I shouldn't have let it gone this far, but there is something about doing this with him that feels like it's exactly what I've been waiting for my whole life.

I focus my attention on him.

I have never satisfied a man to a point of pleasure, so I just do what comes natural—mimicking what he just showed me. I kiss him senseless from his lips, to his neck, and then to his nipples. Biting and tugging him to the edge of escape. The feel of his body beneath my roaming hands is such a turn on, and even more when my fingers wrap around his long, thick, voluptuous cock.

By now, the water is getting cooler, and I feel my senses standing on edge—begging for more of what I just had. I think I feel my coochie heating to the point of explosion again. Yes. I do. He's fondling my clit and pushing inside me, with not one, but two fingers this time. I stroke him faster with a grip he loves, and within seconds we are gasping for air and coming all over each other. This amazing man has just introduced me to the amazing world of foreplay, and we didn't even have to go all the way.

What an introduction...

Chapter 14

We shower until the water runs cold, but the heat between us is still here. Our bodies embrace and soak up the intoxicating body wash that we are both covered in. It smells of Conner, and now I smell like him. Ah, breathtaking and scrumptious.

By the time we make it out of the shower, our bodies are relaxed and satisfied. The mad craving we have for each other is content, and the thirst is temporarily quenched—*or is it.*

That was *fabulous*—out-of-this-world I want to do it again kind of fabulous. I didn't know I had it in me to come so hard; guess it was the man behind the fingers. I wonder if he's up for a repeat.

Seriously.

Secretly begging fate for more future action, my inner self tries to calm my purring kitty. *"Listen here you; we have manners, so use them. If he wants seconds, he'll come back for more. Now, be a good girl and settle down."* My body trying hard to obey; I feel my sex clench in.

Until next time—*please let there be a next time.*

We dry off and get dressed. I wear one of his T-shirts like a dress, and he wears his running shorts that show off that sexy tight ass of his. We are a sight to appreciate, and there is no denying the factuality between us. Our paths have crossed, and we are *falling* in love.

Making our way through the penthouse, we listen for any sign of bad weather. The storm was brutal, but finally has settled to a light mist of rain; you can see the sun trying to peek through the clouds.

Conner grabs my hand and walks me to the covered balcony where we sit, talk, and take in the breathtaking view as the sun sets upon the ocean. His strong masculine arms are wrapped around me, and his head is resting on mine. The moment is perfect, and then he brings *it* up.

"That was some shower, huh?" His voice a low whisper; his embrace more intense.

Not sure of how to take his comment, I can't help but wonder if he is feeling guilty. "I don't regret it Conner. I would do it again in a heartbeat to let you know how I feel about you."

I know he's thinking about my innocence and how it's now tainted by his hands, but I truly do not regret it and would do it all over again to be that close to him.

He lets out a deep breath and kisses the hairs on my head. We sit here admiring the view until the sun is completely gone, and then my stomach growls...*why does it always do that around him?* I'm hungry for him, not food. We both laugh, and he guides me up and into the kitchen we go.

We opt to have a light dinner that consists of grilled cheese sandwiches and chicken noodle soup. There is just something about rainy weather that makes you crave food like that; at least it hits the spot and shuts up my belly.

While sitting across from this vision of beauty, I recall the words he spoke earlier. "So, why were you so worried about me?" I couldn't resist asking—curiosity getting the best of me like always.

His peaceful look turns to distress, and he puts down his spoon. "When I arrived back to the penthouse, you weren't here. Leilani had already left, and all I could think about was you fighting this storm alone. I am still trying to figure out why you didn't have Finn drive you."

I visualize him out running around in the rain; looking for me on the beach, maybe somewhere outside on the grounds, or even along the strip. He was drenched when I found him. Why wasn't he being chauffeured around? It doesn't matter. I take a deep breath and exhale.

"He's your driver, not mine; besides, I needed to walk off a little stress." His curious eyes are trying to see through me, but he can't figure me out.

Don't do it, Hannah! My subconscious is screaming, and I'm not listening. Conner Dawson is going to think I'm a desperate and pathetic woman when I get done, but here goes nothing…the words are spilling out of my mouth before I take time to contemplate what his reaction might be. "You left without a word. I thought you were trying to escape me." My eyes search his, looking for just a hint of truth behind what I had just said, but nothing even close.

His brow raises—his face is a serious shade of aggravated passion. My heartbeat speeds past the steady rhythm of normal and is now thumping harder causing my face to flush crimson. *Is he pissed or turned on by my words?*

"How could you think that?" he asks, his tone showing a trace of bitterness.

My heart now sinking—why did I not bite my tongue?

He takes a deep breath and continues.

"I am a man who demands to be *respected*, but I am also a man who shows *it*."

I watch him as he watches me; listening closely with not just my ears, but of course with my eyes.

"There may be times that I'm a real ass, but I am not a heartless piece of shit. If I didn't want to see you anymore, I'd be man enough to look you in those celestial eyes of yours and fess up." He pauses for a moment; debating whether or not he should go on.

All I can do is wait and hope he does. I'm speechless and *he's not pissed*—just frustrated. I remain attentive—allowing his words to absorb and his stare to penetrate straight through to my soul.

He huffs, running his fingers through his hair as he props his elbows on his knees; he wants to tell me something, but then again he doesn't. Sitting up, his back now against the chair, his gaze is still locked on mine. He can trust me; he has to know that. *Is that why he's hesitating?* I begin to squirm…*why is he still gaping at me like that?* Taking a deep breath, he exhales and his words begin pouring out of his mouth.

"Hillary isn't well. A couple of years ago, she fell hard for a guy named Matt. He lives at one of the other islands, and he is nothing but trouble."

He's struggling with his words; pausing again before he goes on.

"That loser is hooked on heroin, and now my sister is too."

My eyes widen. That explains her tethered look; *the night at Joes*—the windblown hair and smeared make-up. My mind rewinds back to the day on the plane. The bruises were from shooting up. No wonder he's so desperate to get *Hooked on a Better Life* up and going. *It's all because of Hillary.*

"You haven't seen her this week because I took her to the local rehab center. Hillary admitted herself and promised to stay, but she didn't. She checked herself out and went straight to him. Long story short—they got high, got in a fight, and she grabbed his keys without him knowing."

Oh, this can't be good.

"There was an accident. I only left because I had to make sure she was okay," he says—his words covered in fear and his expression darkens with a trace of fury...now he's pissed thinking about the addict that has corrupted his sister's world.

My mouth drops and my heart stops for a split second, and suddenly I feel so selfish. "Oh no, Conner, is she okay?"

He puts my hand in his and raises it up to his lips for a quick kiss. Shaking his head and closing his eyes, he remembers the phone call. I watch him, searching for a clue of how she is.

"After a few minutes, Matt realized she was gone, and then he heard the sirens down the road. She was found unconscious and bleeding from her head about a half mile from his house."

I push my chair back and walk over to comfort the man I now adore. Sitting down on his lap, I wrap my arms around him; hoping he would let the fear of losing her leave his mind. "I am so sorry, Conner. I had no idea." Whispering the words in his ear, I fondle the back of his neck; trying to relax him and doing my best to put his mind in a better place.

"Thank you, Hannah. I'm glad to say she is going to be fine. She was alert when I left, and Dr. Williams has already signed the papers to have her admitted back into rehab—once she is well enough to be moved. This time she cannot check herself out; I'll make damn sure of that."

He pauses again.

Crap. What is it now?

"I have more bad news, though. I won't be able to fly back with you tomorrow. I'm going to stay here until Hillary gets settled in; just in case she needs me."

Of course he will.

"Here is exactly where you should be. Please don't worry about me," I insist.

He runs his fingers through the back of my hair and then leans me closer to him, finishing dinner with the best dessert ever. A sweet tender kiss from the most passionate man I have ever met. It is delectable and better than cheesecake. My heart is content and my belly is full; our lips part, each set adorning a massive grin. My *happy* is back, and so is his.

"Oh, and Hannah…as far as escaping you goes—not happening. You have given me a glimpse into my future, and you're right there in it. So baby girl, hold on tight and get ready; this rides not over—*it's just getting started.*"

My womanhood is sweltering and begging for a taste of the tongue that just landed in my mouth. He kisses me hard, and my hands get tangled up in his hair. Straddling him comes natural. I begin rocking back and forth—making him harder than he already is.

He bites my lip…gasping for relief, his hot breath hits mine. "The things I want to do to you, Hannah," he growls.

My mouth still on his, I growl back. "I can't wait, Conner."

He grinds into me one last time, and then lifts me off of him. "One day, baby girl, one day; but for now, let's turn this down a notch before you do something you're not ready for."

Wow…he's got this respect thing down pat.

"Why don't you go get ready for bed while I call the hospital?" he asks.

My blood is racing through my veins—my heart is pounding—my mind is in overdrive. His restraint...where does it come from? I've never had to fight my own body as much as I am now. I have never wanted a man so much in my whole entire life. Either lust has taken over my senses, or I am truly in love.

Leaning over, I slide my tongue across his lips and into his mouth...*damn he tastes good*...and hesitantly I pull away.

"I'll be right back, Mister Dawson."

"I'll be here waiting, Miss Stone."

Before leaving the table, Conner calls to check on his sister. After hearing a good report, we hit the couch in search of a good movie. My attention is on him more than the television screen. It is no doubt that he's easier on my eyes than the bloody horror flick he chose.

The storm begins to brew up again outside, and the steady rhythm of rainfall is falling on the roof. It seems harmless until lightning strikes, and the roaring sound of thunder follows closely behind it. I jump, causing him to hold me tighter.

Cuddling up to Conner Dawson is the perfect sedative. It is no surprise when my eyes close, my mind wanders, and I'm spiraling down from a dream-intoxicated orgasm. He is becoming a part of me, and there is no controlling my cravings even while I'm sleeping.

The next morning, I wake to find him watching me from the wicker chair only inches from the bed. I can't help but wonder how long he's been there, or if he even left at all last night. I vaguely remember my head hitting the pillow, but I do remember him lifting me in his arms and carrying me here.

"Good morning, Sleepy Head," he says.

I laugh at his name calling...rubbing my eyes and smiling at the same time.

"I thought only angels could sleep so beautifully," he whispers. His voice is low and serious, but it is scrumptious nonetheless. I'm breathless, and his *words* are charming.

I rise up, and he holds out his hand to help me out of bed. I can smell the scent of freshly brewed coffee, and that means Leilani is in the kitchen doing what she does best.

"Why, thank you, Mister D. You aren't too hard on the eyes yourself." We laugh at each other; then things get serious.

"I thought I would ride over to the airport with you if that's okay."

He brushes a wayward strand of hair from my eyes and tucks it behind my ear. I breathe him in...*he's already showered and smells divine.*

"I would love that, but don't you need to be getting to the hospital?" I ask.

"I have already called and checked in on Hillary. It will be okay if I'm running a little late," he insists.

Nothing will make me happier than to have him see me off, but I know it will also make it harder to leave. "Conner, I would love for you to come along."

"Then it's settled. I will call Finn and tell him we will be down within the hour."

I look at my phone, and it's already seven o'clock. My time in Hawaii is over as is my time with *him*.

Suddenly, I'm depressed and faced with what I'm going home too. No Conner and one determined stalker. *Ugh! Why can't I just stay here?* Conner leaves me to freshen up and pack. My time with him is limited, and I do not want to waste a minute of it. I'm ready in no time. I take one last look at my room and walk out—leaving it behind. I make my way to the foyer and place my luggage by the elevator.

Conner comes in seconds later decked out and showing off his massive sex appeal. He's sporting a pair of those tight-fitting jeans that I have come to love and a hot pink polo. Only a *real* man can wear that color and get away with it. He is definitely that man...*every luscious mouthwatering inch of him.* It is going to be harder to leave than I thought.

He stops in his footsteps and watches me as though he is memorizing my every feature. "Hannah, you look amazing."

I couldn't help but wear the sexy turquoise dress that I had bought while I was out shopping the other day; courtesy of Mister Dawson himself. The dress is perfect and he notices. The neckline is low cut and great for showing off just the right amount of cleavage—enough to make a man drool and left for wanting more. The length falls right below my knees and has a slit that goes all the way up the side showing off my sun-kissed legs. It is strapless, and I am *panty-less*.

Maybe, just maybe I will leave him breathless. I hope so. I want him to remember me taking *his* breath away. Perhaps if I leave him with a memory like that, he won't forget me.

"I'm ready whenever you are," I say. I'm lying through my teeth, but I know I can't stop time.

I walk over and hug Leilani bye. The food she has prepared smells as good as always, but I better not touch it.

Well, maybe I better. I recall passing out after the flight here due to the lack of food. I grab a piece of toast and a *to-go* cup of coffee and walk towards Conner. I take a bite and then slowly feed him one too. Yes. It is such a freaking turn on watching him chew. I inhale him and the last bite.

We walk to the elevator, and I turn to wave bye. "Good bye, Leilani."

She waves and winks at me. "Aloha, Ms. Stone, I hope to see you soon."

I can see it in her face that she knows what's been going on. I smile, and we exit the penthouse.

The elevator ride is quicker than I like. No stops. Just straight down to the lobby. The doors open, and I find myself looking for Henry. I want to thank him for all of his generosity. He was a complete gentleman to a complete stranger—a real class act.

There he is, doing what he does best in the middle of the lobby.

"Henry!" I yell.

He turns and looks at me, next at Conner, and then excuses himself from the other guests and walks towards us.

"Ms. Stone, are you leaving us so soon?" he asks.

"Yes. A girl has to work if she wants to come back for a visit."

His lips curl up.

I sit my bags down and hug him. "Thank you for everything."

"It was my pleasure. I look forward to seeing you soon, Ms. Stone."

I release him and notice he is looking at Conner. He nods his head and smiles at his boss. Unspoken words are shared between them, and I'm left wondering. *What was that all about?* Maybe he was giving his approval. I can only hope.

Finn is at the limo waiting, and he sees us coming. "Good morning, Mr. Dawson. Ms. Stone." He tips his hat and a grin spreads across his wise face, showing off his wrinkles and warming my heart.

Our words are perfectly united as we open our mouths at the same time; *again.* "Good morning, Finn."

We all three laugh.

The driver pops the trunk open and takes my luggage. After nestling it safe and sound into the back of the car, he glides over to open the door. I look at Conner, and there's that contagious smile of his again.

"After you, beautiful," he breathes.

I am utterly and irrevocably in awe of this man. Is he real or am I dreaming? My erotica's have consumed so much of my life lately; it is almost hard to tell what's real and what isn't. I climb in, and he follows me. His hand takes mine and he squeezes it— sending a shock straight to my pleasure area and bringing me back to reality. This *is* real. *He* is real.

Finn shuts the door and off we go.

One hand still linked with mine, his other controls the remote to the privacy window. He pushes the button while looking at me. Slowly, the black glass slides up along with the music, and Conner and I are all alone—*so to speak.*

Within seconds the remote is out of his hand, and he is lifting me out of the seat. My right leg is to his left, and my left is to his right. I'm straddling him and longing to say *giddy up cowboy.*

Not a word is spoken, but he's reading my mind. *He's so good at that.* Both our bodies are reacting to the attraction that can't be tamed—not right now anyway.

His mouth moves in for a taste, and his hands are wrapped around my ass. He pushes me into him, while kissing me as though he's fighting to stay alive. Desperately slamming his lips to mine, he feeds his thirst. Sensuous moans leave his mouth, vibrating their way past my lips to somewhere deep and hidden between my legs.

Wow. This is hot.

His fingers begin to move back and forth, gathering at the material of my dress and moving it out of his way. Careful not to expose my bare-butt, his body trembles with desire. His teeth graze my lips when he lets out a low growl. He knows my girly stuff is wide-open and waiting.

He can't resist—and I am so glad.

Lifting me up an inch or so, giving him just enough room to get a handful, he begins fingering me and making me cry out into his mouth. *It feels so good?* In and out, over and over again; I don't just feel how wet I am—he does.

A soft whisper leaves his lips, making me want him even more. "Damn it, girl. You're making me crazy. I want you—so bad—*ah, ah.*" His seductive moans echoing in my ears.

The pad of his thumb begins to vibrate against my clit and his long skilled fingers keep thrusting. My body jerks, my eyes roll back, and here I go. I bite his bottom lip and unravel all over his hand.

What away to say goodbye.

We arrive at the airport, and the jet is fueled and ready for takeoff. After exiting the limo, we stand there staring at each other. I don't want to go, but how can I stay? I can't stay. That's the problem. He has his sister to care for, and I have a stalker to deal with. Worry is all over my face, and he sees it.

"The flight may be long, but you will be back in Nashville before you know it, so don't stress out okay."

Flight, I'm not worried about the long flight. I don't want to leave you.

My mind is screaming, but he can't hear my thoughts. My heart is racing, but he can't hear that either. Screw it. I drop my purse, and I'm in his arms within seconds.

He lifts me up in the air, spinning me and kissing me with that voluptuous mouth of his. Our tongues entwine, and so do our hearts. I kiss him with every ounce of my being. If the ride over here doesn't leave him wanting more, maybe that will.

Hesitating, I pull my lips away; my tempered breathing tickling at his ears—my words a gentle whisper. "Until our paths cross again, Mister Dawson."

He puts me down.

"I can't wait until they do, Miss Stone."

I turn and walk away as gracefully as I can. It takes everything in me to not turn and run back into his arms. I refuse to turn around because if I do, I will not go.

I board the jet and leave the best thing that has ever happened to me behind—*him.*

Chapter 15

The flight is long, but seems even longer than before. I'm restless and missing Conner already. Ugh! I have to focus. My stomach churning into one big knot of nervous tension isn't helping things. Taking a deep breath, I close my eyes momentarily. When I open them back up, I look down at my wrist.

Checking my watch—one more hour and I'll be *home sweet home*. I can do this. I can get off of this plane and face what I left back in Oak Hill. *"Think, Hannah. Think."* I demand myself. There is a crazy stalker who wants to take the one thing you have that money can't buy—your sweet, blissful innocence.

Looking out the window, my head in the clouds just like the plane, my mind wanders; remembering the last twenty-four hours and not what's waiting on me back home. Not only were those the hottest, most passionate moments of my entire life, but the man who shared them with me has left an imprint on my heart; not to mention my womanhood.

There is no doubt I have found the *only* man I want exploring my forbidden cavern, and I'll be damned if anyone else does. My thoughts get carried away again, and I'm conjuring up a plan or at least trying to. How do I stop a sick and twisted moron who has the upper hand? He knows who I am, but I haven't got a clue as to who he is. First things first. Get home safely and be aware of everyone and everything.

Finally, we've landed.

To my surprise, Baylee is waiting for me at the airport. I look at her, and she is holding a poster board above her head. The brightly-colored letters spell out my name. *HANNAH BROOKE STONE*. I laugh at my friend who seems lost without me. I smile. She smiles. "What are you doing crazy girl?" I ask.

She looks at me, adorning that beautiful face of hers, and the words start rolling off her tongue—along with a tear or two onto her cheeks. "I missed my friend; not to mention, I have been going crazy with worry. When I got your text with your arrival time, I knew I wanted to be here," she says in a low whimper.

"Awe, Baylee. Thank you for being such an amazing friend." Her embrace is welcoming; it is so good to be off that plane and in her arms. I missed her too.

We walk and talk our way throughout the crowded lobby. She catches me up on her week, and I promise to catch her up on mine, but first I need to get home and unpack. We go our separate ways, and I head towards the covered garage in search of my car. It is dark and fear is hitting me. I walk faster and can't find it. Where did I park my convertible? I hear footsteps. Crap! *Where are my keys?* I remember putting them in my pocket. I take them out and push the fob.

Lights are flashing and the alarm has been activated. Thank goodness it is loud and only a few feet away. Running as though my life depended upon it, I finally make it. I look around, and two vehicles down I see a woman getting in a dark colored SUV. I can't tell who she is because she is facing the other direction. I can breathe. It isn't him. That freak is going to drive me crazy, and that is not on my bucket list of things to do. No. Not happening, not in this life time anyway. I start my car and speed out of the scary garage, trying my best to leave the fear behind.

I pull onto my street and everything looks normal. No sign of swaying tree limbs or stalkers leaning up against my apartment building. I take a deep breath and pull into a parking spot. Looking in every direction, I take one last quick glance around just to make sure nothing is out of place. Everything looks good, so I get out.

I unload my luggage and put off packing until tomorrow. I'm worn out from the flight, and all I want to do is relax. I text Baylee to let her know I made it home safely and will talk to her tomorrow.

Only minutes later, I'm snuggling beneath my own blanket, in my own bed, and my mind is racing. As tired as I may be, my mind has other plans indeed—it's going to be a long night.

I toss and I turn. I fluff my pillow—flipping it from one side to the next. Looking at the clock—thirty minutes have past—*and then another thirty minutes goes by.* Huffing and puffing until finally…I'm out cold.

I'm not surprised that my dreams are of Conner Dawson. The man who has single handedly captivated my attention. He is doing what he does best; taking my breath away with his touch. His body is hot, and I can feel his heated masculinity as it bores into my backside—stroking me with his hands and his hard lengthy manhood. His bare skin lies perfectly next to mine, connecting with me in ways that leave me breathless and full of desire. My womanhood is pounding with every beat of my heart, and everything in me wants this.

I roll out of his embrace to straddle him with full heated passion, but when I look up I am face to face with blackness. Conner's beautiful face is replaced with nothing. What the hell is going on? I am being taken by a stranger, and I can't wake up from this nightmare. I struggle to fight his strength, but he is overbearing. I can't break free from his hold. I toss and turn, fighting with every ounce of my being. He can't have what is Conner's. I will fight him off, and I will win. I have to win.

Suddenly, my eyes open, and I am safe. My pillow is saturated with wetness from tears and sweat, and the room is lit up from the rising sun. I sit up and rub my eyes and my face—assuring myself it was *only* a nightmare.

I get up and head straight for the shower. I stand there letting the hot steamy water flow all over my entire body. From head to toe, I want the stench gone—*like it's really there.* I cover myself with anti-bacterial soap, leaving no spot untouched. I scrub hard, almost too hard, washing away the filth that had invaded my dreams and my body; the body that only one man is allowed to touch and devour. I am his, and from this moment forward, protecting my virtue has to be my highest priority.

It is Tuesday morning, and it is time to face the overwhelming clientele at the law firm of Jenkins, Jones, and Smith. To this day, I don't understand why people marry only to divorce. Marriage is a unity between two people, a bond that is connected by love and passion; a desire that is taken for granted and discarded like yesterday's newspaper.

Most of their stories are the same. They fall out of love and get tired of fighting over stupid things like what's for dinner or for snoring too loud. Whatever the case may be, sometimes I just want to tell them to fight for what they once believed in. But that is not my job. I have to listen to their stories, type it up, and make it presentable for the court. Then it is the judge who will sign the papers— leaving the couple to start all over. Most people will fall in and out of love with someone new, never realizing they are going down the same path as before. They will be selfish and want more than they are willing to give. In the end, it's all the same. *Broken hearts and broken dreams.*

Before I know it, the clock says twelve o'clock—it's time for lunch and Baylee is anxiously waiting at my office door with her keys in hand.

"How does Mexican sound?" she asks.

The food sounds great, but not so much the thought of being stalked by one. I think back on the stalker and the delivery boy...remembering the word *Chicano* and thinking that's too close for comfort. It really pisses me off too. Some of my closest friends are of Mexican descent. The not knowing who *he* is makes me doubt people I shouldn't.

"I was kind of hoping for Chinese. Do you mind?" Squeezing one eye shut, I peek through the one slightly opened.

Remembering the roses, the poem, and the stupid jerk that sent them, I cross my fingers hoping she will say yes to the oriental food. I'm thankful the creep hasn't resurfaced since I've been home, but I do not need any reminder that he exists. His absence is a welcome, and I can only hope he has moved on.

"Yummy! Sounds great," she purrs. Chinese is her favorite...I should have known she would be up for it.

I grab my purse, and ten minutes later we're across the street at the China Chop Buffet. They serve everything from sushi to crab legs and memories of my date with Conner come to mind. I'm smiling, and Baylee notices.

"What are you thinking about, Hannah? You're blinding me with those pearly whites." My grin widens.

Letting her squirm with wonder, a minute passes and I confess.

"I have met someone," I whisper.

Dropping her fork, she looks at me wide-eyed and gasping. "I knew something was different about you!" she exclaims. Baylee's excitement is heard all over the crowded restaurant. I calm her down by placing my hand over her mouth—while looking her squarely in the eye.

She restrains her provocation to the best of her ability.

"Who is it, Hannah? Tell me!"

I bite my lip, remembering the man who is the topic of my conversation. I am enthralled with the pure-decadent sweet memory of him. He is enticing and consuming my thoughts.

"Hannah Brooke Stone! Spill it; you should be ashamed of yourself for depriving me of such important details!"

Leaning in closer, I mouth the words she's dying to hear.

"Conner Dawson." His name rolls off my tongue and lands right between my legs. The appellation alone gets me all hot and bothered. I wanted him more than food or water— even air. Who needs all that when I can devour *all of him* with just one tasty mind-blowing kiss? *Ah.* Suddenly, I'm yearning to be back in Hawaii. The place I left the only man to ever make my womanhood swell and throb and clench with sweet delicious pleasure. I remember the shower, the limo ride, and before I can reminisce too much, Baylee is pulling me out of my fantasy.

"Why does that name sound so familiar?"

She's going to flip-out when I tell her.

"Do you remember the week before, at Joe's Place?" I ask, remembering the night myself.

"Uh, huh," she says, nodding her head with those intense eyes aiming my way; she's dying to read my mind.

"The man singing...the one Joe called his friend..." Baylee stops me from finishing and is screaming underneath her breath.

Somebody give the girl a prize. She's figured it out.

"You. Have. Got. To. Be. Freaking. Kidding. Me—*the singer?*" I nod, while sipping my sweet tea. "The heartthrob that left us all drooling like idiots," she cries out—trying hard not to be heard.

"Uh, huh," I nod. A thirsty grin spreads across my face, and my straw is still between my lips. I can't help but look around the room. Wondering if anyone realizes what I wish was in my mouth instead of the plastic I am drinking through. I blush at the thought of his cock being there; shaking my head— I put my attention back on my friend.

"Hannah! You lucky hooch, you!" Her slang is far from the truth. She knows me and my well-protected virtue all too well. "So, tell me more. Did you...you know...do the do?" My private moments are just that. I choose to tell my friend only the basics. What happened in Hawaii—stays in Hawaii.

"We had an amazing week. Don't worry. My innocence is still locked up and penis free." She laughs, but can't refrain from telling me how crazy I am not to have given it up. If only she knew how close I was to letting his manhood venture where no other ever has.

The hour goes by fast, and Baylee hangs on to every word I say. I tell her everything I want her to know, and the rest I just reminisce about. My memories with Conner are private, and not even my best friend deserves to share them with me.

We're back to work by one o'clock, and clients are anxiously waiting. Quitting time is still four hours away, and it cannot get here fast enough. All this lingo of divorce and break-ups is the last thing I want to be reading about. My relationship with Conner is brand new and exciting. I want to gloat like a young girl in love; not work my fingers to the bone typing up stories like this. I don't want to be left wondering if it will end before it even gets a chance to flourish.

What time is it already?

I glance anxiously at the clock in the corner of my computer screen—*CRAP!* Only ten minutes have passed since I looked last time.

Locking my eyes on the email that just popped up, I click on it, and it's from Baylee. Leaning over to look out my door, I see her doing the same in her office. Her bouncy curls framing her face, her lips a straight line, and her conniving eyes looking into mine; she's so damn pretty—*even when she's up to something.*

I mouth the words *"What?"* and she mouths *"Look at the email!!"*

So I do...*very carefully.*

The subject of the email reads: *Look what I found.*

There's an attachment. I open it. My mouth drops open. My eyes are in shock. My heart skips a beat, and my stomach flutters. *Is it him?*

Yes, it is.

His flawless body all dressed up in a tux, and he's at the grand opening of his casino; his 21st birthday present from his mega-*gazillionaire* dad. He looks so good standing there on the red carpet and grinning like he had just won the lottery. This picture was taken a little over five years ago, and the article came from the local newspaper there in Honolulu. He was very handsome then, but even sexier now.

My happy grin turns upside down when I see *her.* A girl to the right of him, only inches away with her hand resting on his back. She's model material and much more glamorous than I am. I would be stupid to think his past didn't include a woman of such beauty. Suddenly, I'm wondering how far back she goes into his past, or if she even goes *back* at all. Surely she isn't still a part of his life.

Refusing to be worried, I delete the email before jealousy consumes me. He has a past just like I do; that's all it is. Emailing Baylee back, I tell her the same—also, to quit playing around on the internet and get back to work. I'm ready to go home. I have enough things to worry about, and I refuse to let his past mess with my head. Conner and I are both mature adults. If there was another woman, he would tell me. I'm sure of it.

Finally, the last client leaves at four thirty. That leaves me just enough time to finish up my paperwork.

One last keyboard click to save the file, and that does it...*I'm all done.*

I check my phone before leaving, and I have a text from my mom.

> *Hey honey. I haven't heard from you in awhile. I'm cooking your favorite for supper—lasagna. Hope you can make it here around six. I love you bunches.*

My face brightens up—showing off a massive grin. I really miss my mama. A visit with her is just what I need to help take my mind off of all the drama in my life.

Chapter 16

The smell of lasagna is enticing, hitting me in the face when I walk through the front door. I saunter through the living room and across the hall, and there she is. Ms. Lindy Stone herself. My beautiful mom is standing in the middle of her country style kitchen in front of the sink, and doesn't know I'm here.

The room is decked out with light brown walls covered with rooster paraphernalia and under her feet...well, simple bamboo flooring. There's music playing from under the cabinet radio, and that explains why she didn't hear me knocking at the door. My mom not only blessed me with her looks but taught me everything she knows when it comes to cooking. She is a great cook, and I can't wait to dig in.

I lean over the round oak table to smell the vibrant red tulips that brighten up the room. I laugh, shaking my head at the reality of the artificial beauties that look freshly-picked.

I wish I had inherited her decorating abilities.

Mama's patience and beauty are treasures that not many people have, and my dad was a crazy man to let her go. I stand there for a moment admiring this amazing woman before I interrupt her.

"Mama," I call out, my voice and footsteps now louder than the radio. She drops the plastic bowl in the sink and begins wiping her hands on the apron I had bought her for Christmas. I didn't mean to startle her, but I did. I don't think it was from the sound of my voice though, but more of the old wooden floor that was creaking beneath my feet. She turns around to face me.

"Hannah, you sweet, sweet girl of mine." She strolls over to me, still talking and cleaning her hands. "Where have you been hiding?" She grabs my face and kisses my forehead. My heart skips a beat when I realize how lonely her moments at home must be since Landon and I moved out. I wish that she could find someone to love her the way she deserves, a man that could give her what every person longs for; love, happiness, and *passion*.

I hate the fact that she never got over my dad leaving; although she would never admit that he is the reason she still lives alone in the same house they shared together as a young couple. To hear stories of the people who knew them well, you would have thought that they would have grown old and gray in this very house and still as much in love as the day they got married. Things change though…my dad's disappearance is the cold hard reality of it.

"I've been around, mom. What can I help you with?" She motions to the fridge and tells me to start on the salad. I grab a head of iceberg lettuce and two tomatoes. This is the perfect side to go along with the lasagna and mashed potato casserole she is cooking.

"So, how are you doing, Hannah?"

I study her face to see if she knows something, but there is no proof that my secrets are out. Surely, Landon didn't tell her about the stalker, and there is no way she could know about Conner.

"I'm good, mama. You know, work is keeping me busy like usual." She listens close as she goes back to finishing up the mouthwatering meal she is preparing. Every word heard—even the unspoken ones too. Knowing my mom like I do, I'm sure she's listening to the *sound* of my voice, searching for a glimpse into my private life.

I can't resist telling her about my trip. I'm sure she's picked up on my tone by now and is curious as to why I'm so happy. Of course I'll leave off the part about Conner, and why I left Oak Hill so suddenly.

"I just got back from Hawaii." Her eyes light up, and so does my face.

"Hawaii. Wow. You must be getting paid pretty well after all, and from the looks of it, you must have had a good time. You're glowing."

Mama is always worried I'm not making enough money to survive, but what she doesn't know is that Mister Dawson took the financial burden off of a vacation I really couldn't afford. There is no doubt he is the reason behind the glow I'm now wearing. I decide to keep those details to myself. I'm not ready to talk to her about my love life. She would only worry that the same scenario would happen all over again; just like with Kris. Her heart breaks when mine does and I am not the only one left to pick up the pieces of my shattered life. She is.

A half hour passes and dinner is served before I know it. The chit chat between me and my mom had entertained us both, and the minutes were passing by fast. We are joined by my brother within seconds of setting the table. "You're just in time Landon," says my mother.

Mama embraces her son with a motherly hug, and she has to step on her tiptoes to kiss his cheek. He is tall like my dad and looks like him too. My mom is reminded of the man who left her with a son who has his face. It has to hurt, but the love she has for us outweighs the pain of our dad leaving her to raise us alone. She loved him so much, but that was not enough for a man who wanted more than just a good wife and a wonderful mother for his children. I can't help but roll my eyes, remembering a man I probably wouldn't recognize. Enough of those depressing thoughts, she is better off without him.

Mama says grace, and then Landon and I eat like we're starving—all while she savors the sight of us and not the food she prepared. She would cook like this every night if we promised to come and eat it.

We clean our plates, and together we clean the kitchen. Our bellies are full and so are our lives; it is moments like this that we appreciate the most. No matter what my dad has spent his life doing, we three have each other, and that is all that matters.

We laugh and talk and look through scrapbooks from our younger years. Mama is lit up with joy having her two *babies* under the same roof—oh, how time flies. It seems like just yesterday when we were running around the backyard, and Landon was pulling me by my pigtails. Those days are long gone—now we're all adults, and time has no conscience…it just keeps tick-tocking away—never promising us tomorrow.

That stupid arrogant stalker—how dare he make me waste one precious moment of my life worrying about him?

It's ten o'clock before I know it, and Landon and I both have an early schedule tomorrow. "Mom, thank you for the amazing meal. It was great. Just like you." I kiss her cheek and hug her tight.

Next, I lean over to my brother to hug him.

"We need to talk," he whispers. He's pissed and has hid it well from both me and my mom. We say our goodbyes to mama and head out the backdoor. Landon walks me down the steps, and that's when he lets me have it.

"Why the hell would you leave and not tell me anything, Hannah? I have been worried sick."

How could I have been so thoughtless?

"I'm sorry. I was scared to tell anyone where I was." He gives me that *are you serious look,* and I try to ease his thoughts. "I am the one in danger. I was only trying to keep everyone else safe, so I figured the less you knew the safer you would be."

There's that look again—harder this time.

"Stop while you are ahead, Hannah. I am your brother; you know the older and very protective one that could be annoying while we were growing up. Hell, I am even an officer of the law, and I can protect you." His voice is low, deep, and convincing. He is right. He is good at his job and I know it, and he is the best brother a sister could ask for.

I look back toward the door, hoping my mother hasn't overheard us. I motion him to move further away from the house, and we walk to my car.

"I'm sorry, Landon. No more secrets. I promise." He squeezes me tight. *He really was scared.*

I should be ashamed, but dang it, I was scared too. Actions have circumstances, but my thoughts were too consumed to worry about who would miss me while I was gone. *Note to self: be more considerate.*

He huffs, releasing his anger and remembering what got him that way in the first place—his love for me. Sometimes I can't help but wonder if he feels like he has to play *father figure* to me, instead of just being the brother I look up to. Whatever his reason is, I can't help but admire the man my mother raised.

"No more secrets, Hannah, seriously, or I'll have to start treating you like a child." We both laugh and then say goodnight.

The next day flies by as does the rest of the week. I caught myself doodling on my notebook. The paper is covered with hearts and his name. ***Conner***. I wonder why I haven't heard from him all week. Then I remember we never exchanged phone numbers. That has to be it.

To my surprise, he wasn't the only one absent in my life. The stalker was only a memory now. I haven't needed rescuing all week. The stalker has finally moved on, and my life is back to normal. Normal is good, but normal could also be boring. I am back to reading, watching movies, and surfing the net. My thoughts are consumed with calling Henry and talking him out of Conner's phone number. I don't know what to do. Thank. Goodness. It's. Friday. I have the whole weekend to figure things out.

Friday night is a blur. I spend it doing my usual. The latest erotica I choose isn't holding my attention like I'm use to, but then nothing compares to my exotic week with Conner. I flip through the channels on the television and nothing catches my eye; same thing online…*nothing new there either*. The temptation to call Hawaii is overwhelming, so I call it a night and go to bed. As much as I *need* to talk to

Conner, he has to contact me first. Only then will I know for sure that he feels the same intoxicating feelings I do.

In the blink of an eye but really twelve hours later, morning has shown up and I wake up feeling overly rested—almost like I slept too hard. There had been no dreams to wake up to and reminisce about. Oh how I wish he would have consumed my dreams.

I miss him. His beauty. His smile. His manhood longing to enter my forbidden cavern. I laugh at the thought, but it's true. My private place is *forbidden* to anyone other than him. What if that is why he hasn't called me? Perhaps, my virginity is too much for him. Maybe he longs to be with a woman more experienced than I am. I remember our window shopping and his heated gaze…I shake off the thought. That cannot be it. He respects me for waiting…*doesn't he?*

I grab my tablet off the end table, and I cannot believe it is almost noon. I go straight to my favorite social networking site, and there is a new request along with a new message. I gasp at the memory of the last one. The stalker. Maybe it's him again.

I put the device down—refusing to check it just yet. Getting out of bed, I head to the bathroom, and within minutes I'm back sitting cross-legged on top of my blanket. The tablet is in my lap, and I'm staring at the screen. Here goes nothing.

With one eye open and the other closed…I touch the icon.

My heart races with excitement. I can't believe what I am seeing. It is Conner. I accept the request immediately—checking out every detail from his comments to his albums. He is absolutely stunning.

Refusing to give jealousy a reason to rouse up and show her ugly head, I haven't searched into Conner's past via the web. I have had only a memory of his gorgeous face, and now my eyes are looking at him. His picture is current, and I recognize the hot pink polo shirt he wore the last day I was with him. Then my eyes are drawn to his background photo. It is the luau, and *we* are in it. Conner is standing behind me with his arms around my waist. The hula dancers and fire knife dancers are behind him. We were dancing to a slow song, and I remember it well. It was an amazing night, and he shared it with me. My eyes are drawn back to the message that I haven't opened. I click it and pray it is from him. It is.

Conner Dawson   **07-13-13**
8:32 am

Hey, baby girl.

I hope you are doing well. I'm sorry I haven't contacted you before now, but there were complications with Hillary. She is okay, so don't worry. That aside—I miss you.

I long to hold you in my arms and kiss that sweet mouth of yours. First things first though. I'm going to be busy the next few weeks, but as soon as I get the chance I am Nashville bound. Dad is working on a huge project, and he wants me to head it up. As much as I want to come there now, I have a responsibility to him. Please understand.

I want to see you. Hell, I need to see. You have consumed my thoughts. I can't stop thinking about that beautiful sexy body of yours. You are the first thing I think about when I wake up, and the last thing before I go to bed....and as far as my dreams go...well, use your imagination. They have been incredible...lol—hope that leaves you smiling. I gotta go take care of business. I'll be thinking of you. *wink*

P.S. I need to hear your voice. Either call me or give me your number. My cell is 817-555-2314.

My face is hurting; intense smiling can do that to a person. He misses me as much as I miss him. I have to message him back, but what do I say? *Come to me now and forget your dad.* Oh yeah. I'm sure that will go over well. My words have to be perfect.

7-13-13

My hero,

Finally, you come to my rescue—lol. No, seriously though. I'm happy to hear your sister is okay. I have missed you more than I could ever explain in a message, and I wish you were here. My body longs for your touch, and I'm getting hot and bothered just thinking about it. What have you done to me, Mister Dawson?

I will count the days until I see that sexy self of yours again in person. Until then, I have my dreams, and you are the star attraction. Mmmmmmm. Now, you use your imagination, and I bet you'll be right. Hope that leaves you hard and thinking of me. My cell number is 901-455-1021.

XOXOXO

P.S. Waiting to be rescued...again ☺

I hit enter.

"Breathe girl...breathe!" I demand myself. It's not too much. Just enough to let him know you're thinking of him. Yes. Short, sweet, and to the point. I didn't want to sound desperate, and I *don't* think I did.

A little flirtatious flare mixed in with the truth never hurt anybody, right.

Oh heck!

My cell phone is on vibrate, and it's buzzing profusely. The number 817-555-2314 flashes across the screen. It is

Conner. It is him. I have to get it together and answer the phone, but suddenly my breathing is more erratic than ever. Crap! Breathe, Hannah, Breath! My inner self now calling the shots.

In through my nose—out through my mouth.

Slow and easy. I swipe the bar.

"Hello."

My heart is racing, and I think I am going to hyperventilate. I try to steady my breathing as I hear him taking long deep breaths of his own. They get more rapid as he says my name in a raspy voice that makes me steaming hot.

"Hannah, baby girl, are you home?"

"Yes," I answer him.

"Great. Are you alone?" he asks, his tone somewhat mischievous.

Where is he going with this?

"Yes." I listen closely as he hears my response. His moaning is such a turn on.

"Even better. Now tell me what you are wearing."

I look down at my saggy pajama pants, but I don't think that's what he wants to hear. I lie, but *only* because I think I know what game he is playing. My subliminal essence giggles with delight thinking about how much fun this is going to be.

"Only my panties," I whisper.

He breathes harder—*panting even.*

"Take them off," he demands.

Without hesitation, I do what he tells me. I pull off my bottoms; taking my thongs down with them.

"Okay. They are off." I look around the room as if someone's watching, but the only eyes on me are the ones I see coming from my reflection in the mirror. *This is so freaking kinky.* I love it. I shiver anticipating his next demand.

"Good, baby girl. Now listen and do as you're told." He gasps...taking a deep breath—letting it out slow and easy.

"I'm listening." I cannot believe he has such control over me. I never would have imagined me doing this. I guess he's bringing the woman out in me that's been hiding somewhere deep inside my body...*craving to come out and play.*

I am that woman.

Is it getting hot in here or is it just me?

"I want you to lie on your bed, and put your phone on speaker. Once you do that, listen carefully, and do just what I tell you. Do you understand, Hannah?"

"Yes, sir, Mister Dawson," I say.

I do it.

"Okay. You are on speaker."

He's breathing even harder, and I can only imagine that thick voluptuous cock of his all wrapped up in his hands. He's horny, and he's building up a climax as we speak.

"That's a good girl, Hannah." His voice is like a hot-caramel-fudge-creamy-delight; sweet and thick and *ah*— driving me crazy and making me hungry for an orgasm.

"Now, spread your legs apart, and put one hand on your heated-twat and the other one on your breasts," he demands.

I pull my T-shirt over my head and do as I'm told. I let out a hot breath, hoping the sound alone will allow his skin to crawl with desire.

"Okay, they are there," I murmur.

I can't help but take a second to squeeze my legs together, feeling the pleasure building up down between my thighs, and quickly I open them back up.

"That's good, baby girl," he pauses, taking a deep breath and letting out a sensuous moan. *"Ah, ah, mmmm...*are you as hot as I am?" he says, seducing me intensely with his groans.

"Uh, huh," I mumble the words.

"Good, I'm glad. Want me to make it all better?"

"Uh, huh," I mumble again.

He laughs, rough and sexy like.

"Okay. I want you to massage your boobs, around and around, until you feel like you're going to scream for mercy;

one hand on each," he says, his voice getting lower…deeper and more seductive.

Tearing my hand away from down there, I do as I'm told.

"Ah…Conner, I'm doing it…*you're doing it*." I close my eyes, imagining him here with me. His heavy breathing is interrupted by the slapping sound of his hand gliding up and down his manly pride—*now I'm really turned on.* The sensation is spreading through me like wild fire and only an orgasm will put it out.

I cannot help but gasp.

He lets out a low growl. "Okay, now lick your forefinger and your thumb; get them good and wet and then tug on your nipples."

Okay—*good and wet.*

"Ah. I'm tugging." My breathing is more erratic than ever, and it's all because of him. He is doing this to me. With my eyes still closed, I imagine him lying here with me. I can almost feel the heat of his body next to mine…the thought makes my sex suck in all on its own. "Mmmmm…*It. Feels. So. Good.*" I whisper between barely parted lips; making him fully aware of how turned on I really am.

He growls between heated breaths. "I'm glad. Now, trail your fingers down your body, moving the tips in tiny circles, making your skin sensitive to your own touch—*my touch.* Keep heading south until you've found that hidden treasure buried between your legs."

Wasting no time, my fingers skip over tiptoeing and race to the finish line.

"I've found it." I say breathlessly.

"Fabulous, baby girl…now spread those lips apart and massage your clit. Imagine it's me doing it. I want to hear you come with me. Push your fingers inside your heated womanhood, and tell me how hot you are." I groan. He groans.

"I'm so freaking hot." I whisper the words, but I know he hears me.

"Good. Now rub it harder. Faster this time, but take a moment to move your fingers in and out of your hole; soak up the juices. Now, give your throbbing clit what it needs. Rub it baby...*just like I would.* Do it until you come, and tell me when you do. Come for me, Hannah."

I rub it faster and faster. The heat is building up, and I'm right where he wants me. I'm at the edge of no return.

"I wish I was there to lick you to ecstasy."

That's it. His words make it happen.

My body twitches; shaking to the rhythm of sweet bliss as I begin to climax.

"Oh. Yes. Yes. I'm coming. Ah, Conner."

My womanhood is exploding, and I can hear his breathtaking moans as his joystick slides in and out of his tightened grip—he's finding his release with me. My body tenses with every throbbing jerk of my orgasm. It's hard, and it's delicious. I never would have thought phone sex could be so satisfying.

Breaking me out of my orgasmic trance, his voice is the soft landing I need to spiral back down to reality.

"Hannah. Are you okay, baby girl?" His breathing heavy, but controlled.

"Uh, huh," I say breathlessly.

He laughs at my breathless answer.

"Good. I have a little mess to clean up, so I'll talk to you later. Okay." He sounds so *in control,* and I'm left limp...floating on cloud nine.

"Uh, huh," I whisper.

He laughs again, and then there is only silence.

Spellbound and satisfied—*I think I like this side of him;* good looking, rich, sophisticated, respected, and *naughty.* He really is the man of my dreams.

Chapter 17

Wrapped in a blanket of bubbles, I realize I'm leaning against the shower wall instead of standing beneath the running water. I can't help myself. The memory of what just transpired has consumed me and shows on my lips…I can't quit smiling. That man is getting in my head and turning my world upside down. Even thousands of miles away, he knows how to bring out *the woman hiding inside the girl*—and I hope he never stops.

Rinsing the lather away, I turn off the faucet and climb out of the tub—body cleansed—mind still in the *"gutter"*, but nevertheless, I am freshly showered and dressed in no time.

I leave the bathroom and make my way to the kitchen with nothing but the man behind the call on my mind; that was crazy. Just goes to show he is a kinky hunk-of-burning-playboy after all. I bet he can't wait to pull out the big guns; balls and chains—whips and handcuffs—cinnamon flavored massaging oils. *This could get interesting.*

I shake my head and pour myself a cup of coffee; remembering that I'm a *still* a virgin and not quite an experienced woman. Though, it is only smart for a girl to prepare herself for what may come…and I have to admit, it is a yummy notion.

Pulling my thoughts away from a hot-enticing love affair, I focus on the real world. I decide to tidy up around the apartment, and then visit with my mom. Maybe we can go shopping. Her birthday is coming up, and I would love to buy her a new outfit.

I make the call, and she is more than anxious to go.

After taking an hour to get ready, I'm out the door. The light flow of traffic made it even easier to navigate my way to her house, and I'm there in no time. Two miles north and three turns right…only one red light in between the tree-line streets, and I'm back at the place I grew up.

Beep. Beep.

I lay on my horn letting her know I am outside. She is ready and waiting with her purse in her hand, and she is out the door and in my car within seconds. "I'm so excited, Hannah. We haven't had a mother-daughter day out in ages."

She is right. Suddenly, I feel like a horrible daughter.

"Me too, mom," I say, smiling her way—my heart leaping into my throat. "Where shall we start?"

"Let's eat first. I'm famished!" she exclaims.

I knew it. She always did like to eat first, and then walk off the extra calories while shopping. We have lunch at a quaint little sandwich shop that serves her favorite. A delicatessen right across the street from where we will be spending the rest of our afternoon. "I would like a Chicken BLT on a toasted bun, hold the mayonnaise—add a smidgen of ranch, and that will do it." That is exactly how she orders it, while I opt for a bowl of their famous broccoli and cheese soup. As I sit across from this awe-inspiring woman, I admire her heart-of-gold. Despite the fact that she never remarried, her love affair with people keeps a smile on her face...and also very busy. If she's not working at her second job that she no longer *has to have,* she's volunteering at the local mission helping to feed the hungry. As awesome as that is, I still long for her to find that special someone to grow old with—Landon and I aren't always going to be around, and one day she will get tired.

"This sandwich is delicious. I haven't had one in ages," she says.

Smiling her way, I watch as she dabs the dressing away from the corner of her mouth. We both laugh.

"The soup is pretty good too." I sip from my spoon...blowing before I do.

Lunchtime passes quickly, and now it's time to move on to the fun part. Shopping. We go to the mall—checking out the sales in some of our favorite stores. I'm in the dressing room and mom is two doors down. I have just slipped out of a stunning black dress and find myself longing to have Conner's approval. While debating whether or not I should buy it, my phone beeps. I have a text, and it's from him—the man who never leaves my thoughts. I smile, open it, and read his words.

I miss you already.

I love it. He wants me. I look in the mirror at my half naked body, and I long for his touch. The only clothing adorning my hour glass figure is my black lace panties and matching strapless bra. I can't resist—*it's my turn to play.*

I take a picture of myself, replying with a forward and attach the provocative photo. I know that will make him *rise* to the occasion. I laugh at my carefree thoughts. This is so much fun.

Shopping with my mom, and you caught me undressed, Mister Dawson ;) I miss you more.

I wonder if that's too much. I don't care. I love putting him on the edge of escape. If that picture doesn't do it, I wonder what will.

He's quick to respond.

HANNAH STONE. I am going to DEVOUR you the next time I see you. Be ready.

Mmmmm. The thought of him with his mouth on my womanhood enters my mind, and I'm throbbing at a very inconvenient moment…he's so bad.

Sir, you are going to make me do things I shouldn't do in a dressing room. So, please, watch your mouth, and be a good boy.

I smile and hit send.
Within seconds, my phone beeps again.

*Oh, I'm good alright. I can help you if
you want me to...lol.*

Did he just *lol* me? Does he really think I would do that here? I remember our morning rendezvous, and I know he's serious. As scrumptious as it sounds, he better settle down—things are about to get wild. My nipples are hard, and my lion's den is heated and growling for attention. What is this sexy, vivacious man doing to me?

*Down boy. Down. Not now, maybe later
;)*

*We'll, okay then. But if you're feeling a
little naughty, be sure to send me a video. I
would love to watch you make yourself
come.*

I'll keep that in mind, Mister Dawson

*Eyes on the lookout...hand ready, Tiger
Boy is on the prowl; ready and growing as we
speak→growling over here*

*Sounds tempting, you big bad tiger you;
is there anything else that turns you on that
you might want to share? Uh-oh...Gotta go,
we'll finish this later...mom's outside the door.
By the way, I like this side of you. It makes me
want to get on all fours, purr like a kitty, and
rub up against your leg or something. Later,
Mister D.*

*If only you knew, Miss Stone, if only you
knew...and I'll hold you to it—the finishing
and the rubbing.*

Playtime is over, and I dress hurriedly. That's the third time mom's said my name. There's a knock on my dressing room door. "Hannah, are you in there darling?"

I open the door all hot and bothered, and she can tell. "Honey, are you okay? You're so red." She puts her hand on my forehead checking to see if I have fever.

"Mom. I'm okay. I worked up a sweat trying on all those dresses. That's all." I lie through my teeth and never reveal the truth. The truth is the sexiest freaking man alive wants to make me come like it's nobody's business. Right here in the dressing room.

"You just look so flushed. Why don't you sit down and rest a while."

I roll my eyes. How dare Conner Dawson turn me on while I'm with my mother? Ugh! "I'm okay mom. Let's go checkout." I take the dress she chose out of her hand, insisting to pay for it.

The rest of the afternoon flies by. We shop until it is time for the matinee to start—deciding to watch a movie. It is the perfect ending to our wonderful day together…then it's time to drop her off and go back to my lonely apartment and an even lonelier bed.

My dreams are consumed of him. I wake up before sunrise, and I'm starving for more of yesterday's dirty talk. It was hot, sensuous, and made me feel so alive. Then I remember our time together in Hawaii.

A naughty grin spreads across my face thinking about the scrumptiousness of it all. If he can make me come that hard with words and fingers, I can only imagine what he will do to me with that lengthy mouthwatering cock of his. I think about how thick and seductive it gets when he loses control around me. My cooch is longing for it now. The thought of it going in and out of me, filling me with so much manliness length. I'm going to get off just thinking about it. I realize my virtue may be in trouble. I'm not sure how much longer I can hold on to it with *him* in my life.

I really truly want him. All of him—*inch by inch*—head to toe. Great! Now I'm turned on and craving a much needed orgasm. My kitty is purring and demanding to be rubbed. *Guess I better be a good girl and take care of her.*

I reach under the bed in search of my little vibrating wonder, and I'm startled by the knocking at the door. *Seriously,* right now—at this hour. Who could be here this early in the morning? I look at my phone, and it's not even five o'clock—4:27 to be exact. I grunt a sigh of disappointment, and I make my way to the living room.

I look out the peep hole, and I can't make out who it is. There is a tall, masculine silhouette, but not a glimpse of the mystery man hiding behind it. It's still dark, and now I'm freaking the hell out. Who can it be?

I run to the kitchen table and grab my pepper spray from my purse. Then I grab the baseball bat my brother gave me out of the closet.

There's the pounding at the door again.

Bang! Bang! Bang!

Suddenly, the stalker consumes my thoughts, and I start to hyperventilate.

Crap. My phone—where the hell is my phone? I'm searching frantically for that little piece of technology that could help save my life. I remember now. I left it charging on the end table in my bedroom. I run to get it, and I dial Landon's number. I don't have the chance to hit send because that's when I hear it.

That voice…could it be? Can it really be him?

"Hannah. It's me, Conner. Please open up," he says, his voice low but desperate.

The second I hear him say my name, my heart jumps for joy. That warm tingly feeling that I have come to love consumes my body, and as overwhelmed as I am that he's here…I'm shocked just the same.

I walk back to the living room and turn on the outside light. It is him. I unlock the deadbolt, and he swings open the door before I have a chance to turn the knob—kicking it shut as he enters.

He embraces me with his strong masculine arms and has his lips on mine before I have the chance to say hello. It is the most seductive mouthwatering kiss ever; full of passion and hot, sensuous, sexual desire. I return it with the same force, and he knows I'm ready for him to keep his promise. My womanhood is begging to be devoured. I can feel the beat of his heart as it pounds away next to mine…his erratic breathing slipping between his pursed lips.

"I want you, Hannah. I can't get you out of my head…"

His mouth still pressed against mine, my girly stuff shimmers with delight as his bulge presses forward.

"I'm going to make you come, Hannah…so hard, you're going to beg me to stop," he threatens.

His threat sends my clit into a sweltering frenzy...*damn I hope he keeps his promise.*

Quickly, he lifts me in his arms with one arm supporting my back and the other beneath my ass. His luscious, voluptuous mouth is on mine, and his teeth are gently biting away at my lips. He carries me down the hallway in search of my bedroom. Shit! My virginity. What do I do? I'm not prepared…

He kicks open the last door of the room on the left. He's found it. My room. My bed. He's hard and ready, and I'm scared and turned on at the same time. Could this really be it? Do I give it all to him and say the hell with my wedding night? My gift to the man I will spend the rest of my life with.

I want him to be that man. I'm so ready to do *it* with him. I want to feel him stretch the lips of my coochie apart as he enters me slowly—starting with the thick head of his manliness. I want to feel him tremble with passion when he enters where no other man ever has. The tightness of my virtue will be more than he can handle, but he will not lose control. I know that he will *rescue me gently*. He will take away my virtue, and I will no longer long for what I have been missing; hardcore passionate love making with a man who leaves me utterly breathless. Conner is that man.

While his tongue dips into my mouth, swirling around and around, my senses are yanked back to reality when I feel him stripping my clothes off. He throws every last piece of clothing on the floor beside the bed. This man does not play around, and he does not lie. He *really* is going to devour me.

I'm naked and my body is longing to be taken. He lays me on the bed and frees himself of the clothes that covers all of his sumptuous sex appeal.

His dark gaze gives his arousal away, but if that isn't enough his erection is letting it be known. My eyes are staring at his crotch, and my womanhood is screaming *please enter with caution*. His cock is so hard, and there's so much of it that he has a hard time freeing it from the black pinstripe boxers he is wearing. Finally, it springs forth—his briefs now falling to the floor. My eyes widen and a wicked grin crosses his lips.

My kitty tightens up and throbs at the same time. He crawls on top of me and grinds *it* all over my sex. He moves up and down my thighs. All while looking me straight in my eyes and not saying a word. He watches me close, wanting me to give him some kind of a sign. He's waiting for me to tell him to stop, but I can't find the words. His intense gaze gives up, and he focuses on the body beneath his.

He teases me for what seems like an eternity, and then down he goes. I feel the heat of his breath, blowing slowly while he nuzzles at my breast; the tip of his nose circling my areola— gently licking and biting my nipples until they have perfect erections of their own. His expert hands have spread my legs apart, and I'm wide open and waiting.

His fingers glide up and down my body, and my hands roam up and down his backside. I can feel his body shiver with desire as he groans into my bosom...he's fighting off the urge to slam into me at this very moment.

"Damn it, Hannah...I want you so bad..." and he bites me hard—once, twice, almost a third time but he stops himself— allowing his teeth to gently graze my nipple this time.

I gasp as he trails his fingers through the soft curls of my well-groomed bush, looking for the cavern he came here to explore. Slowly, he pushes one finger inside me; gently, passionately, and exactly how I like it. In goes the second...he begins thrusting—causing my juices to flow. I gasp as he takes turns fondling my clit with the perfect rhythm, and then he moves his fingers back inside me, making me wetter with every push.

"That's my girl. Show me how much you want me," he murmurs.

I can't say a word. All I can do is moan with anticipation.

He moves his luscious tongue around and around, twirling in circles and making my girly stuff dizzy. *"I'm down here!" she yells.* My clitoris is throbbing and needs to find relief soon. I feel like I'm on the edge of a major sexual explosion, and I realize he is so much better at this than I am.

His mouth is moving slowly away from my breasts, and his tongue circles down and around my navel. Over and over again he massages my kitty with his long competent fingers; giving it his undivided attention. Such expertise. He knows exactly what I want and *how* I want it.

His appetite increasing, he's yearning for a taste. His mouth moves lower, along with the rest of his body. Before I know it, he's got my legs bent with my knees in the air, and his hand is no longer teasing me...it's gone. I rise up to look at him, and he's looking back at me with an intense hungry gaze. He raises his hand to his lips, gently licking each of his fingers, and then I see nothing but the top of his head. It is in between my legs, and his tongue is devouring my innocence.

"Oh...Conner...yes...that's...it," I moan. My body responds to every flick of his tongue...swirl upon swirl, he's driving me crazy—my back arching and lifting in the air. Running my fingers through his hair, I find myself holding his head in place. I don't want him to stop. I gasp. He sucks me gently. I call out his name again and he ravishes me even more, gliding his tongue over and over my throbbing and needy clitoris.

He pushes his lengthy fingers eagerly into my womanhood; feeling me as I'm on the verge of a climacteric explosion. Faster and faster he pushes, *in and out—again and again.* This is it. I'm ready to come, and it's going to be hard.

"Oh...baby...here I come!" The words escape my mouth, and he stops licking and starts sucking my swollen throbbing clit. The man is sipping the orgasm right out of me.

My body trembles...jerking with each throbbing orgasmic pulse. I squeeze the sheets with each one of my hands and arch my back even higher than before; unraveling away in his mouth...I can't help myself...the words have left my lips while my head was in the clouds. "Please, Conner...stop...I can't...*ah,* no...don't stop...please don't stop," I whisper breathlessly while spiraling down from the orgasm to top all others. It's massive—pure satisfaction is coursing through my veins.

The climax may be drifting away, but the arousal is still there...swirling down deep inside my womanhood. Slowly, the rhythm of my heartbeat settles calmly between my legs, and I long to give him what he just gave me...little do I know, he's got something else in mind.

I'm shocked at what he does next, but I have to say it turns me on all over again. He's on his knees, and he's going to find his release all over my breast. He's stroking his long, thick manliness right in front of me.

Seconds later, his manhole is spurting hot wet semen all over my nipples, and he's rubbing it in with the head of his cock. His head is tilted back—his hair is swaying back and forth from the ceiling fan right above him. A few moans, growls, and deep breaths later...he's done, and I didn't have to lift a finger.

His body is exhausted, and he lays it right on top of mine—his naked body on top of my naked body. There is nothing between us but the result of the massive orgasm he just had right before my eyes. It's soaking into his skin as much as it is mine. He's breathless, and we're both satisfied.

"I told you to be ready," he whispers.

"Yes you did. I just thought I had a few weeks to prepare myself." I smile.

"I'm full of surprises, Hannah," he chuckles breathlessly.

I rub my fingers in his hair and realize I have some of *it* *on* my hand. "Are you in the mood for a shower, Mister Dawson? I think *we* have a mess to clean up."

He rises up, and the stickiness pulls from my skin and clings to his. "Yes, Miss Stone. I think we both could use a little soap and water."

Our laughter fills the air.

We climb off the bed, and he follows behind me into the adjoining bathroom. I leave myself wide open for what happens next. His strong masculine hand smacks my ass, leaving a passionate sting and causing me to let out a playful scream.

"I couldn't resist baby girl," he laughs.

Chapter 18

The flowing hot water cascades all over our naked bodies, and I can't believe I am standing here with him. He is real—every sensuous inch of him. The heartthrob before me is just as human as I am—money, power, a thriving business doesn't change that. He's the whole package, and he's here hiding away in my world for a change.

Peeking back at me, he sees that I'm admiring his perfect body—*I can't help myself.* Head to toe, he rids himself of any evidence of the finish that escaped his body just minutes before, and the man looks sexy even doing that.

"See something you like, Miss Stone?" he asks. His smooth talking words rushing over me like the hot water coming out of the spout above.

"You could say that," I respond.

Actually, the word coming to my mind is more like madly-crazy-mind-blowing-wow-kind-of-LOVE what I see. *Is that even a word?* Inwardly, I giggle at my girly stuff as she agrees. *"If it's not, it is now."* And *we* continue gazing at his tight ass…his muscular physique…the whole package.

Rinsing away the last of the lather covering that buff body of his, he gapes at me with wanting eyes. He grabs the loofah from my hand, and starts circling my breast with seductive swirls. Over and over again, up and down my waist…down to my toes and up between my thighs—stealing a kiss from each side before covering them with soap.

Letting the loofah fall from his grip, he massages the suds into my skin with his bare-hands. Moving slowly up my body, he allows his fingers to rest down there…circling my tiny hairs and cleansing the cavern between my legs. The moment is as steamy as the room itself, and damn if I'm not craving what he just gave me minutes before.

He lets the water rinse away the bubbles from my body, but he never removes his hand.

"You don't mind if I make you come again, do you?" he asks in a rough sexy whisper.

It doesn't matter if I mind...my body is begging for it.

"Please do," I plead.

I gasp at his wandering fingers.

"I'm glad to hear you say that. I would have done it either way."

A passionate sting causes my sex to clench in. He's there...gliding...pushing...swirling a perfected path to an orgasmic bath. My pulse races as he leans in, taking a mouthful of my breast and sucking the sweet pleasure right out of me. Blissful, breathless, heated words leave my lips as he tugs away at my nipples and at my clit...he's done it to me again, and I'm exploding into a million pieces of satisfaction.

"Oh...Sir...*I...love...the...way...you...do...that.*" I say breathlessly.

Gently biting his way up to my mouth...demanding words finally leave his lips—"I'm glad you think so, now bend over because I'm fixing to come all over your ass."

My eyes widen and my cheeks suck in...the ones on my backside that is. He sees the surprise in my face and soothes me with his gentle hands.

"Don't worry, Miss Stone...I know you're not ready for that—*yet.*"

I gasp at the thought, but I can't resist his instructions—trusting him with my most private area, I bend over. Grabbing a hold of my ankles, I feel his erection sliding up and down my crack. Teasingly, he allows the head of his cock to rub up against my pink-puckered-ravine, and his stroke intensifies. Breathlessly and full of passion, his moans echo among the shower walls. I can feel the heat of his finish flow over me just like he said it would—spurt by spurt as though there is no end to the orgasm letting loose.

"*Oh, Hannah*...I can't wait until the day I do that inside of you," he growls.

His words alone make me want to come all over again.

Taking a moment to come back to his senses, he finishes what he started. Cleansing away the evidence and taking time to wash my hair.

How does he do it? With every touch I crave him. Every look I desire him. Each kiss I thirst for more. He is the personification of power, passion, even life—and right now, I am the victim of all that he wants. *I wouldn't have it any other way.*

He grabs the shower head and rinses my body clean.

"All done," he says.

Conner turns off the water and out we go. I'm cold and he knows it. Not only am I shivering from the cool air, but I'm overwhelmed with the feelings that are consuming my body—most of all, my heart. It is full of emotion—infatuation, obsession, mostly *love*; a strong, undying, and irresistible kind of love that makes me feel so alive.

My thoughts are interrupted by his words.

"Let's get you dried off."

He takes a towel from the shelf and wraps it around me.

"Thank you," I whisper.

Suddenly, flashes of our first night together flood my mind. We were getting ready to walk along the beach, and he placed a blanket over my shoulders to keep the chill from invading my skin— now here he is showing me the same sort of care.

Conner is making all of my dreams come true. It seems as though I have been waiting an eternity for a man to come along and complete me. I have never felt as complete as I do now—he has to be that man. I know now I never really loved Kris. He was more of a trophy I could call mine. He was easy on the eyes but nothing like the real live essence before me. Thank goodness I had enough sense to protect my virtue from a womanizer like him. Finally, I have a face to put with the man who will unlock the treasure that lies between my legs. Conner Dawson will be that man.

Here we go again. I'm in his arms and over his shoulders this time. He runs to the bedroom and gently lays me on the unmade bed. Lying down beside me, we are now face to face.

"You are so beautiful, Hannah. Inside and out," he says, propping his elbow on the pillow and resting his head on his hand.

He moves my wet hair from out of my eyes and glides his index finger slowly down my face. The softness of his fingertip lines my lips, and I can't stop what I do next. My mouth opens slightly. My tongue moves out between my lips, and I begin taking full advantage of the moment.

I entice him more and more with the movements of my tongue. Up and down his finger I go. Every wet, moist, teasing flick makes him gasp and wanting more. I suck hard, and I bite gently. He's on the edge and loving it. His breathing is erratic, and his manhood is crawling up my waist. The hotter he gets, the more he grows. The tip of his penis is barely an inch away from my breast, and once again, I'm aware of how *huge* he is.

I want to please him—just like he did me. I pull away, preparing myself for my next move. I can't resist the yearning desire any longer. My body is screaming to please him...*every* inch of him. I've lost all self control. I'm straddling him within seconds. My heated womanhood is in control. What lies beneath it is pure joy. I can feel his manliness jerking and wanting to crawl inside me.

My erratic behavior is interrupted by heavy breathing and a raspier than usual voice. "What are you doing, Hannah?"

My eyes meet his.

"I've never wanting something more than what I want right now."

He looks at me with a craving that only I can satisfy.

"What do you *want*?" he asks, his eyes growing darker as he hangs on to my every word.

"Only you, Conner. Only you." My voice is raspy as is his. He can't hold back. His mouth is on mine, devouring me like he's been starving for days. He stops briefly, but only to make me long for him even more.

"I want you too, baby. Only you. Always, only you." Our bodies are shaking and craving to be joined at the hips. I know it. He knows it. He flexes his manhood, and every ounce of me knows this is it. He lifts me up, and I'm willing and ready to take in *all* of him. To my surprise, he sets me on the bed with nothing beneath me but the sheet and mattress that it covers. "Not now, Hannah. I will not take your precious virtue just yet."

My heart is racing, and I'm so confused. "I don't understand."

My face is in his strong, masculine hands.

"There is a time and a place for everything, Hannah. This is not ours." He kisses my forehead and wraps his arms around me. My head rests on his chest, and we are soon fast asleep.

Hours pass and it is ten o'clock before I wake up. I quickly look beside me to convince myself it wasn't a dream. There he is. *Sleeping peacefully.* His beauty shines through even with his eyes closed. I don't want to move, but I have to pee like crazy.

As quietly as possible, I slide out from underneath the sheets, and my feet hit the floor. I go to the bathroom to relieve myself, and I debate whether or not I should flush the toilet. I don't want to wake him while he's sleeping, but I refuse to leave it unflushed. Here goes nothing…I close my eyes and hope he doesn't hear it.

I wash my hands and brush away the morning breath that has invaded my mouth. Running my tongue across my teeth, I can taste the leftover cinnamon flavored mouthwash. Smiling at my reflection—I'm a happy girl and a *kissable* one.

I splash my face with cold water…making sure I'm wide-eyed and alert at what I'm about to walk in on.

Turning the knob, I open the door.

"Good morning, beautiful," he blurts out.

I jump.

He's standing there, leaning on the wall with his arms crossed.

"Good morning yourself, sleepyhead," I laugh.

He walks towards me showing off his morning erection, and I stand there pulling my hair up in a ponytail. His mouth closes in on mine. He is so freaking succulent. His mouth moves across my cheek and over my ear. He caresses each and every inch of my lobe; it sends me over the top. I'm covered in heated chill bumps, and then he whispers to me exactly what I'm thinking.

"I'm starving. Let's eat."

Without a word, I smile and look down.

"For bacon and eggs, you sex fend." He laughs and goes to the bathroom to calm down his manliness. The toilet flushes, and I hear the water running. He's brushing his teeth. I guess he found the spare toothbrush I left on the counter for him, or he's using mine; either way, I don't care.

I sit on my bed, waiting on him to come out. He's done. My eyes can't help but wander *there* when he opens the door. The erection is gone, but there is still a massive bulge underneath those boxers. He sees me looking and shakes his head.

"I've created a monster." He reaches for me.

We both laugh.

I take his hand, and we head to the front of the apartment. He goes to the living room in search of a ballgame, while I go to the kitchen. I'm thankful for the open floor plan more than ever right now. I can see him from in here.

"So, how do you like your eggs?" I ask.

He smiles and arches his eyebrows up and down, fast and sexy. "Hot and wet. Just the way I like you."

I laugh and shake my head at his dirty dialect.

"Translated to kitchen talk, I would say that means *over easy*." Looking back at him, I wait on his answer.

"You read my mind, baby girl." He flashes a mischievous grin, and after a second I get it.

Over easy.

"You're a bad boy, Mister Dawson. Just so you know, I can do bad all by myself, but I do kinda like it when you help me." I wink at him.

We laugh at our playful lingo, and I go about cooking—leaving him to his ballgame. I feel very much at home in the kitchen, so I've got the food ready in no time. Ten minutes later that is.

"Breakfast is served." I hand him a plate that adorns two eggs over easy, two slices of bacon cooked to perfection, and a dry piece of toast. He's impressed.

"The girl can cook. I might just have to marry her." He laughs, focusing his attention back on the television screen. My heart drops. I know it's a joke, but I lavish in the pure decadent thought of being Mrs. Conner Dawson. I decide it's time to change the subject. Now.

"So, how did you get away from work?"

He glances my way when I sit in the recliner across from him.

"Dad's preparing me for my future position as President and CEO, so I'm taking full advantage of the role. I changed the meeting for Monday afternoon instead of Monday morning."

He takes a bite out of the crisp bacon.

I'm curious to know why, *like I already don't*, but I want to hear him say it. "And just why would you do that, Mister Boss man?"

He chokes on the orange juice he is drinking; laughing it the rest of the way down. "Do you really have to ask?"

I nod, finishing off a sip of coffee.

"Curiosity is a mean, mean thing, Mister Dawson. Sometimes you just have to know the answer before it kills you." My comment is straight to the point, and he knows it.

He stares at me, reminded of why he made the sudden change.

"Alright, but you asked for it. I was hungry for that tight little *pussy cat* of yours. I had to know what it tasted like, and I couldn't wait any longer."

Crap. He was right. I did ask for it. I'm embarrassed and excited all at the same time.

"Well, okay then. That says it all." A grin spreads across my face as I remember the *early* morning I shared with him.

"So, how much longer do I have you for?"

He looks confused.

"I meant to say, what time is your flight?"

He devours the last bacon strip on his plate; washing it down with the rest of his juice.

"My flight leaves at noon tomorrow."

Yes! That means I have him to myself all day. My girly stuff starts sucking in and out—over and over again, anticipating more bedtime action of course. Conner Dawson and a little kegel workout...wow, I see a major orgasmic moment in my future. I hope he doesn't notice that I'm squirming in my seat; it's his fault my body is acting this way.

Clearing his throat, he gets my attention. "I don't mind getting a hotel if you don't want me to stay the night here."

My jaw drops and my little *exercise* is over. He has lost his mind. "Oh, no, Mister Dawson, you are not leaving my sight until you get on that jet and fly away."

A grin spreads across that perfect face of his; showing off his blinding pearly whites.

He gets up to carry his plate to the sink, but first he takes time to give me a quick peck on the lips.

"That was delicious, and so are *you*."

Damn! There it goes again. My coochie is going to be primed up and ready in no time. His words hit me right down there, sending my little natural reflex into motion. I can almost hear her calling out...*Come and get it!* Closing my eyes, I try to calm the sexual tension that is building in me, and remind myself of why my body is longing for more. It's all because of *him*.

"Why, thank you Mister D."

I hear the water running, and he's washing the dishes. I go to help him, and when we're done the kitchen is cleaner than what it was before I cooked. We leave a spotless room and make our way back into the living room.

Another question is eating at me, and my curiosity once again gets the best of me. Sitting next to him on the couch, I can't resist. "How did you know where I live?"

He picks up his smart phone and waves it at me.

"These little wonders can do just about anything. I put your name in my search engine and there you were, approximately seven miles outside of Nashville. You never told me you lived in Oak Hill. All this time, I thought you lived in Music City."

"Well, you never asked me, Mister Dawson."

He pulls me close, and I lay my head on his lap. *On his lap, of all places.* There it is cushioning my head, and I can't take it. I rise up before *it* does. "So, do you want to get out of here for a little while?"

"What do you have in mind?" he asks.

"I thought maybe we could go shoot some pool or take a walk. It's up to you." He looks good enough to eat, and if I don't get him out in public, I might just take a bite out of him. Figuratively speaking, that is.

"Pool sounds fun. I am a little rusty though." Clearing his throat, he admits there is something he isn't perfect at after all.

"Conner, I promise to take it easy on your balls—if you want me to." I wink at him, and he does the unthinkable. He grabs his sack as though to protect it.

"Please do, Miss Stone. Please do."

I shake my head, laughing until it hurts.

We decide to ride down to Joe's Place in my convertible, since Conner took a taxi to my place from the airport. He's got lots of pool tables there, and the place shouldn't be that crowded on a Sunday afternoon. The drive is about thirty minutes from my apartment, and Conner is full of information. I find out that he and Joe graduated from college together, and they were fraternity brothers. They were inseparable during their college years and have remained friends since graduation—the best of friends as a matter of fact.

We pull up, and I was right. There are only seven cars in the parking lot, and one of them belongs to Joe.

Conner goes in before me.

I decide to text my boss and Baylee to let them know I'll be in tomorrow, but it will be after lunch. My attention is swayed from my phone to the man in the bar. I can hear Joe greet Conner when he walks through the door.

"Well, look whose back. What brings you to Nashville again so soon, my friend?"

Then, I walk in.

Joe laughs and looks at me and then back at Conner. "Oh, I see. Hello, Hannah."

He tilts his head back at us...waving us in.

He's behind the bar and hanging wine glasses upside down in a case above the counter. He's a nice looking man in an intimidating kind of way. He's works out. You can tell by his overly huge biceps—*the ones covered in tattoos*. His ears are both pierced, and he's almost completely hairless. There isn't a strand on his head, none on his face except for his jet-black eyebrows, and I can't help but wonder if he shaves down *there* too. I roll my eyes. *What am I thinking?*

His voice is deep and raspy. He fits in perfectly with this place he calls his. Conner shakes his hand when we make our way to him, and he has two ice cold drinks waiting on us. I look around, and he's the only one working. Kendall is nowhere in sight. Thank goodness. I can't help how I feel about her. That hasn't changed. She isn't on my top list of friends, so it doesn't hurt my feelings that she won't be here to serve us.

We spend the next half-hour talking at the bar, and then we make our way to the game we came here to play. The room is starting to get a little crowded so if we don't get a table now, there may not be one to get.

Conner lays a handful of quarters on the closest one and smiles at me. "That should keep us busy for awhile."

He is right. The afternoon has slipped away and the evening has made an appearance. It is six o'clock already, and the place is full of anxious people ready to party it up. I had forgotten about the Sunday night karaoke crowd that comes in. Oh. Now that would be fun. I can't help but wonder if he would want to join the others, so I just come out and ask.

"Joe is getting ready to start the karaoke sing-off. Are you in the mood for it?"

His eyes bore into me with pure-decadent-gratification, and he says what I want to hear.

"Sure. I'm up to doing anything you want me to do."

I kiss him, and he pulls away showing off a devious smile.

"One stipulation—you have to promise to sing with me," he says wryly.

I gasp, knowing good and well I wasn't blessed with a singing voice.

Wow. Now what do I say?

"I. Think. I. Can. Handle. That." My words bathed in nervous tension...I can barely hold a tune singing in the shower alone, much less in front of a room full of people. I was hoping *he* would sing...not me. I roll me eyes at myself; *the things I get myself into.*

Six people take center stage before we get the chance. While we wait, we dance.

Thirty minutes pass—*it's our turn.* I take a deep breath...he takes my sweaty hand. I'm nervous, and now he knows it.

He leans down, dosing me up with whispered confidence.

"You got this, baby girl...just follow my lead."

The song we chose is a beautiful melody. It is sure to have couples embracing each other on the dance floor, or, if I totally screw it up, Conner and I may be left dodging food, bottles, or whatever else the crowd can get their hands on.

The music starts, and I take a deep breath.

Luckily we both know the words, making it easier to concentrate on each other and not the screen. I love listening to him sing, but I love watching him just as much. He's a very passionate man…on stage and in bed.

My heart is beating to the rhythm of love, and my voice is doing pretty well at carrying a tune…*I can't believe it.* But then again, look who I'm singing with; he's my very own personal comfort zone. I'm so proud of myself for being able to keep up with him. He's got an amazing voice. It is his voice, not mine, that has the room captivated. Just a few more notes and the song will end perfectly, and I'll be able to steal him away for an encore of my very own.

You have got to be freaking kidding!

Right before the last few words leave our lips, it happens—I can't believe what I'm hearing. That unforgettable, badass tone is drowning in redneck tension; causing all eyes to be swayed to *him*. Just hearing his voice makes me wonder how in the world I put up with it for so long, and how in the hell did he sneak in past me?

"Get off of the floor! You suck!" My eyes scan the room searching for him. There he is at a table close to the doorway. It is Kris, and he is drunk.

"I guess he doesn't like a good ole country love song, huh?" Conner says, placing his hand on my back and leading me to our table.

I look at Kris and then at Conner. I have to get him out of here. I know that look on Kris' face. He is in the mood for a fight, and he just found his target.

"I'm ready whenever you are," I say desperately.

Conner looks at me surprised—arching his perfect brow.

"Are you sure?" he asks.

I nod.

"Yes. I'm sure."

"Then let's go," he says dryly.

We get up and head towards the bar, but Joe is swamped with customers. We opt to just wave bye, and Joe waves back.

We aren't even out the door yet, and Kris makes his move. He smacks my ass, and there is no denying it pisses Conner off—royally. His nose flares and his eyes darken. He grabs Kris' hand and has a hold on it so tight you can see the color draining from it.

"What the hell is your problem, dude?" he asks fiercely.

His first instinct is to protect me, and I know that my hero will do just that. I look at his face, and his perfect emerald irises are burning a hole into Kris. His eyes are twitching—his teeth grinding.

"It will do you well to keep your hands to yourself. Now, apologize to the lady, and we will be on our way."

His temper is rising…it's almost like I can see steam coming out of his ears. I've never seen him like this before.

"Go screw yourself, you sorry piece of shit," yells the man that I thought I once knew. *I was so wrong about him.*

Kris jerks his hand out of Conner's powerful hold, and what he yells next catches me off guard. Now, I am the one *royally* pissed.

"How about you keep your hands off of my girl?"

He thrusts his index finger into Conner's chest with hard vigorous hits, and a maddening look engulfs my date's eyes as he pushes it away. I look around the room, and our drama has everyone's attention. Mister Sexy himself is beyond angry, and his eyes are searching me for answers.

My temper flares. *How dare Kris put me in this position?*

"Kris, you know that we are finished! We have been for months. Why will you not leave me alone and let me live my life?" He looks at Conner and back at me. Frustrated, he knows I'm right.

"Get the hell out of my face you teasing little whore. I don't know why I even care. You are not going to open that tight little twat up for anybody anyway."

My jaw drops.

To top it all off, I get a glimpse of Kendall in the corner—laughing and enjoying the show. I cannot believe he just said that, and out of all the people here, she's the only one getting off on it. *How much more pathetic can she be?*

Conner comes to my defense and takes my *ex-loser* down. He throws a right handed punch that sends him across the room, and Joe is waving to us as our cue to leave—now. I can hear him yelling at Kris and telling him to *get out and not come back* until he sobers up.

Fear sets in, and I am scared senseless that I may have just lost the one man I want to keep.

Chapter 19

The drive back starts out quiet, as if I'm all alone. Not only is he pissed, but he's confused, and that makes for an unhappy Conner. I don't know how to break the silence, but I have to. He has to know that Kris means nothing to me.

The craziness of what just happened has put an edge of concern on our newly-found-love-affair. If I lose him now, I swear I am going to give up on love all together. It's not worth all the pain that comes along with all the passion, or maybe it is. Of course it is. He is worth everything, and I will not lose him over that sorry excuse of a man.

My car comes to a screeching halt as I pull off at the nearest barren back-road. Surrounded by tall trees and a gravel road—this is the perfect hideaway to plea my case. Putting my car in park, I leave the engine running and turn to face him.

"Conner, he is my past. Please, don't just sit there—say something, anything," I beg.

Endless moments pass, our thoughts drowning in a raging emotional flood—my heart feels as though it's going to beat out of my chest and his nostrils won't stop flaring. He's breathing hard and trying even harder to figure out what just happened. He needs answers that only I can give him.

As he looks my way, I can see that polished darkness has taken over his vibrant breathtaking irises. He turns back around without saying a word—looking into the black night that is only lit up with the full moon and the stars shining down.

"Please, Conner. You have to trust me."

My eyes are tearing up, and I have no control over what just happened back there, but I do right now. I remove my seatbelt and climb over to sit on his manly lap. Cars are passing by with headlights beaming brightly on the other side of the wooded path, but I do not care. This man is my only concern. My hands are caressing his perfect face and moving it to look directly at me. My eyes are on his, and his mouth is close to mine. So close, I can feel the heat of his tempered breathing—each breath hitting me like a whispering wind.

Gentle and controlled, he's calming down. He is right where I want him but more of where I need him. His urge to destroy the man from my past is settling somewhere far in his mind, and the woman straddling him is getting his undivided attention.

His voice is a mere whisper, with a slight hint of bitterness—but at least he's finally opening up to me. "Hannah, my sweet precious Hannah, I cannot lose you, not now, not ever."

My face is in the palms of his hands, and his fingers are spread across my scarlet-flushed cheeks. My blood is boiling, recalling Kris' earlier actions. *He put this in Conner's head, now it's up to me to get it out.*

"You will never lose me." I confess the undying truth. "I haven't been his for a very long time. I was never *really* his; not the way he wanted me to be."

Taking in a sharp deep breath, I feel his chest expand— and he releases the air just that quick. Exhaling and watching me with those sparkling eyes of his—they're back.

He listens to the words that are coming straight from my heart. There is no denying the truth. The opened windows to my soul say it all. "I never loved him. I didn't know what love was until…"

He shuts me up with a lip-locking kiss that sends tears down my face. Our tongues are entwined, twisted and consuming each other. It's more than being mouth to mouth and drinking each other in. It is being able to taste the pure decadent desire that we have for each other; not to mention the saltiness of my tears that have made a path straight to our lips.

He holds me close, tilting my head to the side and running his mouth along my neck. His gentle nibbling has given way to mouth watering kisses, and before I know it, he is sucking the area right below my ear and close to my nape. *It feels fabulous.* I can't help but quiver from the passion.

My breathing is erratic as he moves his tongue back and forth from my neck to my ear, breathing hot heavy breaths, and making me long to have such splendid attention shown elsewhere. My back arches as his hands slide up my shirt, and his nails bore into my bare skin. He pushes me into him; my breast pressing hard against his bulging chest. His embrace is forceful and welcoming. I don't want him to let go. I never want to know what it feels like for him to not want me. I savor this moment in time and nothing more matters—only the life I want to build with this hardcore passionate man.

He lights the flame that is burning a hole straight to the center of my heart, and his obsession with me is on fire; as well as the sexual tension that is filling the air. It's suffocating us both. I can't help but notice the windows fogging up from the heavy breathing…it's shielding us even more from the oncoming traffic and giving us the private moment we both need.

Fast and furiously, he peels away the halter top that covers my assets and is preventing him from what his lips are searching for. My strapless bra is ripped away, thrown in the back seat, and finally his pursuit is over. He releases my tits and my nipples protrude—anticipating the teasing flicks of his tongue and the sensational suction of his mouth. He's licking and sucking; heating up my very existence by focusing solely on my bosom.

"Oh, Conner," I whisper.

I strip him out of his shirt.

"Oh, Hannah," he growls.

His mouth finds his way back to mine again—nibbling away at my lips and making me love it…*such sweet torture* this man is putting me through. Easing up, he dips his tongue into my mouth. I kiss him harder than before—riding him while we are both fully clothed from the bottom down. The bulge of his manhood caresses my clit over and over again. The sensation of the rubbing back and forth makes me wetter with ever stroke. That is it. I cannot take anymore. One more glide sends me into a forced climax. He holds me as my body quivers from the intensity of the orgasm, and I can't control my hunger.

Gently grazing his lip with my teeth—I bite a little harder. I can't let go. He tastes as good as he feels.

He's done it to me again. I found my release with him.

A few hot breaths later, I release my grip on his mouth. He kisses me gently—on my nose, forehead, and the ruby red cheeks that match my swollen lips. His liberation can wait; I am his only worry.

Resting on his lap, my head now on his shoulder, I continue to spiral down from the climacteric event that just took place—forcing myself to let go of the orgasm that is now lingering in the midst and waiting to resurface.

He runs his fingers through my hair, moving it behind my ear. Softly grinning, a whisper leaves his lips as he leans in closer. "So, how many times does that make for you today?" His soft grin turns to a chuckle. He's found his happy place again, and it's making me come—anyway he can do it.

Lifting my head, I can't help but join him. Our laughter floats through the air, and I'm so thankful we are working our way past the unpleasantness of what took place tonight. Calming down—my laughter now only heard in my words. "I lost count, but thank you for keeping track of my orgasms, Mister Dawson."

"Get use to it, Miss Stone," he promises. "I can't wait to see how many different ways I can make you get off." His hungry eyes give me a glimpse into my future...*and I realize I can't wait either.*

I grab my shirt from the floorboard and put it on—leaving my bra in the backseat. He pulls his shirt over his head, and I slide off of him and back into the driver's seat.

"Let's go baby girl; I hear a cold shower calling my name." He winks at me and places his hand on my neck—up under all of my hair.

The moment is perfect, and then *his* words are haunting my thoughts. Suddenly, I hear Kris' wretched voice echoing in my ears; *teasing whore*—is that what I am? *No! It's not.* I cannot believe he is so selfish that he would put that in my head.

"Conner, are you sure that is all you need?" I ask.

Pulling onto the busy highway, I keep my eyes on the road, but my ears are listening closely to his body language. He speaks, and I hear the way he's breathing. He is in control.

"I want all of you, Hannah. Hell, I *crave* you and *need* you more than anything else, but I will not allow you to give yourself to me just because that ass-wipe put it in your head that you are a tease. I know you better than that."

Only for a second, my right hand leaves the steering wheel, taking hold of his—stealing a gentle squeeze. I'm speechless.

Not another word is spoken the rest of the way home. We are both deep in thought. As I drive, he caresses the back of my neck with tender-loving-care, and I realize I don't know how I have lived my life without him. I feel like he is a part of me and always has been. He was made for me, and I was born to love him. Fate led us to each other, and our future has been locked with destiny's key. Nothing and nobody will tear us apart.

I pull into the parking lot of the small apartment complex, and he gets out of the car.

"Stay put," he says.

The breathtaking, domineering, Mister Dawson himself, struts over to my side and opens the door and holds out his hand. Our fingers interlace, and his squeeze makes me gasp.

Men everywhere should take lessons from this awe-inspiring man. *He really knows how to treat a lady.*

Standing to my feet, he shuts the door behind me.

The summer sound of crickets chirping is interrupted by a nearby dog's bark. Something has startled the four-legged creature, but what? Surely it wasn't us. Our eyes look over the area, trying to steal a glimpse of what set the canine off, but nothing shows itself.

Conner puts his arm around my shoulders.

"Let's get inside," he demands.

Walking side by side, we make our way up the lighted sidewalk, and finally we are inside my apartment. It's late, but that doesn't mean we'll be going to sleep any time soon. Looking down, I notice the hard-on he had is now only a bulge beneath his zipper. *Maybe we will be going to sleep.* Conner has no need for a cold shower any longer; his manliness has given up the fight all on its own. I fight the temptation of feeling bad. Over and over I remind myself...*I am not a tease...I am not a tease.*

"I'm going to grab something to drink. I'll be there in a minute," I whisper.

I go to the fridge, and he goes to shower anyway.

Great...cold bottled water—but I need it ice cold.

After pouring it over a glass full of frozen cubes, I guzzle a huge drink before walking out of the kitchen to calm my unquenchable thirst. I didn't realize how thirsty I was. I guess that little workout in the car dehydrated me a little. I smile remembering what he did to me with my panties still intact. That man really is crazy good at everything.

I take another drink while leaning over to turn on the stereo—flipping through the songs until I find the perfect station. Soft music, a good-looking man, and a comfy bed—screams romance if I do say so myself.

Grinning ear to ear, my heart flutters along with my belly. I never knew love could feel this good. I hear the bathroom door open, and his footsteps are tiptoeing to my bed. Listening as he climbs in, tells me that's my cue to shut out the lights and head that way.

Standing in the doorway, admiring the view, I'm consumed by his beauty.

"You look pretty good lying in my bed, Mister Dawson."

"I would look even better if you were lying next to me, Miss Stone."

I purr like a kitten.

"In a minute, Mister D, it's my turn to shower—I won't be long."

I share my drink with him, and off I go.

Faster than the water running over my sweat-drenched body, I'm clean and smelling divine within moments—fresh breath included. I jump out of the tub, drying off in swift motions using the same towel he did.

I breathe in, inhaling his scent.

Choosing to slip on his T-shirt instead of my robe, I make my way to the man waiting on me. His face lights up when he sees me enter in the room wearing nothing but his shirt.

"You look damn good wearing my T-shirt, baby girl, but I think we both know you will look better out of it."

His words alone are tugging at the material and making my body long for his. "I think so too." I agree and pull it over my head; showing off my bare naked body and causing his body to react—his hard-on is back and standing at attention.

Taking the glass off the nightstand, he takes a huge gulp of the ice water. *Suddenly, he's hotter than he was just a minute ago.*

I climb in bed, skin on skin with the man of my dreams—and he disappears beneath the sheets.

A sudden chill sends goose bumps racing all over my body, and it's not from the air conditioner. It's coming from the ice in his mouth that is trailing all over my breasts, my belly, and above my freshly-groomed hairline.

I wiggle beneath him as he hovers over me.

He's managed to move my arms over my head, and he's removed the ice from his mouth. With one hand gripping my wrists, his eyes grip my heart.

"Do not pull away...do you understand, Hannah?" he asks in a low demanding voice.

I stare at him hard. He's serious.

"I understand," I whisper.

"Good girl...if you do...oh, baby girl," he growls. *"If you do*—I will bend you over, spank that perfect ass of yours, and I will make you beg for mercy."

Damn, if that didn't send a tingle straight to my womanhood.

He stares at me.

"I won't pull away," I promise.

His manliness jerks—begging to be touched.

I grab hold as he maneuvers his body around to where his head is now in between my thighs—his cock only inches away from my mouth. I want a taste, but what if...*ah,* my bottom lifts as he opens me up—teasing me with the ice in his mouth and shocking my clit into swelling anyway. *I wasn't pulling away...I was lifting up.* He's a big boy...surely he knows the difference.

I focus my attention on *it*—gripping tighter as he flexes between my curled fingers.

I stroke him once, twice, three times, and that's all it takes—he's spurting all over me, and I'm not too far away. Between the heat of his breath and the coldness of his mouth—the sensation is a perfect blend. I'm coming before I know it, and he's drinking me in until he's had enough.

Returning to my side, he grabs the towel that I had laid at the end of the bed. Gazing my way, he wipes away the finish from my bosom.

"You listen well, Hannah. I appreciate that, but I was hoping to bend you over and hear you beg."

I exhale.

He laughs.

"So, how many times does *that* make?" he chuckles.

Rolling my eyes, I wrap my arms around him...pulling him in for a *who-gives-a-damn-kinda-kiss-goodnight.* Forcing my tongue out of his mouth, I pull back and look into his piercing gaze.

"I'll take as many as you want to give me."

"Damn it, girl," he moans. "That's exactly what I wanted to hear you say."

Our late night thrills made it easy to doze off. It wasn't long after our eyes closed that we were both wrapped up in each other and sleeping the night away.

The night ended perfectly.

Chapter 20

Even the sweetest of dreams have to end. *Why do they have to end?* I can hear his voice...he's so close. If I open my eyes, he'll go away. I don't want to wake up, but that smell...that sound...the temptation is too strong. Slowly, I blink...and I blink again. Rubbing my eyes, I focus. My dream was good, but this is even better. *He's still here.*

"Good morning, beautiful," he says, sitting on the bed beside me with a tray of food.

Smiling, I blush. "Good morning."

Yawning and stretching my way up, I take a deep breath—inhaling my very first ever breakfast in bed. Glancing at the tray, the food looks delicious. Fresh strawberries, melon, and a warm croissant wrapped around a piece of bacon. My mouth waters—for the cook, not the calories.

"I thought you might be hungry," he breathes.

Biting my lip, I lean in for a taste.

"Indeed I am, but for this—not that," I confess.

My mouth open, I graze his bottom lip—licking it from one side to the next.

He releases a hungry growl, his breath hitting mine. Balancing the tray with his left hand, he places his right one around my neck. Pulling me closer, he seals his mouth over mine for a luscious good morning kiss.

I back away, licking my lips and tasting the fresh fruit he's already tried.

"*Mmmm...so good,*" I murmur. "So sweet—so yummy."

He laughs out loud and proceeds to feed me a strawberry with his bare hands. I chew slowly and swallow seductively—inviting him to taste the deliciousness with me. I lean forward and kiss him again. He moans into my mouth. I moan back. Pulling away and hating it, I glance out my bedroom window and notice the sun has barely made an appearance. It's early. The clock on the wall is ticking away, and the time is only a few minutes past six a.m.

"Why are you up so early? I thought your flight left around noon."

The thrill...the passion...our time together—it will soon be over. He's right here, right now. I don't want him to leave. *Why can't he stay?*

He feeds me another piece of fruit, and answers me while watching me devour it. "Did you really think I was going to spend my last few hours with you *sleeping*?" he asks.

Now, I really don't want him to leave.

I scoot closer to him...my body yearning to feel the warmth of his skin upon mine. I take the tray out of his hands and put it on the table next to my bed, swallowing the food more hurriedly this time.

I grab hold of him. "Lie back down with me," I insist.

I pull him close, and he climbs in under the covers. Cradling my head in the bend of his arm, our gaze focuses on one another. I run my fingers through his chest hairs while he twirls my curls with his. He's wearing only boxers, and I am still panty-*less*. Yet there's so much more to the relationship we are building; we are consumed with each other's minds as well as our bodies.

So, we talk...we laugh...we sneak a kiss in between the croissant we are sharing. His dreams are much like mine. He believes in working hard, and he refuses to be a freeloader and mooch off of his wealthy father. He puts his all into his casino and the rest of the business, and he has a great deal of respect for the man who has raised him alone since he and his sister were born.

It's only now that I find out that their mother died from complications only two days after their birth. He has no real memories of her; only the ones that his father planted in his brain as soon as he could walk, talk, and understand.

He watches me...a sadness blanketing his face that he quickly pushes away.

"Her name was Lillian Mae Dawson," he continues. "She would have made a great mother...if given the chance. My father used to video her a lot when she was pregnant. Sometimes she knew he was doing it, but sometimes he would capture those special moments when she had no idea. Once, she was sitting in the nursery only a week before we were born—rocking back and forth and singing to us while we were still in her womb. She had such a beautiful soothing voice. It's crazy, but sometimes I swear I think I remember it...then I recall I'm only remembering the video that I've watched a thousand times."

As he speaks about her, his face lights up only the way a mother can make a child's face glow. He never knew her, but he loves her anyway.

Okay, if I didn't think he was perfect before, I know he is now...that story just earned him another kiss.

Sealing my lips over his, I kiss him gently.

And he pulls away laughing.

"Enough about me," he insists. "I want to hear more about you."

Using my fingertips, I brush away the wary blonde strands of hair that have fallen in front of his gorgeous tell-it-all eyes. "Well, Mister Dawson, there's not much to say," I confess.

He rolls his eyes at my comment.

"Sure there is, out with it," he demands.

I watch him as he watches me. He's serious. I smile—realizing just how persuasive he really is. I think he could talk me into anything.

I huff. Gracefully, but yes, I huffed. Dreading the words about to leave my lips—*here goes nothing.*

"Okay—long story short. I grew up without a dad, and a mom who worked two jobs to make sure my brother Landon and I were well provided for. She may not have been able to give us riches or wealth, but she gave us something far more precious than money can buy. Her strength taught us how to be strong, and her gentle heart showed us how to love. Two things some people will die never knowing. My virtue has remained intact because I truly believe that part of me is a priceless gift that only one man should know. Lastly, I work in a law office that handles only divorce cases, and I pity the clients who give up on a love that they once believed in. So, with that being said…not only am I clumsy, but I'm also a hopeless romantic."

I'm breathless and worried, but there's no need to be.

His compelling vivid eyes are grinning right along with the curves of his kissable mouth, and I exhale. He's speechless, but he looks happy. Better yet, content. My response pleased him.

Leaning in, he kisses my worry away.

He pulls back, only to get a better look at me.

With one finger, he moves the fallen hair from my face to behind my ear; then repeats the same step on the other side. I must really look a hot mess. Maybe it's time to freshen up.

"I'll be right back. I hear the bathroom calling my name," I laugh, but he doesn't.

Those eyes. *Where did that mischievous glint come from?*

I try to get up.

He won't let me.

His gaze is on fire…I think I may be in trouble.

Pinning my hands over my head, he jumps up and straddles me.

"So, tell me, Hannah…how bad exactly do you have to go pee?"

What the…what does he mean how bad do I have to go pee?

I look at him like he's crazy.

Tilting his head, his brow arches up high over one eye.

"I said, how bad?"

"Like a dam is about to break loose in my bed if I don't get there pretty quick," I say, my voice husky.

His brow dances.

"Has no one ever taught you restraint, Miss Stone?"

"Huh?" I ask, confused.

That mischievous look moves from his eyes to his lips...now he's wearing it in his smile.

No, not that.

His hands; one keeps me pinned down to the bed while the other trails a tickling path over every inch of my belly—hitting my overly full bladder along the way.

I writhe beneath him—he has no mercy.

I can't help but laugh and fight to release myself from his grip, but I'm helpless. He has me right where he wants me and loving it.

"Conner, please stop," I beg, giggling even louder, hysterically even.

I'm laughing and lying at the same time. As much as I love his hands on me this way, it's pretty urgent that I get to the toilet—fast; *especially* now. Either by the look on my face, or the plea in my voice...he knows it. Releasing me from his grip, he jumps up...landing both feet on the floor. He stands there broad shouldered...like a sexy-macho-tickling-tormenter-hunk of sculptured perfection. He holds one hand out to me, and I grab it and get up—very carefully.

My smile is wry and to the point, but my eyes are playful and he knows it. "I'm going to get you for that," I promise.

He arches his brows up fast and steady—his way of telling me to come and get it.

"Go ahead and take care of your business, baby girl. I'll be right here waiting." He smacks me on the ass and off I go.

After relieving myself and freshening up my kitty, I take a moment to look at the starry-eyed girl staring back at me in the mirror. *Is this really me? Am I living the life that I've always dreamed?* Closing my eyes and letting out a breathtaking sigh, I appreciate the reality of my answer. *Yes, it is me.*

I grin at my reflection and go back to cherish the limited time that I have left with my very own *play-boy-prince*. He may not be royalty, but in my book he is...and at this very moment, he is all mine—at least for the next few hours anyway. I open the door to an eyeful of beauty. With each arm above his head and one hand on each side of the door frame, he is standing there waiting on me; just like he said he would be.

Grinning ear to ear, I can't help but burst out laughing—calming myself quickly.

"You are one crazy good-looking man, but you know that already don't you?"

Brows raised—smile gleaming—*he really is gorgeous.*

"Good-looking, maybe," he says, tilting his head with a slight hint of doubt on his face. "But I am crazy for sure. I'm crazy for you, Hannah Brooke Stone."

Jerking me up and throwing me over his massive shoulders, he lands me on top of my warm well-slept in bed.

"So, Miss Stone, I recall you saying something about getting me back..."

I don't have time to respond; he's got me pinned again and torturing me with my one true weakness. I'm ticklish, and he's found me out.

"Conner. You. Are. Going. To. Pay. For. This."

Laughing and wiggling uncontrollably, he releases my defenseless arms and lands his mouth on mine. After a toe-curling kiss and a heated moment between my legs, he pulls away.

"Am I forgiven?" he asks.

My answer is easy and self explanatory. I bite my lip and bat my eyelashes—slow and flirtatiously. The seductive reply earns me another kiss and a whisper to the ear. "I'm going to give you something to remember me by while I'm gone," he says, his voice smooth and sexy.

My heart skips a beat and then picks up speed—fast and hard. *Is this it?* He's on top of me, and I remember my bare essentials are still uncovered—my womanhood is his for the taking. With his mouth on my neck and his tongue gliding up and down and all over it, his hands are moving south and spreading my legs apart—very far apart. I breathe in and exhale. *I can do this. I want to do this.* Hell, we've done pretty much everything else. Why not just go all the way?

His lips are wet, and his mouth is hot; his tongue is well trained, and I'm getting hornier by the minute. Slowly, he leads his mouth south. Stopping briefly to nurture my breasts and getting their standing approval. My nipples are hard, and he knows just how turned on I am. A quick flick of the tongue and a gentle bite to each one, he leaves them protruding and wanting more.

Slowly, he grazes at my sensitive skin...nipping away...licking, tasting, going lower and lower. Making a perfect path to my well-groomed kitty, she's purring hard to be tasted. His manly hands spread open the lips of my womanhood, and in he goes—head first and his mouth wide open. His long, thick, hot tongue teases me with gentle strokes to my clit, and then he swirls it around and around...faster and faster, causing my bottom to lift in the air. My hands are in his hair, and my body is twitching with delight. It feels fabulous.

"Oh, Conner, you make it feel so good," I breathe.

He's turned on even more with my words and seducing moans. I can hear it in his erratic breathing. His expert fingers find their way to my hole—in goes one and then the other. In and out, he pushes and pulls.

He strokes his tongue perfectly and right on spot, and then I almost jump out of my skin. He's found my shiny bedroom buddy, and it's crawling up my womanhood. That little-buzzing-vibrating-sensation sends me over the edge as he massages it into my needy clitoris. I feel so defenseless as my body tightens up, and I begin climaxing beautifully. All I can do is hang on tight.

Spiraling down from an amazing orgasm and catching my breath as I go, I'm astonished at the things he can do with his mouth, those fingers, and that little toy. Slow and easy he kisses his way back up; a peck to my belly and one for each of my tits. I lay there with my eyes closed, and I can feel his gaze on me—his hard cock still nestled in his boxers and resting on my belly. Our eyes meet, and I reach up to thank him with a quick kiss—getting a taste of *me* while I'm at it. It's passionate and sweet...like *strawberries.* I smile remembering breakfast.

"I think you and I are going to get along just fine, Miss Stone," he murmurs, his breathing as ragged as mine.

The buzzing sound finally fades away as he turns it off. He *does* like adding a little kinkiness to the bedroom, and I can't help but anticipate what else he has in store for me. My mind...my body...my whole being is in a sexual whirlwind because of him. I want to experience everything with him....love making and wild crazy sex.

"I think so too, Mister D."

He's in need of an orgasm, and I'm going to give him one. I roll gently out of his embrace, and turn him over on his back. I lean down—whispering in his ear. "I would like to give you something to remember me by too, Conner, so hold on tight and get ready." I can feel his body tensing up; waiting and anticipating my next move.

My tongue glides over his ear lobe, and the heat of my breath hits him hard. His chest expands and he lets out a low growl as he releases the hot air. I move my fingers over his nipples—rubbing, tugging, and teasing him. With gentle kisses and gentle bites, I head to his massive manliness. It's on guard, hard, and ready to meet the back of my throat.

The head of his penis is peeking out of the top of his boxers, so I do the right thing and set him free. Pulling down his briefs and kissing his belly, I can feel his hairs graze my face. I have made it to my destination and staring into the eye of Mister Manliness himself. I gasp at the sight of it, but there is no stopping me now.

Starting off with wet kisses and tongue twirling licks, I tease the whole length of his shaft while trying to figure out how in the hell I'm going to take all of *it* in my mouth...and it's still not done—*I think it just grew another freaking inch.*

I swallow hard.

Slow and easy, I wrap my mouth around the tip of his cock. My tongue traces the lining of his glory, and I focus primarily on the sweet tender spot beneath the head. He tastes so good; it's almost like having my very own *red-velvet-fudge-candy-cane*. I pause for a moment. Licking my lips and tasting him.

I can hear him groaning with pleasure, and this makes me want to please him even more. Down I go, taking him in an inch at a time…trying carefully not to switch on my gag reflexes. Up and down, moving my mouth over the length of his long thick cock and stroking him with my hand as I go. My grip is tight and firm, and my mouth is inexperienced but faking it. I think by his body language he approves.

"Oh, Hannah…just like that," he moans.

He lets out a deep breath…the heat of it sweeping over my bare skin—tickling my back and making me smile. *He likes it.*

I can feel his hands in my hair, and he pulls my long strands to one side to keep them out of my way. Over and over again I move my mouth up and down, tracing each vein of his manhood with my tongue. I start sucking, and he starts quivering.

Grabbing my vibrating wonder, it's my turn to play.

Switching it on, I place it beneath his balls, massaging and bobbing at the same time. His body jerks, and he's on the edge of pure ecstasy. He tries pulling my head away so that he can find his release in midair, but I won't let him. I suck him hard and stroke him faster. Any second he's going to fill my mouth with the result of his much needed orgasm.

There it is. Spurt by spurt. I feel the hot liquid hitting the back of my throat and sliding down to fill my belly. His body shakes off the orgasm while I finish what I started. I swallow the last of it and raise up to see his expression.

His head resting on the feather pillow, his eyes are closed…cherishing the sensation. Then he opens them. Our eyes meet. He looks heavenly. While licking my lips, I crawl up the bed to be face to face with him. He kisses me— *tasting the result of his climax.*

After a long lip-locking embrace, he pulls away.

"You're a natural baby girl," he whispers breathlessly.

I blush. I'm glad he thinks so.

Thank goodness.

A naughty grin spreads across my tired cheeks.

The next hour we lay in the bed saying goodbye the only way we know how. Hands on and all wrapped up in each other. Kissing, laughing, talking, and promising to keep in touch. Then the inevitable happens. It is time to get up.

Conner drags me out of bed, and we get dressed. I straighten the collar of his shirt, and he hesitantly zips up my salmon-colored dress. Our time at my apartment has come to an end, and as much as I hate sending him off, it is inevitable. It is time to take him to board his plane.

Pouting all the way to my car, I *try* to suck it up and be a big girl. After all, he is making a woman out of me.

The last twenty-four hours have been amazing. I don't want them to end, but they have to. He has got billionaires to woo, businesses to buy, and a father to impress.

I load up in the driver's seat of my car, and he joins me on the passenger side, and off we go. The traffic is light and we make it to the airport way too quick.

Ugh! I don't want to say goodbye.

His jet is fueled and ready for take-off when we arrive. I have to let him leave; no matter how much I want him to stay. My car is parked, and for a minute we both sit there staring at each other.

He breaks the silence.

"I'll call you once my flight lands in New York, and I get settled in."

I'm stunned. For some reason it never occurred to me to ask where he would be going. I guess now I know.

"New York, huh?" His eyes take on a look of confusion, and he raises his brow.

"I didn't tell you where I was going, did I, baby girl?"

I shake my head.

"No, I wasn't sure where you were headed. All I can comprehend at this moment is how much I don't want you to go."

I'm pouting again.

His look is intense and focused. He doesn't want to leave me either.

"I'll be in New York for a few days, then I will be flying into Japan for approximately two weeks, and finally I'll finish up at my office in Honolulu. Three weeks tops and it will be time for another weekend getaway. I'll be back in no time, Hannah. I promise."

Now I'm really pouting—*that's almost a month.*

He leans over and kisses my forehead, my left cheek, my right cheek, and finishes off with the perfect goodbye kiss to my lips. My heart races and I feel so flustered. Three weeks is a long time to be away from him.

Teary eyed and a trembling heart, I hug him tight.

"Don't forget to remember me." My words a sheer whisper.

"Never in a million years, Hannah." He kisses me again, and then steps out of the car—leaving me longing to leave with him.

I opt to let him walk away—refusing to follow the man behind that strut. If I do, I may jump on that plane with him and never look back.

Chapter 21

Here goes nothing. I take a deep breath, and in through the doors I go. Not a client in sight, but he is. *Great!* No, make that a double hellacious crap! His piercing gaze is forcing me to make eye contact with him. My heart slams into my throat as I look at my boss from across the room.

"Good afternoon, Hannah." Mr. Jenkins stands there tapping his watch with his index finger.

"Good afternoon, Mr. Jenkins."

"In. My. Office. Now," he demands.

Baylee looks my way with an arched brow and worried eyes. She shrugs her shoulders, and I keep walking.

I can't help but worry myself. My vacation time wasn't scheduled when I left for Hawaii, and neither was this morning. I guess I haven't been handling things very professional lately, and now I'm going to feel the wrath of a pissed employer. I walk into the huge spacious office and shut the solid cherry wood door behind me. The room is filled with sport paraphernalia—*Tennessee* football to be exact. Being that my boss man is an avid fan of our home state's team, his office adorns the orange and white legacy colors.

"Yes, Mr. Jenkins?" I ask.

He gestures at the chair in front of his desk.

"Have a seat," he demands.

I sit and cross my legs—fidgeting my nervous fingers as I try to control my breathing.

"Hannah, your behavior has been erratic lately."

I agree.

"Yes, sir—I apologize."

I'm being scolded by my boss, and inside my head I'm screaming the words, *if you only knew*. Just get to the point already.

"I understand you've had problems with someone stalking you. Is that still going on?" he asks.

I almost forgot about that jerk. Why did he have to bring him up?

"Actually, no, I haven't heard from him for a couple of weeks now. I think maybe he has moved on or got bored. Either way, I'm glad he's not focusing on me anymore."

He sits in his chair with his hands clasped—fiddling his short fat thumbs and studying my body language for an answer that my mouth hasn't spoken. "Well, you are an excellent employee, and I would hate to lose you, but in the future any vacation time has to be scheduled with me. Understood?"

I shake my head vigorously, with a look that says I'm begging for forgiveness.

"Yes sir, Mr. Jenkins. I will be sure to remember that." My words creeping out between my lips like I'm scared to death. *This is worse than when I got called into the principal's office back in grade school.* That voice inside my head starts screaming. *"Get a grip already Jenkins—you know this is out of character for me!"* If only I could say those words out loud.

Debating whether or not he's said enough, he watches me intently—making me that more nervous. With my right leg over my left, I anxiously start tapping my foot. *Crap! He needs to dismiss me already—my nerves are getting the best of me.*

"Is there anything you would like to say?" he asks.

"No, sir, you have made your point, and I respect that."

"Very well, off you go. I have files waiting on your desk. Please prepare them to my expectations, and bring them to me when you're finished," he demands…a touch of anger still in his voice.

"Yes sir." I get up and walk out of his office—embarrassed that I'm a grown woman being scolded.

Glad that's over.

Once the door shuts I let out a huge sigh of relief, and Baylee is all up in my business. "I want details, and I don't mean what just happened in the boss's office. What is going on with my girl?" she demands.

I clamp my hand over her mouth to hush her up, and I lead her into my corner office. The area is pretty plain— white walls, an inky black leather chair behind a mahogany finished desk, and the computer that sits on it. The walls hold framed football art and some of the star players of the 2013 season. Of course Mr. Jenkins decorated the place, but I did add a little personal touch of my own. My favorite quote sits to the left of me in a black wooden frame—reminding me to live by the words closed in by its glass.

Don't take life too serious— just the things that really matter...like love.

I quote this daily, and try to live by it—sometimes I do, and sometimes I don't. Today I am. When I think of love, I think of Conner. I do love him, irrevocably and matter-of-factly. The thought sends tingles all through me. Like tiny feathers arousing my senses—tickling me from my head to my toes. I smile, and Baylee is impatiently waiting on me to get my head out of the clouds.

"Out with it, Hannah, I want to know what has you all *giddy* and running late for work." My grin widens, and I can't hold back.

"He came to see me," I whisper, my voice showing excitement even in the low murmur.

Her mouth opens wide, and she starts jumping around— showing off her own relentless pleasure for my newfound love-life.

"He likes you, he likes you." Her words make me all warm and fuzzy—though she is humorously canny with her teasing. Deep down, I know she's right. He does—*actually, I think he may love me.* Even though they are unspoken words, his actions are screaming L-O-V-E. After all, he did fly all the way from Hawaii just to *bathe my kitty*—or should I say *taste my cookie.*

Ah. Sweet, sweet memories of our early morning rendezvous sends my thoughts into overdrive—*mind out of the gutter, Hannah. There is a time and place for that, and now is not it*...my inner self reminds me. Rolling my eyes to get the thought out of my head, I put my attention back on my friend.

"I think you're right," I say.

She hugs me, and I hug her back—we do a girly dance and are interrupted by a deep voice.

"Ms. Stone, those files aren't going to work themselves up. Get busy," he demands.

Mr. Jenkins is in a mood today. He's never grumpy and demanding—always laid back and easy going. Baylee and I pretty much run the office to his liking, but not today. I wonder what's bothering him—it can't be the half day of vacation I took this morning.

"Baylee, don't you have files of your own to be working on?" He eyes her speculatively.

"Yes sir," she says.

Our boss stands there demanding to be respected and waits on her to leave. Once she does, he goes on about his business—leaving me to mine.

Sitting down, I lean back in my chair, and look up at the ceiling. Work is the last thing on my mind—and here is the last place I want to be.

Jeez, Hannah! Get it together.

Sitting up straight, I try to shake it off. My hands, my head, my whole body is shaking him out of my system. *Yeah, like that will actually work.* Focus, Hannah. People are depending on you to word their divorce decrees just right—*alimony, child support, who gets this, who gets that—how depressing.* There are seven new files on my desk—that means it will take up most of my day, and I will be off work and back home to my empty apartment in no time.

He's really gone.

I take a deep breath, scrolling my way to the template saved on my computer.

I huff, allowing concentration to settle in—*finally.*

Number one.

I gasp a heavy breath, and open up the first manila folder. All the clients want the same things, and this one is no different—*neither are the next six.*

Although, file number seven explains my boss's mood. Charles Ford, his best friend of thirty years, is getting a divorce—and it's ending after three and a half decades of marriage. Guess that proves even a lengthy wed-lock can deconstruct—*hearts can grow apart.*

I hit the last key, and it's all done. The Ford's names will go on the docket with all the others, and their lives will be open to a whole new world. I can't help but feel sorry for them.

Sealed up and ready for delivery, I take the files to Mr. Jenkins' office. He's not at his desk, so I put my finished work in front of his computer. They will be the first thing he sees when he sits down.

I glance at my watch, and its ten minutes till quitting time. *Where is Baylee?*

I poke my head in her office, and she's not sitting in her usual spot. I look around the waiting area, and she's not there either. I hear the door of the ladies room shut, and I turn to see her trying to compose herself. She's been crying. *What the hell happened to her?*

I hurriedly walk towards her, and she sees me coming. She tilts her head to the side and her stunning face has taken on a shade of melancholy. My first instinct is to grab her and hug the sadness away, but I don't think that is going to work.

"What's wrong, Baylee?" My tone is emphatic with worry. I don't like seeing her this way.

She sniffles, blots her eyes with a tissue, and manages a few words. "Err…meet me at The Tamale Shack around six. We'll talk then." She swallows hard, trying even harder not to tear up again. Her face is flustered from all the crying she's been doing, and her eyes are bloodshot and swollen.

Her words were muffled—telling me she's been crying for a while.

The Tamale Shack is known for the best drinks around, so she must need to vent over a strong one. I put my feelings aside and agree to meet her at the popular Mexican restaurant.

"Okay, honey. I'll see you then." I give her a tight squeeze, and we go our separate ways.

I rush home to change out of my work clothes and to check my tablet for any messages—email or otherwise. I haven't gotten any texts from Conner, so I don't know why I would think he would contact me any other way, but I have to check.

Nothing. I glare at my tablet, willing it to show me what I want to see. Still nothing. Ugh! Why hasn't he called or something?

"Suck it up, Hannah. Enough with the pouting—maybe he really hasn't had time. You have a friend in need so get it in gear, and go find out what's wrong with her," demands that little voice in my head.

I do what my subconscious tells me and change into something more appropriate for the local pub and grill joint. Tight fitting jeans, white fitted tee, and a casual ponytail—laid-back and informal enough? Nope…something's missing. Glancing in the mirror, I realize what it is. *Where is my hot pink ball cap?* I search my room over and then my closet. There it is. Now, this is spot-on-perfect, and I'm ready to meet up with Baylee.

I'm racing out the door, and suddenly I realize I left my keys lying on my bed. I run back to get them, and its then that I hear a *swoosh* coming from my tablet, and then another one. That's a video chat. It has to be him. My heart picks up speed as I'm running to my bedroom to answer the call. I'm nervous and excited all at the same time. It's only been six hours since I dropped him off at the airport, but I swear it seems like weeks since I've seen the man I now crave.

Nervous hands—anxious heart—I almost drop the tablet before I can answer it. *Deep breath. In. Out. Slow and easy. Okay.* Finally, I pull it together long enough to swipe the bar on the screen.

After a few seconds of loading, there he is—perfect and freshly showered. He's sitting on the edge of a massive king size bed in what must be a five star hotel—*I bet his family owns that one too.*

His hair is wet and wild, and his chest is hardly dry...showing off droplets of water as they roll down his perfect lean abs. His manhood is covered by an itty-bitty white towel that he has wrapped around his waist, and he is vigorously towel-drying his hair. I watch as the muscles in his forearms and chest flex with every move he makes. He's breathtaking.

"Hey, baby girl."

His voice is so ruthless, but sexy-hot nonetheless. It's tugging at my wayward attention span, trying hard to pull me out of my climacteric moment, and suddenly I'm aware this is *live*...he's right there on the screen talking to me.

"Hi," I swallow hard—not nervous, just turned on. "I'm glad to see you arrived safely," I say anxiously.

"Yeah, me too—the flight here was smooth, but the meeting not so much," he snaps.

"I guess things didn't go as you planned?" I squint my eyes, but never allow them to fully shut out all the hotness on my screen.

I really hope things went well.

"You know, the same ole same ole. We want to buy, and they don't want to sell. It's just so damn frustrating because they *will* give in eventually. They all do. It's all about money and how many zeros are on the check."

One of the things I had found out about Conner during our morning talk was the foundation of his father's business. He is an investor and wants his son to follow in his steps. If Conner had his way, he would invest all of his time and energy into music…but out of respect for his dad, he focuses on the mega-workload that the business entails.

Early on, Mr. Edward Dawson invested his money into anything that said *vacation getaway,* and it has made him a very wealthy man. He owns hotels and casinos, and a variety of property in all fifty states. Not only does he have an airline, but he also owns a huge cruise line of ships that sail all over the world—including Mexico and Canada. *Dawson's Adventurous Cruise Lines…a vacation away, a place where memories are made, and a time you will never forget.* With a motto like theirs, no wonder they are going strong and growing bigger every day.

"Everybody is out to make a dollar more than the next guy, I guess you'll have to pay the business tycoons what they want," I say. He snarls with frustration, but deep down he knows I'm right.

My own words just jerked me out of my little fantasy world. *Conner Dawson really is a powerful man…and heir to his dad's wealth.* The day he inherits it could be the end of our *love affair.* He will be so busy, how will he have time for *us*—much less little ole me?

Stop it, Hannah! I tell myself to focus on the man on the screen. We will face that day if it ever comes.

"Yeah, I know, but dad's going to be pissed. On a lighter note, I cut a deal with the others. I'm going to the ground breaking first thing in the morning. It looks like *Hooked on a Better Life* is going to happen."

"Great, Conner. I know how important that is to you. There was no doubt in my mind that you wouldn't make it happen."

"Thank you for the confidence, but I admit I was beginning to wonder…anyway, enough business-talk." He changes the subject by the look on his face before the words ever come out of his mouth. "You look good, Hannah. I love you in your ball cap…gives me an even better glimpse of that perfectly-pretty little face of yours."

"Thank you," I murmur.

Leaning over the side of the bed, his eyes move from mine to on the floor. He's looking for something—and giving me a show. I can't help but tilt my head, trying to get a better glimpse of what he wants me to see...*even if it's not on purpose.*

I blush, when he catches me trying to sneak a peek.

"I can't help but notice how sexy you look all wrapped up in that rag...*I mean towel.*"

He cuts his eyes at me even harder. "I can take it off if you want me to...just say the word, baby girl."

My eyes widen, and I can't help but bite my lip. I look at the time, and it's almost six o'clock, so this will have to wait—as much as I hate it.

"Maybe next time, tall, dark, and delicious. I have a date with my friend Baylee. She's expecting me in just a few minutes."

The vivacious playful look on his face is taken over by a look of confusion. His eyes are no longer pulling me in, but instead they are unreadable. I think he's upset, but why? *Baylee is my best friend. It's not like I'm going out on a date with a man.*

"Are you okay, Conner?"

He cracks a refined smile, and there it is again. The look I love. "Yeah, baby girl. I just want you to myself, that's all."

My heart is racing again, and I can't help but release the air that is choking me.

Breathe, Hannah, Breath!

"I feel the same way, Conner. I promise I'll call as soon as I get in. A couple of hours tops."

He stands to his feet, no longer sitting on the bed, and down to the floor goes the towel. *Boom.* His manliness falls down between his legs and just hangs there. He's getting dressed right in front of me—one foot at a time into each hole of his boxers, and then into his jeans. He *so* did that on purpose.

"You're a bad boy, Mister Dawson. I have to go before you get me in trouble," I laugh.

He laughs.

"Later, baby girl," he says, fastening the last button of his fly.

Even that is freaking sexy.

I hesitantly turn off my tablet and race out of my apartment. I'm going to be late, and Baylee is going to be worried.

Chapter 22

Baylee and I pull up at the same time, and it's a good thing. If the inside is as full as the parking lot, I may have been here all night looking for her. Glancing at my watch, I see why—*it's happy hour*. The large sombrero sign is glowing with red, green, and white lights. The purple and yellow letters flashing across it confirm the event—half price drinks for the next two hours.

Walking towards her, I push the clicker on my keychain—locking ole faithful up safe and sound. She does the same to her candy-apple-red sports car.

We are both sporting a more casual look that is more fitting for our after-office-hours adventure—me in my jeans and fitted tee and Baylee with khaki shorts and a bright green halter top. She looks good—no sign of tears or smudged mascara, maybe she's okay now. I hope so.

"Hey girl, I was worried you were already here."

She cracks a half smile across her stone-cold face.

Something is really eating at her, and I am not amused—*I want my friend back.*

"No, not this time…I was running late myself," she says bluntly.

Our eyes skim the area as we walk beneath the breezeway. The benches are full of people waiting to be seated—mostly with parties of eight or more. *Great!* It will probably be two hours before we even get in the place. *Now would be a perfect time to have Conner at my side. I'm sure he could get us in without the wait.*

"We can go somewhere else if you want to," she says, her voice fighting to be heard. Not only is the place overcrowded, but the music playing is louder than it should be.

"I'm here for you, Baylee. You tell me what you want to do." I yell, only to become the center of attention.

An announcement over the intercom interrupts the music, and all eyes turn my way—but only for a second. Everyone is too enthralled with their own conversations to worry about ours.

"There's no waiting at the bar—two seats available now," says the voice.

No one budges.

A minute later, the announcement is made again—*still, no one budges.* That settles it. Those seats are ours. Baylee and I go to claim them before someone decides to break up their party.

We walk in, and the place looks the same as always—beautiful Mexican décor everywhere. The walls are painted golden yellow and are covered with sombreros, artwork, and traditional Mexican dresses. It's very authentic looking—you almost feel as though you are visiting the country and not a local eating place.

Our attention is swayed from one direction to the next when we are greeted by Manuel, our *friend* and the manager of the restaurant. Not only is he fluent in his native tongue, but he also speaks perfect English. Seeing him reminds me that not *everybody* is as sick and twisted as the stalker. There are good people and bad people *everywhere.* It doesn't matter what nationality you are. Deep down I know that, but self-consciously I think I had almost forgotten.

"Hola, senoritas."

I smile at my friend—pushing the prejudice thoughts out the door. I refuse to let anyone influence the way I feel ever again.

"Hola, Manuel," I say.

Baylee manages a thin-lined smile.

"It's happy hour. You muy Bonitas sitting at the bar tonight?" he asks.

"You bet we are." I answer for both of us.

Baylee is speechless, and her eyes are gazing blindly at nothing in particular. She is literally in another world. I lock my arm in hers—leading my friend to our seats as Manuel motions for us to follow him to the burgundy colored countertop. She may look like my friend, but she is not acting like it. *Something has got to give.* We take our seats, and we both grab a drink menu—staring at it, but not *really* looking at it.

Enough is enough. I lay the menu down—*it's now or never.*

I huff.

"Honey, tell me what's wrong," I demand.

Her eyes are glassy, and tears are filling them up fast.

Oh Crap!

One escapes the corner of her eye and rolls onto her cheek before she has time to wipe it away with the tissue she has balled up in her hand.

She clears her throat.

"Today, when I was working on my files, I came across a client by the name of Mr. Andy Peterson. He is divorcing his wife because she cheated on him."

She sniffs and uses the tissue to wipe away the liquid now draining from her nose

My look shows confusion, but I'm listening to every detail.

She double sniffs.

If she doesn't stop doing that, I'm going to be doing it.

Poor Baylee.

"Not only did the woman defy her wedding vows with her infidelity, but she gave birth to a son who is not biologically Mr. Petersons," she sniffles *again*.

This is the kind of thing we deal with on a daily basis. I don't understand why this case has her so torn up. "Baylee, honey, we see stories like this every day. You know that."

She hiccups, crying harder—then blurts out the core of her heartache.

"The child's father is *Ty-Ty-Tyler Watson*," she stutters her way though his name.

She blows her nose.

My mouth drops open, and the massive shock sends waves that about knock me off my seat. I hoped that I was hearing things, but I wasn't. *Oh no.* Not Tyler. The one and only man that Baylee has been totally infatuated with for the last ten months—border line in love with more like it.

My heart goes out to her. I'm left struggling for words—I think I'm in more shock than she is. "How do you know that for sure?" I ask.

"Mr. Peterson had a DNA test done, and he names Tyler as the father in the papers."

My mind wanders.

That explains it—he's stripping to pay child support.

"I'm so sorry, Baylee. Have you talked to him about it?"

She looks at me like I'm crazy, and snaps.

"Seriously, Hannah. That's confidential. You know that I can't do that."

Ouch. Since, grade school, Baylee has never snapped at me. *What was I thinking?* "Of course it is. I'm sorry."

There has to be some kind of an explanation. I remember the way he looked at her that night. He has feelings for her too—*I know he does.* I have to reassure her, but how? For the life of me, I cannot fathom how to make this better for her. Grasping at straws—I ask my next question.

"Do you know how old the child is?"

She's ready—almost too quick. I guess she's memorized the file.

"He's barely six months old and ..."

The words choke her up, and she can't finish her sentence without clearing her throat.

"Harrumph, harrumph."

"I'm sorry, Hannah. It's not you—I'm so angry she has *his* baby." *She sniffles again.* "And I know it's not the baby's fault, but I don't know how I'm supposed to compete with his child."

Now, I understand—it's not the mother she's worried about. It's the product of *their* affair. An innocent baby that has no say so in the matter.

"Baylee, it's going to be okay. I'm sure Tyler just wants to be a good father to his son. Besides, I know he has feelings for you. I saw it in his eyes back at the club that night. Just give him time, he'll come around."

I reach over and hug her, and she wipes the last of her tears away.

"Do you really think so?"

She's cheering up—the look of despair leaving her eyes and being replaced with a *little* hope.

"I know so."

She hugs me back, and we motion for Manuel, who is now behind the bar to come take our orders.

The food was good, but my frozen slush was better. My drink of choice was a virgin margarita, and it went perfect with the cheese tamale I had for dinner—not to mention it cooled my mouth down from the salsa that had way too many jalapeños in it.

I think Baylee is back to her old self—*without any heavy drinking may I add.* She's laughing and talking Spanish with Manuel, and it's frustrating because I only understand about a fourth of their conversation. I think it's time for me to go. Besides, I promised Conner I would call him within two hours, and it's been exactly that. I'm running behind, but I had no other choice. Not only is Baylee my very best friend, but she is also like the sister I never had. I will be here for her no matter what, and I am confident she would do the same for me.

"Well, guys, it's been fun, but it's time for me to be going." I look at Baylee, as though I'm asking for her permission.

She swings around—stepping off of her barstool. She is also ready to go.

Thank goodness.

"I'm right behind you, Hannah. Mucho Gracias, Manuel. We'll see you later, amigo." She leaves a ten dollar bill on the counter for our favorite waiter and the exact change for our bill. "This one's on me, Hannah. Thanks for coming out with me tonight."

"Thank you, Baylee. Next time I'm *taking you out*."

We wave goodbye to Manuel.

"Gracias...buenos noches, Senoritas." He waves and pockets the tip.

We laugh and exit the building—going our separate ways.

"See you in the morning, Hannah!" yells Baylee.

"Bright and early, dear!" I yell back.

Before starting my car, I check my phone for any messages. I have two, and they are from him. I read the first one.

I'm bored and missing you desperately. Call me.

The hugest grin ever spreads across my face. Conner Dawson cannot be bored. How can a man like him not find something to get into? Wait a minute. *I don't want him getting into anything, but me. I'm glad he's bored.* I read the next message.

Still bored and missing you, but now I'm horny too...lol.

I. Laugh. Out. Loud. He is so crazy, and I love it. I respond to the second message.

Why, Mister Dawson, I think I like you that way.

Flirting with him is like an aphrodisiac. A natural high that puts my spirits on cloud nine and sends sparks of pleasure all through my body. Closing my eyes, I inhale—remembering the sweet smell of him as though he were right here with me. I miss him too. The thought of not seeing him for three weeks kills my summit. I'm pouting and longing for his touch already.

Starting my car, I pull out of the paved parking lot into the quiet streets of Oak Hill. The sweet sound of love is playing over my speakers. It's a great song, and it's almost like the lyrics were written to tell my story. I listen closely to the chorus.

I love the way you make me feel
The sound of your voice is so surreal
Your kiss is etched in my memory
Breathless memories of your lips on me
Your touch is tattooed on my heart
I knew I loved you from the start

The drive home was short and sweet, and I'm patiently sitting here waiting on Conner to text me back. Thoughts of him in New York suddenly drowned out everything else I'm thinking, and I can't help but wonder if he's out on the town living it up with some floozy. *Argh! Jealousy will get you know where, Hannah Brooke. Don't do that to yourself.* Once again, my subconscious is right. Maybe he's just in the shower. No, that's not it. He had just finished his shower when I talked to him earlier. My heart's going into panic mode, and I grab my phone to check the time. Okay. It's only been twenty minutes since I sent him a message. Instead of willing the phone to do something, I choose to walk away from it.

That man may be everything I want, but I will not worry myself over this. He will text me back. I'm confident he will. I leave my cell charging and decide to pamper myself before calling it a night.

First, I pour myself a tall glass of white wine from the bottle that I keep in the fridge for special occasions. Without hesitating, I take a big gulp and swallow it slowly. After sitting the glass down on the counter, I realize something's missing. Music—I need *something* to listen to. I turn on the stereo system in the living room—loud enough to be heard in the back of the apartment but not enough to bother the neighbors. A long soak in the tub is just what my restless heart needs—I grab my wine and walk back to my room.

My darkened bedroom is lit up bright. *What the heck?* Headlights are beaming through the window, and it seems like they are aiming right at me. I walk over to it, and slowly move the curtains to the side—taking a peek to see who it is. My eyes are stunned at the familiar vehicle facing me. *What the hell is Kris doing here?*

He's looking straight at me and has that familiar look etched across his face. He's pissed. He revs up the engine after seeing me, and then throws his truck in reverse. Backing out and squealing tires as he zooms out of the parking lot.

I storm away from the window and back track my steps—making sure all the doors and windows are locked tight. Memories of the stalker are suddenly haunting me again thanks to my ex. Surely it's not him. It can't be.

Finally, everything is locked up tight, and nobody is getting in—not tonight anyway. A hot relaxing bath is calling my name even more now. The running water is steaming, and the eucalyptus oil that I added to the bath smells up the whole entire room. The candles are lit, and things are peaceful again.

I begin stripping out of my clothes—kicking them to the side. My wine glass is on the floor, and I step over it to get into the tub. Before washing off, I just want to relax. I turn the water off and lie back with my head resting on the luxurious bath pillow I bought for myself—the perfect indulgence for nights like this. *This is just what I needed.* The hot water is opening up every pore I have, and my skin is drinking in the oily heated cocktail. Ah. I'm so sleepy. I yawn, and close my eyes just for a minute to relax—never thinking I would fall fast asleep.

Sleeping in a tub full of water is not a good idea, but it is exactly what I did. After about an hour of relaxing and sleeping, I wake to wrinkled skin and cold water—*burr*. I'm freezing, and chill bumps are covering me from head to toe. I reach over and pull the plug—letting out some of the coldness and replacing it with a fresh stream of sultry water. Ah, much better.

Grabbing a loofah, I lather it with my favorite soap—one with almond and coconut oil. Trailing every inch of my body with it, I scrub and massage the areas that need it the most with relaxing circular motions.

All finished.

I rinse the soap from my body and hurriedly get out of the tub. I'm still cold, and I get dressed quickly to warm up.

While leaning over to blow out the candles, Conner comes to my mind—*of course.* My first move is to check my phone. Back in my room, I grab it from the charger. He did text me back five times, but none are within the last thirty minutes.

I read the first one.

I love the fact that you like me that way baby girl.

Huh? Oh yes. I scroll up looking at my last message.

Why, Mister Dawson, I think I like you that way.

I smile when I look at his message before that.

Still bored and missing you, but now I'm horny too...lol.

Scrolling down, I finish reading his messages.
Second message:

Sorry I didn't text back sooner. Can you believe my cell died and that I left my phone charger on the plane? Luckily, the gift shop downstairs was still open, and I bought the last one they had.

Third message:

Hello, Hannah?

Fourth message:

Baby girl, I'm getting worried. Should I be?

The last message says it all. I won't be talking to him tonight.

Not sure why you're not texting back, maybe your phone played out too—whatever the reason, I hope you're okay. I'm still bored and missing you, but not so much the other anymore. Worrying about you put a stop to that. I have to be up at five in the morning, so I'm going to call it a night. If I don't hear from you before then, I'll talk to you tomorrow. Goodnight, sweet girl. I'll be dreaming of you—every succulent bare inch of you.

I could kick myself for *sleeping in the tub* and for *missing his text.*

I'm tempted to call and wake him up. Maybe he's not asleep yet, but what if he is. Forget it. I'm calling it a night too. I go to bed pouting, but he too is in my dreams— *every inch of his perfect body.*

A girl couldn't ask for a better night's rest. Cuddling up to my pillow, I sigh in my sleep—*best dream ever.*

Chapter 23

I wake up emotionally distraught—some goodnight's rest that turned out to be. Massive cramps have invaded my body, and my heart is begging to hear his voice. Remembering his message and early morning endeavor, I'm sure he doesn't have time to take my phone call. It's seven o'clock, so I bet he's right in the middle of the ground breaking event that got him up at the crack of dawn…and crap if I'm not running late. *Dang phone*…my alarm didn't go off again.

Uh! I feel so yucky this morning…*bloated, tired and moody.* That can only mean one thing. *She's* here for her monthly visit. Oh, I hope I'm wrong.

With one eye open and one eye shut, I slowly drag myself out of bed—taking my phone with me out of habit. The wine is screaming to be released from my body, and my bladder is beating me up over it. I didn't have that much to drink, but I sure feel like I did….and this dang water retention isn't helping.

"Ouch!" I yell out after bumping into the wall. I'm too sleepy to be up this early…*why do I have to be up this early?* Oh, that's right. I have a job. *Ugh!* And I keep on stumbling my way across the room.

One big yawn and a few footsteps later, I finally make it to the cold porcelain seat. I'm so freaking tired, and I yawn again while trying to go through my messages. I'm staring at the last ones he sent, and before I know it, my fingers are tiptoeing over the screen and replying to it.

Sorry, didn't mean to worry you. Took a bath and relaxed a little too much. I can't believe I fell asleep in a tub full of water. Anyway, good morning, Mister Dawson…hope work isn't kicking your butt too bad. Sending hugs and kisses your way.

I hit send and put the phone on the counter beside me.

Finally, my bladder is empty and my sneak peek down yonder proves my suspicion...*she's here.*

"Aaargh!" I cry out as if that will make *her* go away. Starting my period is not what I wanted to wake up to...some week this is going to be.

Hellacious crap! My phone's buzzing, and I'm bare-assed and still on the toilet. Glancing at the screen, I notice that it is Conner. *Double hellacious crap!* I have to answer it. If I don't, he will really freak out—even worse, he may get pissed. Taking a deep breath, I answer the phone—still sitting on the cold ceramic seat.

"Hello, handsome."

"Damn it, Hannah! What were you thinking?"

I'm shocked and listening...his unnerving tone blaring over the loud bull dozing sounds I hear in the background.

"Can you even fathom the thought of what could have happened to you?" He exhales a scared breath. "If I lost you..."

His breathing is erratic, and he's overreacting. I have to calm him down.

"I'm okay, baby. It was stupid, and it won't happen again. I promise you."

I'm pleading, and frustration is finding its way deep inside my groggy head now. I roll my neck—back and forth, trying to wake up—also to release some of the tension that's taking over my body. *Damn this time of month.*

"Please, don't be angry with me," I say breathlessly—now fully awake.

He lets out a low whimper—releasing some of the anxiety he is feeling. *"Angry?* Baby girl, angry is far from what I am," he said softly.

This time I exhale—hearing a trace of relief in his voice.

"Your text scared the hell out of me. The thought of never seeing your face, hearing your voice..." he pauses, "well, that's a reality I refuse to ever come to terms with."

My heart catches in my throat— screaming I love you, but the three undying words never escape my mouth. Neither do they leave his lips—*the ones I love kissing so very much.*

"You are mine, Hannah, and if I have to lock you up and throw away the key, I will do it to keep you safe."

I'm his?

A confusing look crosses my face that he can't see. He's never been this way with me. So dominating and demanding of me. I feel protected, yet controlled all at the same time. I like my freedom, but I love him more—not to mention, this love affair has taken control of both of us. Whirling us around and around and catching us both off guard. I'm sure he's overwhelmed, overjoyed, or over something—just like I am. *This is all happening so fast,* but *time* doesn't understand *love* and *love* makes its own rules. Who are we not to follow those *rules?*

I exhale a delighted breath—moving the phone just enough so that he can't hear the air escaping from my barely parted lips.

"It won't happen again, Conner. You have my word."

His breathing has calmed, and his voice is a whisper compared to what it was a few minutes ago.

"Thank you for understanding, Hannah. I'm so different with you in my life. I like me this way, and it's all because of you."

His words are overwhelming, not to mention my raging hormones, and before I know it I'm tearing up.

"I love my life with you in it too, Conner. Just thinking about you takes my breath away in more ways than I could ever explain."

Silence now on each end, we both sit and contemplate the other's thoughts—each trying to analyze the others words. *Does he really love me? Why won't he just tell me? Is he wondering if I love him?* I don't know, but what I do know is I'm going to be late for work if I don't get a move on. Not everyone is their own boss—*like the man on the other end of the phone.*

"Listen, I hate doing this, but I have to hang up now. I'm already running late for work."

His breathing gets a little off again, but I think he's still okay. "I understand, baby girl. Please take care of you for me."

I grin at his words.

"Consider it done, Mister Dawson."

He hangs up without saying bye, and I rush to get ready for work. I have forty five minutes to get clocked in, and it takes twenty minutes to drive to the office. Today will be a *Plain Jane* kind of day—no make-up or fancy hairdo. A pony tail and casual knee length dress will suffice.

I grab the red slenderizing one from the closet and pull it over my shoulders—opting to wear black sandals and a long black beaded necklace around my neck. I'm ready and out the door in no time.

When I get to my car, I see the unthinkable. I scream and look around the area—searching for anyone or any evidence. *"No freaking way!"*

The window on the driver's side of my car has been broken, and there is shattered glass everywhere, and that's not the worst part. Down every side, the words *teasing whore* have been spray painted in huge black letters. Mr. Jenkins is going to probably fire me over this, but there is no way I can make it to work on time. I have to call Landon—it's great having connections with the police. *I just wish I didn't need one.*

First things first—I take a picture of my vandalized car and decide to send a group message to Conner, Baylee, Landon and my boss.

> **I was leaving for work, and this is what I found. I'm sorry, but I'll be late.**

Attaching a picture of the horrific scene to the text, I hit send.

I can't help but wonder if it was smart including Conner in the message—especially after his reaction to my text this morning. There is no doubt he would find out later, and then he would be upset with me for not telling him. I'm glad I included him.

While the message is on its way, I call my brother. The phone is ringing, and I'm standing there in unbelieving awe of what has happened to my car. I feel so violated. *If I find out whose sorry ass did this, I swear…* Suddenly, the words Kris said to me at the bar that night invades my thinking…*teasing whore.* Is he the one who has been tormenting me? *It has to be a coincidence.*

My thoughts are interrupted when I hear my disoriented brother finally answer. Great, I woke him up. He's yawning and trying to pay attention. "Yeah, Hannah, what's up?"

He yawns again.

I clear my throat. "Did you get my message?"

His phone beeps.

"I just did, hang on."

I hear him yell. "What the hell?"

He puts the receiver back to his ear. "Hannah, are you okay? What happened?"

Before I can answer, I'm getting a beep.

"Hang on." I look at the screen, and it's Conner.

Shoot. I put the phone back to my ear.

"Landon, please just call the office and get someone over to my apartment. I'll be outside waiting. I have to go now." I hang up and take the other call.

"Hello?"

There's that overly heavy breathing again.

"I can see right now that worrying about you is going to give me a coronary, Miss Stone. Are you okay?"

I roll my eyes at my car.

"I am now that I'm talking to you." My nerves were on edge and biting at every nerve ending I had left, but not now. His voice is calming me and soothing my anger to a minimum.

"I guess work will have to wait. I'm calling to get the jet fueled, and I should be there before lunch."

I gasp with anxiety. The thought of him back so soon excites me, but I can't let him leave his job to do it.

"No, Conner. I will be fine. My brother is on his way, and he's use to taking care of his little sister. Please don't let your father down because of me."

He's thinking hard. Almost so hard I can hear his emotions brainstorming—*trying to decide what to do.*

"Are you sure you will be okay?" he asks.

"I promise. My brother will be here any minute, and as soon as we make an official report, I'm going to have him escort me to work."

His voice is raspy and in control again. "Okay, but this is your second strike, Hannah. One more time and I'm stealing you away from the rest of this crazy world and hiding you away in mine."

I flush, remembering our time in Hawaii. I don't think I would put up much of a fight. "Sounds like a deal, Conner. I might even provoke you so you'll have to take me away."

The tension has faded, and we both laugh and say our goodbyes—promising to talk tonight. Silence is on the other end of the phone but not right in front of me.

Landon is here and he's furious.

"Hannah, what have you done, and who the hell have you pissed off?"

I glare at my brother with a look of betrayal. How could he think I made someone do this to my car?

"Did you seriously just ask me that?"

His mouth drops, and his hands fly in the air. "First the letters, then the messages, and now this—*do you not see a pattern here?*" He demands an answer, but I'm still in shock thinking it could be Kris.

Is there really a connection? Crap! I remember the beaming headlights last night. I have to tell Landon, but what if it's not connected, and he throws Kris in jail for nothing. My head is starting to pound, and I start pacing the sidewalk. Here it goes. I'm setting my ex up for something he may not have done.

"Listen, Landon. I don't know if this means anything, but Kris was here last night. His headlights were shining through my bedroom window, and when I pulled the curtain he saw me. He revved up his engine and raced away." Pointing beside my car, I show him the tire marks left by the 4x4 that Kris was driving.

Anger is in my brother's eyes, and if there's one thing I know about him—he will make Kris pay by throwing him in jail before he has time to ask why. I pause before telling him the rest...reading the filthy words all over my car.

"There's something else, Landon."

His eyes widen.

"Of course there is, Hannah, what is it?"

"Those words on my car...they are the same words Kris said to me the other night at Joe's Place."

My brother's face is a blistering shade of red by now, and it's not from the sun peeking through the cloudy sky. Before he has a chance to start cursing words I don't want to hear, a patrol car pulls up, and Landon fills the two officers in.

Afterwards, I look through my car and find that nothing is missing. Everything is still in its place, and then I notice that little round object in the floorboard. It is a baseball, and it must have been what was used to break the window.

Memories of the same kind of worn out balls hitting my apartment window invades my thoughts—realizing there may be a connection, I try to think of anyone who plays the game. This was definitely not an act of theft; just irrevocable meanness by someone who has it out for me...but who?

The report is finished, and the drive to work is the private time that Landon needs to lecture to me. I am his twenty-two year old sister, not his daughter—so I tune him out the best I can. If my vandalized car is connected to the stalker, then that means the jerk hasn't forgotten about me after all? I shake my head—trying to get the thought of it being Kris to go away. He hates baseball, but that doesn't mean anything. It can't be my ex-boyfriend. *It just cannot be.*

Before arriving to work, I tell Landon about my apartment windows and ask him to take it easy on Kris. My gut tells me it's not him, and I trust it more than the words painted on my car.

We're here. Finally, I've made it to the job that pays my bills. Hopefully I will still have a paycheck this time next week. I look at my brother, and the anger is still there. He's pissed thinking that someone he used to consider a friend would cause his baby sister such anguish.

"It's going to be okay, Landon. Don't do anything stupid. We need the truth so don't just assume anything—promise me."

He rolls his eyes but knows it's true. He has to go by the book, or whoever is harassing me may never pay for what they have done. "Agreed sis, call me if you need me."

We say our goodbyes, and I take the dreaded walk into the office.

The morning passes by smoothly, and Mr. Jenkins isn't mad after all. He and Baylee are both glad to see that I'm okay. Maybe he's back to himself, and the grumpy side of him stayed home. I can only hope.

At five o'clock I will be stuck hitching a ride with someone, hopefully my best friend, but I will worry about that later this afternoon. It is lunch time, and I'm famished.

I'm getting ready to go to the break room and eat the tuna salad I left here from yesterday, and my feet stop dead in their track. When I turn to go out my office door, I'm greeted by a young woman carrying a beautiful bouquet of red roses.

Really?

Baylee is standing behind her—here to help me back up when I pass out with fear I'm sure.

"Ms. Stone, I have a special delivery for you ma'am."

Why me? Why won't he leave me the hell alone, and what's up with the freaking red roses this time? They look different than before—more elegant and definitely more expensive.

I'm dazed and lost in thought, and then I hear my name again.

"Ms. Stone."

I look at the woman who must be in her middle to late forties, and she's looking at me like I'm the one crazy—if she only knew.

"Yes, I'm sorry."

I grab the roses, and she hands me a small black box with it. I'm so stunned I don't even think about tipping her, and she's gone before I realize I hadn't. Sitting the flowers down on my desk, curiosity gets the best of me, and I open the box.

I'm more confused than ever. *Why would he give me that?* I search for the card and there it is...right between two roses on the other side of the bouquet. I open the sealed envelope without nicking myself this time—thank goodness. I've got enough bleeding going on down between my legs, and I don't need any more anywhere else.

Sliding out the card, I'm genuinely thrilled with the words that I see. My held breath is released, and my eyes scan the words—grinning as I read them underneath a whispered breath.

My dearest Hannah,

I may be over a thousand miles away, but please let me at least try and protect you from here. Accept my gift and make me a happy man. Enjoy your new ride as much as I enjoy giving it to you. It's parked outside and sitting on a full tank of gas. What are you waiting for? Go check it out.

Conner

I pick up the box, looking at the key, and am absolutely in awe. The man got me a car. *My heart races.* He really got me a freaking car. I run to the door of the lobby and open it to an eyeful of beauty. Parked outside is a 2014 silver Cadillac Escalade—top dollar, loaded, and adorning a huge red bow. Baylee is standing behind me gasping for air.

"Are you kidding me? He got you that?"

I look at her with unaccepting eyes.

"I can't keep it. It's too much." Now, she's looking at me with a hint of crazy in her eyes.

"You are not giving that back. Have you forgotten who the man is behind the gift? The cost of that is only pocket change to someone like him. Let's go check it out."

She's right. I remember Henry's words back in Hawaii— *I was expected to accept it.* That was Conner's expectation of me then, as I'm sure this is now.

Baylee's excitement shows in her eyes as she admires the parked beauty. I grin as it peeks through mine too. I can almost feel my eyes curling up into a smile.

"What are you waiting for?" she asks.

I glance her way, wonderment all over my face.

Astonished is one thing, but stupid I am not. The words are rolling off my tongue before I know it. "Oh, come on already. I'll race you."

Laughter fills the air, and Baylee and I run like crazy to the car. We strip off the bow and jump in the huge SUV. We choose to test drive my new ride instead of eating lunch. It's perfect, and so is he. *He really is.* How have I ever lived my life without him in it? I gasp—having that expression down pat by now, a wide grin spreads across my face…yep, I got that one down pat too.

Baylee turns up the music—testing out the sound system. One word—AWESOME. My new car drives so much smoother than my decade old convertible, and I love the leather seats. It's a dream.

Our one-hour lunch zoomed by, and so did the rest of the afternoon. I leave the office and go home—locking my new ride up with the fob attached to the keychain.

The first thing on my agenda when I get inside my apartment is to call and thank the man who has swept me off my feet. Conner Dawson is the quintessence of true love, perfection, and he's all mine. I smile and search for my tablet. This thank you deserves eye contact—so video chat it is.

Chapter 24

I **hit call on the** screen and the tablet is ringing, but there's no answer. He must still be working. I guess a simple text will have to suffice.

> *A perfect rescue once more Mister D.*
> *You're amazing, and so are my gifts. Call me*
> *when you get a chance.* *

I hit send.

An hour passes, and I've already eaten a bowl of cereal, showered, and now I'm staring at my phone. *Hannah, he is a very busy man. You know this. He will call!* My subconscious is screaming, and I can't help but long to hear his voice—see his face—*admire his body.*

Where is my book? That will occupy my time and take my mind off of him—maybe. Actually, probably not, but I have to try.

I read the first paragraph of the eighteenth chapter.

> *His chest is hard, but his cock is harder—thrusting into me over and over again with breathtaking pumps. My body is his for the taking, and he is on fire—not to mention the hotspot between my legs. Our hips sway back and forth, taking each of us a step closer to the perfect climax. It won't be long now—as we unleash our undying desire to please each other. Our bodies jerk, and here it goes. My nails bore into his naked ass, and he leans over me groaning with pleasure. Even after he releases his massive orgasm, he's still got a*

hard on—making him the perfect sex toy until I
spiral down from mine.

My reading is interrupted by the buzzing of a video call. I lean over to grab the tablet off the stool—taking a deep breath before answering it. I hit accept, and there he is.

"Hey, you," I whisper.

His delectableness shines through, even in the three-piece jet-black suit that is covering all of his masculinity from the neck down. *That tie*—it matches his intense emerald eyes. *Damn, he's gorgeous.* Suddenly I'm longing to have the silky material wrapped around my wrists—confining me as he has his way with me. His face looks fiercely macho with signs of a stressful day, but he's still handsome as ever. If only I could pull him out of the screen by his neatly kept ponytail—drag him to my bed, and ride him like the man-stallion he is—so strong, so beautiful—*so big.* I'm sure a mammoth orgasm would calm his tensed body.

My sex clenches in—begging me to quit teasing her—*just please me already.* Inner self now scowling at my girly stuff—a girl can dream can't she.

"You look good enough to eat, Miss Stone." His voice is tired and raspy—he's in desperate need of winding down, and he's looking at me with wanting eyes.

I laugh, looking down at my nightshirt. It's shortly above knee length, with a v-shaped neck—perfect for teasing him with my barely hidden assets.

"Sounds tantalizing, Mister Dawson—you really shouldn't tease a girl when you're so far away."

He cackles out a seductive laugh and speaks the immaculate truth. "Now, I think we both know that's not enough to stop me, Hannah."

He's right. His recent visit proves that.

His emerald beauties bore into me—tearing away at the material that embraces my body and giving him full view of what hides beneath it. I bet *he's* the one wishing he could pull *me* out of the screen right about now.

I flush at the thought—if only it was possible.

"Well, then, what are you waiting for?"

Now, I'm teasing him with inviting eyes and seductive talk. *Oh Crap!* I almost forgot about *it.* There is no way in hell he is getting close to my blood-tainted kitty for at least a week. I have to change the subject before he's on a plane with a destination straight to my bed. "I'm just kidding, Mister D. As much as I would love to thank you in person for the gifts you didn't have to give me—you have a job to finish."

His breathing gets heavier, and his massive sexual appetite is showing through his dancing eyes. His voice is stern, velvety, and demanding—causing me to tingle right *there,* and I'm desperately contemplating his next touch.

"I am aware of that, Hannah, but I enjoy taking care of you—so get use to it. And it was my pleasure, so you're welcome." He exhales a deep exhausted breath.

"I want my head between your legs—right now. I can taste your sweet juices just thinking about it, and it's the perfect remedy for getting work off my mind." Squirming—he adjusts his manhood. Wiggling in my seat, I try to calm my own desires...I would *die* if his head was right there—*right now.*

Closing his eyes, he inhales deeply—no doubt he's remembering my scent. Crap. My eyes squint, thinking about the tampon plugging off the bloody visitor that is standing in the way of a very hot-kinky moment in my life. *The things a woman has to go through.*

I huff.

I want to please him with an x-rated show, but I can't. Not like this. Think, Hannah, think. Desperate times call for desperate measures. I have to find a reason to hang up with him.

"I can't wait to feel such sweet pleasure, Mister D, but now is not a good time to get me all hot and bothered. I have to call my mom before she goes to bed."

Disgruntled and feeling deprived—he huffs and gives in.

"Fine, baby girl, I got this covered. Don't worry about me—I'll be thinking about you while I'm in the shower." He winks at me, and that's it. I'm turned on and bleeding—time to hang up.

"A man with a plan—glad to know I'll be the star attraction in your mind-blowing fantasy. I'll leave you to take care of your business. Goodnight, gorgeous."

His eyes close and open right back up. "Goodnight, babe."

I end the call and take a moment to compose myself before calling my mom.

Taking a deep breath, I dial her number.

My conversation was short and sweet with her—just long enough to catch up on each other's day, tell her about the new man in my life and to say goodnight. Of course, I chose to leave out the craziness that's been disrupting my life—*stalker-style*. If she knew someone was out to get me, she would have me moved back home in two seconds flat. She was overjoyed to hear about Conner and can't wait to meet him. *Glad that's over.* I've never been one who liked to keep secrets, and Conner Dawson was a big one.

I look at the clock and realize it's still kind of early. I pick up my book to finish the chapter I had started earlier, before calling it a night. I read until I'm too sleepy to go on—my tired eyes closing and my book cuddling up to my chest.

My dreams are all about him and his head all up in my bloody business. *I guess in all reality, that was more of a nightmare. Gross!* I shake the image away as I awake to the loud music playing from my alarm—*another day, another dollar*—my very own recorded tune. I drag my tired butt out of bed and make my way to the shower to freshen up. This time of month is harder than usual. I'm really tired, moody, and ready for *her* to go away.

For the next five days, my emotions were all over the place, and each morning the wakeup call between my legs was a reminder of how much I hated this time of month. Thank goodness my evenings were different. He would call and make everything better, just by the sound of his voice. My nights were filled with tender, loving, enticing talk. Conner and I were just two people sharing our hopes and dreams with each other, but even better—we were falling more and more in love.

We both knew that our relationship was running full speed ahead, but we were also both ready to take it on. Neither of us wanting to hold back—we wanted more and couldn't get enough of each other. Being the mature adults that we are, we decided nothing would keep us apart. We were going to make this work—so what if he traveled the world over and lived in Hawaii.

Like always, I loved listening to his stories. He told me about all the adventures he went on as a young child—to the Smokey Mountains, the Grand Canyon—even his trip to France when he was a young teenager...but also how his dad had started introducing him to the world of investments at a very young age. It was when he turned sixteen that he knew his love for music would only be a hobby, because his dad had *bigger and better* plans for him. Having the utmost respect for his father, and as hard as it was for him to put his dream on the backburner, he knew deep down that's what he would have to do...and he did.

My heart went out to him as he told me about his love affair with music, but I let him know real quick that I was more than willing to sit and listen to him sing me a love song any time he wanted to. He loved the fact that I loved to hear him sing, and sometimes late at night, he would even sing me to sleep via *speaker phone*. As tough as he tries to be on the outside sometimes, I know the real Conner Dawson. He is a die-hard romantic, and I think I may have met my match.

The next two weeks drag by with an occasional unknown call from the jerk that wouldn't go away. *If I ever find out who he is…*the thought disgusts me.

My dreaded days were filled with the same ole same ole at work, but my nights—*totally different.* They were consumed with Conner and our heart to heart conversations. Of course, we took time to tease and please each other with our sensual, sexy, dirty talk, and that helped to ease the lonely nights; but his touch is only a memory that I now crave. I have fallen so in love with this man—as I know he has me. Why won't he tell me? Why won't I tell him? He's due to be here tomorrow night, and Saturday can't get here quick enough.

Friday morning is crazier than usual at the office. Our part-timer called in sick; and that means the workload will be double on me and Baylee today. I don't know how much more I can take of this job—*it's so irritating.*

My mind wanders from focusing on divorce cases to planning my evening. I promised to go to Joe's Place with Baylee. She claims she could use another girl's night out, and like always I couldn't resist her plea. It won't be hard to keep my word since I won't be talking to Conner tonight. He will be too busy tying up all the loose ends on his recent business endeavor and getting ready to come back to me—he made that perfectly clear last night. Ugh! I miss him so much…now if I could just get through this busy Friday, I'll be wrapped in his arms before I know it.

Okay…back to transcribing Mr. Jenkins words.

While I'm working hard at the office and getting depressed as I read the sad words of a desperate house wife, I begin second guessing my job. *Is this really what I want to do for the rest of my life? I don't think so.* I don't know how much more I can work at a job that I don't believe in. I understand people fall in and out of love every day. That is life. It's just that some of their stories end so completely selfish—just like the one I'm working on now.

Mr. McGraw is divorcing his wife because she hasn't been able to lose the unwanted weight after giving birth to their recent daughter. The baby girl is barely a year old, and he thinks his wife should have the same girly hour-glass figure as she did before getting pregnant. *What a loser!* I feel so bad for her, but it's not any of my business. I hurriedly work up the file and end my day with putting it on my boss's desk. It's time to get out of here, do some major career rethinking, and get ready for my night out with Baylee.

Thanks to my new ride, the drive home is smooth and pleasant, and as I pull into my parking spot I debate on what I'm going to wear tonight. Decisions, decisions—a girl and her wardrobe tend to disagree at times, and I feel like I may have one of those nights.

Locking the door behind me, I make my way to the couch. I plop down and begin unraveling from a very stressful day—relaxing and getting the nerve-racking day out of my system. I need a little me time before facing the loud music and massive crowd that is sure to be at Joe's Place.

Uh-oh!

Relaxation settled in, and I had no control of what I did next...yes, I did it. I closed my eyes and went to sleep. *Crap!* My phone is ringing and it's Baylee. The screen says it's eight thirty, but that can't be right. I glance at the clock on the wall. It's right. I answer, and she's excited.

"Get a move on girl. I've been laying on my horn out here for at least five minutes now," she insists.

I use extreme caution when I tell her what I've done. "I. Kinda. Fell. Asleep."

Her voice is surprised. "Seriously? Well, I'm on my way up. Hurry and unlock the door."

I let Baylee pick out my clothes while I'm in the shower. She's got good taste, so I know she'll choose something to my liking. And of course she did. I walk out of the bathroom and lying on my bed is a flawless, flowing, white strapless dress. It has the perfect detail—adorning hot pink and turquoise flowers imprinting the border's edges—both at the breast line and at the hem. My breath catches when I see the flower clip resting next to it. It was my first gift from Conner, and it matches perfectly with the dress and the new pink boots I've been dying to wear. I'm reminded of the luau, but I don't have time to let my thoughts linger. I have to hurry.

Thirty minutes pass by quickly, and I'm ready and we're out the door in no time. Baylee follows behind me, whistling before she says a word. "You look S.E.X.Y. girlfriend." She spells out the word *sexy,* and I'm flattered she thinks so...*if only he were here to witness it.*

Glancing her way, I remind my friend of her own beauty. "Look who's talking. You're pretty damn hot yourself." We laugh and jump in my Escalade and take off—leaving her car parked next to where mine was sitting.

Chapter 25

While pulling up at Joe's, we notice quickly that the parking lot is jammed-packed. I can see right now that we won't be as lucky as last time finding a good place to park. "Over there, next to the bright-yellow jalopy."

Baylee points to a vacant spot at the end, close to the wooded trail that leads right into the middle of nowhere.

"Eh...are you sure? It's pretty dark and dangerous looking down there," I say, turning my nose up at the twenty-year-old-hoopty-classic.

She giggles. "Hannah, don't be a scaredy cat, just park."

Her laugh reassures me, and if she's okay with it I guess I am too.

Here goes nothing.

As I get out of the car, I can't help but scan the area— looking for the jerk that has invaded my life, and put me up to doing a dirty dance with fear itself. It sucks not knowing who the creep is, but I will not let him get in my head tonight.

We walk through the grass and make our way up to the paved parking lot. The sound of music is floating through the air—grasping hold of the wind and doing the tango. There's a light breeze, making it a beautiful night. Even my friend is more carefree than her usual happy-go-lucky self. She really likes the night life, but for some reason she's even more excited tonight. I can't help but wonder what's up with that.

By the light of the moon, I see her face—it's glowing. Dimples in place—pearly whites showing—eyes twinkling— the girl is absolutely stunning. That's it. I want to know what's going on.

"What is up with you, Baylee? You seem especially surreal this evening."

I watch her face, looking for a hint of what has come over her.

"Nothing, why?" she asks.

"Are you sure something's not going on that you want to talk about?"

She shakes her head no, never looking me in the eye, and steadily continues prancing up to Joe's—*cowgirl boots and all.* Finally, after a nanosecond, she can't hold back— giggling out loud now, she stops me midway to our destination for a heart to heart talk.

I knew it!

"I wanted to wait to tell you, but I can't. Oh, I hope I'm not jinxing this." She's ecstatic, glowing, and dancing in place.

"Tell me already!" I exclaim.

"Tyler and I had a long talk after work today." My eyes widen—almost as big as my smile.

I'm listening—ears wide-opened.

"He called me right after I got home and asked if he could come over, and of course I said yes. Well, he was only five minutes away and knocking on my door before I even had time to change clothes," she says breathlessly—she's so excited.

The look of defeat is in her eyes. Tyler has smooth-talked his way back into her life. I just hope this time he doesn't leave her broken-hearted. I continue listening to her closely.

"The baby is his and has become a big part of his life since the paternity test two months ago. That's why he had to get a second job, and that's why he kept standing me up. Sales have been down at the car lot, so he had to take on the extra work. He wants to support his son—emotionally, financially, totally one-hundred percent."

I look at her nodding my head.

Okay, I'm dying to ask a question, and the words are out of my mouth before I have time to stop them. "That's great, for the baby at least. Where does the mom fit into the picture?"

Baylee rolls her eyes—not at me, that look was meant for the mother.

"She doesn't. At least not that often anyway; they agreed to meet at Tyler's parent's house every other Friday. That way he won't have to face *her* alone."

"So, how do *you* fit into all of this?" I couldn't help but ask; I mean this is my best friend's heart hanging on the line.

She takes a deep breath—letting it out easy.

"We both agreed to take things slow this time; just until we can *both* adjust to baby Jaxon being in our lives."

She looks so happy.

"That's great, Baylee. I told you to give it time; I knew he cared. So, where is he anyway?" *Me and my questions— one day I am literally going to put my foot in my mouth.*

"He's going to meet us here later. I hope you don't mind," she says.

"Are you kidding me? I wouldn't have it any other way," I exclaim.

I smile and embrace her with an *I'm-so-happy-for-you-kinda-hug*, and we continue making our way up to the entrance.

People are everywhere—crowding all three decks outside and inside. I find myself trying to figure out why in the world she wanted me tagging along tonight. If Tyler's meeting her, why would she need me around? I refuse to ask...maybe she's just nervous. I leave it alone and decide I'm here for back up...just in case. Ty's history with showing up isn't the best, and if he doesn't, she will not need to be alone.

Struggling to make it past the crowd, I'm trying to make my way through the entrance with her only a few short-feet behind me. I feel her hand touch my back—tugging at my dress.

"Hey, Hannah, let's just go to the top deck. The fresh air is great tonight."

Thank goodness. We turn around and make our way to the outside stairs—climbing them until we are at the top. There is an open bar just a few feet away, and we walk over to get an ice cold drink to quench our thirst. *That was some walk.* It's a pleasantly warm evening, with an occasional crisp wind blowing in. Our drink of choice is a frozen piña colada—dressed up with a pineapple slice and a cute little umbrella.

Standing here, watching the stars twinkling in the night sky and admiring the moon shining down—it is a perfect summer night—*if only he were here, it would be breathtaking.*

The cool breeze continues to swoop in, and lightning bugs are flying around everywhere. I breathe in deep—*then deeper;* it's almost as though I can smell *him.* I look around—hoping he would be near, and then I recall his promise to be here tomorrow.

My heart smiles and Baylee sees it spreading all over my face.

"What are you thinking about, Hannah? You're grinning like it's nobody's business, and I'm making it all mine," she laughs.

I laugh.

The music stops.

We both turn around looking for a reason why, but nothing. Then, I hear him speak. My heart races right into my throat, and I choke on my frozen drink. I cannot believe he's here.

His voice is deep, *sexy* deep.

"How's everybody doing tonight?"

The crowd goes crazy—screaming, whistling, and demanding to be entertained.

My eyes find his. He's center stage and only about thirty feet away—holding a guitar in his hand and sitting on a barstool. Our eyes are locked and in place—we both grin ear to ear.

He's back, gorgeous as ever and dressed in my favorite jeans and black, tight, fitting tee. My heart clenches with desire—beating my sex before she has a chance to. That shirt is hugging him—embracing the man beneath it, and I'm dying to do the same.

Thoughts of my bare skin wrapped around his bare skin sends chills from my head to my toes. I try shaking it off, but the feeling is determined to stay. I'm tingling all over; especially from my heart to below my waist.

He laughs into the microphone and begins speaking again. "I promise to sing, but first I'd like to tell you a little story."

I'm breathless and the crowd is restless. I listen carefully as he begins.

"About two months ago, I met a girl who stole my heart."

Women start screaming. *"Me. Me."*

He laughs again. "Sorry, ladies. I'm a one-woman-kind-of-man, and I'm all hers." He winks at me, causing me to inhale deeply—slowly I release my breath between slightly parted lips.

Continuing on...

"Anyway, this girl has changed my world, and I don't care if it's been two months or two years—I can't stop thinking about her."

The crowd cheers him on, and he grins.

"Time is defined as an indefinite existence...it doesn't have a heart, but I do, and now she has mine. She's always on my mind—even in my dreams. Hell, I couldn't even get any work done this week because I was too busy writing her this love song." A huge grin spreads across my face, and he's got my undivided attention.

He begins picking away at the guitar strings—slowly...beautifully...*so gracefully.*

"It's called, *You'll Be My Rescue*, and Hannah...you're mine."

Tears fill my eyes—my throat burning with whispered words. *I love you, Conner Dawson...I love you...I love you...I love you.* Though he never hears me...those unspoken words haven't left my lips, but they will tonight and everyday for the rest of my life.

Baylee puts her hand in mine—squeezing it gently and winking at me. She knew he was going to be here. That's why she was determined to get *me* here.

His deep sultry voice continues on—speaking words that melt my pounding heart. "Hannah Stone, this is for you. *I love you, baby girl.*"

His last words were like a whisper, but loudly heard over the microphone with a perfect landing straight to my heart. It was a perfect way to end his story telling and a perfect way to begin the song. He continues picking at his guitar and strumming a melody that is truly music to my ears—*my heart*—my whole existence.

This is *the* butterfly-effect-kinda-moment I've waited on my whole life. The feeling is consuming me...swirling around and around deep inside me from my head to my toes. I can feel the fluttering pulsing through my veins so hard it's vibrating from the inside out. My skin...my breathing...my heart...my everything is wrapped up in this moment. His *love* has embraced me and I can feel it. He's sitting there. I'm standing here...and *I feel it.*

As he picks at the strings, he hums to the beat.

Naturally, I begin to sway to the breathtaking sound.

Looking around, so is everyone else.

I look back at him.

He's watching me. That gaze...it's so intensely beautiful.

I wink at him.

He winks back.

This is it.

As the words start to roll off of his tongue, tears begin rolling onto my cheeks. The lyrics are absolutely breathtaking.

Girl, loving you comes naturally
Like breathing, dreaming, and wanting you
I'll be your hero, and you'll be my rescue
We'll take flight in the wind like angels do

I can see us now, walking barefoot in the sand
And we'll make love like only we can
Skin on skin, breathless and connected
Underneath the stars and always protected

Mmmm, mmmm, mmm, mmmm,mmmm, mmmmmm, oh yeah

Dreams come true and lovers unite

Reality steps in and memories are made
I'll be your hero, and you'll be my rescue
We'll take flight in the wind like angels do

Break free from the fear and hear my song
I'll be your strength and you'll make me strong
Baby, all we need is each other's love
Guiding us through this journey called life

Mmmm, mmmm,mmm, mmmm,mmmm, mmmmmm, oh yeah

I want to love you hard and hold you tight
Embracing the moments and sharing the nights
I'll be your hero, and you'll be my rescue
We'll take flight in the wind like angels do

Time has no limit when it comes to true love
Paradise is forever, nothing else matters
With trust and forgiveness, we'll make it through
Listen to the beat of my heart say I love you

Mmmm, mmmm,mmm, mmmm,mmmm, mmmmmm, oh yeah

I'm left breathless and dying to be in his arms. My body language is screaming come to me, but he sits there—finishing the flawless song. His fingers continue gliding over the strings of the guitar; all while his eyes are directly on me.

The song ends, and the next thing I hear is a big bang and a crackling boom. I look up in the sky, and I'm utterly blown away. My heart is exploding right along with the luminous light show.

In sparkling letters spell the words:

Marry Me Hannah

I'm shocked, stunned and overwhelmed at the sight of the astonishing firework display. My eyes didn't know what happy tears were until I saw those words. I begin crying uncontrollably. Baylee hands me a tissue, and I pat my eyes dry—carefully, trying not to get mascara everywhere.

Quickly, I look at him, and he's sitting there looking like he's desperate for my answer. The crowd is cooing and going wild. They loved it, but not near as much as I did. This hot-dreamy moment tops any of my romance novels, and it's all mine—my very precious, idealistic moment up under the stars.

My eyes leave his, but only for a fraction of a second. I look back up at the sky to watch the glittering words fade into the night, all while wondering if fate and destiny really do exist, and if they are looking down on us at this very moment—approving of Conner's proposal. I think they are.

Gracefully, I bring my eyes back down to earth, and they find him walking right towards me with open arms. My heart is screaming at my feet. *"Run to him, you lucky girl you."* But my mind is still in shock, and I'm utterly paralyzed due to nothing but pure decadent excitement.

This is the moment I've waited for my whole life, and it's happening at this very moment. I etch the memory in my mind, and deep in my heart for safe keeping. The beauty of this instant is surreal and has been kissed by fate. My destiny is with him, and I will spend the rest of my life loving him unconditionally.

Seconds before I'm face to face with him, my mind releases the hold it has on me, and I jump into his masculine arms. Conner's lips are on mine, and he's spinning me in the air. As our mouths part and I'm still in his tight-loving-embrace, I whisper the one heartfelt word that he wants to hear.

"Yes."

He kisses me again and swings me around until I'm dizzy.

After a thousand nanoseconds of drinking each other in, he puts me down, gets on one knee, and places *it* on my ring finger—the biggest, most beautiful, sparkling diamond ring I have ever laid my eyes on.

I stare into those tell-it-all-beauties of his with tears in mine, and confess my feelings. "I love you, Conner Dawson. I have loved *you* my whole life."

And he kisses me again.

The crowd is applauding—men along with hundreds of women with looks of envy all over their faces. The moment was splendid until I look *his* way. My heart stops when I see Kris eyeballing me from the bar. He downs an ice cold beer and slams the bottle down on the counter—taking off and more pissed than ever before.

Kendall is behind the counter and cleans up the mess he made—shaking her head and giving me the evil-eye. I will not worry about their stupidity right now; this is my time, and they will not ruin it. I can't help but gloat in this moment as Conner wraps me up in his embrace, and I look around the deck with all eyes still on us.

Baylee is standing close enough to steal a hug from me, and I can't help but hear Conner when he thanks her.

"Thank you, Baylee…by the way, it's nice to finally meet you in person."

"Likewise," she says with a nod of her head.

I giggle.

She chuckles.

"You are the best friend ever," I assure her.

"No, you are."

She squeezes me tight and releases me back to the love of my life.

He wraps his strong arms around me, pulling me closer—as though he's holding on for dear life. I can feel the warmth of his breath on my neck and up to my ear. *It tickles.* He leans in closer and whispers sweet words of his undying love straight to my heart—sending my skin into overdrive and fighting off thousands of goose bumps. "I love you, Hannah. I have since the very first night I laid eyes on you."

I exhale.

"Me too, Conner—with every breath I take, I love you."

Our lips lock, and we begin swaying to the music of the jukebox. It's a fast song with a rocking rhythm. We are moving our feet and shaking our butts before I have the chance to say hello to Tyler. He must have just gotten here, and he has wasted no time pulling Baylee out to the dance floor beside us. She's glowing even more than before, and it's because of him; *she really has it bad.* I look at Tyler as he watches her; *so does he.*

My attention leaves them and focuses primarily on him. The man who has just about made my every dream come true. We dance the night away while my mind races ahead in time—thinking about our wedding night. I truly can't wait to give myself to him—*all of me.* My virginity will finally be rescued, and I will be his—always and forever.

Chapter 26

By the end of the night, we are all standing around breathing hard and ready to go home. There is nothing like dancing the night away with friends and the one you love. Tyler is raring and willing to take Baylee home when he realizes she rode here with me; which is absolutely perfect because I can't wait to get *tall, dark, and romantic* back to my apartment.

Conner gets my attention.

"Hey, babe, I've got to hang around for just a few minutes. Joe and I have some quick business to discuss. Do you mind?" He asks, but that doesn't stop me from wanting to get him home.

"I don't mind. I'm going to go ahead and walk out with Baylee and Ty to get the car; I'll pick you up at the door." He pulls me close, landing his mouth on my forehead and marking it with a wet kiss.

"Perfect, baby girl, I'll only be a few minutes."

He releases me and walks to the office.

The three of us head out of the building and say our goodbyes at Ty's car. He's parked half way down from mine, and I insist on them not walking me the rest of the way down. I'm too excited to be scared, and they are too into each other to care either way. I wouldn't want to ruin their moment anyway, so I keep walking as they beep and pull out of the empty parking lot. The crowd cleared out pretty fast; I guess while the four of us were all caught up in our conversation of football and next year's super bowl. I look at my watch, and it's already half past three. *Wow!*

Almost to my car, I unlock the doors with my clicker—causing the headlights to flash and a quick beep to sound from under the hood. I open the door and climb in, dropping my car keys as I go. *Damn it!* They went under the vehicle.

On bended knee, I begin to panic and start searching for them in the grass. There's not much light, and I'm having a hard time. I move my hand over the whole area, from the front tire to the back tire.

There they are.

I go to grab them and when I do, I hear something moving around on the other side.

Shit!

What is that?

Who is that?

I get a nauseous feeling when I realize it is footsteps, and they are coming around quickly with me still on the ground. I try to make it up fast enough, but the man with the hidden agenda gets to me before both of my feet are touching the grass. I'm putty in his hands as he covers my face with a cloth saturated with chloroform. I'm out in seconds and in the backseat of my own SUV, driving away from the bar—*Connerless.*

Drowsy and confused, I can't open my eyes; nor can I make out the voices I hear in the background. *Who is that man?* He speaks with broken English, but I'm not sure what nationality he is—maybe Hispanic; yes, that's it. I recognize his accent. But the woman, I know I heard a woman's voice too. There it is again. I listen while fighting to open my eyes. I think I recognize it, but I'm too tired to fight the drowsiness any longer. Everything goes black, and I'm out in a flash.

Time is passing by, but I'm not sure how much. Grabbing my head, I finally begin to open my eyes again…just a little at first. I have such a headache. It must be from the chloroform. I look around the room, and it's cold and dark. I'm lying on a concrete floor with a blanket as a bed and a thin pillow under my head. There's a bottle of water sitting on the floor beside me, but I'm too scared to drink from it.

I hear muffled voices. They are trying to be quiet and undetected, but it's too late. I recognize the woman. I'm floored with confusion. Why would she do this to me? Kendall is the one behind all of this, but why? The two kidnappers are fighting about what to do with me. The man, whom she refers to as Carlos, is not up for the plan she has in store for me. *Thank goodness!*

I gasp, letting out a whisper of a cry. Tears fall and I'm scared to death. Why does she hate me so much? I sniffle and wipe away the tears—not sure what to do next.

Looking at my watch, I see that it's 5:30 in the morning. I've been out for two hours. Shit! Conner must be freaking out—not to mention Baylee, Landon, my mom...*my poor mother*. I know Conner has contacted them by now just to see if I'm with them. By now, he knows that I'm not, and I'm sure he's searching for me.

The door cracks open, and I no longer hear them talking. In comes one foot and then another.

I swallow hard.

It's the man—Carlos, I presume.

"Senorita, are you okay?" he whispers, trying hard not to be heard.

My breathing picks up faster, and my heart is ready to beat out of my chest. It hurts, and my nerves are shot, and this man has the audacity to ask me if I'm okay.

Calm down, Hannah. Don't piss him off more than he already is—my inner self on her hands and knees begging...pleading for dear life.

"I'm okay. Why am I here?" I ask.

He coughs and hesitates before speaking.

"The girl wants you broke in—hardcore and painful. That is the exact way she wants you to lose your virginity to *me*. She's pissed because I won't do it. She said something about making you suffer—just like you have made her." He exhales. "What have you done to piss that hot-tempered puta off?"

I'm confused.

"Nothing that I know of—I just don't understand." I cough, and he hands me the water.

"It's okay. I promise, Chula."

I take the bottle, and the top is still sealed. Thank goodness, because I am dying of thirst.

Carefully, I untwist the top and take a sip, then a bigger one. All along while watching him closely, but no closer than he's watching me.

Leaning in, he moves the hair away from my face.

I think I'm going to throw up...*this can't be happening.*

Jerking my head, he pulls away.

"I'm sorry, mamí, don't be afraid," he insists. "I'm going to help you...I promise."

"What?" I ask, more confused than ever.

"Pendeja," he mumbles.

"Huh?" I ask, still freaking oblivious to what's going on.

"That stupid ass girl lied to me," he huffs. "She told me she was doing this for love—I thought she loved you...guess I was wrong. My familía just really needs the money, and..."

We hear footsteps.

It's her.

"I have to go, but I will be back...and just so you know, I don't rape women, so don't even worry yourself," he whispers, leaving me alone in the darkness. He steps out, shutting the door and locking it with a key. I'm stuck in here with no windows. The only light I have is the crack beneath the door.

Desperation may have been in his voice, but that sick nauseous feeling is still somersaulting away in the pit of my belly. *If he won't take my virginity, will she find someone else to do it?*

I hear her voice—screeching out louder than she meant.

"What the hell are you doing in there, Carlos? Did I not tell you to guard the door? I never said open it." She screams at him, trying to keep her voice low and unheard.

"Si, Senorita," he says.

Kendall's voice is angry, and her temper is flaring hot. "One more time Carlos, and you will not get paid, understood."

"Si, Senorita, I understand," he says reluctantly.

For a moment there is silence, and then I hear the scrambling of feet; lots of thundering footsteps heading my way.

"Hands in the air! Now!"

The police are here. I let out a massive breath of air and wait patiently to be rescued.

"Where is she, you sorry piece of shit?" he screams, his words piercing my heart. It's Conner, my *hero*. He's found me.

The next thing I hear is the massive sound of a punch in the face and a loud thump on the floor. There's no denying that would be Carlos's limp body I see lying in front of the only crack of light I have. Conner knocked him out cold. I guess it served him right…he may not be a rapist, but he is an abductor.

I can hear Kendall screaming in the background.

"You'll get what's coming to you eventually, Hannah Stone. I promise you that much."

"Handcuff her and take her away." The officer in charge demands.

"Yes sir," says one of the other officers.

I hear the doorknob rattling, and I can tell his hands are shaking, but he's got the keys and working his way to bring me to safety.

Finally, the door opens, and there he is.

"Hannah, oh Hannah…my sweet, sweet Hannah."

On bended knees, he grabs me up in his arms and kisses every inch of my face with sweet, gentle, butterfly kisses— then stands carefully…carrying me out of the room and onto a field of grass.

I look around, and people I don't know and people I do, are all around the abandoned baseball arena…that explains the old *baseballs* and *broken windows*. They begin screaming my name—my friends, my brother, and even my mom.

I can't speak.

I bury my face in Conner's chest, and he hurriedly walks past everyone. I can't talk to anyone right now, and he knows it. They will have to wait—as much as I hate ignoring them. At least now they know that I'm safe, so any explanations will have to wait until later.

My SUV is parked on the other side of the deteriorating chain-linked fence with the keys still in the ignition. Conner puts me inside on the passenger side, seat belting me up before getting in the driver's seat.

"Are you okay, baby girl?" he asks breathlessly, fear still in his voice. "Can I get you anything? *Did they hurt you?*" his last question a whisper that I barely even heard.

I shake my head.

"I'm okay. Just a little shaken and confused—I was out of it most of the time from the chloroform."

He's pissed. His breathing is erratic. His glare is ice-cold, and his jaw is clenched so tight I think I hear his teeth grinding together. Rage is consuming him for what they put me through.

"They. Will. Pay. Hannah. I will make both of them pay," he says, his voice glazed over with darkened fury.

He is more determined than ever to keep me safe.

Slamming his hands on the steering wheel, he curls his fingers around the leather. A half second later, he places his head on his knuckles—he's beating himself up for not protecting me, I'm sure.

"I'm okay, Conner. I just want to get to the bottom of this. How did you find me anyway?"

Slowly, he removes his hands from the leathered wheel and glances my way—his knuckles softly grazing my face. Moving down, I can feel the palm of his hand touching my thigh—rubbing it with dominating controlling strokes. He squeezes my leg—*tighter than I'm use to.*

"I'll always be here for you, Hannah, never doubt that. I made sure to have a GPS installed on your car before delivering it to you. I almost didn't, but now I'm glad I did."

I place the palm of my hand on top of his and quickly he reverses it; placing his on top of mine. His protective side is showing. He wants to be in control. "Let's get you home and in bed," he demands.

I glance his way, and a crazy thought enters my mind—one he's not going to like. "No, take me to the police department," I blurt out.

This time I am the one demanding.

He looks at me hard; a confused and worried look peering through his heated gaze.

"Please, Conner. I have to talk to Kendall, or I'm never going to get this night out of my head."

His breathing gets heavier, and his nose flares with each passing breath. Oh my. I've hit a nerve.

"I don't want you anywhere around those people, Hannah." His voice is tense, and so is he.

Once again, he has both hands on the steering wheel—gripping it tighter and tighter; so tight, I can hear it squeaking. He wants to please me, but he wants even more to keep me safe. He's caught between a love and hate situation, and I have put him right in the middle.

"She may be locked up, but that will not stop her from the mental abuse. Please, leave it alone, and let's go home," he pleads.

Releasing his grip, he starts the ignition and then runs his fingers through his tasseled hair. He's frustrated, but so am I. Confused, he squeals out of the parking lot— speeding way too fast on the winding road.

My heart listens to him, but my mind refuses to.

"I promise not to let her get in my head. This has been going on way too long, and I have the right to have my questions answered."

Crap! I hit another nerve.

His nose flares even faster than before; his breath catching in his throat.

"What do you mean *going on too long?*" he asks through gritted teeth.

I huff.

"I never wanted to worry you, but this all started around the same time I met you. I've been getting unknown calls, flowers with creepy poems, and letters on my windshield and…"

He stops me.

"All this and you never told me. I don't understand, Hannah?"

"Conner, I was scared to tell you; scared I would lose you." I turn my head, looking out the window into the darkness.

He pulls over onto the side of the road and puts the car in park, then takes my head in his hands and turns me to face him. "You're never going to lose me, baby girl. Not then, not now, not ever." He leans in, grabbing my chin and cupping it in the palm of his hand, and finally locking his lips on mine. Slowly, his lips move away. "I love you, Hannah, more than I have ever loved anybody in my entire life. I will die protecting you if that's what it takes."

With one hand on each side of his face, I gaze into his eyes. "It's not going to go that far; I won't let it." His eyelids close, and my hands fall away from his gorgeous worried face.

"You have five minutes. That's it. I will arrange it, but only on my terms," he demands, slowly opening his eyes back up.

I stare at him…hard and confused—*terms?* "Okay, what terms are those?"

"I will be right there with you; to back you up and to knock the complete shit out of the bitch that set you up." He's really pissed. I have never heard him talk like that, but at least he's giving in.

"Okay, your terms. I will see her on your terms." He makes a quick phone call and makes it happen—a meeting between Kendall and the two of us. We both stare out the window…speechless and tormented. Our minds are racing, trying to figure this scenario out—*hopefully we are only minutes away from knowing.*

We pull up at the station.

An officer is waiting at the door to take us back. We go through the normal security procedures—empting my purse and his wallet and pockets.

Shortly afterwards, we're buzzed through. The walk to Kendall is a short few feet away, and she sees us coming. She's been crying. Her cheeks are smudged with black eyeliner, and mascara is all the way down both sides of her face. Sitting there immobile and looking like a mere hollow image of her old self, I can't help but wonder if she is really this stupid. My heart almost goes out to her, and then I remember why she's here. She is the guilty one, not me.

My gut instinct tells me she's got her game face on— maybe she's trying to play her pity card. Game face—pity card—*who cares?* I'm in control now, and I want answers.

Two seats are in front of the visitor's station, and a glass is the only thing between us that prevents any form of physical attack, but Conner is right; I need to play it smart to prevent her from playing with my head. He whispers in my ear, reminding me of my time limit.

"You're five minutes starts now."

I blink and nod my head once, letting him know I understand, and I sit down in front of my tormentor.

"Kendall," I say.

Her look is mean—almost intimidating.

"What do you want, Hannah? Have you not caused enough trouble?" She asks, her voice smothered in fury.

Me? Did she really just say me? I take a deep breath, trying to control my anger. *How dare she blame me?*

Her gaze is now even more horrid. If looks could kill…she would be a happy woman—I'd be stretched out on the floor...*lifeless*. She will not scare me away. I give her a revolting look right back.

"Kendall, please tell me why you hate me, and maybe I won't have them throw the book at you."

Her laugh is meaner than her look—almost like that of a wicked old witch. She really is crazy. She's not saying anything, just laughing that same freaky weird-ass laugh.

"Let's go, Conner. This was a waste of my time." My words calm, cool and collected—backing away from the window, I stand to my feet and begin walking away.

Just as we're about to go through the opened doors, she bellows out.

"I really love him you know, but he will barely give me the time of day because of you. *Kris only has eyes for his precious Hannah.* And every time I thought he was ready to move on, you showed up—taking his attention from me, right back to you."

She cries out in agony, and deep down...I really do *almost* pity her. We keep walking, never acknowledging she had said a word when she actually said everything we needed to hear. Conner grabs my hand, and we leave.

Later that day, I make a phone call to Landon and ask him to make sure Kris' name is in the clear; thankfully, he had already taken care of it first thing this morning. He also spoke to Kris, man to man, friend to friend—letting him know he didn't have a chance reuniting with me. After a long talk, he agreed to move on. *Thank goodness!*

Maybe now my life will find some sort of normalcy. The *stalkers* are locked up, Kris is *finally* truly in my past, Baylee has Tyler, and I have Conner...perhaps now we can all live life like there's no tomorrow. Never looking back on regrets, but cherishing every day as if it were our last.

Chapter 27

Autumn is showing her true colors—leaves are falling, and there is a chill in the air that has scared summer into hiding. It's hard to believe that August has slipped away, and now September is only about a week away from ending. The days are passing by fast, and our wedding is just around the corner—seven days to be exact.

It's been over four weeks since the incident with Kendall, and luckily she is still locked up. Those tormented days are now in my past, and today is the first day of the rest of my life—my future with Conner awaits and I couldn't be happier. I'm so glad we chose against the long engagement. *Why wait when we're ready now?*

It's a beautiful morning waking up in the arms of the man I am going to marry. My head lying on his chest and his heart beating away—I listen to its perfect rhythm. Thump—thump—thump. He's told me on more than one occasion now, that his heart beats for me...he's such an idealistic romantic. I smile listening—allowing myself to believe that it is true.

Conner continues to sleep as I continue to bask in all his beauty. He really is a beautiful man—*inside and out.* There's no doubt he is a man of many colors—and I love each and every one of them—the business man—the song writer—the passionate lover—the kinky dominant...*especially the passionate kinky dominant lover.*

My kitty purrs for her good morning rub. My inner self pats her—reassuring her there will be plenty of time for that on the honeymoon.

Trying to focus on the actual ceremony and not the wedding night has been harder than I thought it would be. My heart longs to be his wife, but my body craves to be his lover in every way. The desire has been eating away at both of us, but our love has fought the fight, and we have managed to keep my virginity intact.

We have decided to tie-the-knot at our new home—right on the beach. I will walk down a sandy aisle as a single woman and walk away as Mrs. Conner Dawson. Our first night as man and wife will be spent at the house, and the rest of the honeymoon is a secret Conner refuses to share with me.

My mom loves my future husband and is overjoyed when we tell her the wedding is going to be in Hawaii, but not so much when I tell her that is where we will also be living. Conner hasn't left my side since the abduction, so having us here has her a little spoiled. He also insisted that I quit my job since I wouldn't let him tail me to work every day. Of course I did put in a resignation, and I insisted on helping to get the new girl trained. She was very smart and picked up quickly, making my job that much easier to leave.

Now, if I can just break myself away from his loving embrace, I can get up and focus on tying up the loose ends of our wedding. I try slipping out of bed, and his grip tightens.

"Oh, no you don't, Mrs. Dawson."

I can't help but giggle, and then let out a sigh of defeat.

"Mrs. Dawson, huh?" I ask?

He rolls me flat on my back and climbs on top of me—teasing me with his soft voluptuous lips. My breath catches as he glides his tongue up and down my neck and all over my breast—leaving my nipples defenseless, protruding, and begging for more wet-lip action.

Kissing his way back up—finally his eyes meet mine.

"Yes, Mrs. Dawson. I don't need signed documents telling me you're my wife. In my heart, you already are."

I kiss him.

He kisses me back.

I pull away and look deep into the windows of his soul, the opened windows that are full of raging hot passion; not only for me but for this thing we call life. He's living it to the fullest, and he's invited me to share it with him till death do us part. Soon our hearts will be one, emotionally, physically, and *legally*. I can't wait.

"You're perfect you know that right, Mister D."

A grin spreads across his face.

"You make me perfect, Mrs. D."

We laugh, and suddenly I feel his massive hard-on thumping away at my inner thighs; slowly inching its way toward his prized possession. It's knocking at my womanhood—dying to slide on in.

"Only seven more days, Conner, and you will fill me with all that manly pride."

He grins, taking a peek beneath the sheets and growling as he looks back at me.

That look—that sound—damn, he's got Sexy fighting for his title back.

Getting a grip, I finish my thought.

"Thank you for your patience, even though sometimes I know it was almost more than you could bear."

He groans with heated desire—thinking about our wedding night I'm sure.

"My pleasure, baby girl, now get dressed before I devour you."

He releases his hold and up I go. I don't know what his fetish is with spanking my ass, but there he goes again. I'm barely out of the bed and rubbing the passionate sting away that his masculine hand left on my behind. It turns him on. I know it does, and I would be lying if I said it didn't me. I cackle an amusing, flirtatious laugh, and he lays there moaning pleasure sounds as I walk away.

I shake my head and turn around.

"One day, Conner Dawson—one day I'm going to smack that tight sexy ass of yours and make you beg for more."

His arched brows do that thing I have come to love, up and down, over and over again, fast and sexy as hell—making me fall in love with him all over again. "Please do, Hannah, I can't wait until you do."

His smile is contagious. I'm grinning ear to ear—leaving him sprawled out naked on my bed with only a thin white sheet between his mouthwatering manhood and my wandering eyes. *He looks scrumptious—good enough to eat.*

I have to get out of this room before I'm back in bed with him.

My body may be yearning to be close to his, but I have got to get busy finalizing the last details of our wedding. I go to the living room and grab my laptop. The first thing I pull up is my calendar. Every day for the next week is full.

Day 1-September 23

Starting this morning at ten o'clock, I will meet with Amelia St. Julien, the world renowned wedding dress designer from France. Conner flew her in a week after he proposed, and within forty-eight hours she had not only sketched my most desirable wedding gown, but also had a sample made. He insisted that I have the dress of my dreams, and from the pictures she has emailed me, it looks like I'm getting it. I just hope it fits as perfect as it looks; I've lost five pounds this week due to lack of an appetite and a nervous stomach. *Wedding planning can really be very stressful.*

After the fitting, we are scheduled for a light lunch at Baylee's parent's house—followed by a no-holds-barred bridal shower this evening. *I'm still trying to figure the theme out.* I'm so thankful to Baylee's mom, Mrs. Parker, for opening her home up to us on such short notice.

Day 2-September 24

A shop-until-you-drop kind of day—my gift from my mom; the shopping part will be fun, but the time spent with her will be priceless, and that's a gift in itself.

Day 3-September 25

Packing; *the thing I dread the most.*

Day 4-September 26

Final farewells to friends and family—*no, this is the thing I dread the most.*

Day 5-September 27

Fly to Hawaii and get unpacked.

Day 6-September 28

Meet with the caterers at noon and finalize the menu for the luau-themed reception—*I can't wait to see the cake.* Later that evening, we will have a small rehearsal dinner at the house.

Day 7-September 29

OUR WEDDING DAY!!

I really shouldn't wish my life away, but I honestly can't wait until that day gets here. I long to share more than Conner's last name…I want our bodies to connect in a way they never have. I want to share my innocence with the man that I will love for the rest of my life.

I glance at the time, and it's already eight o'clock. I exit out of my calendar and close my laptop, thinking I had better get a move on. We're supposed to pick Mrs. St. Julien up at the airport shortly before ten and then head to my mom's house. Of course Conner will not be allowed to stay while I'm trying on my dress; that is unless he waits in the car. The thought is humorous. *He will probably sit in the car.*

A smile spreads across my face as I hear the light sound of footsteps tiptoeing close behind me. It's as though I can feel his eyes moving up and down my body—he's getting closer. I take a deep breath in, and that confirms his presence.

Conner leans towards me, freshly showered, looking gorgeous, and smelling heavenly. His scent is hovering over me like a blanket of fine silk. I am longing for him to cover my body with his until I smell just like him, and it is as though he can read my mind. Within seconds, he wraps his arms around me, and suddenly I am high on Conner Dawson…the most addictive drug I know. The thought of losing him would be like an addict without their fix; there is no doubt I would have withdraws if I went a day without his touch. That can't happen. I won't let it. I bury my face in his chest, inhaling the man I have come to love immensely more than I ever dreamed possible.

Slowly, I trail my head up, breathing him in even more as I will his mouth to cover mine—finally lip locking him and placing my hand on the bulk of manliness beneath his zipper. I stroke him, up and down—ending with a gentle squeeze and catching him off guard. Instantly, he's hard and turned on. His eyes are burning with desire, and he inhales—letting his breath out soft and easy.

"Why, aren't you a frisky little thing this morning?"

He kisses me hard, tasting my morning breath. *Thank goodness he's so turned on he doesn't notice.* He jerks me out of the chair and into his arms—tearing his mouth away from mine.

"You're in trouble now, little lady."

He walks back to my room and stops at the bed, throwing me on top of the sheets. Quickly he frees my body from every inch of clothing that covers it. My body is craving his touch. His hands glide up and down my waist and then down to my thighs—all while covering my bare-naked body with seductive butterfly kisses. His breath is hot. I feel the warmth of his tongue as he trails it all the way down *there*; my purring kitty is waiting to be bathed with wet, sensuous kisses.

I gasp.

He's almost there.

Oh no, he bypasses it and goes straight down to my inner thighs. His kiss is slow, passionate, and turning me on like crazy. I can't help but let out a provocative moan—maybe now he'll head back north and take time to show my womanhood the attention it needs.

No such luck, he's still going south.

He raises my right leg up in the air with my knee slightly bent—kissing my calf, my ankle, and the tips of each one of my toes. My breathing picks up. This is pretty freaking erotic. I jump, arching my back in the air and gasping for sweet relief. His tongue glides between each toe before covering his mouth over the big one.

Oh. My. Goodness.

"Oh, Conner, please...*I'm begging you!*"

I plea for mercy, but it doesn't matter. He loves controlling me this way.

My body quivers as he sucks and gently bites—sending goose bumps all over my hot craving body. I can't take much more. His teasing is driving me absolutely wild. I raise my head to look at him—our eyes meet. His brow arches and does that thing that drives me crazy...all while my toe is still in his mouth—his tongue circling, swirling, and teasing me.

"Conner, please."

This time, he can't resist. A gentle last bite and then he kisses a path directly to that very needy hot-spot between my legs—*his very own all you can eat buffet.*

Finally, he buries his head in my nicely trimmed bush, flicking his tongue over my love-button like an absolute genius. Such sweet pleasure as he ends my torture—sending me straight past oblivion and right into a celestial awareness. My body lavishes in the orgasmic shower—feeling more refreshed than ever.

Ah! What a magnificent climacteric event. He slowly licks me through it—with gentle strokes, heated breath, and right up until the very last fabulous orgasmic pulse. *Wow!* Helpless and satisfied, he pins my body under his, kissing me and sharing his breakfast—*twat a la carte.*

Pulling away, he gently gives my forehead a peck and stands up on the floor. He holds his hand out to me and helps me up. "Get ready, baby girl. You don't want to be late trying on that dress." He winks, and I look at him like he's overdosed on coochie juice.

I could feel his manhood throbbing up against me, yet he expects nothing. He never ceases to amaze me. I turned him on and *he made me come.* That man has restraint—more than I realized.

His arms are crossed, and that amazing buff body of his is leaning on the door frame watching me get ready. I'm in the bathroom and his reflection from the mirror shows he is staring me up and down. Standing only in my bra and panties, his hungry gaze is eating away at my half-naked body.

"See something you like, Mister D?"

"Do I ever, baby girl," he says.

With raised brows and eyes blazing, his lips curl up into an *I'm still hungry* grin, and he's saved from his torment by the ringing of his phone.

Taking the call, he walks away.

"Hello? Uh, huh. Okay, give us thirty minutes and we'll be there. Love you too, sis. Bye."

He returns, smacking me on the butt *again,* but this time has good reason. "Hurry that sweet ass up, babe. Hillary's at the airport."

Oh crap. I cringe at my forgetfulness. *I forgot she was released from rehab last week.* Since then, she's been in New York visiting her dad and the new site for *Hooked on a Better Life*; and now she's here to be fitted too. Luckily, Mrs. St. Julien has Hillary's size down pat; her one-of-a-kind designs hanging in Hillary's closet prove it. She is one of the designer's best customers; it was Conner's sister who referred the well-known fashion stylist.

"Great, I'm glad she made it," I say. "What does she think of the new project anyway?"

He rolls his eyes. "She claims that she will be signing up as the very first volunteer. If people hear her story, maybe she can impact someone to sign on to the program. We're all hoping for a chain reaction. One addict changes their life…spreads the news…then another follows that same path. As far as Hillary goes, you just never know about her. I'll believe it when I see it. Like I told you before, I'm determined to change the world for the better…especially now. I do not want our children growing up around all that chaos."

"For your sake and hers, I hope she's serious. And you're right about not wanting our kids to grow up around all that garbage. We could just put all ten of them in a bubble and keep them at home for safe keeping," I laugh.

His eyes widen, and he swallows hard. "Did you say ten?"

"Yes, I've always wanted a big family…I must have forgotten to tell you that—*my bad,* Mister Dawson." Forcing my smile back, I want him to think I'm serious. Leaning in closer to the mirror, I apply the last of my mascara—sneaking a peek at Conner's shocked expressed.

"Wow, we're going to have a baseball team, Hannah," he says, the color draining slowly from his face.

Looking back at him, I laugh out loud. "I'm kidding! I only want two kids, and that's after I turn thirty."

Quickly, his cheeks heat up—his color is back.

"You had me there for a minute, Hannah," he admits. "Thirty is perfect…that means I have you for the next eight years to myself. *Oh, the fun we are going to have,"* he growls, coming up behind me and placing his hands around my waist. His breath…it's so hot…he's blowing the back of my neck and here I am supposed to be getting a move on.

"Do you want me to hurry, or do you want to play?" I ask teasingly.

"Damn, I almost forgot…hurry it up, baby—we'll have all night to play," he winks.

"Ok, I'll finish up here. Will you grab my black and white polka dot dress from out of the closet?"

He winks. "I can do that."

"Thank you, honey…oh, and grab the black stilettos too, please."

Honey? Where did that come from? I don't know, but he likes it. His grinning gaze proves it.

I finish applying the last of my make-up, and I'm dressed in five minutes flat— we're out the door in six.

Hillary and Mrs. St. Julien have run into each other at the airport and are waiting by the outside gate when we arrive unnoticed. Both ladies are loaded down with luggage. I eyeball the back of my Escalade and try to figure out how it's all going to fit. Conner sees my worry.

"Don't panic, Hannah. If we have to put some on top, we will."

His smile calms my nerves, and I remember the luggage racks. *I'm still not use to having those.*

Hillary sees us and begins waving—jumping up and down. "Conner! Hannah! Over here."

We wave back, smiling at her excitement. *She looks good*—beautiful even. She's wearing a navy mini-dress that lies right above her knees; *oh, and I love her big white floppy hat. Note to self: Buy one tomorrow; it will be the perfect addition to add to my wardrobe for Hawaii.*

Mrs. St. Julien looks lovely in a one-of-a-kind tailored gray jumpsuit with a black silk blouse underneath it. *I'm sure she designed that herself.* She greets us with a hug and a kiss on each cheek; starting with my fiancé.

"Conner, it's so good to see you again."

My turn…

"Hannah, darling, are you ready for the big day?"

"Yes ma'am, Mrs. St. Julien. Thank you so much for flying all the way here. It means so much to both of us."

"My pleasure, Hannah, and call me Amelia; I'm not an old woman yet," she cackles, and she's right.

Although her eyes show lines of wisdom, she doesn't look a day over forty; which is ten years her younger.

I glance toward Conner and his sister. They're deep in conversation; catching up on business and her time spent getting *detoxified*, I'm sure.

They notice my wandering eyes—*it's so obvious she changes the subject.*

"Dad's eager to get you back in the office and put you to work. Personally, I think he just misses you," says Hillary.

They both laugh. Hillary's attention moves from her brother to me. "Hannah, how are you?"

"I'm great—a little excited and nervous, but great nonetheless. How are you doing?" I can't help but notice the scar above her left eye, and then I'm reminded of her wreck in Hawaii. *I'm so glad she's okay.*

"I couldn't be better, Hannah. Thank you for asking."

I get the feeling I'm being watched, and my eyes go straight to Conner's. He looks upset; almost worried. His mouth is a fine hard line and his eyes are cold and staring directly at me. He breaks the mood.

"Ladies, I think we had better be going now." We all grab bags and head to the car.

The ride to my mother's house is loud; women laughing, talking, and catching up on the latest Hollywood gossip. Conner sits in silence, still adorning that look of worry all over his face. *What is eating at him? Should I be worried?* I'll get to the bottom of this, but first I have to get him alone.

I can't help but notice Baylee's car in the driveway when we pull up. She beat us here, but only by a few minutes. We each grab a bag and make our way up the beautifully bricked path that leads to the entrance.

My mom opens the door.

"Ladies, Conner, please, come in." Conner sets the bags in the foyer and is on his way back to the car within seconds. I can't take it any longer, and my curiosity is giving me a headache.

"Mom, please take my dress. I'll be right back." Her glare shows confusion—so does mine.

"Okay, honey," she says.

"Conner, wait up." I yell, running up behind him.

He turns, looking out of his mind, yet madly in love. He grabs me—embracing me with a hug that steals my breath.

"Oh, Hannah, baby girl are you having second thoughts?"

His voice is a low deep whisper and wrapped all up in disbelief. *What? Where the hell did that come from?* Now, I'm really confused.

"Baby, no, why would you think such a thing?" He hugs me tighter, and I hug him back.

"Back at the airport, you said you were nervous. Would you like to tell me why?" His question is as serious as the look on his face.

I pull away, looking at the darkness that has invaded his sight-seeing-beauties. Placing one hand on each side of his face, I speak with utter sincerity.

"I'm nervous that I won't be good enough for you."

Leaning in, he gives me a hard succulent kiss; taking my breath away again. His tongue circling mine, assuring me I'm good enough.

Our lips part, slowly, and his voice is in a raspy whisper. "Hannah, you're perfect; the epitome of perfection actually. I'm the one who should be nervous, not you." He leans his head down on mine, pressing against me, and we both close our eyes while breathing each other in.

"No worries okay, Mister D."

"No worries, Mrs. D."

Our moment is over with a gentle peck to my forehead, and he's off again.

"I'll be waiting in the car."

I knew it.

I smile at him and make my way into the living room with curious eyes on me.

"What?" I laugh.

"You two love birds are precious," says my mom. I smile.

Baylee interrupts us. "So, I want to see this million dollar dress that's going to make my girl look like a princess."

My eyes widen. I can't believe she just said that out loud in front of Amelia. Thank Goodness Mrs. St. Julien is not offended.

"I can't wait to see Hannah wearing that one-of-a-kind jewel either," she laughs.

"Well, then, what are we waiting for?" Hillary cackles and grabs the bag with her name on it. "Which way is the changing room?"

I grab my dress. "This way, girls," I say, prancing towards the back of the house.

I lead them to my old bedroom. After walking in, I can't help but tear up. Mom hasn't changed a thing. My four-post canopy bed is still sitting in the corner with all my stuffed animals on it, and posters of my favorite country stars are all over the walls. *I'm really all grown up now.* I sniff, fighting back the tears before anyone notices.

"Let's do this," I breathe.

My mom follows me into the adjoining bathroom to help me change into my dress. Carefully, we unzip the cover, and we're both speechless. The gown is amazing—*million-dollar amazing.* The strapless bodice is lined with two carets of iridescent pearls—encasing countless carets of elegant, breathtaking, sparkling diamonds from the breast line to the waistline. The bottom half is a long, flowing, silk chiffon that reaches all the way to my ankles. It has a perfect slit on each side that ends right above my knees. The border of it is etched with the same iridescent pearls, swirling with patterns that scream beautiful. Right below my navel, is a flawless chiffon band that is made to tie into the perfect bow right above my butt. The opened back is shaped like a heart, lined with white twenty-four karat gold and bright radiant diamonds. It's exactly what I wanted.

Hurriedly, I slip out of my clothes and into the most amazing dress I have ever laid my eyes on. It's a perfect fit; hugging my breast and showing off my girlish figure. I look at my mom, and she's crying.

"Mama, please don't cry." I hug her, and she cries harder—trying to control it.

"My little girl is getting married. You're going to make the most beautiful bride, honey," she sniffs and I sniff. We're both crying now. "Let's show the others," she says, turning the knob.

She opens the doors, and my bridesmaids are adorning their hot- pink chiffon dresses. Their strapless knee length attire is a perfect fit too. The girls look amazing. And their reactions to me are nothing more but flattering.

Baylee is the first to speak. "Oh, Hannah, you *really do look like a princess*. You did an absolute fabulous job, Mrs. St. Julien," she exclaims.

I agree. "I couldn't be more pleased, Amelia, thank you again."

Hillary exhales, loudly so that all eyes are on her. "Hannah, my brother is going to fall in love with you all over again—just saying."

Her compliment sends fabulous tingles all over me.

"Let's see the back," she says.

Slowly, I circle the room to show it off. They all stand there in awe; wooing over the most extravagant wedding gown ever...*and it's all mine.*

"Okay, honey, let's get you out of that before you catch it on something."

With mama's hand on my back, we go back into the bathroom to get me changed.

Conner has patiently waited outside and is ready to escort me to Baylee's house for the rest of the afternoon. He hesitantly leaves me there to drive Amelia to her hotel where she will spend the night and head back to France tomorrow. From there, he is meeting up with Landon, who will be keeping him company until I call him to come back and pick me up.

It's been a beautiful, breathtaking, amazing day so far— *now it's time for the fun part.*

Chapter 28

The luncheon goes by fast, and it's five o'clock before I know it; then it's a quarter after. Fifteen minutes later and it's already half past the time when the party was supposed to start.

Baylee stands there with the silk blindfold in her hand, watching the clock, and we're both wondering where everyone is. So far the only guests to show up have been the ones who were already here: my mom, Mrs. Parker, Hillary, and of course the hostess herself.

I huff disappointment.

"I'm sure they're all just running late," sighs mama.

"Of course they are, darling," says Mrs. Parker.

Baylee taps her fingers on the solid oak countertop.

"You know what, who needs the others when the best is already here," she says. "Let's get this party started."

Scuffling my way, it takes her about thirty seconds to cover my eyes with the blindfold and lead me to the entertainment area downstairs. Evidently, she's got the placed decked out for this so called *no-holds-barred* bridal shower, and she wants me to be totally surprised when I see it. I may be the *guest of honor*, but my heart goes out to her for all the work she did. I really hate the others didn't show up.

Allowing our moms and Hillary to go in front of us, I'm only steps away from seeing what all this fuss has been about.

"Okay, Hannah, stop here...let me get that thing off of you, but keep your eyes closed until I say open them," she demands. "This is going to be a picture-perfect moment, and I want to be sure to get a snapshot."

A compassionate grin peeks out from the corner of my lips. *Now I really feel bad for her.*

Slowly, she uncovers my eyes and instructs me that I am not to open them until she counts to three.

"Three it is," I say.

She giggles.

Then huffs.

She giggles again.

Wait. That wasn't her.

She clears her throat.

Okay…now that was her.

"Alright…here we go…1…2…3!" she yells.

"SURPRISE!"

I'm blinded by flashing lights…not just one, but several.

Adjusting my vision, I can't believe what I'm seeing.

I am truly, utterly, over the moon, happy. Everyone who was supposed to *show up* at the front door had snuck in the back entrance.

I'm overwhelmed and my teary-eyed expression proves it.

Laughter fills the air, and it's LOUD. There has to be at least fifty people here. Even the spacious area is no longer the huge room it usually is. Thanks to old friends, family, and the five of us it's crowded…and I love it. *Now this is what you call a party.*

Rolling my eyes, raised brows and all, I shake my head while laughing at my friend. *Hilarious.* I've never seen so many erotic displays in my life; to the left—to the right—even hanging from the ceiling. It's actually kind of cute…in a perverted kinda way.

"Wow, Baylee, you really out did yourself," I cry out—happy tears literally leaving the corners of my eyes.

I wipe them away.

"I know, right," she bellows. "You have to admit, it does scream *bachelorette party.*"

"It most definitely does," I agree.

To the left is a *help-yourself-buffet* with enough food to feed an army. Pinwheels, casseroles, dips, and …oh my, *is that what I think it is?* My eyes are drawn to the centerpiece. Cocking my head to the left, my stare moves from the bottom up all the way to the tip. Standing upright and detailed to perfection is a huge penis cake—*hairy balls and all.*

Amused, I shake my head at my friend *again.*

"Only you would do something as crazy as this, and I love you for it."

She embraces me with a hug, and puts a *Bride to Be* banner over my head; slipping it over one shoulder and letting it rest there and hang around my waist on the other side. Then she places a cute little tiara with a veil hanging down right on top of my head. Guess that makes it official...*I'm really getting married.*

After a few minutes of socializing, my friend drags me to the buffet—and it smells wonderful...especially the pecker and balls combo. Baylee insists that I try her creation, and I can't help but laugh out loud.

"These are mouthwatering—try some," she insists.

With a fork, she places a smoked weenie and two barbeque glazed balls on a plate and hands it to me.

"Eat up."

I snarl my nose.

"Pecker and balls?" I ask curiously.

Her brows arch, and she's got a devious glint in her eyes.

"Uh, huh," she says.

I take a bite.

And another one.

One more and all three pieces are gone.

She's right. *They were mouthwatering.*

I look around the room. Everything is decorated in hot-pink, black, and silver—some of my favorite colors. I really like the paper mache lanterns hanging around; seems like they balance out the rest of the decorations.

I'm almost embarrassed when I see my mom and Mrs. Parker watching me as I'm admiring the décor, but they look to be just as amused as I am. *Thank goodness.*

Just as I'm about to eat another ball, I'm jerked away.

"Come hither, woman, let's get you something to drink."

Baylee guides me to the punch bowl and hands me a cup. Dipping the ladle, she stirs the pineapple and peach schnapps concoction—causing little orange flavored ice penises to surface.

Now, I've seen it all.

As she fills my cup to the rim, I realize how into this she is. Baylee could probably plan parties like this and make a better living than what she does at the law office.

Just as I'm about to take a sip…she stops me.

"No, not yet…here, you have to drink through this," she snorts, placing a pecker tipped straw in the cup and to my lips.

Okay, scratch my previous comment. *Now, I have really seen it all.*

The room steadily fills with friends—some old ones and some still fairly new. The table to the right is full of surprises for me to share with my soon-to-be-husband, and I'm tickled-pink and anxious to see what's hidden away in all the packages.

Grabbing the first one, I get started.

Oh, snap!

That damn bag just moved.

"What the heck is that?" my cousin Tori asks…referring to the double-headed vibrating dildo that I just slung in the floor. I kid you not…I swear I thought that wiggly sixteen-incher was a snake.

Eyeballing my friend Heather…the present giver…that was her exact intention. She has such a comedic personality and her joke worked. The room is echoing with laughter.

Once my heartbeat goes back to normal, I continue on.

And an hour passes.

The afternoon is long gone, but the evening is just getting started. One by one, I continue opening gift bags and cutely wrapped boxes. My presents are ranging from skimpy lingerie, to sensuous warming oils, and even bedroom games for couples. I blush more with each opened gift, but I really think I'm going to like that dice set. I roll…*he pleases me.* He rolls…*I please him.* The thing is we have to do exactly what's on the little square game pieces. *That's going to be interesting…crazy maybe, but hot and orgasmic nonetheless.*

Looking around, I notice just how much personality is under one roof. Half the women here are either middle-aged housewives or young college graduates…each one showing a side into their own kinky cravings. *I can't help but wonder if they all own the same gifts they're giving me.*

Oh, wow.

The next bag contains a gift set with handcuffs, a blind fold, and an array of vibrators…five to be exact. A one inch—a three inch—a six inch—a nine inch—and last but not least—*the anal stimulator* that causes me to flush scarlet.

Glancing at my mom, she's a shade darker red than I am. Out of all the gifts I've opened, hers is the only one that goes in the kitchen….an apron that says *"Who says cooking can't be sexy?"* and a matching chef's hat.

I smile at her.

She smiles back.

Gah! I really do love her.

Bang…Bang!!

Was that a knock at the door?

Bang…Bang…Bang!!!

There it is again. *Surely Conner's not here yet.*

Mrs. Parker opens the door.

Three very good looking men dressed in paramedics clothing walks in with EMS bags.

What the heck?

I look around the room, searching for anyone in distress—everyone looks fine.

The man in the middle speaks.

"We got a call that there's a woman here *dying to get married.*"

I shake my head. No he did not just say that.

Another guy grabs a boom box out of his bag, and before we know it, music is blaring through the room.

I'm eyeballing Baylee, and she shrugs her shoulders like she had nothing to do with the show taking place before us. Within seconds, the guys are stripping down and dancing around my friends and *our moms*—giving us a show that makes our mouths drop.

Shortly after the entertainment starts, the tall, lean, black-haired beauty closest to me makes me the center of his attention. His half-naked body has pinned me down on the chair that I'm sitting in, and his well-endowed cock is rubbing me in places that only one other man has any right touching. I'm getting a lap dance that most girls would drool over, but I'm uncomfortable, and he knows it. Pulling away he moves on to the next lady waiting to be entertained with his barely covered manhood.

I exhale a breath of relief. *I would die if Conner saw that.*

I look at Hillary, and she's laughing along with the rest of the room—*hopefully she won't say a word.*

To the left of her, I can't help but notice the muscular body being sandwiched in between my mom and Mrs. Parker. Both women flushing crimson, he dances away.

And together they giggle like teenagers.

Sitting side by side, Baylee has a confession.

"You can thank Tyler for this," she laughs. "This was his idea."

"Remind me to thank him later," I tell her.

Oh, my. Now, that's a sight to appreciate.

Cousin Clair-Ashley is booty-bumping with one of the guys. I can't believe it takes something like this to get that girl to let loose. *She's always so uptight.*

After a half-hour of extreme entertainment, my bridal shower has come to an end. I just finished opening the last of my gifts, and it's hard to believe the party is over. It's almost sad...*I have really had an amazing time.* Looking at my watch, I can't believe the time flew by so fast.

Standing at the door, I thank everyone for coming and for their kind gifts—*even the battery-operated ones.* That was some party, but I have to admit...I'm ready to see my man.

As I grab my phone from my purse, it immediately starts buzzing in my hand. I look at the screen, and it is him. Putting it to my ear, I answer.

"Perfect timing, baby, I'm ready whenever you are."

"On my way," he says.

Two minutes later, the man of my dreams is knocking at the door. *He must have just been down the road.*

Before leaving, I thank Baylee and Mrs. Parker again for their kindness.

Hugging mama bye, she stays behind to help clean up the mess.

As Conner and I load up the packages in the back seat of the car, he can't help but notice the handcuffs hanging out of one of the bags. He whispers sensuous words in my ear that send each and every nerve ending I own straight to my coochie.

"I can't wait to see you wearing those," his velvety voice tempting my girly stuff—she braces herself and clenches in for dear life. *Deep down, she can't wait either.*

"I bet you can't, Mister Tall, Dark, and Kinky."

Back at the apartment, we're both restless and standing there with nothing but each other on the other's mind. I look at him and he looks at me; his body willing me to touch it, and my hands can't resist. Within seconds, I am all over him—touching, kissing, and seducing him like a madwoman. I can feel him holding back, trying to stay strong. He growls a seductive groan through gritted teeth, and he's defeated by his own desire.

"Damn it, girl," he breathes. "I can't get enough of you."

The next thing I know, he is taking control of the situation—laying me across the kitchen table and getting ready to eat me until he's satisfied. Up goes my dress and down go my panties...his tongue now making a curvy path around my navel and along my torso. That mouth of his is burning up—hot breath, hot lips...*and that scorching hot nibbling—oh my.* He keeps nibbling and my sex keeps clenching in and out...just waiting to be shown the same attention. A few flicks, grazes, and kisses later...he's there. He's found his happy place between my legs, and he moans as he quenches his thirst. With every luscious swirl of his tongue, I grow closer to what he's giving me...pure satisfaction. *Yes.* Here it goes. I'm coming, and he's drinking my orgasm in—all of it, until I'm totally and utterly finished.

He kisses his way up to my belly, and back down again; stealing one last taste of me before he pulls my dress back down. Moving up, his mouth finding mine, he guides his tongue across my lips.

I moan.

He moans.

Between parted lips and erratic breathing, he whispers sweet words that take my breath away. "I. Have. Never. Wanted. Something. More. Than. I. Want. You. Hannah. You're absolutely delicious."

He kisses me gently, lifting me in his arms and taking me to bed—holding me tight until we both fall fast asleep.

Chapter 29

The next few days fly by like a whirlwind. Mother—daughter day was a huge success; of course Conner was only a few feet behind watching my every move, and mama loved the fact that he was always looking out for me. We got a lot of shopping done, and I even found the perfect floppy hat.

My apartment has been packed up and emptied out. The only things left are our personal belongings; things like clothes, toiletries, and *our new gifts* sitting in the corner by the door. In approximately twelve hours we'll be in Hawaii, and only two days away from our wedding.

Wow.

I take a deep breath—letting it out a little too hard.

This is pretty overwhelming.

"I can't believe it's already time to leave." I look at Conner, teary-eyed but happier than I've ever been in my whole entire life.

"It's a bittersweet moment, Hannah. I'll give you a few minutes alone while I take some of this to the car."

I give him a thank you kiss and off he goes.

Crap!

I promised myself I wouldn't do this.

Wiping away the tear rolling down my cheek, I toughen up.

My eyes look at every crevice, border, and ceiling fixture. Not only will I desperately miss my family and friends, but I will miss this place; my first home away from home. It was mine and now it's not, but that's okay.

I'M GETTING MARRIED!

And I couldn't be more thrilled.

My mind wanders off thinking about my new exciting life with Conner. I can't wait to start the new chapter in my life as his wife. The thought sends my heart racing and my mind chasing behind it. *Wedding day equals wedding night.* I close my eyes—trying to get a glimpse into the future. I'm smiling and gradually open my eyes to see him standing there smiling back at me.

"What's that all about, baby girl?"

I wink at him.

"You'll find out soon enough."

His bright eyes shine brighter. He knows what I'm thinking.

We grab the last of the bags, and I'm the last one out the door. I take one final look, saying goodbye to my past. I close the door behind me, and that's it.

Goodbye Oak Hill, here I come married life.

At the airport, we find some of our guests there waiting. Mama, Landon, the Parker's, and a few others will be flying back with us, and I can't help but notice the older gentleman next to Hillary.

Conner's hand leaves mine.

"Dad, I'm glad you could make it."

Conner walks up to his father and shakes his hand, but his dad wraps his arms around him—giving him a bear-hug of an embrace.

After all this time, I've never come face to face with the man who fathered the man I have come to love. He truly is a work-a-holic.

"I wouldn't miss this moment in your life if the world depended on it." The elder Mr. Dawson's voice is deep, way deeper than that of his sons.

Then he looks my way, eyes focused and demanding to be respected; I can't help but feel a little intimidated.

"So, this is the woman who stole my son's heart; not to mention, took him away from work too." He laughs and his gut jiggles as he embraces me in a bear-hug all of my own.

He's the same height as Conner, but at least thirty pounds heavier and it shows on his beltline. I can't help but wonder if he's an alcoholic, and if that's a *beer-belly* he's toting around.

"Yes, dad. This is Hannah, the girl that I'm going to spend the rest of my life loving."

"Ah, that's so sweet and mushy; I think I need to throw up now," says Hillary.

She laughs and so does everyone else.

The plane is ready, and it's time to board.

"Okay, people, let's get going. It's time to get these two lovebirds to Hawaii." His dad demands and everyone follows him onto the private jet.

The long flight goes by quicker than the first time. With so many people on board and a wedding only forty-eight hours away, we found plenty of things to talk about to occupy our time.

It's eight o'clock in the evening, and we've finally made it to our destination. Honolulu is just as beautiful in early fall as it was back in the summer. *I am really going to love living here.* As we unload the plane and grabbing our bags as we go, I see Finn waiting by the limo; just like before and tipping his hat to say hello. He walks towards me, taking my bags when he's close enough.

"Ms. Stone, it is a pleasure to see you again so soon. Congratulations on your engagement."

He places the bags beside the other ones in the rear of the stretched limo.

"Thank you, Finn. It's *so good* to be back."

We all load up and head to the hotel; the place our guests will be staying for the next few days.

When we arrive, we're greeted by Henry, the longtime concierge of the elegant five-star hotel. He greets us all, either by name or a simple hello.

"Ms. Stone, welcome back."

He shakes my hand, and I pull him into a hug.

"It's good to see you, Henry."

"Likewise," he says.

Conner eyes him.

"I assume the rooms are ready as I requested?" he asks.

"Yes sir," answers Henry. "The vouchers are also ready."

"Great. Please see to it that our guests are well-taken care of," he orders. "Hannah and I will be leaving now and heading to the house."

His sultry gaze looks my way, and I know exactly what's on his mind. He is ready to get me alone.

"Consider it done, Mr. Dawson."

While most everyone was ready for a goodnight's rest, Baylee, Tyler, and Landon had other things on their minds. They can't wait to hit the casino. Thanks to the five-hundred-dollar-voucher courtesy of the owner himself, they are sure to get a good start at their game playing.

"I hear the three-card poker table calling my name," states Landon.

"I hear ya, man," says Tyler. "My palms are itching they're so ready."

Baylee shakes her head at both of them.

"When you high-rollers lose all your money, don't come begging for mine when I'm winning it up at the slots," she teases.

The men roll their eyes.

And we say our goodbyes.

After an intense drive in the back of the limo, we have finally made it *home*.

Finn has been ordered to go back to the hotel…just in case anyone has the desire to roam the strip; I barely have time to get out of the car, and Conner has me off my feet and in his arms.

"What are you doing, Mister Dawson?" I ask.

"I'm caring you across the threshold to our new home Mrs. Dawson," he chuckles.

Giddiness has taken control of my body.

Throwing my head back, I giggle out loud.

I freaking love this man.

Unlocking the door with one hand and balancing me with the other, he kicks open the heavy door with his foot.

I lay my head on his shoulder and in we go. He sits me upright on the kitchen counter and turns to lock the front door. I look around the whole front area of the house: the kitchen, breakfast nook, and living room. It's stunning, and I absolutely love the open floor plan.

Nearby is a luxurious wrap-around sofa sitting in the center of the living room—sandstone and leather with mahogany wood surrounding the borders. Only a few feet away is the focal point of the room—the stone-white mantel that sits there only to be admired. The wall behind it is a vibrant oceanic blue, making it stand out from the other soothing tanned-colored walls.

The floors are made from an exotic Macassar ebony wood; one of the most expensive hard woods in the world.

There are candles resting in tall hurricane vases and exotic flowers sitting on every table. The sleek dark furniture sitting around may be stylish, but the greenery hanging around gives the place an outdoorsy feeling. It feels like home here, and my heart is settling in nicely.

Conner returns to me, spreading my legs wide and standing in the middle of them.

I wrap my arms around his neck.

"It's so peaceful here. Thank you for sharing this perfect place with me."

His hand is under my chin, pulling my face close to his.

"Oh...baby girl...there's so much more I'm going to share with you," he moans.

I lick my lips.

He steals a kiss.

I steal another.

He dips his tongue in one last time before pulling away.

"It's getting late...let's go," he says. "We will leave the bags here and worry about unpacking tomorrow."

That sounds great. I'm wore completely out and ready for a goodnights rest…but first, my body is begging for a hot-water beating. I can't wait to hit the shower.

Conner lifts me up and my feet hit the floor.

He leads me through the living room and out to the breezeway through the glass doors in the living room.

"I thought we were going to bed." My face is covered with confusion.

"We are, Hannah. The bedroom is separate from the rest of the house."

"Oh." Still confused, I let him lead the way.

We go towards the left, beneath the breezeway, and to the huge outdoor room he didn't show me when I was here before. He opens the double doors, and my eyes are in complete blissful shock.

This cannot be our bedroom.

It's more luxurious than the whole house. The floors are similar to the ones inside, but a lighter color. Around the exotic wood flooring are marble tiles that are the same color as the sandy beach, with metallic flakes of gold encased inside each one. The border is the same gold that goes all around each tile, showing off the perfect detail.

I notice that the room is two levels. The first one close to the entrance, has a wet bar, a pool table, and a television viewing area. The second level has a U-shaped, black leather sofa that draws my attention. It's covered with lots of white pillows etched with black swirly lines and there has to be at least twenty of them. It sits perfect in the center of the room facing the huge ceiling to floor glass wall—showing off the amazing view of the ocean.

With my hand in Conner's, he leads me down the huge hallway to the left.

Turning the corner, I can't believe the sight before me.

I blink.

Is this real?

I blink again.

It is real.

The mahogany four post canopy bed…a stone fire pit…an array of blooming flowers…the waterfall and oblong pool. If I wasn't seeing it for myself, I wouldn't believe it. There's a swimming pool in our *bedroom*, and it is literally sitting beneath the stars.

It's so surreal and perfectly romantic.

And the ocean view…it's right there in front of us.

I close my eyes as the breeze runs through my hair.

"Conner, I'm speechless," I breathe, looking his way.

He holds me close.

"There's more." He leads me through a doorway that has a curvature frame, and just when I think it can't get any better, it does. The entrance leads to an exotic bathroom— still outdoors may I add.

"Wow," I exclaim.

He squeezes me gently, leaning down and placing his lips on my forehead. He's pleased that I'm pleased.

"You don't mind showering underneath the moonlight do you," he whispers.

"I can't wait, Mister Dawson."

First, we both take a moment to admire the beauty.

The golden-brown tile on the floor matches the shower's walls—same texture—same pattern; it's simple yet elegant— *stunning to be exact.*

Over to the left, sitting in the corner, is a huge round tub—close by is the even larger walk-in shower, and that's where Conner is now leading me.

He leans over, turning on the sultry water, getting it good and hot before it cascades over our bodies.

The area is closed in by bamboo walls, and the only light we have is coming from the night sky—*the moon and stars* are shining bright, but still not quite bright enough. Conner takes a lighter from the drawer and lights four out of five of the three-wick candles sitting along the wall

That's much better. Now I can see his emerald beauties twinkling as the light of the candles catches each one.

Both hands on my shoulders, he moves them slowly down my body—getting a good grip on the hem line of my dress so that he can peel it away; *and off it goes along with my panties.*

For a moment, he stands there admiring my body before he allows me the pleasure of undressing him.

"The things I want to do to you…*the things I am going to do to you,"* he whispers. His voice so sexy it makes my skin shiver.

My body cringes with excitement, and I throw myself at him. Lip-locking him and tearing away at his clothes until there's nothing left—*except* the bare-assed man beneath them.

He takes control—his dominant self showing. Grabbing my hands, and holding them over my head as he rushes us beneath the water. Facing me up against the wall, he moves the hair away from my neck and states his demand.

"Don't move…do you understand?" he asks.

"Yes, I understand."

My heart's racing—I'm so turned on, and I have no idea what he's planning next. Doing as I'm told, I stand there and wait—heart racing, breathing erratically, and anticipating his next move.

I hear the sound of soap squirting into his palm. Rubbing his hands together, he then places them on mine. One hand on each, he glides the soap down the length of my arms and down each side of my waist—moving to the front and lathering up my breast.

My breath catches…*I love the touch of his hands washing my body.* I'll take those any day over a loofah.

"Spread your legs, Hannah…now," his next demand makes my sex swirl around in her own whirlpool. *Oh my.*

I do as I'm told.

His soapy hands trail down my sides again, one moving to the front and cupping my sex while the other gets a handful of my ass.

I gasp when he spreads my butt cheeks apart—cleansing the area that he's once only teased. Taking one step up under the water, he allows it to chase away the soap while his fingers help to rinse the lather away.

Quickly, I inhale and exhale slowly.

While one of his middle fingers is rubbing away at my swollen clit and making my sublime innocence beg to be taken, the other one is massaging that little puckered hole that's hiding away in a cavern of its own.

And in he goes.

I gasp.

The pressure...the sweet torture...the divine pain—it's unexpected.

My body cringes with delight. *I think I like this.*

In and out, he pushes and pulls—only allowing the tip of his finger to enter at first. When he's sure that my body will accept the whole length, he pushes in deeper—three strokes is all it takes, and he can feel my orgasm as I begin to climax around him.

I jerk....twitch...gasp out loud.

"Oh, Conner," I breathe.

My body stirs from the inside out, becoming limp with ecstasy and coiling against the wall.

His breathing gets heavier.

I start to spiral down, allowing the orgasmic waves flowing through my body to float away.

Leaning into me, he gently bites the tip of my shoulder—causing the sexual sensation to last just a little longer. I can feel his manly pride begging to be touched—throbbing against my back.

Gently he withdraws his hands, and I turn around while I have the chance. His beautiful eyes are full of desire—he longs for what I just had. I kiss him senseless—his lips, his neck, his chest—and down on my knees I go.

Once I've wrapped my mouth around his manhood, I'm bobbing away and he's flexing back and forth—going deeper, harder, moaning his way to a blissful orgasm.

It won't be long now; I feel his flesh jerk with the burning desire to release a big one. Here it comes...I'm ready—*my body* willing to take in his finish while *his body* unravels with each spurt. The hot water cascades over the top of my head, down my face—even in my mouth. I don't let it stop me. I crave this as much as he does. I keep sucking and he keeps coming.

My inner self pats herself on the back. *"We're getting pretty good at this."*

Standing up, his mouth covers mine and we stay put kissing until the water runs cold.

Satisfied, cleansed, and ready for a goodnight's rest, we make our way to the bed. I lay there staring at him until I'm sleeping in his arms, and my eyelids are dancing to the very romantic, exotic dreams of our wedding night.

The next day is a blur. I'm a nervous wreck, but with Conner by my side we make it through the last details of the wedding that is now only hours away. Everything on my list is either on schedule or has been taken care of…*Finally.*

- ✓ Reception…luau theme
- ✓ Entertainment…flame throwers and dancers
- ✓ Cake….three tiers of perfection
- ✓ Flowers…romantic and freshly picked
- ✓ Tables & Chairs….enough for one hundred guests
- ✓ Rehearsal Dinner….done and went off without a hitch

Due to the old wives tale my grandmother use to tell me, I refuse to sleep with Conner tonight. He can't see me until it's time to say our vows, so he reluctantly takes me back to the hotel to stay in the room with my mom. His determination to stay close to me keeps him away from home tonight. He decides the best place for him is to stay in the penthouse with his dad and sister. Before leaving my room, he gives me a kiss to remember him by and away he goes.

Now, time to get my beauty sleep. I refuse to have puffy eyes on my wedding day, and I cuddle up beside my mom in the big king size bed.

She laughs. "Hannah, you haven't slept with me since you were a little girl."

I sigh.

"I remember it like it was yesterday, mama."

We are both sound asleep in no time.

Chapter 30

"**R**ise and shine, darling." One eye opens and then the next. There's my mom looking as lovely as ever and sitting on the edge of the bed.

"Good morning, mama."

I let out a yawn and stretch my way up as my feet hit the floor. Standing on my tip toes and reaching for the ceiling, I let out another yawn. *I feel so rested.*

"What time is it?" I ask.

She looks at her watch. "Almost eleven."

Almost eleven. Did she really say almost eleven? "You're kidding me, right!" I cry out.

"No, honey, what's the matter?" she asks, her voice on high alert.

Scrambling around like a crazy person, I search for my phone.

There it is. I look at the time…she's right.

"I've slept half the day away, and the ceremony is only eight hours away!" I exclaim.

I'm a nervous wreck, pacing the floors back and forth, trying to figure out where I should start the beginning of my day.

"It's okay sweetie; you've got plenty of time," she's says—a slight hint of humor now covering her words.

I take a deep breath and let it out.

"Just relax…I'm here to help anyway I can," she promises.

My rattled nerves begin retreating. She's right…I do have plenty of time…besides, my body needs to be well rested and ready for my wedding night.

A huge grin spreads across my face. I'm glad I slept in.

We make our way into the living room, and I can't help but notice a beautiful flower arrangement sitting on the dining room table. Mama sees my wandering eyes, looking for a card attached somewhere.

"Those arrived for you early this morning. The card is on the other side."

"They are stunning," I boast.

"Yes ma'am, they are," she agrees.

The vase is full of beautiful white flowers: roses, lilies, irises, and my favorite—*lots of baby's breath.*

My heart runs a marathon as I read the card.

My sweet Hannah,

You have touched my heart in a way that I can't explain. Thank you for trusting me with your life, your heart, and your innocence. I will cherish it for all eternity.

I love you, always and forever.

Conner

I exhale.

A tear leaves the corner of my eye, and I know exactly what I'm going to do first. *Perfect my wedding vows.* I spend the next couple of hours doing just that, while my mother irons my clothes and prepares us to leave the hotel and head back over to the house.

I decide to send out a quick text to remind Conner to stay put and out of my sight before shutting the door to the hotel room. We've come this far, and I don't want anything jinxing us.

Thank you for the most amazing bouquet. Mama and I are leaving now. We are going to grab the others and head on over to the house. I'll see you soon. I love you.

I hit send.

Landon, Hillary, Baylee, and Tyler are waiting in the lobby when we get downstairs. They will be traveling with us to the house and the others will come later.

My phone buzzes—I've got a text. It's Conner.

My face lights up.

"Being in love looks good on you, Hannah," implies Baylee.

"I agree," states Landon.

"Awe, thank y'all," I say, blushing and moving on to reading the words of the man who has put this look on me.

Hey, Baby Girl, hope you slept well. Dad and I had an errand to run, so I won't be at the house until around five or so. Have fun getting ready and remember—no cold feet...lol.
*I love you more, and you're welcome.**

A happy grin spreads across my face.

The house has an inviting aroma when we get inside; smells like mulberry. Candles are lit, and the light sound of music is playing over the sound system.

Leilani is in the kitchen, preparing fresh fruit and sweet tea. She insisted on doing that much since everything else was being catered in.

"Leilani, it's so good to see you."

She wipes her hands dry and embraces me.

"You too, Miss Stone; I'm so happy for you and Mr. Dawson. I knew that he would find the perfect girl someday."

She kisses my cheek.

"Thank you, Leilani. I plan on doing my best to be just that."

After introducing my family and friends, I take them on a tour of the house. They are astonished by the breathtaking

beauty of my new home sweet home, *especially the bedroom*.
Baylee insists that she's moving in, and Landon assures her
that if he's not, she's not. I giggle out loud at both of them.

"The view is amazing from here," says my mom as she
points towards the ceiling-to-floor glass wall.

"I know, right. I don't think I'll ever be leaving this
spot."

Baylee is down the hallway still admiring the "bedroom"
and overhears our conversation.

"Oh, I think you will be spending more time here if
Conner has any say so in the matter!" she yells.

I flush crimson, looking at my mom as she blushes
herself. She coughs, reminding Baylee that she is still in the
room.

"Sorry, Ms. Stone, just stating the facts," she confesses,
and she's right. I'm sure we will—or at least I hope so, but
married or not, my mom is standing right here. She does not
need to be reminded that I'm going to be having a *sex life*.

She comes around the corner; now joining the rest of us.

I eyeball Baylee with a *paybacks are hell* kind of look,
and she changes the subject.

"So, Hannah, don't you need to get showered so we can
start on that amazing up-do of yours," she suggests.

I agree.

"Actually, I do." I excuse myself.

With all this hair, it's going to take a good two and a half
hours to get it done. First it's got to be washed, dried,
rolled…then pinned up and braided into the perfect halo
crown. Once that's complete, we will finish it off by
interweaving fresh white roses and baby breath into the braid.
I only hope it looks as breathtaking as I picture it.

I head to the bathroom…they head out back to admire the
beach.

Our timing was impeccable—it took two and a half hours exactly to make my hair flawless…then another hour to get my make-up and nails done. The room is now filled with too many helping hands…and suddenly I'm starting to feel claustrophobic. I look at my phone, and the time says it already after six o'clock. I'm minutes away from marrying the man of my dreams and…oh my, my breathing has become erratic. My heart's doing the *Rumba* while the rest of me is fighting off the nervous tension. My mom sees the look of desperation on my face when no one else notices.

"Girls, if you don't mind, I would like some time alone with my daughter."

They look at her and then at me.

"Of course." Their words are all in sync.

They exit the room, shutting the door behind them.

"Darling, are you okay?"

My mom has one hand on each of my arms, rubbing and caressing them from top to bottom. Then she hugs me. I don't want her to let go. All of a sudden, I'm crying, and I don't know why. I'm not having second thoughts. I think I feel as though I'm abandoning my mother—the one person who has been my rock my entire life.

"Mama, are you okay with this?" I sniff.

She's crying and sniffling now.

"I don't mean to upset you, mama."

"Oh, honey, I'm not upset. The things I've always wanted for you are happening. I see how much that man loves you. I know that he's going to take good care of you and protect you with his own life."

I squeeze her tighter.

"Oh, mama." She pulls away, gently.

"I have some things for you, and I would be honored if you would wear them today."

She pulls out a little white box and opens the cover.

My eyes widen.

"They are beautiful," I whisper, while looking at the perfect pair of earrings.

She smiles, inhaling and remembering her past.

"Your dad gave these to me the day we got married. I've held on to them hoping you would wear them on your wedding day too," she whispers, tears stirring heavier in her eyes.

If I ever get my hands on that man...I swear—how dare he hurt my mother.

Pushing that thought out of my head...nothing is going to ruin this day for me.

I pick the earrings up.

They are dangling with topaz stones and trimmed in fourteen karat gold. I watch as the light hits them, sending glistening sparkles across the room.

Standing there, she admires me as I admire them.

"Something old, something borrowed, and something blue...all in one; I also have something new for you," she insists.

I'm amazed at my mother, she's remembered everything. I put the earrings in, and she places a thin gold necklace around my neck. The necklace is perfect—simple and elegantly adorning one single pearl in the front.

"I love all of it, mama...thank you."

Taking a tissue out of her purse, she wipes away the mascara that is staining the corners of my eyes.

"Much better," she says. "A beautiful woman and a flawless bride—you're sure to make the other women envious."

"I love you so much," I whisper, wrapping my arms around her.

"And I love you, sweet girl, so very much."

I am in such awe of this woman—I can only hope she knows how much I truly cherish her.

Our moment is interrupted by a knock on the door.

"Who is it?" my mother asks sharply.

"It's Landon, and it's almost time to start," he says through the closed door.

"Just a minute!" I blurt out. I still don't have my gown on.

I hurry out of my shorts and T-shirt and pull my exquisite dress over my head. Mama ties my bow just perfect on the back of it.

Okay, now I'm ready.

My mom walks gracefully over to the door, unlocking it and allowing my brother to come in. He stands there looking stunned, as if he doesn't know his little sister anymore.

Picking his jaw up from the floor, he speaks.

"Hannah, you look breathtaking. Are you sure that's you?" he laughs, but I'm not amused. I'm too nervous for jokes.

I throw a pillow at him.

He ducks and misses, and it hits Baylee as she comes through the door.

She yells, "Watch the hair please...oh, and the bouquet!"

Laughter fills the room, and mystic little butterflies fill my nervous belly. I take a deep breath and take the elegant white calla lily bouquet from my friend.

"I'm ready whenever you are," I say nervously.

I look at Landon and he holds out his arm for me to hold on to.

Mom stops in front of us—blocking our way out of the room.

"Let me take one more look at my beautiful little girl."

Her eyes glass over with tears *again*, but she's a strong determined woman who fights them back. She's in control—taking a deep breath before leaving me with a quick peck on the cheek.

"I'll see you outside darling," she says.

Baylee leads her away, and I'm left with the man who will give me away...the most awesome brother ever.

Landon pulls me closer—teasing to take me back to Oak Hill if I'm having any sort of second thoughts. "I can fly a plane you know, we'll be gone before Dawson realizes you've flown the coop—just say the word."

I shake my head at him.

"Number one, you can't fly a plane; number two, I love him, Landon...more than anything."

My last words alone send my skin in a goose bumped frenzy.

Our conversation is interrupted by the sweet sound of music. There are no words, only the instrumental sound of the song Conner sang to me the night he proposed.

I tear up, *again*.

I take a deep breath and hold it.

This is it.

I exhale.

"Here we go little sister, hang on tight and watch your step," he whispers.

I smile, remembering my bare feet. Oh well, it is a beach wedding...*who needs high heels?*

Landon escorts me to the breezeway, and we walk until our feet hits the sand. We both take a deep breath before starting our stroll down the amazing sandy aisle.

The walkway adorns beautiful lighting; just watching the burning flames dancing with each gust of wind is like watching a sweet melody come to life. There are bamboo poles resting at the beginning of each aisle of chairs, and the flame from each one is burning high and bright...almost as though reaching for the heavens. The most beautiful part of the lighted fixtures is the delicate white flowers. I love the way that they are resting on the hot pink chiffon and white lace that is entwined all the way around every pole. It is the perfect path to guide me to the altar.

Immediately, the traditional wedding song played all over the country is floating through the air. I listen closely as the words play quietly over the sound system.

"One step at a time, Hannah," Landon whispers through tightened lips.

Right foot, left foot...I repeat the process as carefully as possible to keep from tripping over my own two feet.

Looking ahead, I can't help but notice the amazing ocean view. It's breathtaking. The sun is setting and the horizon looks splendid with the pink and yellow shades streaming through the sky.

I look at the guests talking amongst themselves and watch them as they point at me. I hear one of the ladies to the left say something.

"She's absolutely stunning."

Then another one to my right speaks louder than the other woman.

"Her dress is exquisite; look at the perfect detail."

My grin widens.

My eyes skim the whole area, looking at people I don't know. They are mostly Conner's family and friends, but that's okay. The people who are most important in my life are here, and that's the only thing that matters.

Finally, I look straight ahead at the elegant flowered arch—covered in pink and white lilies and adorning the perfect amount of greenery spiraling around it. I think somewhere in the back of my mind if I looked there first, he wouldn't be there waiting for me. But he is, standing there looking gloriously divine in stone-washed blue jeans and a white long sleeve shirt that is laced up with strings instead of buttons. He's beautiful, and he's mine.

I'm closer now, only a few short feet away.

He closes his eyes for a split second; opening them back with a glassy tear gaze and looking straight at me.

He holds out his hand, and I take it; releasing my arm from Landon's grip.

I look at my brother.

"Thank you," I whisper and turn my attention to the man I'm here for.

Conner brings my hand up to his mouth, kissing it gently before curling his long masculine fingers around mine.

"You look beautiful, Hannah."

I blush.

"So do you, Conner."

He shows off his amazing smile.

We turn to face the pastor who will read the binding words of marriage for all to hear. Our guests will be our witnesses.

The sun has gone down even more, and so far the ceremony is *fairytale* perfect.

Chapter 31

Casually dressed and wearing a snow white head full of hair, the man of faith before us begins.

"Dear friends and family, we are gathered here this evening to join Conner and Hannah in matrimony. The loving couple in front of you has chosen you to share this very special moment in their lives. Although they have only known each other for a few short months, it was love at first sight for both of them. Their undying love for each other will only grow in the years to come, and through the years they will realize just how perfect they are for each other. Their dedication to each other as husband and wife will make their lives complete; as they will not only become the best of friends, but lovers also. Please, listen close as Conner and Hannah recite their handwritten vows to each other." Pastor Willis looks at Conner to begin.

The water is splashing upon the beach and the birds are singing. Love is in the air, and it's better than oxygen—metaphorically speaking that is. I feel like we are truly being blessed at this very moment.

Conner takes a deep relaxing breath before he starts.

With a gentle squeeze to my hands, he begins as we stand there facing one another.

"Oh, Hannah, you had me the first night I ever laid eyes on you, it's true. I may not have realized it then, but we both know it didn't take long. Our hearts were on a mission...to fall in love, and time didn't matter."

He kisses my hand again, pulling away and looking me eye to eye.

"I look forward to living my life with you; loving you, protecting you, and cherishing you for as long as I live. I promise that you will never go a day feeling unloved or unwanted. Not a day will ever go by that you will feel lonely or scared. I'll always be your hero, baby girl. I exist only for you, Hannah. I love you with every beat of my heart and every breath I take."

Tears are now falling from my eyes, and I have to clear my throat before I can start.

"Harrumph…Harrumph…"

Taking a deep breath…I'm ready.

"Conner, my sweet breathtaking, Conner. You have rescued me in more ways than you'll ever know, and I love you so much for that. I never really knew what true love was until you came into my life."

Feeling overwhelmed, I take a moment to compose myself; closing my eyes and trying to dry my tears. With my hands in his, my eyes open back up to see his glassy-eyed gaze. He is as emotional as I am.

Beginning again…

"You've shown me what it feels like to be loved by a real man, and it's amazing; so much more than I could have ever imagined it would be. You're perfect, and you make me feel perfect. I know that with you by my side, we will be even more perfect together."

He squeezes my hands again…sending my heart into an acrobatic dance.

"Loving you is what I do best now, and I plan on loving you with as much passion as you've shown me for the rest of my life. It's true. You'll always be my hero. I love you, Conner Dawson; with everything in me I know that's true. My heart will always be linked to yours—*today, tomorrow, and always.*"

I can feel tears escaping the corners of my eyes, and they don't have a chance to go very far. Conner's gentle hands are wiping them away—and our guests are in awe of his love for me.

Standing here, I try to figure out how I got so lucky; what did I do to deserve him tiptoes around my head, but none of that matters. He is mine, and I am his; *making us one forevermore.*

Our vows are over, and our lives together are just beginning. As we stand here gazing into each other's eyes, appreciating the words that we just promised one another, our moment is interrupted—*bringing us back to why we are here.*

A massive grin spreads across my face; causing Conner's lips to curl into one of their own.

Pastor Willis is a witness to the love we share. He can see it in our faces, our body language, but most of all our tell-it-all-never-lying-eyes. His hesitation to disturb us is pushed to the side, and he continues on with the ceremony.

"Ladies and gentlemen, friends and family of this lovely couple…as you sit here and watch these two souls promising their lives to each other, can you think of one reason they shouldn't be together? If so, now would be the time to speak up."

My stomach knots up, and my mind is screaming. *Please, no one speak. Please. Please. Please.* Refusing to look around, I wonder if they can hear my thoughts.

For a moment, there is only silence, and then that silence is broken by the flapping of a seagull's wings. We all look to the sky to see it flying by.

"The bird doesn't count." The pastor giggles, showing off his good humor. "Okay, then. I didn't think so, but I had to ask. Now, without any further ado…let's get these two married."

In the distance, we can still hear birds, along with the waves crashing upon the shoreline. I can even hear the muffled sound of a boat's engine—way off in the distance. It's so peaceful, making this instant so surreal that there is nothing about it I ever want to forget. Etching the memory away somewhere far in mind, my heart locks it up and throws away the key, and I promise myself to reminisce about this moment when I'm too old to remember anything else.

My attention is swayed back to the preacher…

"Now, Conner, Hannah, I have something to ask you. After the beautiful words you shared just minutes before, I think I know the answer, but you can humor an old man with an answer can't you?"

Laughter fills the air.

We nod, in agreement.

"Conner, I'll start with you," he stresses.

I can't take my eyes off of my soon-to-be-husband, and he can't take his off of me. We are both ready for this question…we were born ready.

"I do. From this moment, until the moment I take my last breath, I do," he says breathlessly.

Conner's words are heard by everyone, and his hands have a grip on mine that can be felt around my heart; his love embracing me and making the moment even more splendid.

Before I know it, those same I do's have escaped my lips and our guests go crazy with laughter—while they're shedding happy tears, of course. Everyone realizes what we just did, and so do we. *We answered the question before it was asked.*

"Well, okay then. I believe that's the answers I was looking for. Now, this is my favorite part. Conner, you may kiss your beautiful bride."

Again, our guests go crazy; whistling and cheering my new husband on as he seals our future together with a long passionate kiss. Within seconds, he has me in his arms, spinning and twirling me in the air and leaving me breathless, as always.

Our wedding kiss should go down in history as the longest, most passionate, kiss ever. What seemed like forever was really just under a minute, but it was envied by every girl here. They couldn't help but wonder if we had stolen all the romance from the world, because this was the most romantic moment they had ever witnessed.

And then our lips parted, and my feet were in the sand again.

When we open our eyes, the sun has completely gone down, and I see the most amazing thing. Our guests have released lanterns into the air. Some of the neon-colored shapes above us are rectangle, while others are perfect circles. There are even some that are shaped into hearts; *those are my favorite.*

The glowing entities are lighting up the night sky, and it is like a fairytale come true. It is a breathtaking sight— just like my whole wedding day has been. From here on out, nothing can go wrong…and I mean *nothing*; it's just too perfect.

Conner and I, along with all of our guests, made our way to the other side of the house. There we found the perfect setting for a luau themed reception.

The night was better than ideal; it was flawless and everyone had a great time. Dancing the night away and eating until they couldn't hold down anymore food. Our love demanded the attention of everyone. Conner held me tight as we danced only with each other; all night long until the last of our guests parted. The last ones to leave were our immediate friends and family.

Then, we were the only two left—all alone in the huge house.

Standing in the foyer, breathless and hand in hand, we anticipate the moment we've both waited for that is now only minutes away.

Conner leans down and kisses me gently, before leading me through our home. We make a stop here and there, to blow out the burning candles and to lock up all the doors and windows. As we make it out the door to the breezeway, he stops and pulls a key from his front pocket and locks up the glass doors that lead into the house.

Within a second, his hand is back in mine.

We turn left, following the blazing bamboo trail that leads us down the bricked path to *our bedroom.*

Swooping me up in his arms, he opens the doors gently. The first thing I notice is the sweet sound of music playing in the background and the dozens of candles lit up everywhere.

"*Oooh, Conner,*" I whisper breathlessly.

Looking down, I see the beginning of a path lined with white rose pedals—*representing my virtue of course*. "You've really outdone yourself, Mister Dawson."

I'm swept away by the romantic gesture, and I squeeze his neck even tighter than before.

"Anything for you, Mrs. Dawson," he whispers, stealing a kiss that I would've given freely.

Within seconds, he's leading me down the path that will mark the place that we will consummate our wedding vows. I admit that I am a *little* nervous, but this is the moment I've dreamed about since I first laid eyes on him; even more so since falling in love with this amazing man.

As we follow the *path of innocence*, I can't help but notice we bypass the bed. He takes me through the doorway, and carries me straight to the beach. We are only feet away from the house when he puts me down.

The trail comes to an end at a white sheet covered with the same rose pedals that led us here. Dozens of lit candles are sitting around everywhere, and the music can still be heard, thanks to the outside sound system.

"I'm speechless, Conner."

Leaning over, he kisses me and wraps his arms around me in a loving embrace. His mouth leaves mine, and his lips graze both of my cheeks with gentle butterfly pecks—ending with a kiss to my forehead.

"I wanted this night to be perfect, Hannah, just like you are."

I inhale deeply—smelling the salty air, the mulberry scented candles, and *him*. The smell is intoxicating and arouses me more than I already am.

The waves are crashing up against the sand, and our hearts are beating away to the rhythm of love. He kisses me again—harder this time. My lips press into his, and slowly his tongue leaves his mouth entering mine; circling and drinking me in. I'm getting hotter by the minute as he finds his way to my neck...tilting my head to the side and devouring me with gentle nibbles.

Our breathing is getting heavier, more forceful with every breath. The heat of his breath sends chills all over my body; causing me to act the only way I know how. I begin jerking away at his loose fitting shirt, releasing him from the material that is hiding what I want, *no* need to feel beneath my lips. Moving my hands up his bare chest, I grab the shirt and pull it over his head—gracefully letting it fall to the ground.

His breath is hard, heavy, and erratic but no more than mine. We've both been ready for this moment for what seems like an eternity, and now it's happening.

I kiss his chest, licking my way to his nipples—sucking and leaving each one with a gentle bite. I take a deep breath in...inhaling the sensuous scent of him with my face buried in his chest hairs. It's intoxicating, putting me on a natural high.

Letting out a seductive growl, he jerks me around, my back now facing him. He moves my hair from my neck, and he trails soft hot kisses all over it; all while his hands are releasing my body from the dress I'm wearing.

I hear it unzip and feel the silky soft material fall to my feet. I step out of it; now standing only in my white lace *crotch-less* panties.

I can hear the edge of desire leaving his lips—his sultry breath hitting my skin. His hands move around to the front of my body, while his mouth is eating away at my neck and ears. With one hand covering and massaging my breast, his other one has found that open spot between my legs.

I squirm in his embrace, and even more as he whispers to me in between his nibbling. "You feel so good, so hot, and turned on."

I let out a sensuous moan, and suddenly I feel his manhood trying to break through his zipper. I can't take much more and neither can he. I release myself from his hold, turning around and looking him in the eyes. I bite my lower lip and caress it with my tongue, getting my mouth wet and ready for what I'm planning next.

Slowly, I unbutton his fly, and help him out of his jeans and his boxer briefs; throwing them to the side, I walk him over to the *bed of roses*.

The night embraces us with its warmth, and the breeze is perfect—blowing through our hair and over our bodies. The waves crashing against the shore—the night sky canvas…the setting couldn't be more exquisite.

Kissing my way to his navel, I feel his body quiver as he's anticipating my next move. On bended knees, I rest on the sheet, feeling the soft silky pedals beneath me. I kiss his waist, gliding my tongue from the left side and back to the right, all while my hand wraps around his hard, throbbing, manhood. I stroke him up and down with a grip that sends him gasping for air—his hot flesh burning with desire between my curled fingers.

My mouth is hot, wet, and he's dying to feel it wrapped around his cock. I swallow hard, getting ready to take *all* of him in. Slow and steady, I start at the tip. I remember how much he likes it when I spend a little time sucking on the end—while trailing my tongue in circles around that soft tender spot beneath the head. He thrusts his hands into my hair, pulling it to the side so he can watch me devour his pride.

Down I go and back up again, taking his length in my mouth all the way down my throat until it just won't go anymore—repeating the process and massaging his balls and driving him crazy.

"Oh, baby…that's right…just like that," he groans.

He begins swaying back and forth, making his erection go that much deeper down my throat. Meeting his rhythm, he's almost ready—I can feel the throbbing sensation as *it* brushes against my lips. His body trembles, begging to release that salty finish into my mouth, but he stops me before it happens. "No, Hannah, not yet," he lets out a long moan and pulls away.

He bends his knees, coming down and hovering over me, spoiling me the way he always does. I love the way he kisses me, with such tender passionate desire; I've never been kissed that way before…only by him. My skin reacts to each breathtaking kiss, as if it's the first time ever feeling such decadent gratification. He can feel the raised bumps of pleasure that have invaded the outer portion of my body beneath his finger tips, and I can feel him grinning in between kisses. He loves driving me over the edge, and I love letting him.

Down he goes, licking his way around each erected nipple. With his mouth on one and his hand now on the other, I feel my womanhood begging to be touched. I gasp out and arch my back up towards him. It's as though I'm sending out a *come hither* signal from straight down there and leading him to the most desirable destination he knows.

My kitty is blazing, and I can feel it reaching the point of no return as his long, masculine fingers caress my clit—circling and massaging it with expert perfection. I moan and he knows I'm almost ready.

Moving my legs apart further with one of his own legs, his mouth continues moving down until it finds the slit between my panties.

Then it happens.

With one hand on each of my thighs and his head right in the middle…he presses forward. His tongue pushes into me—opening me up even further, he strokes my clitoris over and over again.

Whoa!

That suction…those lips…that tongue…his fingers slipping in and out and circling inside me.

I can't stop myself—*I'm going to come.*

"Ahhh," I gasp.

My body jerks.

"Yes, Conner…"

My words drive him crazy.

He licks me faster and faster.

"Oh, baby…don't stop," I beg.

My hands are squeezing the sheets and filling up with sand and my body is his for the taking. I begin to sway my hips, and then I stiffen…that sensation…it's just too much.

Trying to calm my erratic breathing, I can't hold back and he stays put; sucking me until I finish unraveling in his mouth. My body twitches with complete and utter satisfaction, and when he knows my orgasm is over he kisses his way back up—removing my panties as he goes.

With his weight on me, he reaches over and grabs the remote that controls the sound system. The discs change out, and so does the music playing.

It's our song; the one he wrote me.

Covering my lips with his, he kisses me and pulls away.

His gaze is dangerously sexy.

His heart is racing…his erection is throbbing.

My body is trembling with desire.

"If it's too much, Hannah, tell me," he murmurs.

"I promise," I whisper.

This is it.

The monumental moment has arrived.

His fingers curl around his cock as he slides it around my womanhood—he's making sure *it's* good, wet, and ready to push on through…*and it is.*

Nicely lubricated…here…it…goes.

I take a deep breath at the same moment he slams into me. I want to cry out, but I can't. I won't chance ruining this for him. Instead, I bite my lip and take it like a woman in love. *And he slams into me again—stripping me of my innocence.* His thrusting—it's so hard….there's so much of it—*now inside of me.* That feeling…it's so foreign, yet it feels so natural. My body curls around him…legs and all.

Lyrics are filling the air and words are coming from his mouth. He sings to me while sliding his erection in and out, trying to take my mind off of the lengthy thickness that is now moving at a steadier pace…*I feel so wet.* That could only mean one thing. I'm no longer a virgin, and there's a red mess between my legs.

In and out he pushes and pulls. I can feel every heated, hard, inch of his cock as he fills me with his manhood. I gasp at the blissful sweet pain, but I endure it with great wanting pleasure. Never in my life have I felt so complete than I do in this very moment.

He continues singing, missing a word here and now as he steals a kiss, and as his hips sway back and forth, up and down, and meeting mine. He can't resist thrusting harder, knowing he's put an end to my virginity...a seductive growl leaves his lips between the words of the song. He's trying to calm his wild sexual hunger. Taking a moment to circle his hips—oh my...*that feels so painfully good.* I can feel his body trembling—his muscles flexing and fighting to stay in control. He lets out a sensuous moan; circling and grinding deeper and deeper—his pubic mound grazing my clit and the hard thrusting of his cock—*ah*—it's causing something to build inside me. It feels like I'm going to come again, and it's stronger than any orgasm I've ever had.

It's a firework worthy moment.

Closing my eyes, I think I see the passionate sparks of desire splashing across the back of my eyelids.

My body jerks—tensing up while his is trembling even more than before. We are going to come together—any second now.

I moan.

He moans.

"You. Feel. So. Good. Hannah," he growls.

His breathless words hit home.

He feels so good.

My fingernails bore into his back, scratching all the way down to his tight firm ass. I can't help but squeeze his voluptuous butt, and when I do it sends us both reaching for the stars.

His finish pours into me, and my body drinks it in—*every mouthwatering drop of it.* My girly self bathes in the creamy white concoction—soaking the manly cocktail in and applauding my choice of birth control. *"That little insert lasts for five years...yay us," she says as she does a backstroke and bumps into the little piece of plastic.*

Our breathing steadies.

His movements have gone from fast and hard to slow and easy; he's savoring the feeling as much as I am…and then he collapses with my body beneath his. Our bodies are tired, and our muscles are burning from all the passion we just lived through. *That was some workout.*

I lay there with all his masculinity on top of me until we both have time to wind down from the most amazing climax ever.

It was getting harder to breathe as the minutes past, both of us speechless and satisfied, but with his body still on top of mine I found myself fighting for air. He realizes it and rolls off of me and on to his back; pulling me along so that *now* I'm blanketing him.

"I'm sorry, baby, I could stay that close to you forever," he whispers.

I take a deep breath, feeling bad that I couldn't handle his weight. Then I remember he is built like a machine and my body doesn't compare to all the muscle he's carrying around.

I tilt my head up, facing him.

He moves the hair from my face and tucks it gently behind my ear.

"That was amazing, Hannah."

"I think I saw fireworks," I murmur.

We both laugh, but then he gets serious.

"Are you okay, baby girl? You're not hurting are you?"

My eyes widen. Not wanting to ruin the moment, I touch his face, gliding my fingers across his cheeks and whisper my answer. "No worries, okay."

He closes his eyes and opens them with a look that screams I love you. He takes my breath away when he kisses me, wrapping me up in his arms and standing to his feet.

I pull away—smiling. "What are you doing, Mister Dawson?"

He looks at me with playful eyes and does that thing with his brows; up and down they go and causing an even bigger grin to spread across my face.

"Time to get you cleaned up, Mrs. Dawson."

I wrap my arms around him, expecting to be taken to the shower to wash away the virgin cocktail between my legs; but instead I'm totally surprised when he leads me to the wide-open ocean. Gentle waves invite us in and begin lapping around our naked bodies.

"I love you, Conner," I whisper.

"I love you more, Hannah."

I don't know whether to scream for mercy or just let him have his way with me as he lowers our bodies into the cool cleansing water. *I think I'll let him have his way.* After all, he truly did *rescue me gently.*

I hold on tight and inhale his kiss as he takes me beneath the water, and for a moment we disappear up under the stars and into the ocean—forgetting about the rest of the world and cherishing our first night together as husband and wife.

The End

www.ingramcontent.com/pod-product-compliance
Lightning Source LLC
Chambersburg PA
CBHW070734180626
46818CB00007B/2840